DEVIL'S
CAULDRON

Also by Alasdair Wham:

Fiction

Machir Bay

Bac Mor

Due for release in 2022: The Delivery Boy

Non-fiction

Ayrshire's Forgotten Railways

Exploring Dumfries and Galloway's Lost Railway Heritage -
Published by The Oakwood Press

DEVIL'S CAULDRON

Alasdair Wham

Greenan Publishing

Devil's Cauldron

First published in Great Britain in 2021 by Greenan Publishing, Ayr

ISBN 978-0-9933400-3-1

A catalogue record for this book is available from the British Library.

For further information please contact info@greenanpublishing.co.uk

This book is dedicated to:

Nancy Jackson
11th July 1926 – 5th August 2019

1

I was level with the library when I first saw him across the road, emerging from the entrance to a garage. He moved into the light of the late afternoon sun, casting a long, dark shadow across the pavement, which felt like a dagger pointing at my heart. There was no doubt it was him. His face was etched in my mind forever: straight, long nose perched above a narrow mouth, not overly attractive, dour type. Black hair that now looked dyed, slicked against his head. He seemed at peace, unaware of me as he walked down the road, wearing what looked like an expensive tweed jacket edged with leather piping, smart tan trousers and black brogues.

I was stunned that I had finally found him, disbelieving, adrenaline surging, light-headed. I had searched for him unsuccessfully for many years, always on the lookout. Now I had run into him when I hadn't expected it, on my way to get food from a local supermarket.

Jolted by his sudden appearance, I found myself standing gawking at him but turned away not wanting to alert him to my presence. Desperately trying to regain my composure, I walked on trying not to turn around. Hurriedly, I reached stone steps leading up to a car park at Market Hill near the top of the town, clutching at the handrail gasping for breath, my stomach knotted, head light, dizzy. After all this time I had seen him again. I couldn't believe it. I felt vindicated, others would have to believe me now. Sis would be alarmed, of course, especially after last year, worried about what I was going to do.

Strangely, the wrath I had nurtured for all those years was not my main emotion. I was in shock. I gripped the railings, knuckles white, steadying myself. My mind was a whirl, planning my next move. Obviously, I couldn't just run after him and attack him – first I needed to know more about him, find a place for interrogation, get answers to my questions, but then what?

Soon the familiar rage kicked in, barely suppressed trauma erupting as memories seared in my mind flickered into consciousness. Time for action. This was my opportunity, unexpected as it was, and I couldn't risk losing him. Already he was about a hundred yards away, strolling down the main shopping street in the town – King Street. I crossed over the road and started to trail him, keeping in the shadows, dodging into shop doorways in my amateurish attempts to follow him without being seen.

I was a few yards behind as he reached the local Post Office. He strolled, steady pace, not a care. I could change that. I desperately wanted to. Then he disappeared into a newsagent's. My breathing was laboured as I stopped outside the shop, pretending to gaze at the display of local books in the window but trying to peer inside. And there he was, paying for a newspaper, smiling at the shop assistant. She seemed charmed, oblivious to what he had done to my family.

I leant against the shop window, my head on the cool glass. My breath pulsed against it forming dancing patches of condensation that quickly evaporated. He emerged a minute later and headed down the street, a copy of *The Times* neatly folded under his left arm. He gave no signs of noticing me, only ten feet behind him, and then he stopped at the kerb, weaved between two parked cars and headed across the street to a cafe. I watched him for a minute and then followed. He stepped inside and by the time I reached it, he was being shown to a table by a wooden-slatted wall under a display of pictures of local scenes. There were several empty spaces and I followed him inside.

The waitress smiled, a young girl neat in her black trousers and white shirt, and I pointed towards a seat in the corner a few tables away from him. I sat down, the chair scraping on the tiled floor, but he didn't look up. I grasped the laminated menu from its perch between the salt and pepper pots and looked at it trying to control my shaking hands.

The waitress returned, still smiling, but I was transfixed, studying his composed face as he examined the paper, noting hints of white around his hairline. He must be about fifty, I reckoned, more than old enough to be responsible for his actions the last time we met. So close now. I had to remain in control.

'Americano,' I stated, finally noticing the waitress.

'Anything to eat?'

I glanced at the menu and then the display of cakes on the counter under glass covers.

'A slice of the one on the left.'

'The Victoria sponge?'

'Yes.'

I noticed his attention waver towards me.

'Thank you,' I added.

Now he was opening the paper and folding it at the puzzle page, pulling out a silver-coloured pen from inside his jacket. His expression was studied, focused on the page. Soon he was solving clues, lost in thought, apparently not a care in the world. Don't look so innocent. I know what you did. My stomach, instinctively reacting to my thoughts, tightened again, ratcheting up another peak of discomfort barely noticed as I surveyed him, aware of patches of sweat forming in my armpits and staining my tee shirt, beads of sweat on my brow.

The waitress returned, putting down the slice of cake and placing a fork on a folded paper napkin, whilst I pretended to look at the selection of specials chalked on a blackboard, garnering my brooding thoughts.

'Thanks,' I said, as the coffee was put down. This time he didn't look up. He remained concentrated on his crossword, the top of the pen touching his teeth.

I sipped the coffee and put down my cup, toying with the small fork, but the sponge was not appealing, my appetite gone. Okay, out there, all who doubted me – I have found him. I am now sitting a few feet away from him, deciding what to do. I had anticipated this moment for twelve years, his face seared on my mind as he stood over my father, talking to a shadowy figure. I couldn't hear what he said but he was pointing at Dad, determining his fate as if they were deciding to put down an animal. I didn't hear him utter the words 'kill him', but his expression said it all, a person who was used to issuing commands and being obeyed. His hand was raised and lowered. The shadowy figure stepped forward and crouched down; there was a sharp crack as a pistol was fired. The sound echoed in the cold night air as a hand covered my face, muffling my screams. And no one believed me – police, family or friends.

My face twisted, biting down hard on my lips, as I tried to stop from shouting out 'murderer'. I saw him glance in my direction, but there was no flicker of recognition. I suppose that I had changed a lot in twelve years, my face now swathed with a bushy beard.

I played with the cake, forcing myself to eat another mouthful, the jam and cream filling palatable, the sponge harder to swallow, the flavour now tainted with the metallic tang of blood.

An elderly couple got up to leave, and as they reached the door it was held open by a woman who was entering. She was dressed in a black jerkin and matching black trousers – a uniform. She headed to his table to be greeted with a brief smile as she stood there, not, it seemed, expecting to be asked to sit down.

'How long, Tania?' I had heard that voice before.

'The car is ready, sir. They managed to repair the puncture. I've parked it in St Andrew Street, close to the Kings Arms Hotel. As usual, there were no spaces left on King Street,' she added, not with a smile but with a slight softening of her features, an attempted apology for any inconvenience caused. There was a rapport between them. Tania must be his chauffeur.

Tania was stocky, muscle not fat, I thought, her dark shoulder-length hair streaked with wisps of grey, her face impassive. She knew her place. She was also disrupting my plans. I couldn't approach him now, not when he had company. I quickly supped some of the coffee to suppress my emotion.

'That's good. I'll be out in a minute. Just wait in the car.' He certainly was a charmer, knew how to treat women. Same way that he treated my father, contempt inbred. Now things could change with a bit of luck, I thought, shovelling down another piece of cake, although it stuck in my gullet.

Tania complied, not reacting to the brush-off, and turned about to leave the cafe. I looked around, no one else had noticed his chauvinism. However, no one else had the personal interest I had in him.

After a few seconds, he drained his coffee cup and stood up, putting his pen back carefully inside his jacket, and then, picking up the paper, he beckoned the waitress over and handed her a paper note. He waited while she brought his change. I kept my head down, managing another mouthful of coffee, masking my face.

'Thank you.' He took his change and headed towards the door.

Suddenly, I realised that I needed to pay and follow him, but the waitress had disappeared into the kitchen. I got up as he left and rushed over to the counter.

'Hello,' I said loudly and rapped on the counter. I repeated myself and a face appeared, an older woman.

'I need to pay up, I have to go.'

'Okay, no problem. Michelle, can you settle this gentleman's bill? He's in a hurry,' she added.

Seconds passed before Michelle appeared. Precious seconds. Michelle returned, reached up and took the tab from a clip and checked the menu for prices.

'Everything okay, sir?' She glanced across at the half-eaten cake.

'Yes,' but she was taking too long. He could be away in his car by now. I threw down a ten- pound note and said, 'Keep the change.' I turned and ran out of the cafe. A glance told me he wasn't on King Street. I knew Castle Douglas well – after all, I had lived in it for many years when I was younger – and rushed the short distance to St Andrew Street and looked along it. There he was, walking slowly, catching up with Tania who had not yet reached the car. I lurked at the corner and then quickly crossed the street and tried to walk fast without attracting their attention. I stopped beside an antique showroom as Tania pressed a key fob. The indicator lights flashed on a dark-coloured sports coupe, trimmed with a line of lime along the sill, the vivid colour reflecting off the highly polished body of the car. It looked like an Aston Martin, top of the range, a dream car only for the wealthy. Tania held the passenger door open and, as he got in, I took a picture with my iPhone.

Tania paused as she walked round the car, as if she had noticed my action. I turned away and took a picture of a white plaster bust of some historic figure in the window and pretended to be interested in it, breathing hard to steady my tension.

Minutes later I heard the throaty sound of the sports car starting and turned trying to note the registration number, but a car passed blocking my view. I could only see three letters... AGL. The car turned up Queen Street, which ran parallel to King Street, and was gone. I stood for some time, letting my emotion subside before I continued towards Queen Street.

He existed and he knew the area. I had to find him, so many questions to ask him and then... as my thoughts turned to plotting revenge, I saw the car pass the end of the road. I barely had time to turn away but noticed a lime-coloured stripe on the bonnet. Had Tania doubled back to check up on me? Had he recognised me after all? Unlikely, but I had to be careful until the conditions were right for me to exact my revenge.

2

It was a short distance further along St Andrew Street to the campsite. I passed the Rectory for St Ninian's Episcopal Church and then, a short distance on, the granite church building itself, both places frequented by my mother while she was living here. The road then continued beyond new houses, passing a cemetery on high ground to the right, before reaching the open countryside. I didn't go so far, turning into the Lochside Caravan Park, a sprawling camping and caravan site beside Carlingwark Loch, at the southern extremity of Castle Douglas. A walk through rows of caravans and then over a gentle, sloping hill, led me down to my tent, my red Ford Focus parked beside it. The setting was so familiar: walks around the area with Dad, as a boy; taking a boat out on Carlingwark Loch with him; fishing for pike on the loch; an ice cream from the warden's office afterwards. Above all, I remembered the patience, the attention and the affection my father showed towards me. And I hadn't been able to help him when he needed it.

People said that I had to move on, but I couldn't until the truth was known and accepted. I owed him that. That's why I'd come back – had to come back – year after year, long after the family left the area. The answers were to be found around here.

Today's encounter showed that there could be a resolution. It also made me realise that when I confronted the guy that I had seen today, I needed more of a plan, not just raw emotion.

The tent was pitched beside bushes in the lee of several tall trees, providing some protection from the strong sun. Two windbreaks marked out my territory in front of the tent. I reached inside, collected a bottle of water and flopped on the canvas chair I had left out. In this part of the campsite a U-shaped tarmac road looped round, connecting at both ends with the main access road and a parking area in front of a white roughcast shower and toilet block, all overshadowed by mature trees. To the left of the shower block was a white stone house, an outdoor centre and a skate park with concrete ramps, busy with youths testing their skills.

The site was becoming busy, not unusual for this time of year, and I noticed a few newcomers. A long, tubular tent with side compartments, able to take a large family, had been erected in the wide central part not far from my pitch. Two young girls played outside on pink bikes fitted with stabilisers. The father sat beside a picnic table drinking a beer, a couple of empty bottles already lying on the ground. When he looked up, he startled me. His head appeared narrower than it should have been, strangely elongated. Poor soul must have had an accident.

Two couples, their accents foreign, maybe Dutch, were setting up low triangular tents in-between trees to my right, cycling finished for the day; their bicycles in pairs and propped against each other to stop them falling. The site, near a National Cycle Route, was popular with cyclists, and many overseas visitors sought the back roads and tranquil beauty of this part of Galloway. They would probably be gone early the next morning to continue their explorations.

The occupant of the tent next to mine was not there and I breathed a sigh of relief. I needed peace, not offers of beer or talks about women. Rougvie was a volunteer for a local red squirrel charity, giving up a fortnight to locate red squirrels and remove grey ones – to give the reds a chance to repopulate the area. Worthy work, but, from our chat last night, Rougvie seemed more interested in the freedom from his partner, enjoying the chance to drink local real ale and let his eyes wander lustfully.

Then beyond the man with the squashed head, closer to the loch but screened from it by bushes, was the 'Colonel', as I called him. A stooped, elderly gent, patrolling the grass in front of his tent, leaning on two sticks and walking back and forward constantly, wearing a Panama hat to shield his face from the sun, a large white moustache on his upper lip and a stomach barely held in by his belt. His wife was sitting outside their tent on a low-slung chair, her head in a book, her hand frequently stretching out to sip her gin and tonic.

I remembered when I was a boy, in August when the campsite was usually much busier, being fascinated by the different people who camped here from all 'airts and pairts', as the Scots would say.

I unscrewed the plastic top from the bottle of water and drank deeply, my throat parched, still feeling the acid burn caused by earlier events, and as I looked across the campsite to the cemetery on the far side of the loch, I raised my bottle. I've made some progress at last, Dad. I hope that you're proud of me.

The guy who had haunted my nightmares was real, although I never doubted that. I just hadn't been able to find him before this afternoon's chance encounter. He was familiar with the town, so he probably lived nearby. He was also probably wealthy, with a very expensive car and someone to drive him

16

around – Tania, not the most common of names. And almost an aristocratic manner about him, someone who knew how to order others about. The last thought was based both on today's encounter and my memories of that fateful evening, when he had arrived late and others quickly ceded control to him. It looked like the car had a private registration, so his initials might be AGL. That could prove useful and I might be able to check it out on the Internet.

The photo I had taken on my phone showed him as he was about to enter the car: composed, unhurried, not a care in the world. I wanted to change that, make him explain himself. A few Google searches confirmed that his car was an Aston Martin, capable of two hundred miles an hour; the lime stripe on the bonnet signified that it was an Aston Martin DB11 AMR, a very elite, rare model for those who could afford luxury.

Definite progress and I hadn't even started to implement my plans for this year's visit. Hopefully, the encounter was a good omen. I raised my bottle of water again and finished it, crushed it and threw it on the ground. Time would tell.

3

Rougvie parked his battered black Jeep Cherokee in front of his tent and jumped out giving me a thumbs up. No doubt I was going to learn about his day chasing squirrels or whatever he did. He disappeared into his tent and emerged seconds later using a bottle opener to flick off the top of a bottle of real ale. He wasn't wasting time. I looked away but it was too late, he was already striding towards me, taking a slug from his bottle.

'Thirsty work.' I didn't give him any encouragement, checking my Facebook page on my iPhone instead, but he didn't appear to notice, removing his camouflaged baseball cap to expose a receding patch of red hair glistening with sweat.

'I found two reds today. That's very good – a breeding pair unaffected by the squirrel pox virus.'

'That's something,' I said, with little enthusiasm, hoping to dampen his ardour.

'Big progress, actually, and that's just my first day. My beat is around the Glenkens and south to Loch Ken. I work with landowners.' He glanced at me to see if I was impressed. 'Lord Atchison today, who's able to get funding to reduce the grey population. Very satisfying.' He lifted the bottle to his mouth and drank again. Some beer trickled down his red bushy beard, which he quickly wiped with the back of his free hand, belching as he did.

'Hot today,' he added, changing the subject, ignoring my lack of enthusiasm. I nodded, keeping my eyes riveted to the screen of my phone. He looked around the campsite.

'Hey,' he said, 'look at her. Hope she's staying.'

A girl driving a two-door, white Fiat 500, shaped like an upturned old-fashioned bath tub, was slowly following the tarmac road round the site looking for a place to park. She passed by us, turning away when she saw the two of us looking in her direction.

'That's promising,' muttered Rougvie, quick to offer an opinion.

Finally, she drove onto the grass and parked opposite my tent near a gap in the bushes, beside the loch and a picnic bench about twenty yards away. She got out of the car and looked around for a spot to pitch her tent. She wore bright floral leggings, topped by a lemon- coloured tee shirt. Her blonde hair was bunched on top of her head, held in place by a blue band, black thick-rimmed glasses squared off her face. She walked to the tailgate and opened it. The rear seats were down and the space stuffed with camping gear and bags.

'I must have a chat to "flower girl",' muttered Rougvie, wiping his mouth again. 'I'm not going to miss her in the dark with those bright leggings.' I turned away; the guy was a pain. Rougvie was in his late thirties, at least, the girl was probably not long out of school. My salivating fellow camper was sick.

'Time I started to prepare my meal,' I said, disappearing into the tent.

By the time I was heating baked beans and waiting for the kettle to start whistling, 'flower girl' had almost finished pitching her small tent and was unrolling her sleeping bag. She looked around and then headed towards me. Rougvie would be jealous.

Up close, her glasses dominated her face, offset by a square jawline, but when she smiled her face was attractive.

'Hi,' she said. 'Sorry to trouble you, but you always forget something,' and I nodded. 'Have you any matches?'

I reached down to pick up the box from beside my stove and lifted the kettle, which was now whistling, from the gas ring, whilst handing the box over.

'Thanks,' she said, 'I'm Jess,' but she lowered her head as she spoke, as if to avoid my gaze.

'I'm Finn.'

'Never been here before, have you?'

'Oh yes, every year. It's a tradition. Love the area.' Bland enough, but even so I struggled, surprisingly, to find the words, not because she was having an effect on me but because of all the emotional baggage that a longer explanation would involve.

'I'll return them later,' and with that she headed back to her tent.

Rougvie emerged from his tent. 'That's a good start,' he exclaimed, and I pointedly picked up the plate of beans and shovelled a spoonful into my mouth, ignoring him.

Meal over, I wandered across to the shower block, where there was a laundry area, and washed my few dirty dishes. The park was quite busy, several cars parked facing the loch, picnic tables occupied mainly with people eating fish and chips; mute swans and ducks wandered amongst them looking for scraps. The enclosed play area was busy with children, the shrill sound of young voices carrying on the evening air as they played. All so familiar. I wandered round the path that led behind the shower block by the edge of the loch, the evening sun shafting through the trees, the air pleasantly cool, the loch extending to the south beyond several small islets. This was where the first community in the area was established, the genesis of the town, to exploit the lime-rich clay deposits known as marl, used to fertilise local farms and eventually further afield. Marl fell out of favour and the landowner sold the land to William Douglas, who named the town after himself and expanded it. It was Douglas who planned the town based on the central King Street, flanked by Queen Street and Cotton Street, with many smaller roads connecting them. The history was familiar from my schooldays in the town.

I continued round the path stopping beside a concrete slipway to watch two men fishing, and then, having completed the loop, headed back towards my tent still clutching my clean dishes, passing a small circular concrete base with a metal pin protruding from the raised centre.

'Base for a Blacker Bombard,' a voice proclaimed. It was the Colonel.

'Base for a spigot mortar,' I replied and smiled.

'Good work, lad. Someone in your family been in the forces?'

'No, but my dad had an interest in local history, although he did also work for the Ministry of Defence. Part of the town's defences if the Nazi's invaded.'

'Wouldn't have been much bloody use.'

In my mind there was an image drawn from my childhood, of enemy troops appearing on the crest of the hill beside the cemetery, soldiers huddling in a trench ready to fire the mortar, anxiously waiting for instructions.

'Never used them myself. Suspect that the rounds would have frightened the swans more than the Germans. Joined the Argyll's in the sixties, then saw action in Aden and later during the Troubles in Northern Ireland. Survived all that, then injured my back in a car accident after I left the forces.'

There was sweat on his brow, pain etched on his face, an

effort to move, the moustache throbbing slightly.

'Can't get comfortable. Standing or lying down.'

'Sorry,' I muttered, and he shuffled past me towards the toilet block. He was not the type to want lavish expressions of sympathy.

The box of matches was sitting on my canvas chair when I returned. There was no sign of Jess or, thankfully, Rougvie. The guy with the squashed face now had a pile of empty bottles of beer, many scattered on the ground, others lined up on the plastic picnic table. I saw his wife standing at the entrance to the tent, her arms tightly wound around her, keeping an eye on her two kids, occasionally also checking on her husband, her expression changing and becoming more serious as she did. When she saw me looking across she smiled back, shaking her head at her husband, who appeared, by now, to be slumbering.

4

My iPhone rang, a traditional retro ring, and I picked it up from the picnic table and glanced at the screen. I wondered how long it would take her.

'Hi Sis,' I said.

'Where are you?' The tone was direct, let's-get-down-to-business direct.

'Where do you think?'

'Oh no, after last year?' The exasperation in her voice obvious. 'I warned you not to go back. How could you do that to Mum?'

'But I'm relaxing.' That was a joke. 'Enjoying the fresh air, visiting...'

'Stop.' Her voice sounded loud, brittle. Automatically, I held the phone a few inches from my head. Here we go, I thought.

'The police warned you. You know the consequences.'

Warned, not ordered. I had been unfortunate. Too much real ale and then someone who looked like him, but I couldn't be sure. He had had a drink, so had the people with him. One thing led to another and the police were called. Lucky to get off with a warning. Anything else might have affected my teaching career.

Sis was still warbling on. She was fifteen years older than me, treated me more like a son than a brother, very protective of Mother. Both Sis and Mother wouldn't talk about what happened to Dad, they didn't believe me and were angry with me for dwelling on it, but then neither of them were there. I was hurt that they wouldn't speak about him, dismissing his fate as if it was of no consequence.

'And you know that Mother will be furious. Finn, how can you, year after year? Think of your responsibilities – no wonder Gillian despairs.' The pitch of her voice was rising, emotion taking over, approaching overdrive.

'I have just finished a busy term. I'm tired and I need a few days away. Give me peace...'

'But...'

'I'll speak another time,' and I broke off the call. No way was I going to tell her about today's discovery, it would only inflame the situation more.

Seconds later the phone rang again, the ring tone sounding louder. The man with the squashed head looked up, and I quickly switched the phone off.

• • •

As the evening sun set behind the tall trees, the lights on the concrete lamp posts beside the tarmac road flickered on. The shouts of kids playing had stopped, toys and bikes abandoned, lamps on in several tents, shadows playing against the canvas as people moved about inside. I pulled out a bunch of flowers that I had bought this morning from a florist in King Street and walked to the road which continued past the cemetery. It was a beautiful evening, the reeds near the edge of the loch tilting slightly in the breeze, cattle on a nearby hillside munching grass.

I reached the cemetery, screened by a line of conifers from the road, and stepped through the gates, gravestones at right angles in rows on a low hill in front of me. Some gravestones had collapsed to the ground, others weathered, now indecipherable. There used to be steps leading up to this older section of the graveyard but these had been removed, replaced by a grassy slope. However, I took my usual route and clambered over a low wall passing through the serried ranks of gravestones. The newer section of the graveyard was beyond a stone wall, accessible by a gap beside the gravedigger's wooden hut. To my right, the sun was beginning to dip over the Glenkens Hills, the loch now glowing orange, the campsite now in shade. To my left were fields of crops and then a row of hills, including Screel and Bengairn, forming a natural barrier to the south and beyond them the Solway Firth and England.

I walked round the path that followed the wall. In the new section of the graveyard there were more recent graves, posies of flowers, some decorated with small toys, little windmills and vases. Some of the names were familiar from previous visits. Apart from me, the graveyard was deserted.

My father's grave was a simple polished granite stone, close to the wall:

John McAdam BSc, PhD, FRSC,

Husband, Father, Chemist

Much missed

Mother and Sis had fought over what to put on the gravestone. They decided, in the end, that they wouldn't add dates. His ending, so traumatic, had changed everything in their opinion and I was considered too young to have one. It appeared no one had been there since my previous visit a year ago, my last flowers probably scattered by the winter winds.

My eyes filled with tears as I placed the fresh flowers in front of the gravestone.

'Remember, Dad,' I said, 'I'll find out the truth and let others know.' I held my position for a few minutes, my head lowered, muttering a prayer from my childhood.

As the sun continued to dip, I was aware of a cool breeze blowing in over the farmer's fields, the chill making me shiver. I turned around and thought for a second that there was someone watching me from the gap in the wall, a brief movement lost to the gathering dusk. It was time to leave, my imagination playing tricks. I chose late evening not because I was ashamed of my father but because I wanted solitude, communion with him at his last resting place.

By the time I returned to the campsite it had quietened, the light from the few lamp posts beside the tarmac road more pronounced, pools of light against the encroaching dark. The Colonel had found sufficient respite to go to bed, even if sleep would not be easy, his tent in darkness. The wife of the man with the squashed head was sitting quietly outside the tent reading a book by torchlight. From inside the tent I could hear her husband snoring. She smiled and waved and I acknowledged her. Rougvie's car was gone and there was no sign of Jess.

My mind was obsessed by the encounter on King Street, making sleep difficult. Slowly I was absorbing the fact that I had seen the man who had determined my father's fate. I had finally found him, now I could begin to uncover the truth. In the early hours I drifted off to sleep, the rumble of trucks on the Castle Douglas bypass, heading to and from the ferry to Ireland, ever present. Nearer, the sound of a car speeding through the street past the campsite out towards the countryside. Familiar sounds from my childhood. Nearer still, the sound of someone snoring.

5

There had been rain overnight, the ground wet, the air damp, the sky remaining cloudy and overcast as dawn broke. As I prepared to visit the shower block, I pulled on a sweatshirt to keep out the chill. Rougvie's car was back but the flap of his tent was zipped, so he was probably inside sleeping. As I wandered over towards the shower block, towel and toilet bag under my arm, the man with the squashed face was sitting outside already, a mug of hot milky tea on the table in front of him. He looked hung-over.

'Didn't keep you awake, I hope,' he said, wrapping his hands around the mug, trying to steady the shakiness he was experiencing. 'My wife says that I keep everyone awake. Can't help it, my head got squashed under a truck when I was helping to change a tyre. Trapped, they had to jack up the truck. Lucky to be alive.'

I smiled sympathetically and noticed the entrance flap to the tent move, his wife poked her head out to see who her husband was talking to. She pulled her dressing gown tighter across her chest and flicked a loose strand of hair from her face.

'Tom, your breakfast is ready,' she said, but Tom ignored her.

'Painful, it took them over an hour to free me.'

'Tom,' his wife persisted, 'the young man wants to have his shower. Come in.'

She smiled at me, but I could sense that she was irritated with him. 'Tom likes to tell his story,' she said by way of explanation.

'That's okay, sounds like a narrow escape,' and she rolled her eyes, her husband unaware.

I liked to keep it simple when camping. A quick shower followed by a bowl of cornflakes and some milk, a mug of tea, and I was ready for what I hoped would be a busy and productive day. I wanted to make two quick visits before I left the town, so I decided to walk into Castle Douglas, retracing my route from yesterday. First, I walked to the newsagent that AGL, as I was going to call him from now on, had visited. The shop was located on King Street and I knew it would be open early, best time to buy newspapers.

The shop was empty apart from an older man behind the counter, no sign of the woman who had spoken to AGL yesterday – pity. There was a good selection of local history books and I scanned the shelves to see if there was one on local landowners.

'Looking for anything in particular?'

'Yes, anything on local landowners.'

'There was a book, but it's out of print, has been for many years.'

'Just curious. Do you know a landowner with the initials AGL?'

He shook his head. 'Can't think of anyone. Are you staying a few days? I can ask Ann. She'll be in later and is keen on local history. We get a lot of people in here from all backgrounds. Look at today's papers,' and he pointed to the bottom shelf by the door where this morning's papers were arranged in piles.

'Julian Montgomery has been in a few times.'

I scanned the headlines: Montgomery moved to Foreign

Office, was the gist.

'Might even make Prime Minister one day, the papers suggest. Was in here last month with his security heavies and bought most of the titles. Likes reading about himself, I think,' and he winked at me.

I wasn't going to glean anything here, so I left and headed up King Street to the garage that I had seen AGL leave yesterday. I wandered through the arch to where the garage opened out, with lots of parked cars to each side. A boy – an apprentice, I suspected – with red cheeks, not yet shaving, dressed in grey overalls, came out of a small office.

'Can I help you?'

'Just curious,' and he looked puzzled.

'I saw an Aston Martin coupe, dark-coloured, looked brand new, distinctive lime strip on the bonnet, leave here yesterday. Fascinated by prestige cars, my hobby. Must have been worth a couple of hundred thousand pounds new. Who can afford a car like that around here?'

An older man had emerged from the office and was listening to our chat.

'A wealthy person,' he stated, 'but we never discuss a client's business.'

'Did you get a chance to drive it?' I asked, trying to show enthusiasm, encourage him to open up.

'Yes, twenty yards, and I didn't do more than 5mph,' he deadpanned.

I smiled, accepting defeat. 'Someday I'll return with one.'

'And we will be pleased to offer you any help.'

Defeated again, I left the garage and collected some shopping on my way back to the campsite. I hadn't expected any great success from the visits, it was just an outside chance.

When I reached the campsite, Rougvie was up and had

wandered over to the picnic table, where Jess was sitting eating a bowl of cereal, wearing jogging pants and an oversized sweater with the sleeves turned up. She turned away as he approached, her legs crossed away from him, never a good sign, but Rougvie was hardly likely to read the portents and sat down beside her trying to start a conversation. She ignored him, but he persisted, leaning towards her.

I didn't hear what she said, but I could see her face twist and Rougvie, startled, pulled back and stood up. Seeing me watching he tried to save face and stood for a moment looking out over the loch before turning round and heading back to his tent, head down. With technique like that he was lucky to have a partner. Jess, it seemed, could be feisty.

6

If my first two visits of the day had been long shots, then the next trip was more significant. The person that I wanted to speak to had knowledge of the events of that night; he had been the editor of *The Galloway Observer* at the time. George Park was now retired and living in Dalbeattie, a small town a few miles from Castle Douglas, and had replied courteously to my letter asking to meet him, although he offered little hope.

I left the campsite around eleven. Rougvie had already left without saying anything about his rebuff. Jess, I noticed, sat at the picnic bench flicking through a magazine, looking bored. I didn't know why she was here but she probably wondered the same thing about me.

I drove up Queen Street to the roundabout at the top of the town beside Market Hill, where the train station had once been situated, the site now occupied by a Tesco supermarket, and turned right onto the A711. After a few miles, it led down a steep winding road to traffic lights at a bridge over a river, close to a granite quarry, once the source of much of Dalbeattie's wealth. The grey granite was a feature of many of the small town's buildings.

I was searching for Station Road but missed it and was

heading through Dalbeattie before I realised and started to turn at an entrance leading to a caravan park. I waited to get back on the road and was surprised to see Jess driving past in her Fiat 500, probably taking the back road to Dumfries. I don't think that she saw me.

Heading back into Dalbeattie I soon saw Station Road and eventually found Park's house, a bungalow. It was raining when I arrived and I used my umbrella to cover my head as I walked quickly up the driveway. The doorbell was answered by his wife, grey hair in a bun, warm and motherly, who showed me through to a modest lounge where I waited, taking one of the chairs and looking out through the patio doors to an immaculately tended garden – manicured lawn, rose bushes, shrubs and a water feature.

'Tea or coffee?' she asked, only to be interrupted by her husband entering the room.

'I don't think Mr McAdam will have time for that.' She slipped out of the room, quickly breaking eye contact with me.

George Park was quite small, silver hair neatly parted, lined face cleanly shaven, smartly dressed with a shirt and tie. Park sat down at one end of the settee.

'Well, Mr McAdam, it would have seemed rude to have not agreed to meet with you, but I don't think that I can help you.'

'It's about my father.'

'I realise that, and I do remember the incident. We covered it in the *Observer*.'

Was that all it meant to him – someone's life ended, that'll fill a few lines?

'Two people found dead on a lonely road in a remote part of Galloway. One thought to have been murdered, the other committing suicide, presumably having murdered the first. No one knows why they were there. Both top research scientists.

32

Both worked for the Ministry of Defence near Eastriggs. Worth looking into as a story, could have been a real scandal. Not many in this part of the woods. They had a heated argument and your father shot him.'

'He never had a gun!'

'After realising what had happened he turned the gun on himself,' he continued, ignoring my statement, as if reading from a script.

'He never had a gun,' I repeated, but Park ignored me again.

'Both under a lot of pressure at work, I was told. But no one could understand why he took you with him,' and he looked quizzically at me.

'He didn't commit suicide. I was there. He was shot on the instructions of another man.'

'As you can imagine, there was a thorough investigation. No other conclusion – argument, murder, suicide. His prints on the gun,' he stated it almost robotically.

'The investigation was a travesty. My father was on great form that evening, no sign of depression or anxiety. I never once heard him raise his voice.'

Park leant forward. 'Sometimes you can't tell.' For the first time there was a slight edge of sympathy in his voice.

'I was there. We were going to fish on Loch Grannoch.'

Park interrupted. 'There was no evidence for that. The police dismissed that theory. I spoke to some of them and there were investigators from the defence services, top notch, greatly alarmed by what happened. After all, there could have been implications for national security. They really wanted to know the truth. Your father and…,' he paused, searching for the name, 'Hamilton, yes, that's right, were working on a sensitive project.'

'I never saw another man at Loch Grannoch. I saw what happened on the road. I was in the back of the car.'

Park's tone changed, no sympathy now, just irritation.

'It must be difficult, but you were young and the police said you were heavily drugged.'

'That was later and anyway, who drugged me? It wasn't my father – he was already dead, wasn't he?'

'I am sorry, but it was your father,' the tone now insistent. 'His fingerprints were all over the syringe, and he got the drugs, it was reckoned, from where he worked. There were some drugs missing when they did an audit. Look, I am sorry, this must be difficult for you, but I can't really help. It was twelve years ago, you have to move on.'

He stood up, meeting over, and he ushered me towards the door. Slowly I stood up. What he said was no more than I had expected. Everyone had agreed on the story, not that it bore any resemblance to the truth.

Park stopped at the door of the lounge where his wife was hovering about, the retired editor not pleased by her unexpected presence.

He changed the subject. 'Where are you staying?'

'The campsite at Castle Douglas.'

'Oh very nice,' and turning to his wife, he added gruffly, 'Please show Mr McAdam out,' and he went back into the lounge.

Mrs Park blanked her husband and showed me along the short hallway to the front door, opening it for me.

'You were just a small boy,' she said in a low voice, 'it must have been terrible for you and your family.'

I nodded, sensing that she wanted to say more. She looked over her shoulder and stepped outside, pulling the door behind her.

'I remember George being really angry at the time, said the police were, too. Don't blame him, he can't say anything more. His police contacts meet in the Kings Arms, close to the campsite you're staying in, every Wednesday, early evening, most of them now retired. Maybe one of them can help. George often talked about Mac, he was very friendly. A Mr Urquhart was in charge for the police, if I remember correctly. He visited us a few times, didn't like him.'

I smiled and quietly thanked her, but she motioned for me to leave as Park shouted, 'Mary,' from the lounge.

When I reached the car, I realised that I had left my umbrella and went back to the door. Mary opened it, her expression changed, worried why I had returned.

'I forgot my umbrella,' and she quickly handed it to me when she realised that was all I wanted, her face relaxing. Park was on his mobile by the lounge door looking very tense and immediately stopped speaking when he saw me.

· · ·

I drove back to Castle Douglas with two new pieces of information, the name of a policeman involved in the investigation and where I might find some of his colleagues. Police had come round to our house to speak to us, but it was MOD police who dealt mostly with us and I was interviewed only briefly, despite my protests.

Park seemed to be spouting a line I had heard before, none too convincingly.

This was Wednesday, I suddenly realised. I could go along this evening and meet the policemen who would be there. They would probably be no more forthcoming than Park, but I had to try.

With a few hours to kill, I decided to visit Threave Castle, a favourite haunt, one I often visited with my father to inspect the ruins and to visit the bird hides by the river, trying to identify all the ducks and other visiting birds. The castle was just a few miles from the camp- site. The weather was improving, blue skies emerging, and it would fill in time before the retired policemen gathered.

Arriving at Castle Douglas, I drove down King Street, past Carlingwark Loch at the bottom of the town and eventually reached a roundabout on the A75, crossed it to a narrow single-track road and reached an old farm building and a car park in a grassy field.

I paid my money and walked the long zigzag path through pleasant green fields to reach Threave Castle, located on an island in the River Dee. It had a turbulent history reaching back to the fourteenth century, when it was built. Powerful local landowners, initially the Douglas's, had a love-hate relationship with the Scottish kings and eventually the castle was besieged. Mons Meg, the famous canon, now kept at Edinburgh Castle, was used to penetrate the outer walls. I vividly remember being told about one cannonball that pierced the wall of the castle and whipped off the hand of a woman inside. As a young boy there was much to fire the imagination.

I reached the ferry jetty on the bank of the river, where there was a small boat fitted with an outdoor motor shuttling people across to the island. I put on my life-jacket as instructed and when the boat was full, the boatman manoeuvred away from the jetty and took the short crossing to the island in the middle of the river.

The tower house was five storeys high and surrounded by an outer wall. I wandered about entering the castle, looking down through the metal grill to a dark, damp prison, where light never penetrated. Climbing up the stone stairs to the top there were dramatic views of the local countryside. An hour spent rekindling old memories and reminding myself of the turbulent past, passed quickly and I took photos for my Facebook page. Soon I was back on the boat and walking back to my car.

My mood improved I returned to Castle Douglas, collected a steak and some other items for my evening meal and dropped them off at the tent. The campsite was quiet, Tom was sitting in his usual spot drinking, his wife and children were away. There were a few people enjoying the sunshine at the picnic tables by the loch.

I sat for an hour collecting my thoughts before walking towards the Kings Arms.

7

I walked up the few steps into the hotel. There was a framed picture of Prince Charles on the wall, enjoying a glass of Laphroaig on a visit to the premises, a small bar, empty, to the right and then I was in the lounge bar, a wood-panelled area to the left, an arch leading into the bar counter. Chairs and tables scattered around, all empty. I must be too early.

'Hello, can I help you?' It was an attractive young girl, probably late teens, Polish background by the sound of her accent. I glanced across at the pumps, my hands firmly gripping the edge of the bar counter to stop them shaking.

'Soda water and lime, please,' resisting the temptation for anything stronger. 'Expecting people in?'

She smiled. 'We were very busy with a party at lunchtime.'

'Quieter now,' I said, looking around the empty bar. 'It's just after five...'

'Yes, but normally we have a group,' and her gaze suggested the far corner, 'meeting here on a Wednesday.'

'That'll be the police group. I'm hoping to meet with one of them,' I added.

She nodded, placing my drink down on a drip mat on the counter, taking my money.

'Usually, there are about six, mostly retired.'

I would just have to be patient. I went over to a seat close to where they gathered, and waited, sipping my drink slowly.

A young couple came in with a toddler and a baby in a pushchair, wanting an early meal and ordering some drinks. The young girl went about her business.

A man came in, elderly, florid face, and went straight to the bar.

'Usual, Agusia,' he said in a booming voice and perched himself on one of the bar stools at the counter. Agusia, as I now knew her, poured a half-pint of Guinness and a whisky. 'Tell your dad that I am available to go fishing on Friday.'

The girl acknowledged him, 'Usual time?'

'Yes.' He didn't seem like a policeman, not sure why.

Ten minutes later Agusia was bringing through plates of food for the young family, when another man came in. She nodded in my direction. I took another sip of my soda water and lime, as he went up to the counter and ordered a pint, moving over to the table that the bar girl had indicated was their usual meeting place. He was casually dressed in a short-sleeved shirt and shorts.

He smiled at me briefly as he sat down, sipping his pint. Two others quickly followed, collecting their drinks and sitting down. All looked as if they had been retired for some time. The conversation was general, putting the world to rights, someone mentioned Julian Montgomery and the others laughed.

'He did nothing at the Home Office, did nothing for the police. Expect it will be the same at the Foreign Office. He was up here many years ago and I had to liaise with his security detail. They didn't like him, nor did I. Stuck up.'

'Come on, Mac, none of them are any good.' So Mac was here. 'The guy who is taking over from him at the Home Office is also privately educated, wet behind the ears. What does he know about life on the streets?'

I had my group. Maybe better to act now before others arrived.

Mac was balding, a monk's fringe all that was left, overweight, wearing a creased linen jacket.

I got up and went over to them. They all looked at me, as I imagine police do – and I knew that teachers did – evaluating me, weighing me up.

I focused on Mac.

'I heard you being called Mac and I wondered if you could help me. George Park mentioned your name, said that I could find you here.'

I had their attention and Park's name made them curious. I sensed that they liked him. I pulled back a spare seat and no one objected, so I quickly sat down.

'I'm looking for one of your colleagues.' Wrong tack, they all immediately appeared cautious.

'Urquhart.'

Mac partially relieved the tension. 'Everyone is looking for him,' and the others laughed.

'Especially PIRC,' said the man who had arrived first. When he saw my puzzled look, he added, 'Police Investigations and Review Commissioner.' Urquhart had a reputation, it seemed.

'Why do you want to talk to him?' The mood changed again, more serious.

'I'm Finn McAdam,' and Mac rubbed the back of his neck, an involuntary response.

'You've grown and acquired a beard. I remember seeing your photograph.'

'It was twelve years ago.'

'As long as that? What is it you want to know?' He sounded sympathetic, but wary.

'I was traumatised, so was my mother and sister. They won't talk about it and my recollections are hazy. I want clarity and closure,' and justice, but I didn't add that.

All three had put down their drinks, but I could see the glances between them, no one sure what to say, how to proceed.

Mac led. 'It was terrible to lose your father like that, so I can understand your feelings. Best to let it go, move on.'

'Without answers, that's hard. Please help me.' I tried to add a pleading tone to my voice.

Mac's face softened, but he wanted reassurance from the two others and after a pause, he said, 'Jimmy retired a few years ago. I think he went to live in the Machars, probably the Isle.' He was pointing me in the correct direction but, I sensed, didn't want to take responsibility for full disclosure.

'The Isle of Whithorn?'

'Probably, but latterly he was a terrible drinker. His wife left him. I don't think that he will want to help you.'

'Well, at least I'll have tried. Can I get you guys a drink?' They shook their heads, probably seemed too much like blood money.

'Thanks,' and I stood up, judging it was time to leave them.

After a pause they started to talk, a bit quicker, nervous, wanting to put our conversation behind them. I sat down and finished my drink, looking at my iPhone. Their conversation turned to an upcoming golf competition. Mac got up and went out, presumably to the toilet.

Eventually I got up, thanked them and left, going down the stairs following the sign for the toilet myself.

Standing at the urinal, I was conscious that a cubicle was occupied. I was washing my hands when Mac came out and saw me.

'Difficult to talk openly up there.'

41

'I understand.'

'You don't,' he replied.

'The death of your father and Hamilton haunts us. Total cover-up. Urquhart got the brunt as the lead officer, but we never trusted him. Let's say that he did well out of it.'

'In what way?'

'Leave it at that, okay,' his tone suddenly clipped, as if he realised that he had said too much.

'It was my father.'

'I know, son, but take my advice, go back home and forget about it. You will just be putting yourself in great danger. There are forces out there that would destroy you.'

I stood, taking it in. I couldn't give up, I knew I had to go on.

On impulse, I blurted out, 'Who is AGL?'

Mac's face went ashen and he took a step back before recovering.

'I don't know, son. Just go home,' and this time there was an edge to his voice, there would be no more disclosures.

8

I walked quickly back to the campsite, my mind racing, my stomach in knots. It was obvious that the policemen knew something more had happened, given their reaction. Whatever it was, was above their pay grade, but it left them frustrated, unhappy that justice had not been done. A cover-up. I knew it. The blood pulsed in my arteries, headache starting. I needed to calm down. And then Mac's reaction to me mentioning AGL. Proof, for me, that I had the right person. Progress, but how to proceed from here? The campsite was quiet, Tom and his family away, a pile of empties under his picnic table, Rougvie not back, thankfully. The Colonel paced about. His wife, seemingly oblivious, lost in her book. No sign of 'flower girl'.

I unfolded my chair and flopped on it, fighting to take a step back from what I had just learnt and calm down. I had the modern instinct and took out my iPhone, pressing my fingerprint against it to open it up. Another missed call from Sis and then a text. Trying to be friendlier, she must be worried. Then a few emails, nothing of importance.

I looked at the photos I had taken earlier at Threave Castle. Nothing great. A dark picture of the prison cell, a few towards the River Dee and others of the boat, including a short video of it chugging across the narrow strip of water. Hold on – I peered more closely – 'flower girl', Jess, was on the boat, but I hadn't noticed her when I was on the island. Maybe she was just touring the local tourist sites. I had also seen her heading to Dumfries in the morning. Busy day. Anyway, I had other matters on my mind much more important than dwelling on her. I quickly uploaded the best photos to my Facebook page and, as usual, commented on some posts.

Then I got out my steak and set up the camping stove, cutting up a red onion and starting to fry it, my eyes watering. Tom and his family came back and another family arrived. A father and son, it looked like, were pitching their tent, laughing, bonding. That hurt.

I was serving my steak when Jess reappeared in her Fiat 500, showing no recognition as she passed my tent. Minutes later she grabbed a towel and headed towards the shower block. Rougvie came back, parking his Jeep a short distance away, since I had parked my car in the narrow space between our tents. A barrier, I hoped.

The cooking had helped, distracting me, letting my subconscious whirr away in the depths of my brain, the thoughts that came out no longer jumbled or tumbling over one another. There was a conspiracy, covering up what happened the night my father was murdered. The police had been sidelined and AGL was involved. My next step was to look up Jimmy Urquhart and find out what he had to say. A trip to the Isle of Whithorn was called for.

I was aware of a group of pupils playing about on the slope of the hill beside me but didn't pay any attention. A voice, slightly hesitant, interrupted my thoughts. 'Is that you, Finn?'

I looked up. It was Duncan, a teaching colleague from the school we both taught in a year ago when I was completing my probationer period. A good guy. He was with another teacher and a party of boys. Some of the boys were just finishing fish suppers.

'Good to see you,' I said, standing up to shake his hand.

'What are you doing here?' he asked, curious.

'I was going to ask you the same,' I replied. 'It's a long way from Glasgow. I got a post in Ayrshire, permanent.'

'Good for you. Chemistry, wasn't it?'

I nodded. I looked beyond him, the other teacher was organising the boys, setting up some goals with their jackets and sweatshirts, ready to kick a ball about.

'I'm here with Jim, helping out.' Jim, who was not too far away, heard his name being spoken and waved across.

'We have a small group of boys, with issues,' and he looked at me, knowingly. I understood. 'Taken them away for a few days, trying to help them to mix with each other. Teach them some social skills. They all have difficult backgrounds. We're staying at an outdoor centre just south of here for a week, not the one over there,' and he pointed towards the outdoor centre by the shower block. 'They're still high, so we brought them into Castle Douglas for fish and chips and a kick about.'

'Good idea, burn off some of their energy, maybe get some sleep tonight.'

Duncan was already a dedicated teacher with a heart for this sort of work and you needed that, it was a calling few had. His round glasses on a slender frame gave him an owlish expression and earned him the nickname 'Potter'. His rapport with the pupils was legendary, they instinctively recognised his genuine concern for their needs.

Jim, who presented a slight figure, wiry, his head shaven, was busy sorting out teams – three-a-side. Such a small group suggested that they all needed a lot of individual care and

45

attention. Jim had started the game. Two boys showed no interest, the others were keen.

'Hold on,' said Duncan. 'I better get involved.'

As he ran the few yards to join the game, one boy kicked the ball away and sat down. This was indeed going to require a lot of patience. I admired both teachers. With a little persuasion, Duncan got the boy to collect the ball and the game started again.

I stood and watched. One of the boys, small with thin hair, a white narrow, pointed face, struggled to join in, and when the ball came to him, he swiped at it and missed. The others laughed. His face turned puce, his hands clenched into fists, and he screamed and screamed.

Duncan ran over, indicating that Jim took the others. The boy fell on the ground, his body rigid, tears streaming down his face. Duncan crouched down beside him.

'Come on, Davie, everyone misses the ball sometimes.' The scene played out for a few minutes before Duncan, sensing some change, offered a hand, which was accepted, and he pulled Davie up. He said something that I couldn't hear, and the boy wiped his face roughly on the sleeve of his jumper. Jim shouted to Davie and eventually he ran towards the rest of the boys.

Duncan came over shortly afterwards. 'You know the type. Hellish background, no love, big issues.'

'Yeah.' Every teacher encounters those that society doesn't know what to do with.

'Davie was brought up on white bread and tomato ketchup. Had to be Heinz, mark you. Saw his father beating and raping his mum regularly, and then one night his father went too far and strangled her, throwing her dead body in a bath. The father's now in prison, serving a long sentence. Davie didn't talk for a year and now lives with foster parents. Hopefully, we can help, get him to engage. He is improving,' and Duncan smiled. 'He usually ends up biting people if he gets into a rage.'

One of the boys shouted across, 'Come on, Mr McIntyre, you've got to be better than Mr Black at football,' and Duncan left me, trotting over to join the game. I admired his commitment.

Anger rose inside me, tears welling in my eyes, as I turned away from Duncan trying to hide my emotional response from him. Life was unfair, no one should see a parent murdered. Davie looked about the same age as I had been.

I watched the game for a few minutes, shouted encouragement, even collected the ball when it came in my direction. One boy, thick glasses, carrot-coloured hair, very friendly – Robbie, Duncan called him, as he urged him to rejoin the game – made a point of talking to me. Each of these kids had problems, I could see, struggling to fit in, past trauma blunting their social skills. Duncan and Jim were doing a wonderful job. I wanted them to succeed with Davie and the others.

Rougvie had returned and came across inviting me to a real ale sampling at a local pub, which I declined. Despite his rebuff from Jess he was enjoying himself, talking about the estate he had visited today that belonged to some lord and how to cull grey squirrels. Mercifully, he left early.

After an hour, the football match was getting ragged. The boys, many not used to physical exercise by the look of them, were tired, arguments starting. Duncan came over. 'Time to go, I think, hopefully they'll all sleep tonight. Over the next few days we're going to try abseiling, rock climbing and various day-long exercises intended to get them working as a team.' He paused and smiled. 'The impossible will take a bit longer.'

'You're doing a good job. The boys will benefit but they'll grumble a lot.'

Duncan laughed but then became serious. I knew what was coming.

'If you don't mind me asking, how is Gillian?' But he really meant: where was Gillian?

'We have a few issues, so I thought I'd take time out and nowhere better than this part of the country – I was brought up here.' I wasn't about to share what had happened.

He placed a hand on my shoulder, a gesture of empathy.

'I hope things work out,' his face serious. 'Is she still teaching at the same school?'

I tried to be light. 'And still believing that it is possible to teach young people French.'

Minutes later their minibus left going slowly over the speed bumps. I was haunted by the story of Davie, his face fresh in my mind. At least his father was in jail.

• • •

I was tired, it had been a busy day, and started to prepare for sleep, wandering around the tent, hammering in some loose pegs and the wooden poles that supported the windbreak. The street lamps around the site came on, and I could hear the birds settling down for the night, the dusk chorus, while an inquisitive blackbird, with its orange beak, pecked at some crumbs near the windbreak.

A car approached the site fast, bumping over the speed bumps, past the warden's office, which was now closed, its tyres screeching as it swung onto the tarmac road, headlamps full on, dazzling me as it passed my tent, Jess in the passenger seat. Out jumped a young man, early twenties, shaven head, wearing a white tee shirt, slashed jeans and black boots. He waited for Jess to get out before embracing her. He was taller than Jess and had

48

to reach down to kiss her, which he did passionately. At least I knew what she was going to be doing tonight. He held her firmly and then broke away reaching into the back of his car, a green Mondeo, and grabbed a small holdall and what looked like a carry-out, slamming the car door behind him, as they headed into the tent. A lamp was turned on, casting their shadows large over the canvas. I turned away; I had seen this script before.

• • •

I thought that it was the sound of farmers working late, bringing in silage, the trailers bumping behind the tractors, that woke me but then I realised it was the bass beat of some unrecognisable tune. I sat up and yawned, struggling out of my sleeping bag. My watch told me that I had only been asleep for an hour. The music was coming from the direction of Jess's tent. After ten minutes I knew that I couldn't get back to sleep, so I unzipped the tent flap and eased out. The cold air hit me and I shivered. There was still a light on in their tent and the silhouette of their bodies told me what they were up to. Hopefully, they would soon satisfy their lust. I headed over to the shower block. Just as I was about to reach it, a voice spoke from the shadows.

'Bloody squaddies think that they were the first to discover sex.'

It was the Colonel appearing out of the dark, leaning heavily on his sticks, pacing about.

'Can't sleep?'

He grumbled. 'Bad night.'

'How do you know that he's a squaddie?'

'Look at the car registration. Army. And I am sure that they won't have lent him the car. Borrowed, shall we say. Probably just back from training, testosterone filled. It is always the same.

Young men deprived of female company, making up for lost time.'

'It was the beat of the music that woke me.'

'Lucky you, I haven't managed to get to sleep.'

'Let's hope his passion will soon subside,' and I left him pacing about.

As I returned to the tent, I saw Rougvie on his way back from the pub. Even from a distance he was staggering, shouting something that I couldn't make out as he passed Jess's tent. The shadows showed someone jumping up but being quickly pulled down. Rougvie was so drunk that he didn't even notice me as he fell into his tent.

I lay awake for an hour, the beat throbbing in the night air, and then all went quiet.

9

Someone was shouting and getting nearer my tent, waking me.
Disorientated, I tried to make sense of the shouting but couldn't.
The person was roaring, thumping what sounded like a table. I
scrambled out of my sleeping bag and unzipped the nylon flap,
pushing my head out. The squaddie was standing in front of
Rougvie's tent swearing, demanding he came out, wearing only
his shorts, a large vivid tattoo of a Scottish thistle on his back.
I heard no sound from Rougvie. Probably sensible. He was
thumping Rougvie's picnic table, then he picked it up and threw
it at Rougvie's tent, droplets of water cascading from the surface
as it shook.

I worked my way out, standing in shorts and a tee shirt,
aware that it had rained overnight, my bare feet wet and cold.

'What's going on?' I said, trying to sound measured, calm the
situation down, the teacher bit kicking in.

I repeated myself before I got his attention and he glanced
my way, scowling.

'None of your business,' he answered, an aggressive edge to
his voice. 'Piss off.'

'You're disturbing the campsite, calm down.' It sounded a
lame response and it was.

I saw Tom's wife peering out of her tent, alarmed. The squaddie came towards me, stopping at the windbreak that marked the edge of my territory.

'This is between him and me, no one else. Keep out of my business or you'll get what's coming to him.'

'What's he done?'

'I told you, this is between him and me.'

I cursed Rougvie but I couldn't stand back and let him be attacked. Something about injustice always rankled in me. Maybe Davie's mother would have been alive if someone had stood up to her husband. Maybe my dad would have been alive if I had shouted out, done something and not just watched on.

'Leave him alone,' I said firmly.

Now I had his attention. His face was contorted, his eyes red and inflamed. He grabbed one of the wooden poles that held up the windbreak, pulling it out of its nylon socket, and swiftly pushed the dirt-encrusted pointed end against my throat. The action was quick and he stabbed my throat repeatedly, hurting me, choking me. I stepped back, rubbing my throat, coughing.

'Get the message?'

'No,' that threw him and he then poked me hard on the chest. I grabbed the pole and twisted it. His grip held firm and he pulled it away, trying to stab at me again. I moved to the side. Thanks, Rougvie, I thought. Where was he? Probably cowering in the tent.

'If squaddies get into trouble off-base they get disciplined.'

'Eh...?'

'You are a soldier, the registration number on your car shows that,' and I pointed to it, noticing for the first time that Jess was standing outside her tent, beside the Mondeo, wrapped in her dressing gown, her white face etched with alarm, her hand rubbing her face. I shouted across to her, 'Tell soldier boy to lay off, or I'll contact his commanding officer.'

He rushed me swinging a punch, which I managed to avoid, but I tripped over my canvas chair, slipping, struggling to regain my balance. The second punch hit my jaw and I toppled over. It hurt, the side of my face throbbing. His snarling face was above me, inches from mine. I shouted at him to stop, but he grabbed me. His breath stank, unshaven, white powder clung around his nose.

'I'll tell your commanding officer that you're doing drugs,' I said quickly, in desperation. That stopped him and a booming voice shouted from behind him, 'Private, stand to attention.' It was the Colonel, making his way slowly across. For a second the squaddie froze and I squirmed free.

'Danny, stop or you'll get in trouble,' shouted Jess, and she ran towards him.

Danny cursed as only squaddies can.

'I want to hit him,' and he pointed towards Rougvie's tent, 'for what he said last night.' It was the first coherent thing he had said.

Sweating profusely the Colonel had reached us, leaning heavily on his sticks, out of breath.

'Look at my tent. My wife has a phone,' and I could see that his wife was holding her phone up in the air. 'She will phone the police, if others haven't already done so. You are ruining your career, you are a disgrace to the uniform.' The words boomed, resonating with authority. He had been here before, taking control, restoring order, unflinching.

Danny allowed himself to be pulled away by Jess.

'Come back to the tent,' she said quietly, 'neither of them are worth it,' which I thought was rich, since I had done nothing but try to stop Danny getting into trouble.

The Colonel stood shaking with the effort he had made, his

brow dripping with sweat, not with fear, I suspected, but from the physical effort of reaching us.

He addressed Danny directly. 'I expect you to be off the site in ten minutes. I've noted the registration number and I have many contacts in the army. Return and I'll use them, and smarten up, don't let your regiment down,' he ended, delivering the words sharply.

Danny's face was white, the exertions of last night and this morning's events catching up. He allowed himself to be led away by Jess, who was stroking his arm, trying to calm him down. Suddenly, he broke free of Jess and turned back towards Rougvie's tent but stopped after a few steps.

'Tell him, if he says anything more about my girl, I'll kill him.' The statement was made more to save face, bravado, like macho man must have the last word.

And turning to me, he shouted, spittle spraying from his mouth, 'If I see you with her, I'll kill you, too.'

'None of that, laddie,' said the Colonel. 'Now get yourself together and act like a soldier should – disciplined, not letting the army down.'

The Colonel and I watched as Danny was led back to the tent.

'Disgraceful,' muttered the Colonel, 'in my day he would have been drummed out.'

'Thanks for your intervention,' I said.

'You did well,' and he smiled. We heard the zip of a tent being undone, turning to see Rougvie emerge, wearing only underpants, and quickly running behind his tent. We heard him retching.

'He could do with some army discipline,' the Colonel stated, as he shuffled back to his tent, where his wife was waiting for him.

Rougvie appeared from behind his tent, grabbed a towel from inside the flap and ran towards the shower block, his face drained of any colour, muttering 'thanks' as he passed me. My jaw was throbbing but as I felt it, I didn't think that anything was broken, a small patch of matted blood on my beard. I was suddenly aware of the cold dampness that was permeating my body. I went back inside my tent to put on more clothes.

Coming out of my tent a few minutes later, I saw Tom's wife approaching bearing a mug of coffee and a plastic bag which, it turned out, contained ice. Beside her were her two young daughters.

'Thought you might need these, lots of sugar in the coffee, good for shock.'

'Thanks,' and I was glad to sip the coffee, holding the ice pack to my jaw. 'I'll be okay.'

'That was horrible. You were very brave.'

I blushed slightly. 'Couldn't stand by,' I muttered.

'Very brave,' she repeated.

We were looking across the campsite when we heard a car door slam and saw Danny throw his bag in the back seat of the Mondeo. We watched as he jumped into the front seat, the engine roaring as he spun the car round, and he drove off without looking in our direction.

'Good riddance,' I stated.

'Agreed, and I'm Mary,' she replied, smiling, 'and this is Molly, she's six,' and she pointed to her taller daughter, 'and Zoe, only four.' Both girls smiled shyly.

I smiled broadly at them, probably more in relief now that my ordeal was over.

'I watched you both on your bikes, you are very good.' The girls smiled and Molly turned away, running back to her tent. Zoe clutched her mother's hand.

'Campsites should be quiet places,' and Mary nodded.

Rougvie came back about half an hour later, ashen, grabbing a bottle of water from his tent and drinking thirstily. A few seconds later he stopped and belched.

'Thanks for what you did. Not going to drink so much real ale again…'

'Or make comments passing Jess's tent.'

'I don't remember that. Is that what caused him to be so angry?'

'And violent,' and I rubbed my jaw again for effect.

'Sorry.'

'Be careful. Stick to squirrels.'

He was pathetic and I went back inside my tent to get away from him.

I was glad of the ice pack, my jaw was really sore, a headache starting. No point in heading to the Isle of Whithorn to see Urquhart. It was a long drive and I wasn't up to it. I'd leave it until tomorrow.

Instead, I decided to hang around the campsite for the morning, go into Castle Douglas to get some shopping, and I felt it was time to visit the place where my father was murdered. It didn't change anything, it never could, but it was my duty never to let Dad's memory fade. I couldn't understand why Mother and Sis would never go there, refused repeatedly. They couldn't grieve as I did, they were both too angry.

10

Jess was walking slowly back from the shower block, hair slick and wet, ignoring me as I drove past on my way out of the campsite. I was able to move my jaw but it was swollen, and I felt sure that I was going to have a lot of bruising. Hopefully, my beard would conceal it. A couple of painkillers had eased the headache.

Like the flowers on the grave, my visits to Castle Douglas had certain rituals. Today's was equally macabre – I was going to visit the site where my father was murdered. Reliving it wasn't healthy, Sis said, but in a strange way I found that it did help. Like visiting Dad's grave, the scene of the crime made me feel closer to him, reinforcing my determination to resolve what happened that night – get answers, get resolution, get revenge.

I reached the A75, the road from Gretna to Stranraer, the main road in the area, although that didn't mean that it was a good road. Only small sections were dual carriageways, mostly two-lane, with sections where there were overtaking lanes. You could also encounter convoys of trucks heading to or from Ireland, which could slow you down. The countryside compensated: low, green rolling hills, called drumlins – a local feature left by the retreat of the last ice age – and many fields of contented cattle munching on grass.

Fortunately, I didn't have far to travel, reaching the turn-off for Gatehouse of Fleet after twelve miles. Steep slopes leading up to pockets of trees marked the edge of the Galloway Forest Park to my right. On the approach to Gatehouse of Fleet were the grounds of the famous Cally Palace Hotel, where I once had afternoon tea on Sis's twenty-first birthday. The hotel was surrounded by mature woodlands. I remembered Gatehouse of Fleet – the granite tower beside the Murray Hotel as you reached the town, its narrow main street with a few shops. Continuing south, you would rejoin the A75, as it now ran alongside the expanse of Wigtown Bay.

When we reached the Ship Inn we turned right, soon passing the primary school, climbing into the hills. It was as if Dad was beside me for one of our many question and answer sessions.

'Why is it called the Ship Inn?' he would ask, a smile playing on his face, and I would answer to show that I had listened previously.

'It is located near the end of the canal that linked Wigtown Bay to the town. Boats could sail up close to the town from Wigtown Bay reaching Port MacAdam. The town was once busy with boats, ferrying goods from the cotton mills...'

'Okay,' he would say, raising his hand for me to stop but pleased at my enthusiasm and recall.

'Anyone famous stay at the hotel?'

'Dorothy...' I paused, the surname evading me.

'Sayers, where she wrote…?'

'I know this,' and I searched my mind as he patiently waited, 'The Five Red Herrings.'

'Good.' I never remember him saying anything else but good. We enjoyed each other's company on our frequent trips; such chats and grilling were the norm, enjoyed by both.

'Was there another canal in the area?' The eyebrows would rise as he waited for a response, a warm, encouraging smile on his face.

'Yes, from Carlingwark Loch to the River Dee, to carry out the marl.'

He loved history, places, learning about people. In some ways it was surprising that he studied chemistry.

We were heading up towards the closed Gatehouse of Fleet railway station, almost seven miles from the town it was named after, the distance between town and station once a record for any railway in Britain, he told me. Dad didn't bore with facts, he just absorbed them. Mother never shared his enthusiasm.

'Don't fill his head with useless information,' she would exclaim, exasperated, but Dad ignored her. He frequently did.

I was transported back to that evening. The narrow road twisted, blind corners, farms and cottages competing initially, then woodlands with a broad mix of trees until you reached the treeline and then there was wild moorland, the granite crags of the Clints of Dromore in the distance and beyond them, and towering over them, the majestic granite pinnacle of Cairnsmore of Fleet, the dominant hill in the area. Then, always straining for the first glimpse of it, the Big Water of Fleet viaduct. Remote, its brick-clad piers often reflecting the sun as it did that evening. To some it was one of the most iconic railway features in the country, crossing the remote valley of the Big Water of Fleet, before the railway passed in front of the Clints of Dromore. Many photographers waited to see the plumes of smoke as steam engines fought to reach the summit of the line. The railway had closed in 1965, part of the Beeching cuts, but its legacy lingered on.

We turned right when we reached the station site that fateful evening, entering what was now the Cairnsmore of Fleet Nature

Reserve, the road twisting even more as we lost height, watching out for stray sheep, rumbling across cattle grids and bypassing the visitor centre to approach the viaduct. At 900 feet long, 70 feet high, it was impressive. The brick cladding added later to strengthen it, stopped just short of the curved top of the arches, which were braced with tie rods and rails.

Today, I drove under one of the arches and stopped in a small car park. I got out and breathed the pure fresh air, listened to the buzz of insects on what was becoming a warm day. I walked to the base of the viaduct and clambered up the slope beside it and after a scramble reached the embankment that led away from it. Once I reached the viaduct I walked over the ballast surface, noting its gentle curve as it crossed this remote valley. At the point where it crossed the Big Water of Fleet I stepped up onto the brick-lined side and gripped the rusty railings. Whenever we passed the viaduct, this was the ritual, admiring the Victorian engineering masterpiece.

On that evening we stopped at the viaduct, as usual, and climbed the rough slope to the trackbed. Swallows were flying around it and swooping under the arches, never stopping, a mesmerizing aerial dance, a private performance for our benefit. I gripped the rusty railings of the viaduct and looked down at the river passing underneath, the water crystal clear, showing up the peaty coloured riverbed.

The Forestry Commission had planted trees all over this area after the Second World War, masking the barren landscape, creating the largest forested area in the United Kingdom. Now some of the trees were being harvested, leaving a patchwork appearance. The contrast between this remote landscape and the green lush terrain further down the valley, around Gatehouse of Fleet, could not be starker.

Eventually, that evening, we returned to the car and drove on towards the forest directly ahead and soon turned right, passing a farmhouse and then following the road towards the loch. Loch Grannoch, a narrow loch, two miles long, awaited us. Little did I know that journey would change my life.

I hoped to return and go to Loch Grannoch another day, but today, with my head still pounding, I didn't feel up to it. I just savoured the sweet air, looking skyward for any birds of prey hovering, memories of past and present mingling.

There was always a breeze in the valley, softly tugging at me as I stood there. In winter, a raging gale could blow down the valley, but not today. The familiarity of it all calmed me. I rubbed my jaw, now quite swollen, pondering on recent events and then headed back to the car.

I drove away from the viaduct, back towards the junction at the station. There wasn't a soul, only some sheep. There were a couple of houses at the junction, former railwaymen's dwellings, and then as I drove on I passed by the former station building, remote, haunted, according to my father. The space between the platforms now infilled with gorse, rhododendrons and populated by wildlife, small birds and, by some accounts, adders.

There were conifer plantations to each side and then remote moorland. The woods would return further down the hill towards Creetown. The railway trackbed continued to my right and there, as the road twisted over the former line, I pulled over and stopped.

At the scene of a famous battle there are often signs, monuments, strange burial mounds, whatever. Here there was only a bunch of wilted flowers wrapped in cellophane, flapping in the breeze, which I had placed there a year ago, tying them firmly to a fence post.

Much happened that evening between our journey towards Loch Grannoch and arriving here in the middle of the night, someone else driving our car. My head had been hooded with a hessian sack, my arms and legs bound in ropes. After stopping and briefly being led from the car into a hut, I was bundled back into the car, a man who stank of sweat holding me tightly, as I became more distressed. Thereafter, a further long journey in the car, God knows where, had been endured, my shouts muffled, before we had reached here.

Then through a rip in the sack I saw my father standing, held firmly. Then the sound of a car approaching. I have never been able to identify the type of car. Light-coloured, maybe silver, low-slung but very long, air vents to the side, the bonnet dipping sharply beyond the wheels. What looked like vents on the sloping bonnet but were headlamps, their light dazzling me. I turned away. I could imagine my dad saying: Tell me, what type of car is that? Expecting me to know. Instead, he was being forcefully held. Two people got out of the car. One was the same man I'd seen a few days ago in Castle Douglas, his face stony, no warmth, angry. Something had gone wrong. He was in charge, the shadowy figures holding Dad looking towards him as he eyed up the scene. The car window was partially down, the cold night air catching my throat, tears welling as I took in the severity of the situation. Even at twelve, I knew what was going to happen. Then wordlessly he issued his instruction, nodding towards one of the figures holding my father. Dad was made to kneel on the ground, a hand forcing his head down. A gun appeared, a flash, the retort echoing off unseen hills and silence as my father slumped, his head distorted with the impact of the bullet. My father murdered in front of me.

I screamed, and the man's attention turned to me. Hands gripped me, hauling me out of the car, loosening the ropes that bound me. No gun, but a syringe was produced out of a bag that the driver had grabbed from the back of the car, the needle glinting in the light of the headlamps. My right arm was held rigid, fingers fumbled to find a vein and then a needle was inserted, a pinprick of pain, and liquid fire spread through my body, my thoughts disappearing with a whoosh as blackness descended.

I jumped as the memories ended, the darkness created by them replaced with light, and I was aware that I was alone on a remote road. It was cold, my head ached as I leant against the car, breathing deeply, regaining composure. The other players in that nightmare were bit part characters. I was after the main man – AGL or whatever he was called.

I drank water from a plastic bottle that I grabbed from the car and swallowed more pain-killers. I opened the tailgate and took out a bunch of flowers to replace the previous year's offering. I wouldn't forget, even if others did.

• • •

Driving back by the same route I took my time, stopping at a restaurant and gift shop in Gatehouse of Fleet to have some soup and a roll, and a much-needed coffee. I lingered over the coffee trying to cope with my memories. It was as if I was emerging from a nightmare only to discover that it was all true, but no one believed me. In the car park beside the restaurant I noticed Rougvie's Jeep, which didn't improve my mood.

I reached the campsite late afternoon and showered. Feeling better, I went along to the Kings Arms for a meal and afterwards walked back to the campsite. On impulse, I continued past it and reached the cemetery, the gates always open inviting you to visit the dead. As I walked through the old section and entered the newer part, I saw my father's gravestone and immediately knew there was something different about it. Was it the evening sun that made it appear streaked with yellow? It couldn't be – the setting sun was behind it.

Horrified, I reached the gravestone. Someone had spray-painted it. The message was clear. A single word written across the polished granite – murderer.

11

I could think of no obvious person who would have spray-painted my father's gravestone. I tended to blame Rougvie for everything, by default, such was my contempt for him, but he had no idea of my background story and it was ridiculous to think that he did it. I could think of no one else who had a motive. I was upset and for the first time in a few months I could have done with a drink, but I dismissed the idea. Instead, I reached for a can of Red Bull, feeling the almost instant caffeine boost, the edginess that came with it, crushing the tall, slim blue-silver can when it was empty and throwing it against the windbreak, adding to the pile of crushed cans, exorcising my demons. I watched the sun go down, the activity in the campsite settle and the stars coming out, ignoring the chill night air. The sound of Tom snoring now an accepted part of the background noise. Eventually I crawled into my sleeping bag, having to sleep on my right side, the left side of my face swollen and painful.

Next day had a purpose and a plan which energised me. I tidied up after my breakfast and got ready to leave. I could hear that Rougvie was still slumbering. Jess was up, sitting at the picnic bench beside her tent, watching the world; all dressed up but nowhere to go, it seemed. I waved to Mary as I passed and smiled at the Colonel, who was emerging from the shower block, shuffling along.

It was back onto the A75 and this time continuing past Gatehouse of Fleet, the road now following the coastline. The tide was out as I reached Wigtown Bay, the mudflats at the mouth of the River Cree, banks of shimmering mud, with deep gouges created by water flowing into the bay. At the roundabout just south of Newton Stewart, I took the road towards Wigtown, entering the area known as the Machars, a large triangular area of land bounded by Wigtown and Luce Bays, its northern boundary loosely marked by the A75. Again the land was gentle and rolling with outcrops of rock, fertile land, green at this time of year. Wigtown lay ahead on high ground, which I skirted, and I passed through a series of small villages, reaching the historic town of Whithorn.

'What is Whithorn famous for?'

'The first Christian Church in Scotland, founded by St Ninian, known as Candida Casa or the White House.'

'Good, well remembered.' Memories of Dad were never far away.

I liked Whithorn, its wide main street narrowed at both ends, so that cattle, in medieval times, could be kept safe overnight, penned in.

I left the town behind, passing a large water tower on the outskirts. Many local farms had water towers to supply water to cattle or the farmhouse, due to the undulating ground. Now I drove towards the Isle of Whithorn. Ahead in the distance, I could see the faint outline of the hills of the Lake District, across the Solway Firth.

The Isle was a favourite haunt of my father and I, the Wigtown Bay Sailing Club frequently visited as we mastered our sailing skills, using small boats in the harbour and then eventually venturing out onto the Solway Firth. At the moment the tide was out, boats stranded on the mud, a fishing boat clinging to the harbour wall, its keel exposed. Of course, the Isle of Whithorn was no longer an island. A gravel beach, where the church and neighbouring houses are today, once separated the headland from the mainland. About the end of the seventeenth century, it was filled in to form a narrow strip of land, the sea pressing on both sides, the area today still dogged by flooding at extremely high tides, whipped up by winter storms. The Isle was where pilgrims landed to journey on to Whithorn.

Some things had changed since my last visit, with a new community cafe and shop having opened. There was housing, mainly to the left, some terrace, some individual, all heights and sizes, roofs lined with rows of chimney pots. Some houses stuck out into the sea, as did the church, whose request for land to build on had been rejected by the then landowners, forcing them to build on the shoreline. The road turned sharp right as it continued to the harbour, passing the Steam Packet Inn, a favourite meeting place for locals, literally at the end of the road through the Machars.

I had no idea which house was Urquhart's, but I suspected he would likely be found in one of the bars at the Steam Packet or someone there would be able to help point me in his direction. It was just about lunchtime as I parked the car around the corner from the hotel, close to the harbour, and wandered back along. Both bars were empty, so I walked back to the car, continuing on by a field used as an overflow car park, through a play park and up the hill towards the white tower, a wonderful viewpoint overlooking the entrance to the harbour. Some days you could see England, the Scottish coastline, the Isle of Man, Ireland and even, on an exceptional rare day, the snow-clad peak of Snowdonia in Wales. Five kingdoms, which the hotel owner had used as the name of his range of real ales. There was a light swell on the sea, markers for lobster creels bobbing about. I sat on the wooden bench that surrounded the base of the white tower and thought about my next steps.

It was doubtful that Urquhart would want to speak, especially about the events of that evening, but I had to try. I might glean something, another piece in the puzzle. I waited for an hour, watching a group visiting the now roofless St Ninian's chapel, built in the thirteenth century to welcome pilgrims and then headed downhill towards the harbour and back to the hotel.

The group I had seen at the chapel were now sitting in the lounge bar, a waitress taking their orders. Further on in the public bar, two men were sitting beside each other on bar stools at the counter, sipping from pint glasses, their backs to me.

I pushed through the doors into the public bar and stood waiting to be served. The younger of the two, maybe in his thirties, which ruled out Urquhart, shouted, 'Malcolm, you're needed.'

I thanked him, glancing at the other man. Now, he was a possibility, thinning hair dyed black, badly, face covered with red blotches and I remembered what Mac said about Urquhart's drinking. He didn't respond to my arrival, remaining taciturn and gazing down at his almost empty pint glass.

Malcolm appeared, almost having to duck as he navigated his way from lounge to public bar, such was his height, and took my order for soda water and lime. 'Either of you guys want a drink?'

'I'm going after this,' said the younger one, lifting his pint glass, which was almost drained.

The older man scowled and shook his head. I collected my drink and sat at a table near the window, checking my iPhone but really waiting to see if the older man turned out to be Urquhart.

I didn't have long to wait. Ten minutes later the younger man got up to go, 'See you soon, Jimmy,' he said, as he finished his pint and placed it down on the counter. Jimmy barely acknowledged him and the man left. This had to be Urquhart.

'Malcolm, can I have a chaser? The usual,' he shouted to the barman, who was also serving the lounge bar next door.

A whisky was delivered, no water added and it was downed. 'Another, Malcolm,' and a further whisky was placed on the bar counter. This one lasted only a little longer and then he got up quickly and walked towards the door. He caught me by surprise and I watched as he walked past the window. Quickly I left my drink and ventured out onto the street. He continued towards the corner and I saw him enter one of the houses beyond the church. He never looked back.

My guts were churning, but I had to do something now, so I walked along to the house. As I passed by what was a lounge window, I glanced in and saw the usual three-piece suite, a display cabinet and television, but it was extremely untidy, littered with old newspapers, envelopes, letters and an almost empty bottle of whisky on a coffee table.

Taking a deep breath, I rapped loudly on the door. Eventually the door opened a few inches and Urquhart appeared, looking worse than when I saw him side-on in the bar. His face very lined, deep shadows under the eyes.

'You were in the bar. What do you want?' Suspicion on his face, eyes squinting, mouth tightening.

'Mac sent me for a chat. Thought you could help.' I rushed the sentences out, stating my reasons for the visit.

'Mac?'

'Yes, I met him in Castle Douglas, Kings Arms.'

'I know where he drinks,' he replied gruffly. 'Why do you want to chat to me?'

'I'll explain. Can I come in?' I took him by surprise, as I stepped inside quickly. He stepped back, I think that the drink had befuddled him a little and I walked into the lounge.

'Who the hell are you?' he snapped.

'Finn, Finn McAdam,' I stated, turning to face him.

He drew breath, as if gulping for air.

'I wanted to talk about my father,' I demanded, pressing home my advantage before he could recover. To say that the room was untidy would be an understatement. I could see through the door into the kitchen and out to the sea and hills behind. It was also a mess, surfaces littered with cans, mostly empty, and dirty mugs and crockery.

'I have nothing to say,' he muttered, his face now losing colour, which made the red blotches more striking.

'You were there, you know what happened.' I tried to smile and be friendly, but I was too tense and failed. We stood facing each other, both uncertain what to do next.

I tried again, this time managing to force a smile.

'Look, I need help, Mr Urquhart. You're my last chance. Please tell me what happened. You know I was in the car, watching.'

'I didn't see anything. The case was out of our hands by the time I arrived at the scene. I saw you in hospital,' and he squinted again, as if he was trying to confirm that I was an older version of the young boy he remembered.

'Who took it out of your hands?'

'The guys from the defence ministry. They were there very swiftly, the bodies removed.'

'Is that not unusual? Lots of evidence lost.'

70

'Listen, son, I follow orders. Ask no questions, get on with my job.'

'It was a cover-up. My father murdered.'

'Lots of stories went around. Can't remember much.' The window of surprise was closing as he gathered his wits.

'Long time ago, best to forget about it.'

'I can't. Your colleagues felt that you benefitted from it. How?'

That hit home. He grabbed my arm with surprising speed and strength, propelling me towards the door. 'Get out or I'll call the police.'

'Would you?' I replied coldly, refusing to move. 'Could be awkward questions. Your friends have largely retired, no longer there to protect you.'

I was shoved hard against the lounge door but I stood my ground defying him.

'Get out,' he shouted, his mouth twisting, anger mounting.

'Okay, but I'll keep asking questions and when I get answers, I'll be back,' and I left, taking my time, trying to show that I was not frightened, the door being slammed behind me. I waited a minute and walked past the window. He was already pouring himself a glass of whisky, hands shaking. When he saw me he shouted, but I left smartly.

He was rattled. Good. So as Mac hinted, he had benefitted in some way out of that evening, but why? What had he done? Again too many questions. I needed answers. Where could I turn now? I had chased up a number of leads but still had no definite proof of anything. Time to head back to the campsite.

12

I left the Isle of Whithorn with much to think about, taking
a right turn at the community cafe and onto the back road to
Garlieston, another small village with a harbour, further up the
coast. I could have taken this route on the way down but decided
that it would be too much of a distraction and that I should
focus instead on talking to Urquhart.

A few miles up the road, I reached the site of Cruggleton
Old Church in the middle of a field, its boundary marked by a
stone wall, the church surrounded by tall trees, which obscured
its outline. I parked at the roadside. Memories of a much happier
day flooded my mind, but they were tinged with regret, only
temporarily, I hoped.

Two years before, I waited inside the small church, originally
built in the twelfth century and restored in the nineteenth
century, nervously standing beside the altar, waiting for Gillian
to arrive for our wedding service. The minister stood at the
south door, at the other end of the church, waiting for Gillian
and her father, a local farmer. A few shafts of light penetrated
the narrow windows, dancing motes of dust showing up in their
path.

A small group of musicians played folk tunes on a mixture
of violins, and a cello, hemmed in beside the door, struck up a

Celtic wedding tune on fiddles as Gillian appeared. The small church was crowded and I couldn't initially see her as she entered, the congregation standing, but I soon caught my first glimpse and was rewarded with a nervous smile from under her veil.

By now I had left the car, wandering over to the church, no path linking the road to it and like that day two years ago, I was glad that it wasn't muddy underfoot. The tall trees in full leaf hid the church, which was rarely used. Stuart, Gillian's father, had local connections and the church was especially opened for the occasion. The narrow road beside the church lined with cars and minibuses.

Gillian was looking fantastic, her long brown hair framing her smiling, beaming face, her happiness there for all to see. Her proud father bringing her to the front, people standing admiring the radiant bride. Jon, my best man, nudging me, cracking some inane joke that I pretended to smile at but helped to settle my nerves.

Service over, we stepped outside, the sun shining through the leaves of the trees, creating a flickering pattern of light on her dress. Someone put a garland of flowers over her head and she turned smiling at me, laughing. I was a lucky man. At that moment there was not a dark cloud in the sky. I felt happy, blessed, even my mother was smiling, caught up in the occasion. Sis was standing beside Paul, her husband, talking to some of our friends, relaxed. The portents were good.

Rumour was that Stuart had built a barn, especially for the marriage of his only daughter. It was certainly well-provisioned with multiple power sockets and excellent lighting, too good for his dairy cattle, who I was sure would enjoy a stripped down version of the barn when they were eventually allowed to enter. Tables were set out for the wedding meal and the caterers did him proud. I was glad when the speeches were over. The final photographs were taken once we had been hoisted onto hay bales by a digger hung with ribbons. The two of us put on a pedestal. No expense was spared and I was warmly welcomed into Gillian's family. And I loved her, still do.

We met during a postgraduate teaching course and just hit it off, our friends delighted for us, our mutual happiness apparent.

What went wrong? The black clouds soon gathered, memories of my childhood trauma resurfaced, probably never went away, just temporarily overwhelmed by the positive emotions engendered by the romance. I felt bad, but my moods intensified, we argued and it was my fault. I drank too much, a dram before bed to help me to sleep, stop the nightmares, which didn't work, neither did two drams or three.

Stuart and his wife, Sheila, soon picked up on the atmosphere, although Gillian, initially, was very loyal. Tensions grew between me and my in-laws, lovely people, rightly hurt, after all they did for both of us. How I hated myself.

We were both fortunate to get teaching posts, having successfully completed our teaching courses. Starting teaching didn't help with all the stresses of controlling classes and mastering the curriculum, long stressful days with heavy marking. There was no release of tension at home and the lack of space in our two-bedroom terrace house proved claustrophobic and, ultimately, overpowering. Our friends were unaware of the growing chasm between us, surprised by our announcement.

Gillian moved out just two months ago. We have talked little since, although we do text. Mutual friends say that she is heartbroken. I feel great pain, responsible, yet paralysed in trying to do something about it. We both promised to use the time apart sensibly, to re-evaluate our lives and learn lessons. The message was clear – I had to put the past behind me and show that I could be a reliable partner. She had listened to the story of Dad's murder many times, sharing in my grief, empathising, her eyes filled with tears, but she couldn't understand how my love for her could not overcome the trauma and create a new life with her. At times, neither could I.

The sun had come out, teasing me, creating dappled patterns on the green grass, stirring memories of a happier day. I looked around and took a deep breath. I would resolve my issues and make it up with Gillian. There was no doubt that I loved her. I would certainly accept counselling and...

I heard a car slow down, paying little attention to it, although the engine sound seemed strangely familiar. Seconds later a white Fiat passed the gate as the driver peered in, accelerating fast as she saw me. What the hell was 'flower girl' doing here? She kept turning up: Dalbeattie, Threave Castle, now here. But surely this was a coincidence too far. I ran to the gate, but the car was speeding away. Then another thought struck me – why the interest in me? Who was she?

13

Back at the campsite Rougvie was returning from the shower block as I parked outside my tent. He shouted something that I didn't catch and just ignored, heading into my tent, but he shouted again, 'Finn, do you have a moment?'

I hesitated, which was usually fatal, and turned towards him.

He appeared out of breath as he got near, his towel wrapped around his neck.

'Glad to catch you. Listen, I'm sorry about the other day – my fault. How's your jaw?'

'Pretty sore.' It was not difficult to spot the swelling, the emergence of bruising.

'Yeah, so sorry. Can I make it up? I'm pretty good with steaks. I have a nice couple of sirloins and a bottle of red. Can I cook you the steak and open the wine?'

I closed my eyes for a minute, feeling trapped, but I realised that I was hungry, hadn't eaten all day.

'Okay,' I said, and was rewarded with a big grin, 'but I don't drink. I'll bring my own Red Bull.'

'I'm avoiding real ale myself, was only going to have a couple of glasses of the red. I'll start cooking in twenty minutes.'

It seemed like a plan and it saved getting something for myself to eat and gave me time to have a shower.

I soon showered, changed and crossed the divide between our tents, bringing my camping chair to sit on and a can of Red Bull.

Rougvie seemed pleased, if not a little nervous.

'Have you seen her today?' I began, and pointed towards Jess's tent, curious about my fellow camper and what Rougvie had gleaned about her.

He cleared his throat. 'She left right after you this morning and I haven't seen her since.'

Soon after, I watched as Rougvie cooked the onions, pushing them aside when they were ready and adding the steaks to the hot frying pan. The steaks sizzled, fat spraying, and he quickly turned them over, sealing in the juices.

'Turn forty next year,' he stated, as we watched the steaks cooking, 'bit of a game changer. Wonder what life is about.'

'Everyone does, whatever the reason,' I replied, hoping that sounded suitably enigmatic.

'Not easy to mess around when you have a wife and a kid.'

'Of course, probably time to settle down.' Not that I was the one to pass judgement, given the state of my own affairs.

'Yeah, you're right enough. Stick to squirrels,' and he smiled as he turned the steak over. 'Only a couple of visits to go, a few reports and I head back up the road for another year. Too many greys, not enough reds. I don't know if the reds will survive with the pox about.'

Rougvie turned off the gas burner. 'The steaks should rest for a couple of minutes before we eat them,' he declared.

Both of us looked up as we heard a car drive past. It was Jess returning, studiously ignoring us. She parked and disappeared quickly into her tent.

'Danny was quite a lad, not her type I would have thought,' Rougvie added, 'I thought that she would have gone after he left.

Embarrassment if nothing else.'

That was true, but why did I keep bumping into her as I travelled about?

'She seemed more interested in you than me, anyway, more her age. Asked a few questions.'

Now I was curious. 'Like what?'

'If I knew you well. Where you were from. Asked about your family.'

'What did you say?'

'Just made it up. She soon lost interest and gave me the cold shoulder.'

'Maybe something about the twenty-plus year gap between you two.'

Rougvie looked embarrassed, checking on the steaks.

'Has been a learning curve. Time I realised my age, need to grow up,' and he scooped my steak out of the frying pan with a spatula and laid it on a plate, along with some fried onions.

'Do you want extra seasoning?' I sprinkled my steak further with the salt and pepper sachets he offered.

I hoped that his self-reflection wasn't going to descend into self-pity. I wasn't in the mood to start counselling him.

'So where are you going tomorrow?'

'Sir Archie's estate, near Mossdale. In his woods he has some red squirrels and is looking for funding to exterminate the greys. I am going to do a headcount, estimate the populations and prepare my findings. I'm just a volunteer, let others in the charity make the hard decisions.'

I could never see Rougvie taking responsibility.

'How long does that take?'

'A few days. Start tomorrow. Do you know where Mossdale is?'

'Near New Galloway, not far from Loch Ken.' I had lived

around here but Rougvie didn't know that and he looked impressed.

He nodded. 'Do you want to tag along? I can show you a lot. More interesting than it sounds.'

Rougvie raised his head expectantly, waiting for a reply.

I didn't really want to 'tag along', as he put it.

'Tell me about the estate owner, Sir Archie,' I replied, playing for time.

'Sir Archibald Graham-Linton...'

I choked on my steak and Rougvie looked alarmed.

'Sorry,' I said, wiping my mouth, sitting up coughing.

'Tell me about him,' and I attempted not to look too interested as I tried to regain composure. Suddenly squirrels appeared more interesting. AGL – Archibald Graham-Linton. It had to be him.

'His family have been in the area for many generations. Well-to-do, seems like a nice guy.'

'You've spoken to him?'

'Yes, a couple of times on the phone. Happy for me to start my survey but doesn't want me around the area of the house tomorrow. Visitors, he said. Do you want to come?'

'You know, I'm sure that I would find it fascinating.'

Rougvie smiled broadly. 'Great, we can leave early tomorrow.'

The steak was sitting heavily in my stomach, undigested. My heart was beating fast. I would have loved a glass of wine. Progress, at last and I would want a good look around the place, a nosey, as my dad would have said. And Rougvie would supply the perfect cover.

14

As soon as I got away from Rougvie I was on my iPhone, googling Archibald Graham-Linton. There were a number of items about him in extracts from local papers, including The Galloway Observer. George Park must have met him and no wonder Mac blanched, he too must have been aware of who he was. Why were they covering for him or, at least, not wanting to talk about him?

There was enough on the Internet to identify him as a prominent Galloway landowner, a local worthy with influence, the latest generation of a family who had lived and worked in Galloway for a long time. Landed gentry, money made from coal mining in the north-east of England.

For many years he had been abroad – I wondered why. A couple of years ago he had returned. There he was, cutting the ribbon at the opening of a new garage, present at some local business dinner, opening a care home in Newton Stewart, talking to a primary school class about conservation. He got around, the same smile, always neatly dressed, oozing money and power, glad-handing with locals. No suggestion, however, of political interests.

There was no doubt in my mind he was the person I saw that night. If only people knew what he was really like, could see behind the facade – cold-hearted, someone who could extinguish another's life, which made him a murderer in my book, even if he didn't fire the bullet.

One of the extracts told me that he lived at High Mossdale Lodge, just north of Mossdale village. I hadn't noticed it before and I had travelled the road to New Galloway many times. I checked Google maps and saw that it was off the road and screened by trees. I would be visiting the house tomorrow, I promised myself.

One more thing to do. I phoned Sis.

'Hello,' the voice answered. It was Paul, Sis's husband.

'Can I speak with Sis?' I asked.

Pointedly, he replied, 'Debbie is not in.' He hated me calling her Sis. I had a poor relationship with Paul, a policeman, who had never achieved very much, never promoted, not that I could boast about my achievements. Mid-forties, dour, he'd been married to Sis for about ten years. No children and never any talk about wanting a family. That made me pause. Gillian was desperate for a child.

'Debbie, is at a business function in Dumfries. I don't know when she will be back. Maybe phone back tomorrow.' Sis worked at a bank in Moffat, in Dumfriesshire, had done for many years. Not totally sure what level she was at in the bank, but she seemed comfortable.

'Thanks, Paul, I'll text her.'

'How is Gillian?' He knew fine well, was stirring it.

'You know that we're living apart, but hopefully we can work things out. Thanks for asking.' I hoped that he noted the tinge of sarcasm in my voice. 'Speak soon, bye,' and I hung up.

Quickly I composed a message to Sis. She wouldn't be pleased with the content but despite that, I hoped that she would answer.

15

I woke up instantly alert, aware of what today might bring. I heard voices outside the tent, Rougvie was talking to someone, but I couldn't make out what was said. The other voice was female, but who was he talking to? I squirmed out of my sleeping bag and partially unzipped the flap, surprised to see that Rougvie was talking to Jess. She quickly turned her head away when she saw me and started walking towards the shower block, her flip-flops echoing on the tarmac road.

'Hi,' said Rougvie, 'ready to go in half an hour?' He didn't seem bothered that I had witnessed him talking to Jess. There was something that I didn't trust about Jess, but I didn't feel that I had the facts to challenge her. It could have been an innocent conversation between them but there again, given their past history, maybe not.

I was soon washed, ate some cornflakes and was ready to go. Rougvie was packing some gear – cameras and tripods – into the back of his jeep.

'Do you want to travel with me? You're more than welcome.'

'I might not manage the whole day, so I'll take my own car.' I looked up at the grey clouds gathering, Screel and Bengairn obscured by a blanket of cloud, a weather front coming in.

'Pack wet weather gear?' and he nodded.

'Probably need it. Midges might be bad, but I have some midge repellent ointment.'

I hadn't thought of that and the misery they could cause. Maybe a breeze would get up to keep them away.

Rougvie got into his jeep and drove off, and I followed. There was no sign of Jess. The Colonel smiled as I passed.

We headed up the east side of Loch Ken, north from Castle Douglas, passing through several small villages. To my left, low-lying ground, prone to flooding, then past a busy campsite and activity centre beside an old rusting railway bridge. We reached Ken Bridge, crossing over the Water of Ken and soon arrived at New Galloway. Even in the gathering greyness of the day, the villages all appeared attractive, small settlements among the Galloway Hills.

The Galloway Forest Park fringed the road to the right, a trout farm to the left on the banks of Loch Ken. The hills blanketed by trees were getting higher. I noticed two tall white stone pillars and a small slate sign, too small for me to read but which I was sure led into High Mossdale Lodge.

Rougvie drove on, stopping at the entrance to the Raiders Road, a ten-mile forestry drive that opened up some of the forest to visitors, linking to a road beside Clatteringshaws Loch at the west end. Traffic could go in either direction along the unsurfaced road that followed the track taken by cattle rustlers along the north bank of the Black Water of Dee. It was named after local author S. R. Crockett's book The Raiders, about smuggling in the eighteenth century. The forest drive was popular and available to use on payment of a small toll.

Rougvie pulled over on rough ground beside the start of the road, parked and got out. There was space for me to park beside him. The midges were out already and he gave me a tube of midge repellent to spread on the exposed parts of my body.

Even so, they were annoying and I was soon scratching. Rougvie handed me two bottles of water and a protein bar.

'You'll need these,' he said. 'We have a stiff climb ahead,' and he hauled a backpack out of the jeep, slipping a Canon camera on a strap and binoculars over his head. When he saw me scratching, he handed me an olive-coloured midge hood with a fine mesh covering for my face.

He slipped a camera tripod under his arm and held out his Samsung phone.

'I have a tracker on this and I've entered the coordinates of the latest red squirrel sightings. I want to confirm the sightings by looking for evidence. Take a few photos.'

He seemed genuinely enthused. I smiled warmly. 'Looking forward to this, should be interesting. Lead on,' and I gathered my own backpack.

Satisfied with my response but still, I suspect, surprised by my presence, he clambered onto a low sandy bank and strode out ahead, soon entering the edge of the forest, where silence descended. No other noise except an occasional passing car which quickly grew more distant.

The climb was hard and I was soon out of breath, stooping under branches, feet sinking into soft mossy ground layered with needles, initially, at least, no clear path. I was sweating, calves aching with the effort, but Rougvie strode on, avoiding obstacles, maintaining a steady pace.

He stopped, but only for a second. 'Okay?'

I barely had breath to answer, sticky with sweat and very hot. As soon as I stopped, flies descended in black clouds.

'Let's keep going,' I muttered and on he strode.

Through gaps in the trees, mainly Douglas fir, I reckoned, I could see Loch Ken below and hills beyond.

Rougvie kept glancing at his phone and eventually held up a hand.

'This is the first area,' he stated. 'Look around and stay quiet.'

I crouched, looking for any movement, aware of how hot and sweaty I was. I jumped when Rougvie touched my arm, pointing to a tree about twenty yards away and taking out his camera. He waited for what seemed an uncomfortable eternity. 'There,' he said and took a rapid series of photos. I saw some movement among the higher branches. Rougvie checked the screen on the camera to see what he had captured.

'Got a picture,' and he showed me. 'Confirmation that there is some red squirrel activity. I haven't noticed any greys. All good.' He worked his way slowly around the area, pointing to a nest high in the branches. 'Their nests are called dreys,' he told me, and he stooped to pick up what looked like a chewed pine cone. He photographed it. 'They chew the cones for food,' he explained and he put the cone in his backpack for evidence.

He was looking at the rivulets of sweat on my face under the midge net. 'Don't worry, not too long, we'll soon be out in more open countryside – a bit cooler.'

And on we went, climbing steadily until we reached a firebreak. Below, I could see a loch and a stone viaduct and beside it, a car park with a couple of cars.

'Loch Stroan,' he declared. 'The viaduct was a part of the disused railway that ran through here. It closed in the sixties, as part of the Beeching cuts. There's now a picnic place beside the loch, for visitors using the Raiders Road.'

The weather was clearing, the small front having drifted further north. In the far distance I could spot the distinctive outline of Cairnsmore of Fleet and other hills appearing, blue tinged. I turned to see that Rougvie had sat down on a tuft of heather and pulled out a bottle of water.

'Thirsty work, eh?' He took a small mouthful of water, swilling it around in his mouth before swallowing it. 'Try and keep some water for later.'

The first of my two bottles was already finished. It was going to be a long day.

'Have you heard of 'The 39 Steps'?'

I searched my mind, the title familiar.

'I think that I've seen a film of that name – old black and white movie.'

Rougvie smiled, apparently slightly amused by my response.

'There have been several films made of the book by John Buchan.'

'I'm only a science teacher,' I replied, trying to explain away my ignorance.

'And I'm only a joiner, but I like to read.' He meant no malice. I was warming to him.

'Buchan was a Scot and wrote the book as a "penny thriller", the first of its kind, and it proved extremely popular. Published during the First World War.'

'The hero, Hannay...' and I interrupted him. 'Richard?'

'That's right, was caught up in a tale of espionage and mystery. He escapes from London on a train bound for Scotland, police searching for him, believing that he's murdered someone. Changes trains at Dumfries and gets on the slow train through Galloway. He overhears farmers talking about lambing, at farms just north of here. They get off the train, probably at New Galloway station, which is about a mile west of here, where the railway crosses under the road we travelled down this morning, but further south. Alone on the train, he must have crossed that,' and he pointed to the viaduct by the picnic area, 'before heading, in those days, out into the wilderness. At the turn of the century there were no trees in this area, it was just one big moorland, remote and unfriendly. Hannay got off at Gatehouse of Fleet station, beside a white road that straggled over the moor, in the lee of Cairnsmore of Fleet. No mention of the Big Water of Fleet viaduct, which many wrongly associate with the book and films.'

I knew the area around that viaduct, but it had a more sinister association in my mind and, after all, Buchan's tale was fiction.

'What about the railway route between here and Gatehouse of Fleet station?' I had memories of being driven along a track before arriving at a long wooden hut. Could it have been the railway trackbed?

'You can walk the trackbed. I have done it with my brother. The trackbed curves around that large hill,' and he pointed to a rock-strewn hillside, 'and eventually reaches Loch Skerrow, where there was a halt and a small railway community, totally isolated, no roads to it, only the railway. There were water tanks there to slake the thirst of the steam trains. If a passenger wanted to get off at Loch Skerrow, and they often did to fish, they had to sign a disclaimer, agreeing that the railway company would not be held liable if they got into trouble. Between Loch Skerrow and the Big Water of Fleet viaduct, the main feature was the Little Water of Fleet viaduct, which has been demolished, local builders wanting the granite, but the forest road bypasses the site of it. The Loch Stroan viaduct would probably have been demolished if it had not been used for access to farms.'

'Could you drive a vehicle along the route?' I was now curious.

'With difficulty today. I think that there is a metal gate beyond Loch Skerrow Halt and some bits are very boggy now. But there is a forest road that leads in from a public road, crosses the railway trackbed near the site of the demolished Little Water of Fleet viaduct.'

'Where does that lead to?'

'The Mossdale road eventually if you wanted to take that direction.'

I could have reached High Mossdale Lodge that night, given that was twelve years ago, by either route.

'What distance is it to Gatehouse of Fleet station from here?'

'From the Loch Stroan viaduct, roughly nine miles.' Rougvie looked at me, slightly bemused by my interest.

It's difficult to judge distance or speed when you're being thrown about in the back of a car with a hood over your head, trying not to be sick, panicking about what's happening. If there was a possibility that I was taken to High Mossdale Lodge, then there was even more reason to visit it.

Rougvie seemed unperturbed by the clouds of midges as he sat sipping water and munching on a protein bar. I was getting cold as the sweat evaporated, cooling my body.

'Has this morning been a success?' I ventured, hoping that he might take the hint and we could move on.

'Yeah. Hopefully there was a breeding pair at that drey. Certainly there was evidence, the sighting of one and the chewed cone.' He took his phone out and looked at the screen.

'Let's get going. That way,' he said, pointing behind him. 'Not too far,' and we both stood up. I stretched my limbs, which were stiff after the exercise and then sitting for a while, the sweat now cold against my skin. We headed off first along a firebreak, the view over Loch Stroan left behind. After a few minutes Rougvie pointed out a clearing which had some red wooden cages fronted with metal mesh.

'When they were preparing red kites for release in the area they kept them in these cages. Few people knew about the cages then. No secret now.'

We both heard a couple of sharp retorts and Rougvie stopped, alert.

'Damn. Someone out shooting. I don't know if they should be,' and he picked up pace, glancing again at his phone. His focus was now on getting to the next site, something was bothering him, and I was left to try and keep up with him. Rougvie reached a clearing, again checking on his phone, and stopped. I caught up, out of breath and immediately sat down, pleased to rest.

Rougvie scanned the area and sniffed the air. I caught the faint scent of cordite. Looking up at the branch-lined canopy, Rougvie shouted, 'There's the drey,' and he turned his attention to the ground.

'Oh no,' and he crouched down. I saw what he was looking at – a dead red squirrel, shot.

'Bastards,' he spat out with venom. 'Probably one of a breeding pair. How can people do that? The damage…' and he shook his head. 'I'll report them, they have no right to shoot red squirrels.'

He took photographs of the dead squirrel and the drey.

'Sorry,' I said, aware of his distress.

'I've seen it happen before. That's why we need volunteers to check out what's going on, to be eyes and ears, to protect the red squirrel population.'

16

By late afternoon, we had visited three different possible sites of red squirrel sightings. At the third site we had found no evidence of red squirrels and I was tired after all the physical exertions, interest long gone. However, I had warmed to Rougvie on our foray and thought his dedication admirable and had to admit that the reds were cute. But it was time to leave him and head to High Mossdale Lodge for a look.

'That's us for the day,' Rougvie declared.

'I think I'll take a wander, need the toilet, then I want to return to our lunchtime viewpoint, take in the view and maybe take the Raiders Road back to my car.' It sounded lame and I don't think that Rougvie was taken in.

He studied me for a minute. 'Don't get lost.'

I smiled. 'I'll try hard not to. I've enjoyed today. See you back at the campsite,' and I turned quickly, ducking under a branch and heading away.

Rougvie shouted after me, 'Finn, it's that direction,' and he pointed the other way, laughing.

I waved and went in the direction that he pointed, continuing until he was out of sight and then stopped. Using my iPhone I checked the map and took a compass bearing, who said that the Scouts were not useful, even if things were a bit more high tech now!

It was not easy manoeuvring through the trees and trying to maintain a straight route. The midges were annoying, my sweat seemingly attracting them, but gradually I was getting closer to the lodge, according to my iPhone, and finally the ground started to slip away, quite steeply, and suddenly I was looking down at High Mossdale Lodge. Shielded from the nearby road by trees, it sat in a large natural hollow, the hillside surrounding it also lined with trees. A very private setting. The house sat east to west, at right angles to the nearby road, connected by a sweeping driveway that curved round a large pond, a water feature in the middle, leading to a gravel-covered sizeable car parking area at the front. The house itself was two storeys high, the front constructed from red sandstone, with large bay windows on each side of the doorway, extending the full height of the building. Several rows of chimney pots rose from the slate roof. At each end was a slated conical tower.

A flight of steps led to the entrance, the stonework of which was supported by two columns, topped by a triangular stone feature, with what appeared to be a coat of arms embossed in the centre. While I couldn't determine its age, it was probably over a hundred years old and was well-maintained. The residence of a well-to-do family.

I hid myself among the trees, crouching for some time, absorbing the features, cursing that I had not brought binoculars. Instead, I took some photos with my phone. Thanks to Rougvie, I had found where Sir Archibald Graham-Linton lived. A bit of me was disappointed that I could see no immediate connection with the night that my father was murdered, no moment of insight linking the house, but realistically that was unlikely. Every step forward in my cause required more effort and the odds were seemingly mounting against me. Proving anything was going to be difficult after so long.

I had to know more, search for clues, so slowly I tried to work my way around the hillside in a state of heightened alert, adrenaline pumping, mouth dry, waiting for that eureka moment.

There were a lot of broken branches on the ground and I tried not to snap any. This took time and effort but gradually I worked my way to the west. A branch snapped behind me, a rustle in the undergrowth and I turned alarmed, but it was only some red deer I had disturbed taking off through the woods.

Taking even more care I resumed my progress until I was level with the western edge of the house. Then I saw it, concealed by the trees – a long wooden hut. My stomach knotted, I was breathing heavily. Could it possibly be where I was taken?

That evening we had stopped in a clearing, a pile of logs left to rot, to one side, the southern end of Loch Grannoch seen through the trees, just short of a fork in the dirt track.

'I won't be long. I don't know which side of the loch the hut is located,' and Dad disappeared, leaving me in the car to read my book.

Sometime later I heard a gun being fired, the echo reverberating around the loch. That wasn't unusual in this area and it didn't seem too close. I didn't connect it with Dad.

But time passed and I got out of the car to stretch my legs, wondering why the delay. I had wandered into the trees aimlessly, call of nature, when I heard a vehicle approaching fast. A Land Rover arrived very quickly stirring up dirt, the driver braking as he passed our car, glancing into it and then speeding up and following the track around the side of the loch. I don't think that the driver saw me. I became worried, a bad feeling in the pit of my stomach. Something wasn't right.

Another vehicle appeared, a pickup and this time I was spotted. A man jumped out and ran across to me.

'Who are you?' he demanded. I noticed that he appeared nervous, edgy, glancing around the clearing, even before I could reply.

'I'm Dr McAdam's son,' I answered. 'Can I help you?'

'How long have you been here?'

I looked at my watch. 'About an hour.' I realised now that the answer must have sounded so innocent. He appeared puzzled.

'Stay here, I'll be back,' and he jumped into the pickup, slamming the door, but not before I heard him swearing at the driver. A second later they were gone.

I waited, now becoming concerned, the midges descending in biblical hordes, and so I returned to the car to get away from them. The light was fading and I just wanted to go home, desperate for Dad to show up, when I heard the Land Rover returning, lights now on.

The driver and a passenger got out and ran towards the car. Clutching at the door they opened it and pulled me out, one of them producing a hessian sack that they pulled over my head, making me choke with the dust from it. Rough hands grabbed me, twine bound my hands behind me and then my legs were tied together. The back door was flung open and I was heaved into our car.

I was screaming, shouting for Dad, my voice muffled by the sack, tears welling up. One of them got into the driver's seat, the engine was started, revved up and the car quickly spun around.

Thereafter, I was driven at speed over unmade roads. It seemed a long time, with many twists and turns before I heard the crunching of small stones beneath the tyres and the car stopped. There was silence and then I heard shouting and the driver was out of the car and I was pulled out, dragged along the ground, bumped up steps and flung onto a wooden floor. In the process the sack slipped up and I could briefly see the interior of the hut, metal-framed chairs with faded red vinyl seats, a long trestle table, a darts board.

I was grabbed, 'Don't let him see,' someone shouted and the sack was pulled down as I squirmed, by now crying, sobbing, my mouth dry. I heard the door opening again and knew that someone was standing watching me, assessing the situation.

'Leave him,' a voice proclaimed, 'and step outside. We need to talk.' That was the voice I heard again in the cafe.

There were angry, raised voices, one person furious that I had been brought back here. I tried to free myself from the sack, which reached down to my waist, and through a small rip in the sack saw the interior of the room again. This time I saw a different wall with framed photographs, antlers mounted on a plaque and a line of fishing rods held in slots in a frame, a row of wellington boots beside them, all shapes and sizes.

The door opened and a man's strong pair of hands grabbed me, picking me up from the floor and tossing me over his shoulder as if I was a bag of flour. I was carried back to the car and dumped in the back. I heard voices talking softly, so that I couldn't make them out, aware of torches, their beams like lasers cutting through the dark. And then the car was started, someone now holding me firmly in the back seat, and I was being driven through the night, this time along better roads.

All this played through my mind as I got nearer to the hut. I was now in line with the driveway. I could also see that this side of the house was harled, a dirty grey.

Two cars drove up the driveway, both Jaguars. The leading one, a four-door saloon, blue in colour, the second, an older model with a long boot lid, was racing green. Both cars had more antennas than I would have expected, something different about them. I noticed blue lights embedded in the bumpers. Both cars stopped outside the front entrance and from the second Jaguar two men quickly got out, leaving the driver in the car. They scanned the area and I instinctively crouched down behind a tree before they moved forward to the first car, one of them holding the back door open. A smartly dressed figure got out and as he did Sir Archibald appeared at the top of the steps and waved warmly to his visitor. He walked down the steps and the two men embraced, while the visitor's minders continued to look around. After a few minutes they all went into the house apart from the two drivers, wearing peaked caps, who hung about the cars, one of them smoking. I wondered who the important visitor was, but decided to close in on the hut.

The last time I had been here it was night-time and I only ever saw the hut from the inside. At the front of the hut, facing the house, was a wooden veranda with steps leading up to it and that fitted with my memory – the pain of being dragged up steps. On the veranda were some wicker chairs. The door was at the far end from me and there were three small windows along the front.

On the side nearest to me was a small window with opaque glass, which I assumed was a toilet. The pitched roof looked as if it had recently been renewed, the felt had no moss on it and appeared clean. I crept around the back, where there were a further four windows. Branches from trees overhung the hut and I hoisted myself on one branch, clinging to it, and peered inside. I saw a snooker table with the balls set up inside a wooden triangle and two snooker cues lying on the surface. Craning my neck around, I saw some framed photographs on the far wall. I took a deep breath, peering hard, but the detail was not clear. There seemed to be groups of people posing with fishing rods in some and with guns in another. One was of a man standing beside a car, its wedge-shaped front seemed familiar, low-slung, a powerful looking car. It could be a photo of the vehicle I saw on the night. I had to get inside, answers awaited, I felt.

I worked my way around the back reaching the far end, crouching low, keeping an anxious eye for movement in the house. I climbed on the veranda and reached the door to find that it was bolted and locked with a combination padlock and I could also see a Yale lock. Disappointment surged through me, so close. I checked but didn't see any burglar alarm. All I could do was peer inside, but I risked exposing myself to someone watching from the house. Adrenaline surged and I took the risk quickly taking more photos of the far wall and antlers mounted on a plaque. I took a few more photos but they were not very good, reflections spoiling the images. Certain that I had been here before, I slunk around the back of the hut again and sat down, mind working furiously but other than breaking in I was stymied. There was no cover in daylight; I would have to return later.

After a few minutes I peered out from behind the hut, no activity to suggest that I had been seen. At the back of the house there was a vegetable garden, with neat rows of potatoes and leeks, contained within a low hedge. Further back was a large brick building with a car parked outside an open door, probably a garage.

I had a thought and wondered if the car I saw that night was maybe inside it. A long shot, but it was an unusual car and maybe one that someone with money might keep. It was worth checking while I was here anyway, and I retreated to the cover of the trees and edged around the back of the house. I could now see that a driveway led around the house to the entrance of the garage.

I left the safety of the trees and ran to the side of the garage, working quickly around to the entrance. A wooden door on runners had been pulled back, exposing part of the inside. There were several cars on the far side, nothing special, one minus wheels resting on bricks, but I couldn't see the space behind the door so I chanced it and nipped in. The dark-coloured Aston Martin coupe with the lime strip on the bonnet sat there, newly polished, gleaming under overhead lights, but nothing else.

I was about to walk out when I heard voices. I quickly ran and hid between two of the cars on the far side. One voice was instantly recognisable – Tania's.

'There is space in here for both your cars and there's a tap and a hose by the door if you wish to clean them. Even after a long drive our bosses are quite demanding.'

The other person laughed. 'You get used to their demands, but a cup of tea would be welcome.'

'Of course, come on in.'

I risked a glance. Tania was talking to one of the chauffeurs, his peaked cap held under one of his arms. She was wearing a white shirt and black trousers, her hair pulled back in a clasp.

'Can I put the car in the garage first? Then my responsibilities are over for the day.' Tania acknowledged his request by moving her hand, indicating the space that was available.

I needed to get out before someone noticed me, now regretting my decision to enter the garage. Tiredness had made me reckless and I looked around hoping to find a side door. There was one on the other side of the garage from me and as I heard their voices receding, I ran to it but it was locked. Nothing for it but to exit the way I came in and I ran to the entrance, trying to stay in the shadow.

I waited a few minutes, drew breath, didn't see anyone and

decided to dash towards the safety of the trees. After checking again I started to run, but I heard a click and stopped.

'What are you doing here?' The voice was Tania's.

I was lost for words and turned to face her. She was holding a shotgun levelled at me.

17

Tania held the shotgun steadily in her hands, moving closer to me, studying me carefully.

'I am volunteering with Rougvie,' I quickly stated, 'to identify red squirrel dreys. We've found three today. I was caught short, looking for a toilet, upset stomach, and I saw the garage, hoped that there would be a toilet inside.'

My staccato delivery hung in the air, fooling no one, I feared.

'Why were you hiding between the cars then? I spotted you lurking.'

'I panicked, especially when I saw the Aston Martin. Thought you might think that I was going to steal it. A bit silly, sorry,' and I looked down as if I was embarrassed by my actions, crestfallen, a naughty schoolboy.

Tania didn't respond but I heard a door slam and one of the security personnel I had seen earlier emerged from the house and ran out, running up to Tania but keeping a careful eye on me.

'What's the problem? I get worried when I see guns near my boss.'

'Found him hiding in the garage, claimed he was looking for a toilet.' It was difficult to tell from her tone if she believed me.

'What were you doing in there?' he asked brusquely.

'As I said to the lady, I was helping out as a red squirrel volunteer along with a colleague. We were chasing up possible sightings of red squirrels on the estate. My colleague, Rougvie, has spoken to Sir Archibald. He knew we were going to be around today. My stomach was upset and I was looking for a toilet. Sorry if I have caused a problem.'

The man glanced at Tania, raising his eyebrows, looking for an indication to whether or not she believed me. Troubling for me, he added, 'I saw him hanging around that hut over there.'

'I wondered if there was a toilet there.'

Tania held the shotgun steady, unresponsive, something was troubling her.

'Can I use a toilet, please, this has made me feel worse, and can you lower the gun, it makes me nervous.'

'There is a small toilet at the back of the garage, did you not notice?'

I held up my hands, palms exposed and edged away, turning and walking into the garage.

'I see it,' I said, and ran towards it.

The two of them watched me as I stepped inside the cubicle, pulling the door shut behind me. I stuck my finger down my throat so that they would hear me retching and made a play of pulling the chain and turning on the tap, washing my face.

I stepped outside the cubicle after a few minutes.

'Feeling better?' Again the same look, and she motioned with the gun for me to step outside the garage.

To add to my woes I saw Sir Archibald striding across from the house looking none too pleased, his face frowning, wearing his customary tweed jacket, complete with what looked like a club tie, red with a crest on it, never knowingly underdressed.

'What's this all about, Tania? I told you today of all days I

100

didn't want any problems.'

'I can answer if you let me,' and his attention turned to me.
'I am sorry if I have upset people, but I was helping Rougvie out
with this red squirrel survey – remember, you spoke to him –
and I got caught short, wandered into the garage to find a toilet
and panicked when people appeared.'

The bodyguard added, 'I saw him up at the hut before he
came down to the garage area, acting suspiciously.' That didn't
help, would only make Sir Archibald more wary of my presence.

Sir Archibald glanced at Tania, irritated, wanting her
reaction, but she remained inscrutable.

'I'll leave now. Sorry to have been a nuisance.'

I'd started to walk along the driveway leading from the
garage when Tania shouted, 'Stop.' I hesitated and then turned
around trying to appear puzzled.

'I remember now,' she stated, 'this is the man I saw taking a
picture of the car in Castle Douglas, acting funny.' I tried to show
no emotion.

'Yes, I saw the car in there but that is just coincidence. I took
a picture the other day because who wouldn't. Latest model
Aston Martin, beautiful. Not many around here. I haven't seen
one before of this model.' Again I was conscious that I was
maybe saying too much.

'You took a photo of the car? Let me see your mobile phone.'
'Why?'

'I want to see your photos. That will prove your interest is
only in cars.'

'Hand it over,' he demanded, stretching out his hand.

'No way, you have no right.' It was a stand-off. He held out
his hand again. I blanked him.

'This could lead to trouble,' he stated, and in a sudden
movement the security guy beside Sir Archibald stepped

forward, grabbed me and felt in my trouser pocket, removing the phone. The manoeuvre was unexpected and professionally executed. He handed it over to Sir Archibald.

'What is your passcode?'

'Don't remember.'

He held out the phone in front of him.

'Last chance,' and he stared straight at me, trying to intimidate me.

I shrugged.

He dropped the phone and before I could move he stamped his foot on it and ground it into the gravel surface.

'What's your name?' He repeated his request and the security guy edged closer, ready for action.

'Finn,' I blurted out, trying not to add McAdam. Why complicate the situation.

A look of recognition spread across his face and he smiled at Tania.

'Finn McAdam.'

'Yes, that is me.' This wasn't the time or place, I realised, to tackle him or accuse him of anything.

'I had a phone call about you the other day. I do hope that this encounter is coincidental. Some of the comments you made were very alarming, litigious, and likely to land you in trouble if ever repeated, which I trust they won't be,' he stated, with a perceptible edge of menace in his voice. The security man standing beside Sir Archibald and Tania was now taking a great deal of interest in our discussion, I noticed.

My reaction was inevitable, any attempt to conceal my feelings gone. I could feel my face flushing, hoping that my beard covered it, aware of my aching jaw, not sure if that was my body subtly signalling to be careful, no repeats please. My fists clenched but I quickly unclenched them.

'I saw you that night, when my father was executed on your orders,' I blurted out, my restraint evaporated.

Tania was getting twitchy, the shotgun moving up and down almost involuntarily, the security personnel's expression was slack-jawed. Sir Archibald's face twisted, his mouth narrowing in fury.

'What Park said was true, you are pedalling lies, deranged, needing help, but you are not going to damage my standing. I won't allow it,' his voice growing louder as he grew visibly angrier.

I stepped forward and automatically Tania stepped forward, narrowing the gap between us, motioning me away with the shotgun.

'I will find out the full story of what happened that evening and I will have justice,' and I spat these words out with venom. 'Truth will be told for all to hear.'

Sir Archibald changed tack, which caught me off guard.

'I failed to appreciate the trauma to one so young.' The comment was intended as conciliatory but his unchanged expression of suppressed fury failed to convey that, trying to regain control of the situation. 'The hospital said that you were pumped full of drugs, which must have distorted your memories.'

'Who pumped me full of drugs?'

'I was told that it was your father,' and here came the official line, 'his fingerprints were all over the syringe. All this is common knowledge. I am sorry.'

'Not one bit, you bastard, you're lying. Who are you covering for?'

'I've tried my best,' and he moved his hands, which had been in front of him, swiftly apart in a dismissive gesture.

'Tania, deal with him. I don't want to see him ever again.' So now I was being referred to as a third party, dismissed as a petty nuisance. This guy didn't change.

I was about to explode when I heard a vehicle being driven, tyres screeching as it took the corners of the house, and a Jeep appeared braking hard. Rougvie was driving it and as soon as he saw me he jumped out from the Jeep, leaving the door swinging in his haste.

The security personnel reached for his inner pocket, while Tania appeared confused by a fresh potential target.

Rougvie strode towards us, out of breath. 'Why are you threatening my partner? I was working with Finn today and we got separated. What's happened?' he demanded to know.

'Take him away,' Sir Archibald said, 'our meeting is finished. He was found loitering in the garage. I was about to get him charged with burglary. I will not be working with your organisation again.'

'Good, because someone on your estate has been shooting red squirrels. I have the photographic evidence and the police will be informed. It is against the law.'

I wasn't sure how he had found me but, boy, was I glad that he had. Talk about the cavalry arriving in the nick of time. I stooped down slowly and picked up my phone, the screen was hopelessly cracked.

'I'll be expecting a new phone.'

Sir Archibald looked furious, pivoting ready to walk away, but he turned back towards me.

'I never want to see you again. If I find you on these premises I will take the most severe actions. Be careful, Mr McAdam, very careful. Accidents happen.'

I was about to reply in kind when Rougvie grabbed my arm and hauled me away, pushing me into the passenger seat and firmly shutting the door.

'I won't forget that your people shoot red squirrels,' he shouted, as he got into the driver's seat. The door slammed, the engine was fired up and the Jeep reversed at speed and then spun around, accelerating away towards the front of the house.

'What the hell were you doing there?'

'Looking for a toilet.'

'I know that you think I'm a fool, but even I don't believe that.'

There was silence between us. Eventually, I said, 'Thanks for rescuing me. How did you know I was going to go to the house?'

'I knew you were planning something. Your expression changed when I mentioned Sir Archibald last night. And your story of needing the toilet earlier was, shall we say, not convincing.'

Minutes later he stopped beside my car at the entrance to the Raiders Road. I got out but leant back into Rougvie's car. 'Your timing was brilliant. How did you manage it?'

'You haven't worked that out?' He appeared surprised and was quick to add, 'and you think I'm a fool.'

I shook my head.

'I think you will find out this evening. Leave it till then. Let's get away before you cause any more trouble.'

Before I drove off I checked if my phone was working, but the charger point was broken and the screen unreadable. I'd pick up a cheap mobile on my way back to the campsite and transfer the SIM card, but I had lost my photos.

More reasons to get angry with Sir Archibald.

18

Back at the campsite I noticed that the Colonel and his wife had gone but Tom and his family were still there; Tom slumbering on a chair, empty bottles on the ground by his side. A few other campers had arrived and the site was filling up as the weekend approached. Rougvie was already back and I thanked him again for rescuing me as I wandered over to the shower block, but he said little, distracted as he fried a burger on his camping stove.

I was intrigued by what I was going to find out this evening, puzzled by how Rougvie had managed to turn up in the nick of time but very grateful. Everything had now changed. I had spoken to Archibald Graham-Linton, argued would be more accurate, and disliked him intensely, no surprise there. It didn't just confirm in my mind that he was the man on the road that night but that he was also capable of issuing the instruction that led to Dad being murdered. He was also now aware of me and that made life more complicated, as I tried to unravel the conspiracy around Dad's death.

A hot shower eased the aching in my body and I realised that I would have to work hard on my fitness, as I had struggled at times today to keep up with Rougvie, but the hot water did little to ease my racing mind, as thoughts tumbled out, each vying for attention but none making real sense.

As I headed back to the tent, Jess drove slowly past. I'm sure that she was aware of me but she kept her eyes fixed ahead of her, ignoring me. A strange girl and I couldn't understand why she was staying on or always seemed to be around places that I was.

As I sat down, my new phone pinged and I checked the screen, a text from Sis. Everything suddenly made sense and when I looked up I noticed that Rougvie was wandering over to Jess's tent. She, if not exactly welcoming to him, wasn't hostile any longer.

A few minutes later Rougvie ambled across to me, leaving Jess sitting at the picnic table beside her tent.

'Time to talk, Finn. Come over with me,' and he pointed towards Jess.

Now, after the text and understanding a bit more, I followed him and we all sat together at the picnic table. It was a sunny evening, the sun shining strongly on my back as I sat down, some awkwardness between us all as I waited for someone to speak. It was probably only a few seconds but it seemed longer. I was aware of a swan on the loch, gliding smoothly across the surface, suddenly dipping its head looking for food and then I heard Rougvie speak.

'You are probably wondering what this is about,' I nodded, going along with him, 'but Jess and I got talking, after some initial misunderstanding,' and his cheeks flushed. Some misunderstanding.

Jess was not really engaging, her head held low, eyes narrowed but watching me carefully, showing little emotion, most probably attempting to suppress it. I was tempted to spoil Rougvie's moment but out of new-found respect I didn't.

'Jess's father knew your father. And what happened.'

It was time to say something. 'You are Jessica Hamilton, our fathers worked together.' Sis's text had been timely.

Jess cut in quickly, 'Your father murdered my father,' glaring at me, her chin protruding forward aggressively.

'Not true, Jess. I saw my father shot on the orders of Sir Archibald Graham-Linton, the person,' and I turned to Rougvie, 'that you saw confront me today,' and there was a dawning realisation on Rougvie's face of what had occurred.

'I was told different,' she snapped.

'I was there, witnessed it.'

'Not what the police said. They were sure that Dad had been murdered. Mum was told that because your father committed suicide there was no case to prove, nothing more that could be done, no justice. Said it was about passion, an affair, someone at work. I want to know the truth.'

That knocked me back, couldn't be true, surely. 'We share that quest,' I said, trying to regain my composure, 'but let me repeat, I saw my father murdered. Saw it happen with my own eyes and that guy I confronted today gave the order. I didn't see what happened to your father and I know his body was found beside Dad's, but that doesn't make my father guilty. I am here searching for the truth, like you, it seems. Anyway, how did you know where I was?'

'Facebook, stupid. I am one of your followers, in name only,' she quickly added. 'You post and talk about your life as if you were someone important, you're not. You are just the son of a murderer,' and in a flash one mystery was solved.

'You vandalised my father's gravestone,' and my mood was beginning to change, becoming angry. Rougvie began to twitch, not liking the direction we were taking, tension mounting.

'Yes, and proud of it. Standing there, placing flowers on the grave of someone who ruined my life and that of my mother.'

'My life has also been ruined.'

'Just words to make you sound better. That's the trouble with teachers. Doesn't change anything. The proof was that your father's fingerprints were all over the gun.'

'And they said that his fingerprints were also found all over the syringe that was used to drug me, but it couldn't have happened that way. I saw him murdered first and then I was drugged. Someone else drugged me,' I added for emphasis. I was aware that my voice was getting louder. A woman with two small dogs on leads walked past, glancing at us, frowning, and hurried on.

'I don't have all the answers but there is a lot I can tell you,' and then I had another thought. 'You were following me today. You alerted Rougvie to rescue me. Thank you for that.'

'I saw the shotgun, didn't want you killed before I confronted you,' her face still stone like. 'Rougvie told me how you had suddenly decided to join him on his squirrel hunt and saw the change in your expression when he mentioned about Sir Archibald. He's not a fool.'

'I know.'

'And I followed you. It was me who startled the deer. I thought you had seen me.'

'On this occasion, no, but I had noticed you at Dalbeattie, Threave Castle and near the Isle of Whithorn.' I wanted her to know that I was aware. 'Wondered what you were doing. Texted my sister, remembering that Dougie Hamilton had a young daughter and couldn't recollect the name.'

'I wanted to know what you were up to. I want answers,' and I noticed her eyes glistening. She lowered her head again, trying to avoid any sign of weakness. 'It's not just you who is upset, desperate for answers. Losing my dad has ruined my life, made me a rebel,' and she suddenly stopped, not wanting to reveal anything else.

This I could sympathise with. 'It's not easy losing a parent and you were even younger than me. I can understand your emotions, despite what you think happened.'

'Maybe you should work together.' It was Rougvie, intervening, wanting to be a conciliator, justifying his presence. 'You may still disagree, but there must be an answer out there somewhere and I didn't like Sir Archibald – ruthless, nasty and concealing something. Talk to one another. Finn, you have a lot to share. It might help Jess.'

The sun had dipped below the treeline, the heat of it gone, the swan was now on the far side of the loch. In some ways it would be good not to be fighting the whole world, a disbelieving world, on my own.

Three young men entered the campsite from the direction of the road. They had obviously been drinking, with several plastic bags stuffed with what appeared to be bottles of wine and cans of beer, swearing at each other, shouting loudly, play-acting, the leading one staggering and as he passed leering at Jess, giving her a big smile and a wink. Rougvie told him to piss off and for a moment he stood staring at us, gazing intensely at each of us, and I thought that he was going to attack but one of his friends pulled him back and they wandered on, heading around the back of the shower block where they could drink in peace. I glanced at Rougvie and we were both thinking the same thing, say nothing. They reminded us of Danny.

I quickly switched back to our discussion. 'I'll tell you what I know happened, believed happened, but like you I don't understand the motives that caused the tragedy.' Rougvie seemed pleased. Jess was giving little away but was listening. 'Have you been to the places where it happened?'

'No,' replied Jess.

'Maybe we should go there tomorrow. You'll understand better.'

Jess hesitated, but Rougvie spoke. 'I'll come with you, keep the peace,' and Jess relaxed and he added, 'and anyway, I'm very curious.'

'I'll see you both in the morning then,' and I got up to go back to my tent, leaving them to talk. A few minutes later Rougvie left Jess alone and returned to his tent.

19

Once back at the tent the impact of what Jess had said really hit me. An affair of passion, a woman at work, I found that hard to believe. It wasn't the father I knew. Mum was not a particularly warm type, reserved, something that Sis had inherited, but they loved each other in their own way, never had arguments. I suspect Mum felt that Dad was too involved in work, was seriously academic and sometimes lived in his own world, could be distant. But he was nothing if not loving to me, the son he had always yearned for and being a late baby, a surprise, all the more welcome. He was passionate, not in a sexual way but in an enthusiastic way, always keen to learn, with an enquiring mind.

After Dad died we cleared out his possessions, never an easy task, his clothes going to charity shops in the next town so that we didn't see anyone wearing them. That was the easy bit, but his vast collection of books, mainly academic because Dad didn't read fiction – his idea of a good read was a primer on quantum chemistry – were difficult to get rid of. In the end an old colleague from his university days was contacted and agreed to take them. Mum had organised the books in piles and asked me to box them for her. As I did so I saw his PhD thesis at the bottom of one pile and extracted it, hurt that Mum would throw it out; it was precious, a tangible memory. The black bound volume was dusty, embossed with gold lettering – something about the synthesis of organophosphates, not my favourite branch of chemistry. I opened the manuscript, sneezing as fine dust irritated my nose. No one had looked at the thesis for many years but it represented three years' work.

Inside was a folded letter from his supervisor, a Professor Fred Rankin. He thanked him for being his best-ever student, one with a bright future and pleaded with him to remain in academia, sure that he would get his own professorship very quickly, just be patient. The professor even invited us up to his holiday home near Banchory, in Aberdeenshire, for a few days, but his charm didn't work. I met Fred Rankin years later when he returned to the university to give a short series of lectures. I was an undergraduate at the time and he asked to see me, pass on his condolences, and gave me his business card, if I ever wanted advice. I appreciated that.

I didn't know how Dad replied to his letter but the proof was that he had left Glasgow University shortly after, the dates fitted, and went to work in a laboratory in England. Dad's work thereafter was never discussed. I knew that he worked for the Ministry of Defence, mainly down south – but then at Eastriggs, near Annan, and I was never allowed to visit his workplace.

Someone at work, an affair, it didn't seem likely. Of Dougie Hamilton I knew little other than he was a keen fisherman and always, on the few occasions that I met him, the talk was only of fishing. That evening Dad had received an invite to join him for a spot of fishing. I had never met his family, vaguely remembered that he had a young daughter.

After Dad's death Mum and Sis would never talk about him and that hurt me. I wanted to talk about him, needed to, but they just changed the subject and would say something vague, like he was very clever or he was happiest when working. I wanted more than such platitudes, to honour his memory, to preserve it. Sis would chide me later, 'Don't hurt Mum by bringing up his name, she is too upset to talk about him,' but that didn't ring sincere. I was the only one who seemed to see the best in him and wanted to share that with others.

I sensed where my thoughts were leading me, had to face up to it. Maybe the reason that they didn't talk about Dad was because they had discovered that he was having an affair. That thought weighed on my mind. Sadly, Jess had revealed something that I hadn't known before or was willing to consider.

By now it was getting late, I must have sat for an hour ruminating over what I had been told. The light was fading, the campsite getting darker, a few stars now appearing, the glow of the lights from the lamps posts more apparent. I saw Mary walking towards the shower block, toilet bag and towel under her arm. Tom was asleep, I could hear the slow rhythmic snoring which no longer kept me awake, and so presumably were his two daughters. I don't know how Mary coped, Tom's only activity was drinking, with two young daughters to care for and an alcoholic husband, life could not be easy.

I had showered earlier and with my mind still absorbing Jess's revelation I turned in and after a few restless moments I fell asleep, the physical and mental challenges of the day catching up with me.

Drifting into dreamland, I heard a small voice calling my name softly but repeatedly. Eventually my conscious state emerged and I awoke.

'Finn, Finn,' the voice repeated, the voice of a young girl.

I raised my head, gruffly replying. 'What is it?' Still not sure of who I was addressing.

'Mum wants you to come to our tent, now. Very important. You are in danger.'

My head was clearing. 'What is it?'

'Just come,' a whining edge now added to her voice. I struggled out of the sleeping bag, partly unzipped the tent flap and poked my head through the space. The young girl was Molly, one of Mary's daughters, who pulled at my arm urging me to leave the tent.

'Come on, quickly,' and looking beyond her I saw Mary herself waving, urging me from her tent to come over. This was strange, surreal. If it hadn't been for the cold air, I might still have been dreaming.

I pulled on my trousers, grabbed a sweatshirt and crawled out under the half-open flap. Mary beckoned more frantically and I ran across. She pulled me and her daughter into her tent, which had a living area with a couple of separate compartments off it. From one I could hear Tom snoring. She held up a finger against her mouth indicating for me to be quiet and listened intently. After a minute she said in hushed tones, 'They are not here yet.'

I looked puzzled, but her attention was focused on outside the tent. Eventually turning to me, she said, 'When I was in the toilet, the top window flap was partly open and I heard some men talking. They have instructions to give you a beating, a warning, to make sure that you leave the area.'

'How many?' I wanted to know the odds. I had already guessed who sent them.

'Three, it was the men who were drinking and were wandering through the campsite earlier.'

We both froze, aware of people passing close to the tent. Mary showed her little girl into her compartment. Outside I heard a voice say, 'Finn, Finn.' It was almost a repeat of what had happened a few minutes ago but this time it was a man's voice.

'Thank you,' I mouthed to Mary, 'you've saved me.' I hoped

that I wasn't being premature.

My name was being called again and then all hell broke loose. There was shouting and I heard my tent being ripped, belongings being flung about, but I didn't dare risk taking a look.

After a couple of minutes I was aware of lights in other tents, someone shouting 'stop the racket' and a powerful torch beam shining in the direction of my tent. Rougvie was shouting and I heard him trying to struggle out of his tent.

There was more shouting and someone hit the metal bar against a metal triangle, the camp's fire alarm, which hung under a red box containing fire extinguishers, and then I heard the sound of people running away.

I chanced to look out, my tent was flattened, possessions scattered about. Several people were walking towards it, Rougvie looking anxiously for me, relieved when he saw me emerge from the safety of Mary's tent.

I quickly thanked Mary and joined the group around the remains of my tent.

Rougvie said, 'I suppose no prizes for working out who did this.'

I nodded, 'It was the drunks we saw earlier.' I added, 'Mary heard them, thankfully, when she was in the toilet and took me into her tent or I would have got a battering – a clear warning was intended, she heard them say.'

'I'll help you clear up in the morning,' and he bent down, pulling out my sleeping bag, which had been slashed, its fluffy filling oozing out.

'You were targeted for today,' and it was Jess joining us.

'You're right. Maybe there is more to our fathers' deaths. Certainly no one wants us prying about.'

'It appears so,' and she looked thoughtful.

'I told you the truth about what I saw that evening – my

116

father was murdered in front of me.'

She shivered and wrapped her arms around her, saying, 'You might be telling the truth but I still have a lot of questions I need answered. You are not off the hook. Wonder why no one seems to like you,' was the sting in the tail.

'I also have a lot of questions – in fact, probably more than I had when I arrived here – but they'll have to wait till the morning. Just glad to be in one piece,' but she showed little sympathy, turning away quickly.

'Good idea,' said Rougvie. 'I think they've gone, so bring your stuff into my tent.'

The curious occupants from the other tents were dispersing, moaning about being disturbed, one offering to phone the police, which I declined. Jess wandered away back towards her tent. Mary was still standing outside hers and I went over to her.

'Many thanks, it would have been a lot worse if it hadn't been for you.'

'Yes, I know, but it appears that you have problems. Be careful.'

I heard the sound of Tom snorting and turning over.

'He didn't get disturbed,' and she smiled.

'Never does. He's not a bad man, just not the man he was before his accident,' there was a pause, 'but I still love him and he has given me two lovely daughters.'

Neither of us knew what to say next, so I smiled and headed to Rougvie's tent.

20

I did eventually sleep but was awakened by Rougvie hauling himself out of his sleeping bag and sitting up, rubbing his face, glancing at me, as if he was surprised that I was there. He grabbed a bottle of water, unscrewed the top and drank deeply before he put the top back on.

'Quite a night,' he said, finally acknowledging me. His attention was then diverted by his phone and he frowned as he picked it up, fingering the screen.

'Bastards,' he exclaimed after a second. 'I've just had an email from the red squirrel charity, the group I volunteer with. They no longer need me. Thanks for all your efforts over the years but bye-bye.'

Before I could formulate a response, he continued, 'Guess someone that we both know has been speaking to them. Oh to have power and influence,' he added sarcastically.

'Sorry, I know it meant a lot to you.'

'Yes it did, I enjoyed the work, felt that I was doing something worthwhile. You know what gets me most,' and he didn't pause, not expecting me to answer, 'that someone who allowed squirrels to be shot on his estate is dirtying my name. I won't just take this, I'll find a way to get back at him.'

'Not a good way to start the day, especially after the night we've just had.'

'Yeah, sorry, you have enough problems of your own.'

'Let's make some coffee and then I'll clear up the mess they left.'

Rougvie slapped me on the shoulder, which I took to be an attempt at male bonding, and clambered out of his tent, rummaging around for water to fill the kettle, the stove permanently set up.

The thugs had done a good job of scattering my possessions and a breeze had also aided them. Papers were spread over a large area, notes that I had made clinging to bushes, stuck to windbreaks, tents and more. Maybe just as well that they had not read them. My clothes were damp as I picked them up but would soon dry, the same breeze now working in my favour. I grabbed my toilet bag and a damp towel and headed off for a shower, leaving Rougvie still peering at the email he had received, frowning, as he lit the gas stove.

The coffee revived me, firing my mood of determination. No thug was going to deter me from finding out what happened. I was lost in thought when a voice interrupted me.

'Are we still going to visit the places?' Jess sounded cold and when I looked up her face was set. She was wearing her glasses today, which always made her more severe, hair flopping about her face – no friendliness, no comment about the attack on my tent, no sympathy – wearing ripped jeans and a black tee shirt with a slogan in large white letters: 'Been there – done it'.

'Yes, why not, you'll have more information on which to base your opinions,' my tone suitably cool, I hoped.

She shrugged. 'Okay, let me know when you're ready.'

Rougvie was observing our little cameo. 'I'm more than willing to help out, but we have to work with each other,' he reminded us, although he didn't mention his new additional

119

reason. 'I'll help Finn clear up and then we can go,' and looking up at the sky, he added, 'at least it's a bright day for exploring.'

• • •

I wanted everyone to think that I had left, so I packed my belongings into my car and dumped the tent. Jess was watching us, sitting at the picnic bench, a backpack ready by her side. Rougvie beckoned her over.

'We'll follow Finn. He'll park his car in the town and then join us in the Jeep. Okay?' She nodded and minutes later we were driving away. Mary stood at the entrance to her tent, one of her daughters clinging to her leg and waved as I drove off. I found a space close to the local Co-op shop on Cotton Street and left the car, nipping in to get water and some biscuits. I didn't know how long the day would be. Minutes later I climbed in the back seat of the Jeep Cherokee and gave directions to Rougvie.

'The first site to visit is Loch Grannoch. There have been a few changes there recently as they've started harvesting the timber. The second site is on the road down to Creetown from the station. Do you know how to get to the old railway station at Gatehouse of Fleet from here?'

'I know that area well. My brother and I have walked along the disused railway route several times, it's a great cross-country hike and you can't really get lost. You can direct me to Loch Grannoch, presumably along a forest road from the Big Water of Fleet viaduct, when we get closer.'

'Yes.'

Jess shuffled in her seat but said nothing, fidgeting with her glasses and staring ahead.

We were on the A75 before anyone spoke again, the atmosphere in the car tense. Hostility from Jess, simmering anger from Rougvie, over the email.

'I'll try and explain what I know,' I started. 'Our two fathers worked together for the Ministry of Defence, near Annan. They often went fishing together. I believe, Jess, that your dad even designed his own fishing rods.' There was no response, which irritated me.

'On the evening that my father was murdered we were in the house alone. Mum and Debbie, that's my sister, were out shopping in Dumfries, then going for a meal. Dad was in his study when I heard the house phone ring. He didn't have a mobile. It was your father, Jess, and I soon learnt that he was going fishing at Loch Grannoch. He wondered if Dad wanted to join him – a new loch to fish for both of them, it seemed. He agreed and said that I would have to come along, as he couldn't leave me alone in the house. We got in the car and headed up towards Gatehouse of Fleet Station and...'

'The police said that he didn't have a fishing rod with him, which was a bit strange.' At least she spoke, so some progress.

'I didn't see him pack a fishing rod, he said that your father had enough gear with him. We took spare jumpers, in case it got cold later, some water, chocolate bars, midge repellent. I took the book I was reading. Fishing could mean sitting about a lot and I could get bored.'

Jess listened, unmoved. Rougvie glanced at her now and again, trying to gauge her reaction. If I twisted my head I could see her face in the rear-view mirror, but generally I didn't attempt to give her eye contact. She would just have blanked me anyway. It was maybe her age, I thought. Girls of her age, just left school or about to – and I had met many like her – often lacked confidence, simply didn't know how to respond, awkward with older people and especially teachers, who they often associated with adult authority.

We drove up to the junction where the road turned towards Creetown, next to former railway cottages. The station buildings, unseen, shielded by bushes and trees as we turned right, heading down to the Cairnsmore of Fleet National Nature Reserve and the viaduct.

'Have you been here before, Jess?' I asked.

She shook her head. 'Didn't want to, wasn't sure of the way.' I suspected that this was the first year that she had had a car, so I was not surprised.

We drove past the visitor centre, a former farm building, as we approached the viaduct.

'Do you want to stop?' Rougvie enquired. Jess shook her head and Rougvie continued following the road that led under one of the arches of the viaduct, heading towards the edge of the forest ahead. Each year the scene changed as patches of forest were cleared, trees felled, trunks piled up at the side of the track, with warning signs not to clamber on them. As I already knew from my recent trip some of the trees at the edge of the forest had been felled. The route through the forest was now part of a national cycle route, a sign declaring that it was twenty-five miles to Glen Trool – a long way on dusty roads.

Shortly after we entered the forest, we turned right at a sign that said 'Path Mossdale 8 miles', but we soon deviated from it. After a few miles we reached the southern pointed end of the loch, gleaming blue in front of us, the hills around it mostly tree-lined, with a few gaps where trees had been harvested.

'Stop and pull over.' There was silence as Rougvie turned the engine off, a peaceful silence in contrast to the tense stand-off in the Jeep.

'Let's get out. I am pretty certain this is the place.'

'You should know, if you were here,' Jess stated, rather snappily.

'I was here but things change,' I replied, trying to sound patient. I was getting accustomed to her attitude, but it was a bit wearing. 'There was a pile of logs about here but they've been removed. From here you could see the loch clearly but the bushes have grown, partially obscuring the view.'

'Things do change,' Rougvie said, helpfully, 'but you think this is the spot?'

'The car was parked here, a short distance from where the road forks, heading in different directions along the shore of the loch. He left me behind.'

'Why did he leave you behind?' Jess proclaimed. It was going to be a long day.

'A lot of midges about, just like today, and he wasn't sure exactly where your father was. And I had my book with me, happy to be left since I would be more comfortable in the car. This was the first time he had been to Loch Grannoch and maybe your father's directions were not clear. I didn't always accompany him. His last words to me as he left were "I won't be long". Maybe he was checking the whereabouts of your father, not sure where the fisherman's hut was located. I didn't see another car. He walked over to the lochside, taking the road to the right, obscured by bushes almost immediately.' Part of me did wonder why he left me. I'll never know now but I didn't say that to Jess.

Jess strode off in the direction of the loch. We both followed her. Where the road split, the track churned up by heavy trucks extracting timber, she turned right, following the road along the shoreline but about twenty yards inland. A few hundred yards along the shore was a small wooden hut, the waters gently lapping on the narrow sandy shore, the hut reached by a couple of stepping stones over a burn and then a short wire-covered slatted wooden jetty. She walked fast towards the hut and

123

entered it, looking around, maybe she expected blood stains but, of course, there were none. 'Is this it?' she asked, disappointed. But I did wonder what she expected, as we joined her at the hut. There were signs that someone had had a barbeque recently, empty crushed beer cans but nothing else. I had some sympathy for her, had been there myself, hoping for some clue. I had, of course, visited it much later, years later, but it was just an empty shell then, like today, very remote and not often used, I expected.

'I never got as far as the hut that evening,' I explained.

You heard a shot being fired?'

'Yes. I had been in the car for some time, not sure how long.'

'It had to be your father, if no one else was about.'

'Someone could have been lurking, waiting,' Rougvie pointed out.

'But no one ever saw anyone else,' Jess answered, 'a bit suspicious. The police said that they weren't looking for anyone else. Why didn't you follow your dad, when he was away for so long?'

'Two reasons,' and I showed my irritation, my tone clipped. 'Firstly, I was only twelve and did what I was told and I was reading a book that I was enjoying. Secondly, you sometimes hear shots fired in the forest. Rougvie and I saw evidence of that yesterday.'

Rougvie agreed, 'Don't remind me.'

'The shot didn't seem that close. I didn't connect the shot with our fishing trip, why would I? Thought maybe that a stalker was out shooting deer. Dad never had a gun and I don't see how he could have turned into a cold-blooded murderer by the time he arrived at the hut. He was in great form, excited about the fishing.'

'He could have placed a gun there earlier...'

'But he didn't know that he was going to meet up with your father until that evening and, as I just said, didn't know the exact location. Can I just say again he never had a gun, wasn't interested in them.' I felt I needed to keep making that point.

Jess was still not convinced. 'The police said that they were not looking for anyone else,' she stated, refusing to change her view.

'When did you know that someone had been shot?' Rougvie asked, trying to be helpful.

'Later, at Sir Archibald's house. I overheard one of the men wondering what they were going to do with the body at the hut. They sounded quite wound up, as you would expect. Not every day they have to deal with a dead body. I was terrified it was my father and shouted at them to tell me what had gone on but they shut up when they knew I was listening and didn't answer my questions. They kept quiet after that.'

'From what you've said, Finn, it does seem unlikely that your father would shoot anyone. So let's suggest, for the moment,' emphasising the last three words, before Jess was able to intervene, 'it was someone else. Could it have been an accident? Unlikely,' Rougvie answered his own question. 'Your father would probably have tried to get Jess's dad in the car and head for the hospital.'

Rougvie turned towards Jess. 'Someone murdered your dad, but I can't think it was Finn's father. You were very young at the time but have you heard any rumours about your dad being unpopular? I'm simply trying to find a motive, not blame.'

She was sullen, mention of her age made her feel that she was being patronised. 'Are you a teacher, like him, always superior, think that they know the answer? I hated them at school.'

'You're not at school now,' Rougvie replied, 'and we are just looking for the truth. 'Was your dad unpopular?' he repeated.

Jess cast her eyes down. 'Mum refuses to talk to me about him,' she admitted.

'But you mentioned an affair at work, thinking it was Finn's father,' Rougvie pointed out.

'That's what the police said. There was a woman involved but they said it was his dad who was involved with her. An uncle, when he was drunk at a New Year party, told me, years later.'

I tried not to get emotional. 'The picture you are painting is not one I recognise,' and that probably sounded a bit formal, teacher like. 'If someone knew of your father's plan for the evening they could have followed him and my father turning up unexpectedly complicated the situation. Neither of our fathers sound as if they were likely murderers. They were research scientists, steady types, academics. If the authorities had any suspicions they would not have been allowed to continue in their posts.'

'We simply don't have enough information to reach a definitive conclusion,' Rougvie declared.

'What happened next?'

'A Land Rover appeared driving fast and headed up the track where Dad had gone. I was in the bushes at the time, having a pee, so they didn't see me. A pickup followed and the occupants did see me and stopped to speak, asking who I was before driving on.'

'It can't be coincidence that they arrived so quickly,' Rougvie stated. 'There must have been contact from the scene of the crime to bring them hurriedly to the hut. That suggests a third party.'

'Why?' asked Jess.

'Someone had alerted them. If Finn's dad shot him, it's unlikely that he would have called for assistance. Who were the people that arrived in the Land Rover?'

'I didn't recognise them or the people in the pickup who followed later. The two men in the Land Rover eventually returned and got out and grabbed me. One of them pushed me into our car after tying me up and putting the sack over my head, then drove me to the hut in the grounds of Sir Archibald's house. Sir Archibald, and I'm sure now that it was his voice, was furious, annoyed that I had been brought there. Didn't want a link to him.'

'Sir Archibald is somehow involved. It must have been his men, estate workers presumably, who arrived, but why? Given his reaction yesterday, he's hiding something, knows more than he's admitting. Nothing makes sense at the moment. We need more information,' Rougvie stated again. 'Anything else you can remember that might be useful?'

'Only little things.' Rougvie wanted me to continue. 'The Land Rover had one of these snorkel kits, which allows them to pass through deep water.'

'Quite common in country areas.'

'Later on the road to Creetown, Archibald arrived being driven in an unusual car, part of the reason I wanted to see inside his garage, but it wasn't there.'

'Describe it.'

'It was light-coloured, possibly silver, the nose dipped sharply beyond the wheels, seen nothing like it since.'

'Have you checked websites?'

'Of course. Sounded like a powerful sports car. Lights seemed to come from double vents on the bonnet.'

'I'm not that knowledgeable about cars, but I'll have a look later. My brother might be able to identify it.'

'Thanks, Rougvie.'

'Anything else?'

'When I was at Archibald's house that night, I heard someone refer to Hitler.' Rougvie's eyebrows shot up. Even Jess appeared startled.

'Continue,' Rougvie said.

'That's it. Hitler's bridge, no – Hitler's grave, that was it.'

'I'll take you there just now. I know where it is. Let's get back to the Jeep.'

For once Jess and I looked at each other not with hostility but with puzzlement. Rougvie just smiled enigmatically.

21

We headed back under the viaduct, continued up to the junction with the road from Gatehouse of Fleet and drove past the former station site.

'Not far from here,' I said, as his Jeep sped along the road to Creetown, conifer plantations to each side before they gave way to more open countryside.

'I know,' replied Rougvie, 'I'll take you to the exact spot.' He was enjoying the whiff of mystery he had created and since it had taken the focus off me, the atmosphere in the Jeep was not so tense and I could tell that Jess was also intrigued.

Rougvie pulled off the road onto an area of dried mud in front of a metal gate, just short of where the road took a sharp turn to cross a bridge. The narrow bridge was painted in vertical black and white strips to make it more visible. He twisted his head around and smiled.

'Am I right?'

'How did you know?' I said, as I saw the bunch of flowers I had left just a few days ago, already starting to wilt.

'Hitler's Grave is a local curiosity, carved out by a Polish stonemason during the Second World War. "Polish Joe", as he was named, carved out a figure inside a coffin and underneath carved "Hitler 15.8.40". This is where they brought you.'

Jess looked warily at Rougvie and got out of the Jeep. She stood looking around before joining us as we reached the bridge. We found the small carving, only inches in length, etched on the top of the parapet. Branches of a tree overhung it, the sun filtering through the leaves creating a dappled effect on the carving.

'Polish Joe was driven out of his country because of Hitler and so he hated him. He was sent to help repair bridges on the railway line and found an unusual way to display his feelings. That's the railway the bridge crosses, but the drainage has broken down very badly and it's now virtually a stream.'

'Rougvie's correct,' I said, trying to sound friendlier, change the mood, as I spoke to Jess. 'The car was parked here, between the gate and the bridge. Archibald didn't want me at his house, so they sent me on a journey to here. I was left in the car while they discussed what to do. There was panic in their voices, something gone badly wrong, although I couldn't make out a lot of what they said. Eventually I heard one of them say: "What about the boy?" as if I had been forgotten about. Minutes later they surrounded the car. I was mute with fear. Then a Land Rover drove up, distracting them, and they manhandled a body out. I didn't know that it was Jess's father but it must have been, and while I could see only a little through the rip in the sack I believe that they dumped him near the gate.'

Jess, who had been standing listening intently, now focused her gaze involuntarily on the area near the gate, her jaw slack as she took in what I said. That was where Dougie Hamilton's body was found, so it must have been him.

That night as I struggled into a more upright position, I saw my father for the first time. He must also have been in the Land Rover, now being led, hands bound, head hooded, not slumped but defiant, brave. There was the sound of another car approaching, a throaty sound, a high-powered engine, and the sports car with Sir Archibald arrived. He stepped out of the passenger seat and the driver also got out. In the dark I couldn't read his expression until he stepped into the glare of the Land Rover's headlights.

I was only twelve but I could clearly identify anger on his face, his mouth narrowed as he absorbed what was happening but quickly taking control. Dad was brought from the shadows into the light and unseen hands whipped off his hood. He immediately looked around, probably searching for me. I screamed and he looked at our car. 'Finn,' he shouted, then, 'leave the boy, let him live.'

My eyes filled with tears as I recounted the story. Jess was staring hard at me and she must have seen my eyes brimming with tears. I was reliving the events vividly, as I had done so often. Trauma lingers.

Sir Archibald spoke to the driver and he went back to his car to lift something out of the back seat. Meanwhile Sir Archibald turned his attention back to my father, who stood unflinching, giving no ground. Sir Archibald nodded giving a shadowy figure the go-ahead and my father was forced down on his knees and a handgun was produced.

I shook my head opening my eyes, the playback loop disrupted by the bright sun. Jess and Rougvie were both watching me carefully.

'And you know,' I said, 'I still don't know why and that hurts me more than anything. Why, Jess, did they do it? Kill two men, murder two men, who were on a simple fishing trip. What does Sir Archibald Graham-Linton have to do with it? Why the cover-up? I want answers.'

Jess kicked a piece of gravel into the long grass and stood

silent, tears evident now in her eyes. I gave her space and turned away.

'So why here? What do you think, Rougvie?' giving him an easier question to tangle with.

'I know the answer to that, too. Look on the hillside over there,' and he pointed to the other side of the road, towards a wood and then to the hillside beyond. Do you see the spoil heap, what looks almost like a shale outcrop from here?'

I nodded.

'That's the spoil heap from the Pibble mine, an old lead, copper and zinc mine. Although you can't see it from here, there are the remains of an old engine house the other side of the trees. The area was worked extensively for the metals but it closed a long time ago. Up there are some very deep vertical shafts. The farmer wants no one venturing on his land, it's too dangerous. Fall into one of the shafts and your body falls for some time before it hits the bottom. A great place to bury dead bodies, where they will never be found. I think that they were going to drag the bodies up there and get rid of them but it would have required a considerable effort.'

'But Sir Archibald stopped them.'

'Correct. If two scientists from a top secret research facility go missing and their bodies are not found, that is a major story with national implications for security. If their bodies are found and a story concocted to explain their deaths, a passionate affair, jealousy, very human, that is a tragedy but it is containable.'

'Do you think that there was a cover-up?'

Rougvie paused, not for effect but to think further.

'Looks like it. I believe your story, don't think that you made it up.' Someone believed me at last and that felt good.

Out of the corner of my eye I could see that Jess was appearing less defensive, more eye contact, her cheeks flushed,

132

blinking, emotion not far below the surface.

Rougvie continued, 'I am still not clear what took place at Loch Grannoch but I can't believe your father went there with the intention to murder Jess's father. It does seem likely that Dougie was killed at the loch and he was brought back, with Finn's father, in the Land Rover and his body, sorry Jess, dumped here.'

'You were dragged through the countryside to Sir Archibald's house and then back before seeing your father being murdered, although a cover story was concocted and it was made to appear that your father committed suicide. Jess, what do you think?'

'Not sure. It seems suspicious that Finn's father left him in the car and then there is the unexplained gun shot. But then all these people appear and panic sets in. But why were they killed?'

'That's a big question – we don't know. No motive,' Rougvie said.

'But from yesterday and the reaction at Sir Archibald's house they are hiding something. There has been a cover-up. Add in the reaction of people I have spoken to, like George Park, the newspaper editor, who phoned Sir Archibald to tell him I was asking questions, probing into the events. Then there was Mac, the retired policeman's reaction when I talked to him and mentioned Sir Archibald's initials and let's not forget Jimmy Urquhart, who admitted that the case had been taken out of his hands by security from the defence ministry. The events of that night certainly didn't discourage his drinking, they probably broke him.'

'Our fathers were murdered, Jess, and I don't know about you but I need to find answers.'

Jess remained silent, nothing unusual in that, her gaze directed towards the ground, but I sensed that she was thinking, trying to piece together all the facts, her thoughts about what happened under revision.

'Give me some space,' and she walked over the bridge and around the sharp left hand turn on the other side.

Rougvie raised his eyebrows at me and we stood for a few minutes in silence, listening to the innocent chirping sounds of birds on nearby bushes, before he spoke. 'Life-changing events, Finn. No wonder you are so wound up. The question is, what are you going to do now?'

'Go after the bastard and prove my father's innocence,' the sharp edge in my voice surprised even me. A small bird flew away from its perch, fluttering its wings as it rose in the sky.

'Count me in,' and we both turned, not having heard Jess return.

'I want the truth, but you better not be lying.'

At long last I was being believed, maybe not completely, but at least enough to join my quest for the truth.

22

Jess was sitting on an easy chair, legs drawn up tight against her body, arms wrapped around them, chin resting on her knees. It was difficult to work out what she was thinking. Rougvie was sitting on the step that led up to the en suite bathroom in the hotel room I was staying in, having found a sachet of hot chocolate by the kettle and was sipping the drink, blowing on the surface to cool it. I lay back on the pillows I had stacked behind me on the bed. I had booked a room for the night at the Kings Arms, in Castle Douglas, to give myself a good sleep and because I wanted to avoid the campsite, let them think I had gone. My funds could stretch to a few nights, if needed. We also had privacy to talk.

Both had agreed that we needed to speak more about Sir Archibald or AGL as we had decided to call him. Calling him Sir Archibald or simply, Archibald seemed too respectful. Jess had taken on board what I told them on our trip today and seemed to half-believe me and that, at least, was a start. However, if she was a year out of school and that was all, looking pale and vulnerable, I did wonder how useful she might be and whether it was even fair to involve her. But I had thought that about Rougvie and he had been invaluable today, providing real insights. I couldn't help wondering what Gillian would think if she found out about Jess. Our relationship was totally innocent, based on mutual need, of course, but it wasn't good for a teacher to be found with someone who had just left school. Hopefully, she would never know.

The town clock sounded, jolting me from my thoughts, and I was aware that both of them were looking at me, waiting for me to speak.

'Thanks for today and listening to my story,' I began, 'it actually means a lot that people believe me. Everyone else has dismissed my story of the events around Dad's death, even my mother and sister. After the last few days I realise that there has been a massive cover-up and I am more determined than ever to get to the root of it.'

'Seems like it.' It was Rougvie speaking, and as he put down his mug, he added, 'It just doesn't make sense. Two respectable scientists murdered on a fishing trip and nobody wants to know. My feeling,' and I was beginning to trust his instincts, 'is that it was not a fall out between friends that led to their deaths – that seems very unbelievable – but the explanations reach much higher. It's also interesting that while a lot of people from newspaper editors to the police know more than they are saying, everyone is keeping tight-lipped. The conspiracy of silence must be driven by fear of what would happen to them if they talked. That suggests some important people are involved and AGL is only one of them. I mean ordering the killing of someone and then covering it up is…' and he paused, lost for words.

'…is extreme behaviour which requires powerful motives,' I finished, struggling to find the words that expressed my feelings, sounding like a teacher again.

Rougvie nodded. 'Can't think what the motive could be – it's incredible.'

Both of us turned towards Jess, who was now hugging her knees more tightly, slowly rocking back and forward. She glanced briefly at each of us, the movement stilled. 'I don't know what to say. I always thought that your father was responsible but that doesn't make sense now.'

I smiled, pleased at her comment, but her face did not relax in response, remaining very tense.

'Conspiracies go above my head. You mean like people believing that Kennedy was assassinated by aliens or stuff like that?'

'I suppose we do,' said Rougvie. 'AGL is well connected.'

Suddenly I remembered what Mac had said. 'The new foreign minister, Julian Montgomery, has visited the area in previous years, out shooting on some estate. Maybe AGL knows him but I don't know how that helps us.'

'Maybe not,' said Rougvie, 'but there was someone important visiting him the other day. Fancy cars, bodyguards, greeted in person by our man on the steps of his mansion.'

'Maybe that was the reason he wanted to check my photos and the bodyguard snatched my phone. Check that the VIP's security was not compromised. That's probably why, when I wouldn't give him the passcode, he smashed the phone. AGL just being his usual brutal and ruthless self.'

'Is it totally ruined?'

'Yes.'

'Let me see it.' I got up, rummaged in my bag and handed it over to Rougvie, who fiddled with the buttons. 'There is a little charge left, but the recharging point is smashed. He shook his head, 'the screen is unreadable,' and he handed it back to me.

'Ruthless man,' stated Jess, 'and he knows about you, even sent his thugs to give you a clear warning. He'll stop at nothing. When I thought about it, I realised that you were probably telling the truth.'

Still the caveat but at least she was on my side.

'What did you see at the garage? Anything that he didn't want you to see?' Rougvie enquired, still probing.

'Just his fancy car and a few old wrecks. I didn't see the Land Rover with the snorkel kit. And they let me go to the toilet, so there was probably nothing there that they wanted to hide,' I concluded.

'Okay, what about the hut?'

'I'm sure that it was the hut that I was taken to that evening, framed pictures and antlers on the walls. It looked familiar but I couldn't see clearly through the windows. The photos on the walls were too small. I did think one showed a car similar to the one on the evening but I couldn't be sure. Of course, the photos I took were destroyed with the phone.'

'I wonder if that was deliberate. I mean the destruction of your phone was not just to preserve the VIP's security but because you might recognise some link with the events of that night.'

I thought for a minute. 'The bodyguard mentioned that he saw me at the hut. AGL picked up on that and he is not the type to take chances, especially when he heard that I was fishing around and maybe wondered if I realised it was the same hut. Certainly gave me a warning to stay away.'

'I think there might be something in the hut, a link,' and we both looked at Jess. She blushed slightly, hesitating before adding. 'It must be the same place that you were dragged to and if there is a picture of the car then we might be able to identify the driver.'

'That would help, well done,' Rougvie replied. Jess checked to see if he was being patronising, but Rougvie was smiling warmly at Jess for her contribution.

'Good teamwork,' I said, 'but it means that we'll have to break into the hut to check. AGL will not be happy. I've been warned off.'

'You have to calculate the risks to yourselves against possible gains,' said Rougvie, 'but I don't see another way forward.'

'Nor do I,' stated Jess, lifting her head from her knees and sitting upright in the chair, feet touching the floor, apparently energised.

'I have to go home in a couple of days, stayed longer than I intended to, but I feel that I owe AGL for allowing the red squirrel to be shot. Did you notice any burglar alarm at the hut?' enquired Rougvie. I shook my head. 'I'm a joiner and one of the firm's contracts is with the police. Doors get damaged in raids or some old dear loses her key and we get called out. I'm not a locksmith but a good bit cheaper, so I know how to open locked doors. How was the door secured?'

'There was a Yale lock and a combination padlock.'

'Yale lock, no problem. You would be surprised how unimaginative people are in setting the four numbers for a combination padlock. Most just want to remember the code easily. I am sure I can get in and if not a hacksaw or the old jemmy never fails. However, I don't want to leave visible signs of damage if I can help it. Don't want AGL to discover anything amiss. He knows your name, he can find you. But Jess, he knows nothing about you. Let's keep it that way. Let's be clear, if I break in that's all I do, repayment for allowing red squirrels to be shot. Then I leave you both to search the hut. Do you accept that?'

'Of course, thanks for your help.'

'Tomorrow night?' Jess asked, and I agreed.

'There is a quicker route into his estate over the hills,' Rougvie said, appearing slightly embarrassed. 'I was winding you up the other day, taking difficult routes, since you were

139

treating me like an idiot. I took you around in circles and you didn't notice.'

'Sorry if I gave you that impression,' and I hadn't realised that he'd taken me on a wild goose chase. 'You've been a great help and I judged you wrong.'

'I suppose I was acting like an idiot when I arrived,' and even Jess smiled.

I wasn't sure what I would find in the hut, maybe nothing, but it was our best chance at progress, our only hope.

'Jess, you don't need to come with me, it might be dangerous.'

Jess snorted. 'My father was killed too, not just yours. We go together. Danny has shown me a few things. I'll prove my usefulness.'

Rougvie suddenly choked on his hot chocolate and started coughing. I fought the urge to stroke my sore jaw but maintained a straight face.

We agreed to meet the next morning and they both left the room a few minutes later.

23

A good sleep in a comfortable bed and a big breakfast helped my mood. Jess and Rougvie arrived just after ten and I joined them in the Jeep. Both seemed relaxed, Jess wearing another of her tee shirts with a statement – 'Of course I can'. It seemed a positive statement. She wasn't wearing her glasses, presumably using contact lens, which made her face softer, not so severe. The sunny weather was also helping, the mood in the Jeep different from before.

'We need to plan,' I said. 'Somewhere we won't be seen or overheard.'

'How about Kirkcudbright? It's the other direction from where we're heading later.'

Jess agreed, although I am not sure she knew where Kirkcudbright was, but we reached there half an hour later and found a cafe, allowing us to sit outside near the harbour. The tide was out, boats resting against the pier, the River Dee a slow stream surrounded by mudflats.

The waitress brought us coffee and cakes and we waited until she had gone before talking.

'What we are planning is very dangerous,' Rougvie stated, stuffing some cake in his mouth, which somehow distracted from the seriousness of what he had just said. 'AGL is ruthless, is hiding a secret and has ordered the death of people before. If he finds us back at his estate then he will chase you and the consequences of being caught could be dire. I just want you to be clear about this.'

Surprisingly, it was Jess that spoke first. 'And if we do nothing then he gets away with murder. Not fair.'

'Life isn't fair, Jess,' I stated.

'Let's go for it.' Jess had bought into our plans. 'We're only taking photos,' she continued, 'and if Rougvie can get us in, then we should finish quickly and get away.'

I suspected that Jess and Rougvie had been talking before they picked me up this morning, as Jess was clued in to how we were going to do it, enthusiastic.

'We need to be prepared. Wear dark clothes, take torches, a towel or blanket, water and some sweets for energy and, of course, midge repellent. We'll need backpacks.'

'The tension will drain you of energy,' Rougvie added. 'Are there blinds on the window, Finn?'

'No.'

'We'll do this at night, which is much more difficult. You can easily get lost in the woods. I'll try and think of ways to help you. The towels or the blanket will be useful to mask the flash when you take the photos. You mustn't alert people in the house. Get back to the car as quickly as possible and get away. Seems simple but you must plan for all possibilities. I would suggest that you park the car at Loch Stroan, next to the old railway viaduct, and drive west away from the estate along the Raiders Road when you're finished. That's the route I'll take when I leave you. If you're rumbled they will probably search for your car in a lay-by off the main road first.'

Rougvie's suggestions seemed sensible and we talked for

some time, going over the details. The effects of the hot sun and just watching people going about their everyday lives made our plans seem unreal. Of course I was worried. I was aware that a charge of burglary, if it went wrong, would finish my teaching career and probably my relationship with Gillian and my family. A lot was at stake and we had to get it right.

We had time to kill, hours that would stretch. Our conversation drifted.

'So you are a joiner, Rougvie?' I asked as the waitress brought more coffee.

Rougvie nodded, 'I like it, satisfying when you complete a job.'

'You take pride in it?'

'I had a teacher at school, a Mr McAnespie, taught me woodwork. Old-school type, demanded the best. Kept sending me back if the joint or whatever was not quite right. Didn't like it at the time but appreciate what he did for me now. And you're a science teacher?'

'Chemistry and science.'

'I hated both,' Jess said, ' and school. And the teachers hated me,' she added. I could believe that, I recognised the type, but I showed no reaction. 'I missed having a dad, felt different from everyone else. Not many have a dad who was murdered and other pupils soon found out.'

'And could be cruel,' I said, 'I know that feeling,' but I didn't want to interrupt her, interested in what she was going to say.

'The only way I could make friends was to rebel, be the class clown. I needed friends, I was an only child, and Mum was often drinking to hide her unhappiness. I couldn't take people home and other parents didn't want their precious children...' and I sensed the pain, 'playing with me.'

'It must have been hard,' I said, 'no one likes to be different.'

143

I didn't necessarily blame the parents. They only wanted the best, to protect their children from what they thought might be a bad influence. But someone had to stand up for the children who were different by circumstance or choice. I suddenly remembered Duncan with his crowd at the campsite. These kids needed someone to care for them, take an interest.

'At secondary, I got in with an older crew. Drink, drugs, I did the lot, got the scars. Then I met Danny, who left the school a few years earlier. He cared, protected me, made me feel good.'

I saw in front of me a young, vulnerable girl, life cursed by events outside her control, desperately searching for answers, love, meaning in her life. There were similarities but my father was a positive role model, someone to look up to who inspired me. In that sense I was lucky, but I had still suffered.

We finished our coffee, having sat for hours. I walked to the edge of the pier before we headed back to the Jeep. The fast-flowing Solway tide had swept in, boats floating on the incoming surge, the mudflats now covered. We couldn't let AGL's murky secrets go undiscovered. The prize was to find out the truth, remove the blot on our families, so that we could put the past behind us and move forward.

24

The long, light Scottish summer evenings prevented us from starting our journey early. Eventually after ten the fluffy pink clouds reflecting the waning sun darkened, the blue intensified turning to dark and a few stars appeared, harbingers of a bright, starry night in dark-sky country. We drove north taking a different route, Loch Ken to our right, Rougvie leading in his Jeep, me beside Jess in her Fiat 500 following on behind.

We turned at the entrance to the Raiders Road, the cars stirring up dirt on the dry baked surface. Reaching the car park at Loch Stroan, we parked beside some tall bushes, partly concealing the car from a casual observer driving past.

We took out the torches that we had bought and collected our backpacks. The only sounds were that of an owl hooting, and the rush of water as the loch emptied into the River Dee at the viaduct. We were ready to go. Rougvie crossed the track we had travelled along and confidently headed for a firebreak in the coniferous woods, stopping as we reached it.

'Go slowly, the ground is uneven and we don't want twisted ankles. Aim the torch on the ground just in front of you. No talking, sounds carry.'

The midges were bad, swarming around us, biting, detecting

the carbon dioxide in our breath, they say. I had liberally applied midge repellent but still the massed hordes got through, and it was hard not to react. Soon sweat added to the attraction as we laboured up the hillside, having to remind myself that this was the quick route. I was at the rear, my speed restricted by Jess as she stumbled along. The first twenty minutes were slow, a soft breeze cooling the air and dispersing the midges as we climbed.

Rougvie stopped and turned, pointing back the way. At the bottom of the firebreak we saw the loch, stretching out under the stars. Searching in his bag, Rougvie produced a long glow stick, primed it and stuck the glow stick to a tree with tape on the side we would notice on our return.

'They'll last for hours and might help you find your way, which can be hard in the dark.' The green fluorescent tube glowed. 'Dawn will be around three and you can wait until then, if you wish.' That seemed a long time away, almost four hours. I wanted away by then, the job done.

'Not far now, ten minutes at most.' To our right there was a rustling in the trees and several deer startled by our presence, ran away clattering through the woods.

Rougvie stopped to place a couple more glow sticks as we progressed. I wasn't sure how useful they would be but they gave some reassurance and maybe that was his intention. Jess said little and I could hear her laboured breathing as she carefully made her way. As we left the firebreak progress became harder, having to duck under branches, feet sinking into the soft mossy ground.

I was aware of Rougvie suddenly stopping, Jess almost bumping into him and their torches being switched off, me quickly doing the same. We huddled together, aware of the cold air chilling our sweaty bodies. Rougvie parted some bushes and there below us was the house, a few lights shining near the

146

doorway, the vast brooding bulk of the house in darkness apart from a room on the second floor which was lit up, curtains drawn.

'I think that everyone seems to be in bed or maybe there is a party at the back of the house,' and Rougvie gave a nervous half-laugh. As our eyes became accustomed to the scene we saw more details, the outline of the house with its conical towers and rows of chimney pots, the water feature, the driveway.

Rougvie had manoeuvred us close to the hut, which I could just make out. He now worked his way through the trees towards it, Jess and I close behind, trying hard not to make a sound. A few tense minutes later I saw the outline of the hut looming in front of us.

On the side nearest to us was the window with opaque glass, which I assumed was the toilet. The window consisted of a top pane and a bottom pane, both metal-framed, and probably a simple clip which, when freed, would allow the panes to slide open and shut. I mentally noted that as an emergency escape route.

'I'll crawl along the veranda to the door and see what I can do. Keep a look out for any activity in the house and warn me by whistling if you think that we've been spotted,' and with that he left us crouching, working his way onto the veranda, keeping behind the wicker chairs, and then edging towards the door which was nearer the other end. We waited in silence.

I heard some muffled sounds and knew that Rougvie was working away at the combination padlock, his torchlight shielded from the house by his body and held very close to the padlock. Most people chose simple number combinations, he assured us, but that still left a lot of possibilities. We waited as patiently as we could.

Occasionally, we heard traffic passing along the main road

and got used to that, nothing to disturb us as we waited. Then I felt Jess grip my arm and I knew why. A car had slowed down, its headlights turning in towards the house and suddenly it was coming down the drive, heading towards it. I whistled softly and the scraping noise at the door of the hut stopped. A minute later Rougvie rejoined us, having gone the long way around the back of the hut as the car stopped in front of the house and more lights came on.

We watched from our vantage point as the front doors of the house were opened and someone stepped out. I also saw the driver's door open and a light coming on in the car. A familiar figure appeared – Tania. She went around the car and opened the passenger door to let out AGL. As he headed for the house someone came down a few steps to greet him. Tania shut the passenger door and got back into the car, driving it around the side of the house, its beam briefly lighting up the hut before it turned towards the garage.

'At least we know where he is,' Jess said, breaking the silence between us.

'How are you getting on?' I asked Rougvie.

'Not ideal conditions but I'm systematically working my way through different combinations. I'm trying possible years of birth at the moment – 1950, 1951 and so on. The Yale lock looks easy. My impression is that the hut contains little of value, probably a social or drinking den. There's a bin filled with crushed beer cans inside the door.'

'There's also a snooker table and a darts board, so it's used as a games room,' I replied.

I grasped Rougvie's arm. 'Look,' and we saw the red glow of a cigarette at the back of the house near the garage. Tania must be having a quick smoke before she retired.

After what seemed a long time the red glow disappeared and

I briefly saw a light at the back of the house.

'She's gone inside,' I said, and Rougvie edged his way back to the hut door.

Time seemed to stand still. I was aware of Jess rubbing her arms, warming herself or was it nerves, probably a mixture of both. The night magnified all sounds and I could hear Rougvie's struggles with the padlock and then a quiet, 'Gotcha,' as the padlock was removed. There was some shuffling and I heard the door open and breathing hard Rougvie was back beside us.

'5678,' he stated in a whisper, 'no imagination. The Yale lock was easy.' He handed me a small compass. Keep to that bearing. Don't forget the glow sticks and you'll reach the loch. Good luck,' and he edged past us. Further help would have been useful but he had delivered, got his revenge on AGL. I shook his hand, thanking him by the firmness of my grip. Jess leant forward and hugged him. In seconds he was gone and we were alone.

25

We gave Rougvie a few minutes to get away and then holding up my hand I indicated that I would go first. Slowly I stepped onto the veranda and moved towards the door. I twisted the handle and pushed in, the door swung open easily. I beckoned Jess and we stopped just inside the door, shutting it behind us, leaning against the wooden wall, both breathing heavily. There were no blinds on the window, as I had noticed earlier. As our eyes adjusted, I saw the billiard table and a row of fishing rods. I could make out the shape of framed photographs on the wall. They were our priority. To our left, at the far end of the hut, was the door that led to the toilet. The photo frames were located between the windows. Jess took off her backpack and took out her phone and I did likewise, producing a blanket.

There was a photograph above our heads and we stood up to face it. We agreed that we would not attempt to analyse the photos here but just take a clear picture. I held the blanket over Jess's head and tucked the blanket around her as she tried to focus the picture. There was a flash but little light escaped. Jess checked the photo and we moved to the next one, with no time to analyse what the photos showed, we just checked the clarity. We repeated the process along the wall that faced the house and reached the far end. I went to hold the blanket around Jess again, but this time she pressed the button too quickly and the flash lit up the room.

We both dived to the floor and waited. I crawled back towards the door and looked out of one of the windows. There was a light on in one room on the nearside of the mansion, but had anyone seen the flash?

'Sorry,' Jess said, 'I am sorry. I didn't mean to press so soon,' and I could see that she was shaking.

I gripped her arm gently, 'Hopefully, no damage done,' trying to reassure her. 'Don't worry but let's get on with the others.'

On the wall with the door there were antlers mounted on plaques, which we ignored, starting instead with the photo frames on the wall opposite the door. One of the photos showed a car, possibly the car I saw that night, but concentrating on holding the blanket didn't give me time to pay attention to it, although I felt a tightening in my stomach, a surge of excitement.

We reached the last photo frame and Jess took the picture, checked it and moved from under the blanket. Jess sat down, crouching over her phone, and checked all the photos.

'They all look good, in focus, but I don't know what they will tell us.'

As she stood up, she glanced at the final wall which had a row of fishing rods, held in a wooden frame, and a row of snooker cues. Suddenly she gripped my arm. 'The fishing rods,' and she leant down touching one of them. 'That's my father's rod. He made his own. How did that get here? There are his initials.' She pulled out her phone and quickly took a picture, before I could shield it with the blanket. The flash lit up the room.

'Sorry,' she said, when she realised her mistake.

'Let's go,' and I moved towards the door, dropping the blanket in my haste when I heard noises from the house. Peering out I saw that a light was on at the back and in the still night air I heard footsteps crunching on the gravel. Jess clutched her mouth in horror. We were in danger of being trapped.

'Jess, open that door,' and I pointed to the toilet door. 'Open the window in the toilet and get out.'

'What about you?'

'I'll follow as soon as I can,' and I pushed her, as she seemed paralysed by fear.

A torchlight flashed on the window near us, the person or persons getting closer.

'Now,' I said, and I grabbed a snooker cue and crouched behind the door. Jess barely made the toilet door and was shutting it behind her as a man burst in, his torch lighting up the interior of the hut. He must have noticed the movement as the door closed or heard the click as the door shut, or maybe both, because he roared and ran towards the toilet door. Seeing my chance I stuck the billiard cue between his legs and he tumbled, letting out a yell as he crashed against the snooker table, falling heavily.

I got up and ran out the door, pulled it closed and clicked shut the combination padlock. Another torchlight lit me up and I saw two more people running over from the house. Jumping off the veranda I ran the long way around the hut, ducking under overhanging branches. I reached the end with the toilet window to see Jess struggling to get out. Grabbing and pulling her, I supported her weight as she got out and helped her to the ground.

I checked that we had our backpacks and saw that Jess had thrown hers out of the window. Grabbing it, we started to run, torchlights illuminating the bushes and trees around us as we ducked and dived, trying to get away.

26

I could see more lights coming on and heard people shouting, their voices carrying on the cold night air as we ran around the edge of the woods that overlooked the house. We stayed low, mainly due to the low-hanging branches, crouching, finding it difficult to move fast. The ground soft with pine needles, slippery with moss, especially where it was draped over the roots of the conifers. Lights were now on in the hut and someone was playing a powerful torch beam at the trees, keeping the beam low, moving it back and forwards, looking for movement. Already they were close and the beam swept over us as we hugged the ground, but there was no shout and I was sure that we hadn't been spotted. I suspected they didn't know the direction we were moving in, which was good news. Darkness was our friend.

Jess was already out of breath and I was huffing and puffing trying to catch my breath, the tension not helping. I glanced at the luminous dial of the compass, checking the bearing. I pointed to my right and dipped under a low-hanging branch, tripping on a root as I did. My fall was soft but I scratched my head on another branch, aware of a trickle of blood running down my forehead, adding to my discomfort. Cursing as I got up, I saw Jess looking anxiously at me, willing me to get up unhurt.

I pointed ahead and we crept forward again. I was hoping that the people at the hut would take some time to get their act together before giving pursuit, but I knew we had a fairly long journey ahead, even before we reached the firebreak, made more difficult because we could use our torches only sparingly and then aimed only at the ground. Just at that point I heard shouting, still coming from the lawn in front of the house, angry voices, more torches shining now, a search party forming, but the distance between us and them was now greater and the density of the trees and the undergrowth created an impenetrable mass for the torchlights.

We paused to draw breath. 'We've got to get back to the car.' Jess nodded, still gulping air. 'I don't think the man I tripped up had time to see me. They'll know that there was someone else but not if it's a man or a woman. We should be okay.' I was hoping, trying to be positive. I was sure that they would suspect me and the gloves would be off. I had been warned.

'Where is Danny when you need him?' I said, with a smile, trying to ease the tension.

'Stuck in Germany on exercise, but he would probably want to attack them, not much use.'

I avoided stroking my jaw.

Jess suddenly grabbed my arm and pointed to one of Rougvie's lights, taped to the trunk of a conifer a few yards away, glowing dimly. We edged towards it and I ripped it off the tree, burying it in the moss. I only wanted it to help us. Hopefully, Rougvie would be well on his road home, unaware of what was happening.

A few minutes later progress became easier as we reached a small clearing. We paused again hearing no sound of voices, but in the direction of the house I saw a torch beam catching the tops of some conifers, but it was quite far off. Somewhere in the distance I heard a dog bark, disturbed by the noise at the house. They were coming after us, surprising if they didn't. Checking the bearing again we moved forward, aware of the stars for the first time glowing bright above us in the clearing. I could see our breath and saw Jess shivering. I took out my water bottle and sipped from it, my mouth dry, and offered it to Jess, which she accepted, wiping her mouth when she finished.

'Let's keep going, not far to the firebreak now,' but I was bluffing. I didn't really know where we were. We struggled on, our bodies scratched by the trees, my sweatshirt tugged by the branches. We reached another clearing, stopping to check the compass bearing again, then moving forward slowly but steadily.

Then fewer trees and we were in the firebreak, below us the expanse of water that was Loch Stroan glistening in the starlight but still some distance away. We hugged the edge of the firebreak, picking our way down the slope. We were about halfway down the slope when I saw a torch beam high in the trees and we stopped. Turning around I saw more torch beams playing among the trees a few hundred yards away. We both put our heads down, scouring the ground, picking our way along with renewed vigour.

I could now see the road ahead and bushes that I knew surrounded the car park. 'Almost there,' I whispered and minutes later we reached a ditch beside the road, scrambling across it and with our feet on firmer ground we ran towards the loch and the car park beside it. Beyond was the brooding shape of the former railway viaduct.

Jess fumbled in her pocket for her car keys and quickly found them. I motioned to make as little noise as possible, aware of the lights advancing down the hillside behind us.

The noise of an approaching vehicle stopped us and around a corner headlamps flashed, lighting up the loch and then the disused viaduct as it swung round. We both knew it was too late to drive off and I grabbed the backpack and hauled Jess towards the bushes. She snatched at her backpack and we dived into the bushes as a Land Rover appeared, turning quickly into the car park, almost immediately spotting Jess's Fiat and screeching to a stop beside it. The headlamps played on the small white car, smeared with dirt, which was standing starkly against the gloom of the surroundings.

A man jumped out of the passenger side and shouted in triumph. 'This must be their car, they haven't reached it yet.' So close to getting away. The two of us were crouched only a few yards from the car. He swung a torch beam around the area, missing us. The driver switched off the engine, killed the headlights and stepped out.

'Switch off your torch and we'll wait, catch them by surprise. Sir Archibald will be pleased with us when he arrives.' The other man muttered, 'I wonder what he will do with them.'

We shivered as we hid, too frightened to move.

27

We waited and I could see more torch beams, as a group worked
their way down the fire-break but still some distance away. One
of the men by the Land Rover lit up a cigarette, remaining silent
until a radio crackled.

'Be with you soon.' It was AGL. I recognised his voice. A few
minutes later the two of us, still crouching behind the bushes
and too frightened to make any noise, heard another vehicle
approaching, the car turning into the car park. I recognised AGL
as he stepped out of a dark- coloured SUV. The two men who
had been waiting immediately went over to him.

'No sign, sir,' one stated. 'I don't think that they've got this
far.' I couldn't make out his response over the sound of his
vehicle. A second later the engine was turned off.

'That's better,' he said. 'Are you sure?' I heard no reply from
either of the men. 'There are two of them, the second might
be a woman, not certain,' Sir Archibald continued. 'They must
be caught. McAdam's son is a pest, like his father. Catch them,
hold them until I speak with them. Afterwards, well, it's easy for
people to die out here from exposure, their bodies never found.'

Was history going to repeat itself? Father and son both
murdered on lonely Galloway roads on the orders of the same

man. I felt mounting anger, rage, my jaw clenching, hands turning into fists. I was a pest, for what, seeking justice for my father? The arrogance, the contempt of the man. How Dare He. I wanted to jump out, confront the bastard and go for him. Jess, sensing my anger, grabbed me, twisting my head, holding a finger to her mouth. Her grip tightened as she saw my face, felt the tension in my body. 'Not now,' she mouthed.

The driver got out of the SUV – it was Tania. AGL spoke to her. 'We'll get them,' but it came across as if he was trying to reassure himself. 'Too much is at stake.'

What is at stake? Tell me. Oh I so wanted to know. I felt like screaming. What could justify taking lives, then and now? What was he hiding? Jess maintained eye contact with me, trying to calm me.

'Tania, someone has given McAdam information,' AGL said, and did I detect anxiety? 'Could it be Urquhart? I thought that his alcoholism would have finished him by now. Once we've found McAdam and whoever is with him, pay him a visit. If you suspect he is blabbing, deal with him.' There was both anger and frustration in his voice.

'Will do, sir.' Would Tania do anything requested of her, even sell her soul and for what? Still too many questions, still not enough answers.

'And check whose car this is, should be useful. Anyway, I'm not hanging around here. We won't see them in the dark. You two stay here,' he ordered, 'wait till Jim and Stuart drive along the old railway. They can keep watch here and block them using the old railway track to reach Mossdale. Then head along the Raiders Road and wait at the far end, hidden, so if McAdam and his sidekick go in that direction you'll catch them. We'll search further along the old railway track tomorrow. We'll find them. They can't have got far.'

158

He stepped into his vehicle and slammed the door, his frustration evident, which gave me some consolation. As the engine in the SUV started up, I motioned to Jess and we edged away towards the viaduct, slipping along a path under the first arch, the river in front of us where the waters tumbled out of the loch.

As Tania drove away, I heard another vehicle approaching along the old railway, its lights illuminating the rock face of a cutting before it slowed on the approach to the viaduct. More doors slammed and a voice shouted down to the men still waiting in the car park.

'Didn't see anyone.'

'Nor us,' came the reply.

They had us cornered. Continuing along the railway towards Gatehouse of Fleet station, many miles away, was our only escape route and then only if we were quick. I explained that to Jess. We also couldn't use the viaduct without being seen, so we would have to cross the river where it flowed from the loch.

'The river looks shallow here, a good place to cross.' Jess looked carefully, reluctantly, at the flowing, dark water and then nodded. Like me, she was keen to get away. We took off our footwear, stuffing our socks into the boots and tying the laces together, hanging them around our necks.

As I stepped into the river the cold water took my breath away. Slowly taking short steps, trying not to slip on the slime-covered rocks, I took Jess's arm, feeling her shiver as she also experienced the shock of the cold water. A few more steps and we reached a spit of land beside the first pier of the viaduct, crawling into the long grass and stopping to recover. I waited, holding my breath, but no one had heard us. I had to rub my legs to restore circulation.

'Sorry,' I whispered, 'I wasn't expecting it to be so cold.'

I knew waiting was fraught with the danger of being discovered, so I stepped into the section of the river that flowed between the next two piers. This time the cold was expected but it still made me gasp. The water was deeper, rising to my knees. Jess clung to me and using our combined strength for support, the force of the water tugging at us, wanting to drag us downriver, we made it to the ground by the next pier. We were now some distance from the car park and just had two more sections to cross. The next one was easy, raising my spirits. Almost there, one more to go. This time the water was deeper and suddenly Jess lost footing, almost plunging into a deep pool of water. I held her firmly, pulling her up, our progress hanging in the balance, perched on the edge of disaster, every muscle straining, trying not to splash about and attract attention. With a final effort I dragged her upright and we reached the river's edge, water splashing as we fell on the sandy bank. I pulled her up and we ran up the steep slope, reaching the safety of trees and shrubs.

A torch beam shone on the riverbank that we had just vacated. Over the night air I heard someone say, 'Must have been a fish jumping.' The torch beam shone around the area until the man was satisfied that there was no one around and then he used it to guide himself along the path, under the arch and back to the car park.

I took the towel from my backpack and dried myself, rubbing my legs to get the circulation flowing again, Jess doing the same.

'Let's get away from here, we can talk later,' and she did not demur, recovering from her ordeal. We scrambled up the bank onto the railway track and walked fast, the exertion helping to restore heat to our bodies. The tree-lined route, however, soon gave way to a section of embankment, exposing us to the chill night air sweeping down from a nearby hill. I was aware that Jess was struggling to keep pace with me and I slowed down.

When we had put some distance between us and the viaduct, I felt able to think. 'Do you remember when we drove into the woods beyond the Big Water of Fleet viaduct, there was a sign saying Mossdale eight miles?' Jess shook her head.

'Well, that's the direction we're heading. Mossdale is about one mile west of the viaduct we've just left and we shouldn't need to go as far as the woods with the sign, so maybe six miles to the Big Water of Fleet viaduct. Once we get to the viaduct we can phone for a taxi from the visitor centre there.' I was keeping distances down but it was a long walk not helped by the dark, although the stars gave some light, the route used by farm vehicles and free of obstacles. We trudged on, Jess bravely, not complaining.

'Thanks for helping me back at the car park,' I said. 'I was in danger of losing it.'

'Now I understand. That arrogant bastard doesn't care for anyone. Sir bloody Archibald,' she replied. 'You did well not to jump at him.'

'I'm glad you stopped me,' but my words hung in the cold air now whipping across our exposed route.

We walked on and gradually I was aware that the track was slowly veering to the left, as the sky behind us started to lighten and the stars began to fade. Rougvie – and it seemed an eternity since he left – had mentioned a railway halt near a loch, a water stop for thirsty steam engines in bygone days, where we could briefly rest. Beyond that near the site of a demolished viaduct, a forestry road cut across the railway. People could be waiting for us there. We had to keep moving.

As the morning light intensified and the birds chirped away on the many bushes that lined the route, I saw the loch to my right with tree-lined slopes beyond and was aware of a barren hillside to my left. Ahead there was a row of Scots Pines and a concrete platform in their shadow, and beyond that I could see collapsed brickwork, presumably the base for water tanks and the ruins of some cottages. This had to be the Loch Skerrow Halt and, after what must have been several miles, a place to stop for a few minutes. Jess was many yards behind but lifted her head as I clambered onto the moss-covered platform and sat down, taking off my backpack.

Jess joined me, dropping down on the moss-covered concrete, looking totally exhausted. I took out my water bottle, which was now empty, and asked for Jess's. I jumped down from the platform and walked across the track to where I heard gurgling water and filled our bottles, drinking deeply and refilling mine. What a godforsaken place in the middle of nowhere, just as Rougvie had described.

Jess sat up and drank from the water bottle. I produced a chocolate bar that I had been saving and broke it in half. The hunger pangs were still there when we finished the chocolate.

'Are we nearly there?' she enquired, her voice sounding weak.

'Not far,' I lied, calculating that we were not yet halfway. Maybe Sir Archibald was right, people could die of exposure out here. Our race through the forest, our dunking in the cold water, the long night-time walk, little rest or sustenance, were all stretching us to the limit. I looked at Jess as she lay back on the platform, her clothes streaked with dirt, her face ashen white, eyes open, staring, swiping lazily at a fly that was annoying her. The last few hours had been a nightmare, all for the sake of taking photos which we weren't even sure would show anything. We did know that Sir Archibald was part of a cover-up, of such importance that people had lost their lives. I suppose that we had also learnt that Urquhart was deeply involved. If we got through this we would also need to pay him a visit. Such thoughts I put to one side – survival was the immediate priority.

28

My legs were aching, my body bruised, clothes dirty and still
damp. Worse was the growing hunger pangs which I tried
to ignore but increasingly drained me of energy. Jess was no
better – quiet, exhausted and struggling. The old railway route
stretched out in front of us. To our left was moorland and a rock-
strewn hillside and to our right was Loch Skerrow and beyond
that coniferous forests, which gradually extended towards
the railway trackbed some distance in front of us. A remote
landscape far from any road, inhospitable and I suspected filled
with lurking danger.

We reached metal gates which straddled the trackbed.
Hopefully, they would slow down any vehicles trying to follow
us. Beyond that the trackbed deteriorated, long grasses, marshy
underfoot where the drainage had broken down. Neither of us
had much energy to talk, each of us just hoping that we could get
away. Slowly the trackbed drew closer to the conifer plantations
and at least there we had some cover.

It was an engine being switched off that alerted me, sudden
silence after noise, having been unaware of the noise until then,
difficult to judge how far away. I stopped and Jess who was
following behind almost bumped into me. Ahead the trackbed
was entering a cutting, which would restrict our scope for

escape, the conifers now close on both sides.

'I heard an engine being turned off,' I said. Jess seemed unaware. 'There may be people ahead, waiting for us,' and she nodded, adding a sigh. To our right was a large boulder. 'Hide behind that,' and I pointed to it, 'and I'll check out what lies ahead.' Jess seemed glad for a rest and I walked ahead keeping to one side of the trackbed, ready to dive for cover.

After twenty yards I encountered a forestry track cutting across the trackbed and pulled back quickly, hoping that no one was watching for me. Moving into the woods I worked my way along close to the track, stopping when I heard voices, crouching down, moving the branches of a small bush to the side. Two men were standing beside a Land Rover. One of them was pouring a drink into a cup from a thermos flask, and how I envied him, the other smoking, leaning against the door of the vehicle, a rifle laid on the bonnet beside him. I couldn't tell if they were the same men from the car park last night, hoped they weren't because they would probably be pissed off with not finding us more quickly. From the back of the Land Rover I could hear a dog whining excitedly. Our path, our route to safety, was blocked and I retreated slowly.

The Land Rover was pointing west and the track continued past it and quickly turned left, dipping and disappearing around a corner. The railway trackbed vanished into foliage on the other side of the forestry road. I wondered if this led to the site of the demolished Little Water of Fleet viaduct that Rougvie had described, bypassed by a forestry track. Edging away I made my way back to Jess, describing what I had seen.

'We'll need to work our way around them and try and rejoin the trackbed further on.' Jess naturally did not seem impressed with my plan of action, her face drawn, showing her fatigue, and now I was asking for more effort, but she picked herself up and followed behind me without complaint. I admired her determination.

The sun was now higher in the sky, the heat already building, small patches of mist rising from the trees and rapidly dispersing. More flies buzzed around us as we entered the woods, adding to our woes, but the trees were more spaced out in this wood, so we didn't have to duck under so many low-lying branches. We reached a gap in the forest where a stream flowed, crossing over it quite easily, the water level low, and then we found ourselves reaching another forestry track which seemed to lead further into the forest. That didn't seem a good idea. We stopped and I scouted along it until I reached what I thought was the continuation of the road which bypassed the demolished viaduct.

I could see where the railway trackbed continued, the forestry road winding up to it. That was good as I didn't want to get lost and I couldn't see the Land Rover. I waved for Jess to join me and we quickly moved up to the forestry road. We were making good progress when I heard a vehicle approaching from the direction of the Big Water of Fleet viaduct. We moved quickly into the undergrowth and worked our way up a hillside until I felt that we were safely concealed behind an outcrop of bushes overlooking the road.

The height we reached meant that I could now see the Land Rover through a gap in the trees. A white Nissan pickup drove along slowly past us, leaving a dust trail behind it, driver and passenger scrutinising the surroundings, presumably looking for us. They stopped beside the Land Rover and got out to greet the men from it, all four chatting, looking quite relaxed, while we lay in discomfort, attracting more midges, hungry and tired. They appeared in good spirits, probably confident of capturing their prey. To them this was a game. To the two of us this was one long, nightmarish, unremitting hell, and not for the first time I wondered what the outcome would be. Would I end up like my father, dragged before AGL? I couldn't let myself think like that.

The initial conversations apparently over, I watched as one of the men went to the back of the Land Rover and when the door was opened out bounded a young black and tan German Shepherd, excitedly barking. What looked like the blanket I'd left behind in the hut last night was produced and shown to the dog. It sniffed the blanket held in front of it and paced around. A rifle was produced from the front of the pickup and the rifle on the bonnet of the Land Rover was collected. The men watched as the dog picked up my scent, whining and barking. The chase was on. We had to get away.

29

I stood transfixed watching as I saw more dust being stirred from the dry roads – more vehicles approaching. Jess was scratching her face as the midges descended around us, getting into our hair, our noses, our mouths, driving us crazy.

'Come on, let's go,' I said, tugging at her arm. 'Time we were gone from here,' and I led the way up the hillside as another pickup sped along the old railway track, this time heading in the direction of the Big Water of Fleet viaduct, cutting off our escape route, leaving me wondering how we were going to get away and where we were going to go. Another night out here could finish us, make AGL's statement prophetic. I didn't say anything to Jess, it would only have upset her and she was struggling as it was.

As we climbed, leaving the shrubs and stunted trees that had taken root beside the railway trackbed, we entered into the relative peace of the forest. Most of the trees on the lower slopes of the hillside, between us and the Big Water of Fleet viaduct, had been harvested, leaving only tree stumps. We would easily be spotted if we attempted to go that way. As we entered the forest it was good to be out of the intense heat of the sun. Progress was slow, Jess stumbling, her pace slackened from the previous night. I was beginning to worry about Jess developing hypothermia, her core body temperature dropping, and I didn't feel too good myself.

We reached the crest of the hill and began a descent on the far side, suddenly reaching the treeline. Below us was what looked like a battlefield scene, uprooted tree stumps, dried-up branches littering the ground, with the occasional small tree stripped of most of its branches but left for birds to nest on. A bomb would have created a similar effect. The valley bottom had been cleared of trees and I saw a stream tumbling down from the higher ground. It was only on the higher ground that the trees had not been harvested, a rim of trees surrounding the valley. The quickest route was to cut directly across it.

I heard the bark of the dog somewhere in the direction we had come from earlier this morning, searching for our scent, maybe already following it. We had to cross this valley of desolation and speedily before we were spotted. Even Jess recognised the need for urgency, as we worked our way among the exposed stumps and roots until we reached the stream.

'Jess, you won't like this suggestion,' I said, 'but if we walk up the stream it will make it more difficult for the dog to follow our scent, break up our trail.'

She nodded and again we took off our socks and boots and stepped into the stream. The water was not as cold as the previous night, more invigorating than freezing and we made good progress, drinking deeply as we went, taking the opportunity to refill our water bottles.

Still casting anxious glances behind us we reached the safety of the trees and sat down, drying our feet, putting our socks and boots back on, tormented by the ever-present buzzing flies and midges.

'Better to keep moving,' I said, and I pulled her up and we

walked on. The extraction of timber had led to the creation of many new tracks to allow the harvesting machines access and we soon reached one of them. After checking that we could hear no vehicles, we walked along it, the path of least resistance, reaching a high point overlooking a large swathe of forest, a steep slope beside the forestry road to our left. Below us I could see a dust trail as a vehicle moved about. Given that this was the weekend, and forestry workers wouldn't be about, any vehicle would probably be searching for us. AGL was determined, throwing in all his resources.

We carried on, stumbling on a harvesting operation in a clearance, the machines left abandoned for the weekend, no need for security in this remote part. There was a bulldozer and a machine I recognised from the television which felled the trees, gripped the logs stripping the branches and then slicing the logs into the correct size. Several piles of stacked logs were lined up beside the track ready for removal, towering above us, the usual health and safety signs displayed.

We stood, both of us so tired, taking in the scene. Suddenly Jess left my side and walked as fast as she could towards the bulldozer, hoisting herself up onto the caterpillar tracks and reaching up to the cabin door, opening it and climbing inside, rummaging around. I realised what she was doing and ran to join her as she emerged from the cabin and triumphantly held up a bag of crisps and a packet of biscuits, eagerly ripping the packaging off with her teeth. As I got closer she threw some biscuits to me, scraps gratefully received. Never have biscuits tasted so good, as I crunched them, quietly thanking the operative for leaving them. I knew that we should eat slowly, given that our stomachs were empty, but it was hard not to just munch them down quickly. Our impromptu meal was soon finished, the hunger pangs not totally abated but assuaged for the moment.

We sat in the shade offered by a high pile of logs, neatly stacked, drinking from our bottles, feeling better and more nourished by the minute. The effect of the food, however, made me drowsy, the heat of the sun likewise and I found myself getting sleepy. Jess left me, disappearing behind bushes. I suspected that I knew the reason and closed my eyes for a minute, drifting off, fighting sleep but succumbing.

Only at the last minute did I hear the vehicle approach, exhaustion making me slow to react. An old three-door, grey Land Rover Defender, complete with a black snorkel kit, which immediately revived memories in me, screeched to a stop feet from me. A man quickly jumped out, grabbing a rifle and pointing it at me.

'I get the reward,' he claimed, smiling at me, his tone one of jubilation. 'Where is your friend?'

My mind was now more alert, cursing myself for being caught, as I attempted to stand up, desperately trying to clear my head, working out if I could dart behind the pile of logs beside me and then into the woods. His total attention was focused on me. I was wasting my time.

'We separated last night. No idea,' I replied eventually.

The man shrugged. 'You're the important one.' He must have been in his mid-fifties, hair grey, peppered with white, a smile revealing a missing tooth, giving him a strangely lopsided grin, wearing dirty jeans, a sweat-stained tee shirt and a faded baseball cap perched on the back of his head. He seemed wiry, strong and he had the rifle. I cursed myself again for being caught, glad that Jess was not around and wondered how I was going to get out of this.

He nudged the rifle in the direction of the Land Rover. I shuffled over, taking my time and as he opened the rear door, with the spare tyre attached to it, he reached in and snatched a coil of rope, not letting his gaze drop, the rifle held firmly in one hand.

He motioned for me to climb in and as I did so he put down the rifle very quickly, grabbing me before I could move, twisting me around and holding my hands behind my back. He was tying my hands before I could react and then pushed me further inside.

Something caught his attention, he gave a loud roar, grabbing for the rifle, swearing. I heard a rumbling noise, very quickly growing louder and the Land Rover was hit hard, side-on, the impact rocking the vehicle, knocking me against the far side. The man screamed as there was another blow to the Land Rover, a loud bang, and it rocked further before it finally tipped over, tossing me hard against the side again. I crawled out of the back door onto the ground, dazed and sore, to see Jess snatching the rifle from the man, who was staggering about clutching at his leg, swearing loudly. He had been hit a glancing blow by one of the logs that Jess had set in motion by pushing the top log off the pile, sending the logs cascading down. The man was hopping on one leg, roaring in pain, and Jess easily pushed him over as she gestured with the rifle.

The rear wheel of the Land Rover was at a crazy angle, the tyre deflated where it had been hit by several of the logs. Jess put the rifle down, quickly untied me and I rolled him over, grabbing his arms behind him and holding him while Jess bound the rope around his arms and tied a knot.

'Thanks,' I said, and that seemed totally inadequate. I don't even know if Jess heard me, she was so fired up. Finally, her eyes focused on me.

'I heard the vehicle as I was coming back. I was sure that he would hear me climbing the other side of the log pile, but he seemed so pleased to catch you that his attention was diverted.' She looked at the man, leaning over him, bellowing 'Lie down,' as I went and picked up the rifle, reinforcing the message.

'We'll leave you gagged if you don't shut up,' and the man stopped for a second.

'You'll never get away, you're really in trouble now.'

'Shut up,' Jess snarled, surprising herself with the ferocity of her command and then as if regaining her composure she crouched down beside him. 'Let me check your leg.' She felt it, moving her hands up and down the injured limb, the man squirming.

'It may be cracked but it's not broken, you'll survive. More than you deserve,' she added, no doubt using skills gleaned from Danny's training.

I helped him up and manoeuvred him towards the back of the Land Rover, now on its side, roles reversed, struggling to open the door and push him inside, which led to a further torrent of abuse. I shut the door. The problem was how to deal with him. Could we just leave him, injured as he was? From inside the Land Rover we could hear him moving about trying to free himself.

'He doesn't sound too bad, does he? Lot of injured pride. He'll have some explaining to do to his friends and AGL. Defeated by a young girl. Not good for his self-esteem.'

'Let's leave him,' I said. 'We'll take the rifle and dump it. I wouldn't know how to aim it let alone fire it. Maybe they'll hang back if they think we're armed.'

Jess was drained, her adrenaline ebbing fast. 'Come on,' I said, 'we better move before they start searching for him.' I could see that any energy gained from the snacks was all used up and there wasn't much reserve left for either of us.

As we stood there the radio in the Land Rover crackled. 'Steve, Jasper has picked up a scent. Looks like they are heading in your direction. Keep an eye open and let us know immediately if you see them. We'll be with you shortly. Over.'

There was a pause. 'Steve, please acknowledge. Over.'

Time to go.

Looking down from our vantage point over the forests, I could see a dust trail thrown up by a vehicle, like an invisible dervish creating a dance of dust, seeming to cast a spell over us, encircling us. They knew that we would have to use the roads at some point to make our escape, that staying in the forest would slow us down, use up our energy quicker.

I tossed the rifle high in the air over the edge and saw it bounce down the rocky escarpment and plunge in among the trees on the hillside below. We had to keep going, but where to?

The radio in the Land Rover crackled again, the voice more urgent.

'Steve, are you okay? We'll be with you soon. Over.'

30

We needed no encouragement to leave the scene but even the
prospect of imminent danger couldn't hide the reality that we
were both exhausted, our limbs weary, struggling, suffering from
lack of sleep, our morale dipping fast. I needed a plan B to give
us hope. Options were limited but a plan did form in my mind
– not a great plan, but at least a plan. To the south the towering
mass of Cairnsmore of Fleet blocked the horizon, its steep
northern slopes ruling out an escape route in that direction. I
also remembered the sign near the entrance of the forest at the
Big Water of Fleet viaduct – Cycle route to Glen Trool 25 miles.
Too far, that distance was well beyond us. One glance at Jess as
she stumbled along confirmed that. The only escape route was
eastward towards the old railway track which formed a straight
boundary running from the Little Water of Fleet viaduct site to
the Big Water of Fleet viaduct, with more forest on the far side of
the trackbed.

If we could manage to wait until dark we could maybe slip by
them at the Big Water of Fleet viaduct. Trouble was that darkness
was many hours away and it would be a while before we could
approach the viaduct, which was the perfect pinch point. AGL's
men could just wait for us, blocking our exit, our return from

the wilderness. However, if we could edge around the viaduct making our way along the rocky ramparts which were the Clints of Dromore, the higher ground that overlooked the trackbed, then we could reach the road at Gatehouse of Fleet station. Not an easy route in the dark, especially if we weren't able to use our torches to help us. We would still be five miles from Creetown or seven miles from Gatehouse of Fleet but at least beside a road. Maybe someone would be in the cottages at the junction and we could waken them, get help. Maybe even one of our phones would work there. Here in the forest there was no signal, which added to our frustration. I wanted Jess to send the photos to someone else, so that if we lost the phone or if AGL did his wrecking bit again we would still have evidence. I hoped, once again, that the photos were worth all the drama.

Maybe Jess was reading my mind or working on her own escape plans because she asked, 'Is there a way out of this?' A note of despair in her voice.

We stopped on the dusty track, with the land still falling away to our left and I pointed out Cairnsmore of Fleet and the obstacle it presented, reminded her of the distance to Glen Trool and explained about the viaduct. I don't think that geography was her strongest subject but she listened, her face too tired to express the disappointment she must have felt that a long demanding day and most of the night still lay ahead.

'Let's try,' she replied. 'I don't want to be caught by them.' We agreed on that unattractive outcome being undesirable.

'Until we overcame Steve,' and I almost spat out his name, 'I don't think they knew much about you. Now they do and I suppose they will track your car to confirm your identity.'

'That won't help them, Danny bought it for me and it's in his name. I couldn't get a loan.'

'And Danny is still away?'

176

'Still in Germany.'

'Hopefully, that's a dead end for them.'

Trudging on, I stated, as much for my benefit as Jess's, I suspected: 'I can't give up. Dad was murdered and I must bring the people who did it to justice or I will not be able to live with myself.' This, after all, was my life's purpose since Dad was killed, all-consuming, destructive of relationships and life. 'I've also destroyed other people's lives in my quest. I owe it to them,' I added, wondering what Gillian was doing at this moment. Was she thinking of me or was I now part of her past? The thought of her with someone else churned me up even more. Exhaustion turned to self-pity.

'Sir Archibald Graham-Linton is a bastard,' Jess proclaimed with all the energy she could muster, which was not a lot. There was no elegance in her statement but it was direct and truthful, focusing my mind on the present, which had enough challenges of its own.

I smiled. 'Spot on.'

'I was younger,' Jess continued, maybe encouraged by my response, 'was told little of what happened but knew that I had lost out. Most other kids had dads, a family. I had nothing. I lashed out.'

Jess was not alone. I knew many pupils who didn't know how to cope with loss, who couldn't articulate their pain, learnt to go on the attack to hide their vulnerability.

'It must have been hell for you,' I added sympathetically, 'at least I was older. I knew something of what took place, witnessed it, although no one believed me. Dad was my best friend.'

Jess was studying me carefully.

'When I saw you on Facebook, I used to shout at your photo, swear, place all the blame on you, hold you responsible. Sorry.'

'I understand hurt, it screws you up.'

177

It was important to keep reminding ourselves of why we were doing this.

Nothing more needed to be said so we continued our journey, conserving our energy, listening all the time for approaching vehicles, the sun overhead beating down on us remorselessly, the familiar posse of midges and flies tormenting us, our water bottles needing refilled.

The forestry trail gradually lost height, with upturned roots, trees pushed over, rocks exposed to each side, where the ground had been churned up to create the route, leaving a bleached path shimmering with reflected heat, through green swathes, trees encompassing us on both sides now. Eventually we reached a crossroads, stopping as I worked out which route to take. We wanted east and with the sun almost overhead, it took a few minutes to decide, the compass lost somewhere on our journey.

I pointed in the direction we should take and we headed off, managing only a few steps before Jess halted and tugged at my arm. I was immediately alert. For a moment I could hear nothing, feeling puzzled and then I heard voices. Both of us immediately edged into the woods, jumping over a ditch filled with stagnant water, our feet sinking into soft ground, black water covering our feet quickly. We struggled to be free, soft ground cloying at our boots until we reached firmer ground. We crouched behind the root of an upturned tree, drawing breath.

We heard a vehicle approaching, glimpsing a white pickup truck driving slowly along the road, driver's window wound down, a driver searching for us, peering into the gloom of the woods. Another man was standing in the back of the pickup, rifle cradled in his arms, his face turned towards the other side. Instinctively we clung together, although I didn't think that they could see us.

They were nothing if not persistent. We waited for a few

minutes after they had driven slowly out of sight. But they weren't the source of the voices that Jess had heard. There were other people further along the forestry road and we heard the pickup slow as it reached them. Shortly after there was a sharp exchange, voices raised.

Jess tugged at my arm again and pointed in their direction and before I could say anything she was moving away, working through the trees. I was too tired to follow and sat back. Minutes passed, the flies were unbearable, no doubt attracted by the stagnant water nearby, a breeding ground, not that they seemed to need encouragement to breed.

I lost track of time until I heard a sharp crack, a branch snapping and I twisted around to see Jess reach my side, out of breath.

'There is a clearing up ahead,' she whispered, 'and two vehicles parked in it. Three men standing around, a map spread out on the bonnet of a car and there was also a minibus parked beside it. There were more people inside the minibus but I couldn't really see them from my position. I don't think that they are searching for us, but on some trip. They didn't seem to recognise the people from the pickup who had stopped and were talking to them. I couldn't get too close or they might have seen me, so I don't know what they were saying. I don't think that they got on. The guy who was riding shotgun in the back was having a good look around, peering into their car and the minibus, quite aggressive and the others didn't like it. The pickup was still there when I moved away.'

'We can't stay here,' I said, 'I'm being driven crazy by the flies and I'm out of water,' and I could have added, struggling to stay alert and starving. This was a nightmare and we were miles from safety, on a rollercoaster of despair, my resolution to keep going waning.

179

'We'll creep past them and move on, find some water.' It was now Jess who had found some reserve of energy, fresh resolve, and she reached out her arms to pull me up.

I responded slowly, limbs sore, stiff and stood up stretching. Suddenly Jess looked behind me, frozen, open-mouthed in surprise. I spun round.

'Don't shout,' I said quietly, 'please don't shout,' emphasising each word, but the figure just stood gawking at us, lips trembling.

31

The small boy stood blinking, his narrow face white, streaked with dirt, tear-stained, his thin hair stuck to his head by beads of sweat. Like an elfin creature, discovered living in the woods, he had an otherworldly air. If only I could remember his name, stop him from screaming and alerting the others. My thought processes, dulled by exhaustion, were slow, my mind searching frantically. The name began with a 'D' – Douglas, Dougie, David, no, – Davie.

'Davie,' I finally managed, 'good to see you again.' I kept my voice quiet, trying to be non-alarmist. 'Do you remember me from the campsite at Castle Douglas? You were good at football. Mr McIntyre is my friend. Remember?' Please remember, just don't shout out. I was aware of Jess following the conversation, it gradually dawning on her that I knew this waif.

I stepped forward but he stepped back ready to run, eyes wide. I heard rustling in the trees behind me, someone pushing through the branches. Jess was staring in that direction, alarm etched on her face and I turned quickly. Relief. It was Duncan.

'Have they gone?' I asked. 'The guys in the pickup.'

'Just driven off,' and then he stopped, smiling at Davie, pleased to see him, reassuring him, before he looked at me, an expression of bewilderment on his face.

'So they were searching for you. What's been going on and…' he acknowledged Jess.

'Are you sure they've gone?' I repeated, and he nodded.

'This is Jess, a friend who is helping me,' and I tried to convey that she was not more than that by emphasising the word friend. 'We're in trouble.'

'You sure are,' he said, and his teacher colleague, Jim, joined us, his face showing surprise, simply saying, 'Hello,' but glancing at Duncan, hoping that he could explain what was going on.

'Both of you are in a bad way,' Duncan stated, observing the condition we were in, 'so let's get to the minibus and we can talk further. Come on, Davie,' he said, almost as an aside, not putting more pressure on him, 'you've been a big help,' and he held out an arm beckoning the boy, who slowly edged towards him, not sure why he was not in trouble, and eventually joined us. 'Thanks, Davie,' I heard Duncan say quietly.

The other boys were waiting in the minibus, restless but looking cheerier than the last time I saw them, their faces touched by the sun, showing more colour. Standing by the minibus was a man probably about my age, wearing a wide-brimmed bush hat, who was watching events unfold.

'You found him, sir,' one of the boys shouted, as Davie emerged from the trees.

'He's done well. He found my friends who were walking in the woods.' That was certainly one description of what we were doing. I don't think that any of the boys recognised me from the campsite and one of them stared at Jess, carrot-coloured hair, his glasses had thick lens. I should also have known his name. I could see his attention made Jess uncomfortable and I saw Jim scowl at him and he turned away.

'Finn, this is Mark, he is our leader for our exercise today. He

182

works at the Centre where we are staying.' With the mention of my name, his expression changed, becoming pensive. AGL's men must have mentioned it.

I realised that we looked bedraggled – filthy, our clothes in a mess, our faces scratched, covered in grime, our feet caked with mud, our trousers wet and torn. Duncan as ever was practical, giving us water to drink and getting the medical kit out, producing antiseptic wipes and giving them to us. Mark joined him and went to his car producing some energy bars and handing them over. I realised how tired I was and Jess looked the same, grateful for the support, and Mark seemed to notice this, opening his car door and letting Jess flop down in the passenger seat. I leant against the bonnet of his car and finally slumped to the ground, leaning against the wheel.

'We need to get you some help,' Duncan said, and Mark colluded. 'Both of you are suffering from exposure. Probably should be taken to hospital.' Duncan shook his head, alert to the danger. 'They might find them there.'

'I can explain everything,' I said, 'but we can't be caught by these men. Can you help us escape?'

Duncan indicated to Mark and Jim and the three moved away talking in whispers. I couldn't hear them, almost didn't care, relinquishing responsibility, trusting in others. I had reached my limits, the fight had gone, my eyes closed.

●   ●   ●

A hand gently shook my shoulder, a voice softly repeating my name. Duncan spoke quietly so as not to alarm me. Having given in to sleep my body resisted being woken. Eventually, I opened my eyes and saw Duncan crouched in front of me, his eyes smiling behind his glasses, and when he saw that I was awake, he said, 'We know that you are both exhausted but we must talk.'

I moved my head from side to side trying to relax the muscles in my neck and accepted his offer of another drink, gulping down the liquid gratefully, my thirst nowhere near slaked.

'The men searching for you are from Sir Archibald's estate. Mark recognised them. The Centre sometimes use the estate for trips like today's. They claimed that you had abducted a girl, presumably Jess, and had assaulted one of their workers.'

His expression suggested that he wasn't for believing them, but this wasn't the time for long explanations.

'There is far more to it than that. Jess is here by her free will. Check with her.' I noticed that she was asleep in the car seat, her mouth open, 'when she wakes.'

'You know that I'm married. I didn't assault anyone.' The words weren't flowing freely but they were the best that I could do and Duncan seemed willing to accept them.

I tried again, a fuller explanation. 'Jess and I are united by a family tragedy. We're trying to find out more about an incident in the past. Sir Archibald was involved and he didn't like us asking questions, poking into events that he hoped had been forgotten.'

Mark seemed to make note of that, raising his eyebrows slightly.

'We need help. Can you take us back to the Centre?'

They must have discussed this because Mark spoke next.

'Duncan and I are good friends, we've known each other for many years. He vouches for you and that is good enough for me. But there is a problem,' Mark explained, 'two of AGL's men are waiting at the Big Water of Fleet viaduct, we saw them this morning. We don't know how to get you past them without

184

being seen. We stopped there, the boys interested in the viaduct and they came across, asked us questions, probing. It was obvious they were searching for someone.'

'We'll find a way, Finn, leave it to us.'

'I was so fortunate to bump into you, Duncan,' and I felt emotional, quickly looking at the ground, exhaustion again playing its part.

Duncan laughed. 'We've been driving around all day with the boys from site to site, trying to get them to solve problems, a team-building exercise, but Davie decided to wander when we stopped here,' and he rolled his eyes, 'and we couldn't find him. We owe you one, it must be your lucky day.'

I suddenly realised that some of the dust trails were the result of Duncan's crew driving about, not just AGL's men. Somehow that helped me, our imaginations had multiplied our fears, believing the odds to be even more formidable. I felt better, somehow, more positive.

Once again Duncan, Jim and Mark walked a few steps away and talked. I was in their hands, being in no fit state to help myself. Jim peeled away from the others and looked in the minibus, pausing to banter with the boys who were getting bored.

'It's possible,' he shouted across to the other two, 'not comfortable but possible.'

The other two absorbed the information, looking at each other for confirmation. 'Few alternatives,' Duncan stated, 'worth a go,' and he turned to me.

'Finn, we're going to try and get you out of here and with a bit of luck and the boys' help we might manage.' Surely I misheard Duncan, how could the boys help. My reaction must have shown in my face.

'Don't worry, but we have a little preparation to do first.'

32

Duncan went over to the minibus and spoke with the boys, as I went to waken Jess. She jumped when I shook her arm and swore as I called her name, appearing confused, before she looked around in alarm, then realised that she was safe. Grabbing a bottle of water from the seat beside her, she drank deeply before muttering that she had never felt so tired, her body trembling. I knew that feeling. We both needed help, so the quicker Duncan put his plan into action the better.

The plan was simple: we would be hidden in the minibus concealed under the metal-framed seats, backpacks or boys carefully positioned, covering any bits of us that someone might see. The boys would play a part, encouraged to be lively, distracting, something which would come naturally, I was sure, and they certainly seemed keen. Duncan had spun them a tale. The boys had been working around the forest collecting clues, completing tasks designed to get them to work together. Jess and I had been part of the exercise, he explained, and the boys were to search for us, but with Davie running away and discovering us the exercise had been aborted. One final part remained, to ensure that the boys could smuggle us past the guards at the viaduct. If they did it then there would be a reward, an extra barbeque this evening. It was imaginative, in the circumstances, and needs must, I suppose, and a treat at the end of the day seemed to motivate them.

Jess was not keen, disliking confined spaces, but the prospect of food and a hot shower helped her overcome her misgivings. The temperature in the clearing was still rising, the sun blisteringly hot, the flies just as annoying. It would be hot and uncomfortable in the minibus, but only, hopefully, for a short time.

'Let's get it done,' I said, and I saw her agreeing. I just wanted out of the forest.

Mark was going to lead in his car. We went to the minibus. The metal-framed plastic seats were bolted to the floor and there was limited space under them. We tried various positions before finally deciding to use the ones at the back, where there was more room, Jess taking one side and me the other. The boys were helpful, enjoying the intrigue. Backpacks were piled in the spaces in front of the seats we were hiding under to help conceal us, and one of the boys had the idea of spreading a towel over the seats, but another boy thought that was too obvious. Eventually we were hidden and the boys were happy, buying into their role. Duncan and Jim had done a good job with them, definite progress in a week from the disparate bunch at the beginning of the course.

The sliding door at the side of the minibus was pulled shut, the doors at the back locked and equipment piled against it to discourage anyone demanding it be opened. With Jim driving and Duncan beside him, we left the clearing bumping along the forest track, feeling each pothole, ever more uncomfortable and hot.

'Viaduct ahead, boys,' exclaimed Jim, after what seemed like an eternity but probably was only ten minutes, and the boys who had been talking away to each other went quiet.

'Be yourselves, talk to each other, don't let them think you are hiding something,' Duncan reminded them, but the boys remained silent, their bluster fading.

'Two guards are there beside a pickup,' Jim stated playing along with the scenario, and I could imagine the vehicle parked beside the piers of the viaduct that I knew so well. The Big Water of Fleet viaduct, it seemed, was destined to play another critical role in my life. Instinctively, I tried to make myself smaller.

'They are not the same men as this morning. They've stopped Mark,' Duncan said, the commentary for my benefit because the others could watch. The boys remained quiet, apart from a few nervous comments. It was frustrating not being able to see anything for myself.

'That's bold,' exclaimed Jim, and he added, 'the second guy opened Mark's boot while the first man was talking to Mark, without asking. Thank goodness no one was hidden in there. Mark is not happy. Good, Mark, give them a piece of your mind. Boys start talking to each other, you all look as if you're hiding something.'

'Mark is driving on. Here we go,' said Duncan, and I heard someone speaking. 'We are looking for two people who have stolen tools from a hut.' The story kept changing but the intention was the same – to find us.

'And you suspect us. We are teachers in charge of the boys. Do you think we are organising a crime ring? Get real and let us through,' Jim demanded, an irritated tone in his voice.

'Let's have a look, only take a minute, mate,' the request almost sounded innocent, friendly, but I suspected the velvet glove concealed an iron fist.

'I said, no,' replied Duncan firmly. 'You can see that we have a bunch of boys, who are in our charge, so they are not likely to be thieves, unless you are accusing us, so there is no point in checking.' Silence then: 'You have no authority. They are also hungry and tired, so we will just move on.'

The engine was revved up but didn't move. One of them must be blocking the road.

'This is ridiculous. I am going to report you to the police.' The boys had gone very quiet. I imagined that while one of them talked, the other would be walking around the minibus, peering in. There was nothing I could do but stay still, hoping Jess was reacting the same way.

I heard the sliding door being opened and an angry reaction from Duncan.

'Stop, you have no right to do that.' Duncan sounded annoyed. I heard a door opening, probably the passenger door. I couldn't see anything but I thought that Duncan was blocking someone from stepping in. It sounded like a scuffle and then I heard screaming, loud and piercing. It had to be Davie.

There was an angry roar. 'Get that little bastard off me. The bastard's bitten me.'

Then Duncan's voice: 'I warned you. The boys are on a special trip, to recover from trauma. You have upset them. Davie come here.' Someone entered the minibus and then the sliding door was shut firmly, followed by the passenger door and I heard Duncan saying under his breath, 'Drive on, Jim, quickly,' urgency in his voice.

The minibus lurched forward picking up speed and we were away – Davie still screaming, the other boys still quiet.

'Good work, boys,' Duncan shouted, as suddenly the boys were raucous again, tension relieved. 'Davie, you shouldn't bite, you could get into a lot of trouble,' Duncan said.

'Davie was a hero, sir. He gave it to the bastard, drew blood. Sorry, Mr McIntyre, for swearing, but he saved us,' the boy finished.

'No more of that, Robbie,' and the boy accepted the rebuke meekly. That was the boy with the carrot-coloured hair, I finally remembered. I was aware that Davie had stopped screaming and risked peering out, pushing aside some backpacks. The boys were making a fuss of Davie, leaning over towards him.

'Keep your seatbelts on,' shouted Duncan, ever the teacher.

'We'll let you two out when we get back on the proper road,' shouted Jim. 'Not long now, and they're not following us, you'll be pleased to know.' The minibus was abuzz with excited voices. Duncan and Jim had succeeded in creating a team, the week had been a success. And Jess and I had escaped. I just hoped that it was worth all that we had been through and that the photos revealed a lot.

33

I emerged from under the seat, pushing aside backpacks, sticking with sweat, helping Jess free herself. There was no one at the station site as we reached the junction with the road from Gatehouse of Fleet. The minibus sped on, heading down towards the small town, Mark racing ahead in his car.

'Well done,' I said to the boys, 'mission completed. You're a great team.' Jess said nothing and flopped down on a free seat.

'Don't forget your seat belt, Miss, or Mr McIntyre will have a go at you.' Jess didn't know how to react, boy's banter beyond her at the moment, and I helped her fasten her seat belt. She appeared unwell, shivering and very pale. It was only the adrenaline of escaping that was keeping me going.

We drove through Gatehouse of Fleet onto the A75 and headed in the direction of Castle Douglas, turning off long before we reached the town, turning onto minor roads before entering an estate and ending up outside a mansion house with a modern conservatory attached, extensive lawns reaching to tree-lined slopes.

Jim parked, Davie opened the sliding door and all the boys tumbled out. I helped Jess out, supporting her as Mark appeared with an older man and welcomed us.

'She needs help,' the older man stated, with the quiet authority of someone with experience, and Jess was helped inside and through a corridor towards the back of the house, past a dining room and a kitchen, before we reached a long corridor with bedrooms off it. Jess was taken in one of the rooms, where two women were waiting and the door was swiftly shut.

The older man, who was tall with a mop of grey hair, spoke again, direct but warm, his eyes a piercing blue, intense but friendly. 'Welcome, Finn. I'm Darren Houston, the Centre manager. You are both welcome. I know that you have a story to tell, having been through a lot. I want you to know that we are making no judgement on what has been going on. We will offer you sanctuary, safety, food and medical attention until you are able to leave. Mark let me know that Jess was suffering from exposure, so we've quickly arranged help. The women are trained first-aiders and will assess her and help her. We are quite well-qualified to offer assistance but I will contact a GP if they think it necessary. You don't look too well yourself,' he added, and I was aware that I was leaning against the wall for support.

'We'll check you over, give you some food and drink and give you a room to rest in. That okay?'

I smiled. Kindness was making me emotional again and I was led into the dining room. The warm drink helped and I ate a sandwich before being led to a bedroom in the same corridor as Jess. Mark waited while I had a shower, gave me some pyjamas, attended to some cuts and scratches, wondering what had I done to my jaw. I slumped on the bed. Sleep came quickly.

34

There was the sound of singing in my room, drifting in through the open window. It was surreal, where was it coming from? Tentatively I sat up and put my feet out of the bed, my body stiff and sore but no major complaints. In the en suite bathroom, I inspected the damage to my body, my face sunburnt, scratched and a few bruises, especially my jaw. Memories of getting flung about in the back of a Land Rover as it was tipped over flooded back, explaining a large bruise on my shoulder. The shower was effective in flushing out more painful spots but the cold water was also invigorating and whilst still tired I was on the way back, recovery underway. My clothes had been washed and ironed, left beside the bed, which was a bonus and a short time later I left the room making my way back to the dining room I had seen the previous evening.

Outside the sun was streaming down and I noticed the boys kicking a football about and was pleased to see Davie participating, now a full member of the group. The position of the sun suggested that it was still morning, so I must have slept for well over twelve hours. I made myself a coffee using the hot water urn and looked around. The dining room was fairly basic, trestle tables and wooden chairs. I plunked myself down on a chair and sipped the coffee. Apart from the boys no one else seemed to be around. Then I realised that it was Sunday and the singing made sense – a church service. I remembered seeing a wooden cross near what I took to be an office.

How was Jess getting on, I wondered, recollecting that she was in a worse state than me. Then the big question: what would the photos show and was it all worth it?

At that point a girl in her twenties, probably from Eastern Europe, by her appearance, pocked her head around the door.

'You must be, Finn?' But from her expression she already knew the answer. 'Are you feeling better?'

'Wonderful what sleep can do,' I answered, 'and how is Jess?'

'I have just been to see her half an hour ago and she was awake. We called the doctor out to her but she will be fine. She will probably be along soon.'

'That's great,' I replied. 'Is this a Christian centre?'

The girl smiled and nodded. 'You heard the singing? Did it waken you?'

'No,' I protested, 'I was awake, thought I'd gone to heaven for a minute,' and the girl laughed. 'I'll get you some food.'

There was a heavy rap on the window pane and I turned noticing one of Duncan's boys grinning at me and giving me a thumbs up. It was Robbie. Life was definitely brighter this morning. I was eating toast when Jess appeared, ashen white, wearing an oversized white tee shirt and shorts which made her look even frailer, as if she had shrunk.

'Okay?' I asked, pleased to see her.

'I felt rotten by the time I got here. Never thought that I would make it.'

'I felt much the same but picking up this morning. We're being well looked after. Have you…' and she completed the question, 'Got the photos?'

194

I laughed. 'Reading my mind now.'

Then her face darkened. 'Not sure what they show, the screen being so small, and I don't have my contact lenses back in yet, but I took your advice and when I found a strong Internet connection in my room this morning, I passed them on to Danny and Rougvie as backup.'

'Good. Hopefully, after what we've been through, they'll help us in our quest.' My heart thumped – the photos had to help us, surely our efforts couldn't be in vain.

We were both very tired and would struggle to get much done today but we had escaped AGL's clutches for the moment.

A short time later the boys came in with Duncan and Jim. 'We saved you yesterday, sir,' said one of them as they crowded around us.

'A brilliant job, many thanks. I know who to call on in the future,' I replied, and they all smiled, still basking in their moment of glory, being praised not usually part of their curriculum.

'Lunch in ten minutes,' Jim declared, 'so time to wash,' and he chased them away.

The boys left and Duncan and Jim made a coffee for themselves and joined us at our table. There was an uncomfortable silence. Both were curious, Duncan especially, I suppose, because he wanted to know about Gillian.

'I owe you both an explanation. When I was twelve I saw my father murdered in front of me.' Their faces reflected shock. 'It happened not far from where we were found, on the road down to Creetown. I saw Sir Archibald Graham-Linton give the order.' While they didn't personally know Sir Archibald, his involvement explained a lot.

'My father was also murdered that evening,' chipped in Jess, adding to their bewilderment. 'I was told that it was Finn's father

195

who murdered him, but since we talked things over I no longer believe that.'

'Quite a story,' and they both nodded. 'There was a cover-up and I want to expose them, that's why we took photos in a hut in the grounds of Sir Archibald's house. I believe I was taken there the night my father was killed. There were photos on the wall and we hoped that they might help us. We were taking photos of them when we were discovered and chased.'

'What do you think they would do if they caught you?'

'Hopefully, they won't. They are not nice people,' that seemed an understatement, 'nice' not really conveying the sentiment I felt, 'and the reaction by Sir Archibald suggests that they are hiding something.' I explained a bit more about where our fathers worked, filling in background.

Duncan looked at both of us and I could almost see his mind whirring. 'Get more rest, the people here will help you.' I appreciated him not continuing to probe us, although I could see that he had many questions.

'Thanks, Duncan,' I said, and as I left, 'you were both a wonderful help.'

35

The room was fairly small, entered through the main office, the top half of the divide between the two, a simple glass partition. I got the impression that Darren was somebody who didn't like being locked away, always wanted to know what was going on. Being Sunday the main office was deserted, three desks with computer terminals on top abandoned for the weekend. There was a window in Darren's office which looked out over the driveway that continued around the side of the house towards a tall tree, with handholds for climbing bolted to the thick trunk, with fields beyond.

Darren was clearing his desk, pushing aside some thick files, exposing a shortwave radio on a charging pod. He took his mug, bearing the logo of the centre and tried to rub away the ring mark left behind.

'I've transferred your photos onto the computer, you'll see more detail.' He paused, fixing the two of us with his penetrating blue eyes. 'I hope that you find what you are looking for.' I wasn't sure that we would, time would tell. 'I am not far away if you need me. Just press the button on the radio, speak and someone will come along.'

I wondered what he really thought about us as he edged out of his office. The door shut and we were left alone, Jess sitting on the swivel chair, me on a chair that we had brought in from the main office. In front of us on the screen were the photos that had nearly cost us our lives, waiting to be opened.

'Let's do it,' I said, and Jess clicked on the first icon.

It was a picture which appeared to have been taken outside the hut, of a group of six men holding fishing rods, most in waders, one holding a large silvery fish, who appeared vaguely familiar. All were smiling, happy with the catch. I peered at their faces, Jess zooming in and enlarging each face in turn. I studied them carefully and as Jess turned to me I shook my head. 'I don't recognise any of them. Various ages, nothing remarkable about them.'

There was no date or caption underneath. Not a promising start.

'All hail King Salmon, I suppose.' I had taken a few of the photographs off the wall to check for information on the back but there had been none.

Jess clicked on the second photo. Another group of fishermen, about twelve, huddling together, several with fish held in their arms. Some were laughing as if someone had said something funny. Again no date or additional information.

'Next,' I said, but inside I felt deflated, this was not proving productive.

The third photo was of the row of fishing rods and overexposed. Jess peered at the screen and zoomed in on the rods.

'Dad was famed for making his own rods, at least two of them are his,' and she pointed out a double red band at the base, 'and that will be his initials, just above the bands, although the letters are fuzzy in the photo. DCH – Douglas Collins Hamilton.' I could see the coloured bands and just about make out the initials.

'An uncle told me about his skill in making fishing rods and there are still a few in the attic gathering dust. He was very possessive about them and wouldn't lend or sell them. Years later a dealer travelled up from Wales to try and buy them. Mum sent him away, not interested, and he was offering serious money.'

'So how did the fishing rods appear in the hut? Could he have been using them that night?'

Jess shrugged. 'Don't know, probably never will,' and she sighed.

'Doesn't prove anything except the rods are still being used twelve years later. We are wanting links between our fathers and AGL and this is one, however tenuous. Let's move on.'

The next photo was taken on the steps of AGL's mansion. Two rows of people, fourteen men and one woman in total.

Jess gasped. 'That's my father,' and she pointed to a figure in the front row standing next to AGL, a woman at his other side.

I studied him, a lit cigarette in one hand held down by the side next to AGL, between splayed fingers. He was smiling broadly, handsome, thick hair swept back from his forehead. His arm was around the woman's waist and the woman was leaning towards him. They gave the impression of being more than friends, each enjoying the moment. Jess's eyes were glistening as she stared at the photo and she was biting her bottom lip. I said nothing, giving her space. The picture could tell a thousand possible stories but the most obvious was staring straight at us. Dougie Hamilton and the woman were close. Jess, by her reaction, obviously thought the same.

We also now knew that there was a connection between Jess's father and AGL, they socialised together, were part of a group. Maybe it was as simple as a shared interest in fishing, maybe it was more. I did wonder if my father also knew him.

I examined the rest of the figures. AGL was obviously

199

younger looking, the photograph had to be at least twelve years old. His hair looked more naturally black, the nose, as always, dominating his narrow mouth, giving him a superior look, as if he was looking down at you. I tried to impose that image on the one I held in my memory and they matched. The photo didn't show the coldness that he displayed as he stood over Dad but then surely this was a more relaxed occasion. My usual anger built and I quickly switched my attention to the others.

One of them, in the back row near the end, was not staring at the camera and that attracted my attention. I took the mouse from Jess's hand and zoomed in on him. He had fair, very curly hair, clamped to his head, protruding eyes and even given the quality of the image you could see that he was staring at the woman. Was it just the timing of the camera shot or was it deliberate? More importantly, did it mean anything?

Jess had composed herself and looked at the image. 'Don't know him,' she said, 'but he is a bit weird, wouldn't like to meet up with him.'

'I know what you mean.'

'Finn, I know that the police accused your father of having an affair but an uncle told me that my dad also had a roving eye. Said that Mum had forgiven him a few times, always took him back, but she couldn't stop him from straying.'

'I'm sorry, Jess,' and I touched her lightly on the arm. She appeared distant, not moving, thoughtful.

'I really didn't want to find this out. Why couldn't he have just loved me and Mum,' and the hurt Jess felt was palpable in the room.

Outside the window, I was aware that Duncan's group were standing at the bottom of the tree clad in harnesses, receiving instruction from Mark, getting ready to climb. Robbie was first to attempt the climb, his carrot-coloured hair catching the sun, pushing his glasses further up his nose, girding himself to start climbing.

'Two more photos, Finn,' and I turned back to the screen as Jess clicked on the next icon. The next photo showed a larger group, possibly on the front lawn of AGL's house, taken from an elevated position, maybe the steps of the house or from a stepladder, but what it showed was odd: each person was holding a folded umbrella, all different sizes, different colours, some black, some golf umbrellas with different coloured panels, but all pointing towards the photographer with the tip of their umbrellas, wielding them like a sword. The colour in the photo was faded, suggesting it was older than the rest. Everyone was on their best behaviour, eyes focused on the camera, tightly grouped together. There were about twenty men in all, most casually dressed, the fashions dating them. It was difficult to understand what the occasion was, maybe they belonged to a club. I scanned the faces and only recognised AGL.

'Okay, last photo,' and Jess brought it up.

'Result,' I exclaimed. It was the car from that night with a middle-aged man, thinning hair, ruddy complexion, standing beside it. And a caption this time: 'Murdoch W. Birse with his pride and joy.' He had to be the driver. The lines of the car were as I recollected. Long sloping bonnet with what appeared to be vents, but were probably headlights on closer inspection – that chimed with what I remembered on the night. Two doors, mid-engined, air vent to the side to allow air intake. On the bonnet a badge, an upside-down diamond. Inside the diamond shape was a thistle on a blue background with a name underneath. It was difficult to make out and we expanded and contracted the image until Jess exclaimed, 'Argyll!'

I googled 'Argyll car' and there were pictures of the model. Argyll was a Scottish company which built cars before the First

World War but the company had not been successful and had gone bankrupt. The name had been revived in the mid-seventies for a sports car being built in Lochgilphead, Argyll, no more than a few dozen being produced. A very rare, unusual car which must help us in our quest, if we could trace it. And we had the owner's name, an unusual name. Bonus point.

Jess seemed tired, not yet over the exertions of the last few days, struggling to maintain concentration. The office door opened and Darren appeared, smiling and continuing into his office where we were. 'Sorry, can I look for a list of names for the group who are arriving tomorrow,' and he opened the drawer in his desk and rummaged about.

'Any success?' he asked as he searched.

'Some,' and he looked surprised. 'Good.'

Jess was scanning through the photos and Darren paused, his attention drawn to them. 'I recognise Sir Archibald's house and I presume that is the hut you entered,' a smile playing on his face, another way of saying you broke into it.

'That picture is older than the rest, probably thirty years ago, if I recognise the fashion,' pointing to the photo of the group of men with umbrellas. 'I had a jumper like that once,' he explained. 'That's a young Sir Archibald in the middle,' and he pointed him out, 'and that's Julian Montgomery, now the Foreign Secretary, beside him. They have been friends for a long time, probably went to some fee-paying school, somewhere like Eton. I would date the photo from university days, looking more closely and guessing at their age.'

'How do you recognise Montgomery?' I asked.

'He was here with Sir Archibald a couple of days ago,' and he saw the startled expression on my face. 'Sir Archibald has a trust fund to benefit local charities and he visits them to see what we are doing. The Foreign Secretary was staying with him and so accompanied him. Their photo will be in the local paper next week. He likes to be seen to be doing his bit,' he added.

'That was who was visiting AGL at his house,' Jess said. Darren was confused for a second before he worked out what the letters meant. 'Take a few minutes and look at the other photos,' I added. Darren studied each in turn as Jess scrolled through them.

'That's Montgomery holding the salmon,' he stated, becoming more thoughtful.

'The two of you must be careful. From what you said, it sounds as if there was a cover-up years ago, but you have already stirred up a whole lot of trouble for yourselves and provoked a backlash. And if the cover-up reaches government level then you are out of your depth. They know your name, Finn, and they could cause you a lot of problems.'

'I'm prepared for trouble,' I replied, 'it's a matter of honour, to reveal the truth.'

Darren grimaced. 'Not worth your life, Finn.' He paused to let that sink in. 'What next?'

'We're going to visit Urquhart, the policeman involved in the cover-up. He knows more than he's saying and I think he has been paid to keep quiet.'

'That will stir up even more trouble, if Sir Archibald finds out. Again be careful.'

'I get the message and I'm grateful for all that you have done for us.'

'You needed help, so we couldn't turn you away. Stay as long as you need, you both still require time to recover from your ordeal.'

'I was hoping to collect our cars tomorrow and then we would get on our way,' and Jess nodded, agreeing with me.

'One last thought. Duncan told me that both your fathers

worked for the Ministry of Defence, near Annan, and were research scientists. There is a museum in a village to the east of Annan, dedicated to the history of the munitions works, which played a big part in the area for many years. The munitions works were built during the First World War, when there was a big shortage of propellant for shells. The works were built quickly and extended for many miles along the border between Scotland and England. Later the area was used to store munitions. If your fathers worked in the complex maybe the museum would have some information about what they did, which could help you.'

Jess was interested. 'What is the name of the museum?'

'The Devil's Porridge. Someone famous who was visiting the factory used the term 'devil's porridge' to describe the cordite paste that they were producing. It's very interesting and some of the tour guides who worked there in later years, the nineties, have a lot of knowledge.'

'Thanks, Darren, we'll pay a visit.' Maybe someone would remember our fathers. Certainly Dad never talked about where he worked or took us near the place. A visit would offer another line of enquiry.

I waited until Darren had left. 'Jess, Darren is right, what we are attempting to do is very dangerous. AGL's mob are violent and ruthless. If they get a hold of us it could be dire, maybe even fatal. You don't have to do this,' but before I could finish Jess held up her hand.

'My life has already been mucked up and I want to know the truth. Don't play the strong man who is only trying to save me card. I don't care about the cost, I want the truth with or without you. And something else you should know – Danny is being recalled from Germany, where he was stationed with his regiment, to his barracks near Edinburgh. You put two and two together,' her cheeks flushing, showing colour for the first time since we reached the Centre. 'Someone must have traced the owner of the car and wants to ask some questions. Who has the power to do that?'

'Maybe someone with the influence of the Foreign Secretary,' I answered.

There was no point arguing with her, she was resolute, determined and like me she wasn't about to give up.

36

Soon after we left Darren's office and wandered through the
building and out via the boot room to the rear of the house.
The large windows in the boot room gave a good view of the
buildings at the back and the hillside where there was a zip wire
set up. There were rows of boots and cagoules hanging up and
discarded dirty clothing on the floor.

I spotted the boys in the games room, a separate hut in
the grounds, playing snooker and we continued walking in
silence past the gear store and several outbuildings, including
a garage. Once past the outhouses the track became a country
lane, a minor road running parallel to it, separated by a hedge. I
breathed in deeply enjoying the fresh country air, hoping to clear
my head, put aside my concerns.

Jess was texting as we walked, frowning, lost in thought.

'Danny or Rougvie?' I asked.

'Both. Danny has been given a dressing-down by his
commanding officer and put on a plane. He's angry.' I could
imagine his reaction and it was unfair, an abuse of power.

My phone then rang and she announced, 'That will be
Rougvie.'

I answered it. 'You two have being having a great time, I
hear.'

'You could say that,' I replied, answering in kind. 'You got away safely?'

'I did, home in my bed a few hours later, whilst you were just starting your ordeal. Poor souls. But I hear the photos were helpful.'

'I think we can say that there is a link between AGL and Julian Montgomery, the Foreign Secretary, extending back, maybe as far as schooldays, certainly university and it is still strong today. He was the visitor at the house when we were having our little discussion with AGL. Both are influential, lots of contacts and given what has happened to Danny they are wielding their influence.'

'So it seems. Jess's dad is also tied up in it all, even if only as a sporting colleague.'

I felt uncomfortable talking about Jess's dad while she was around, so I just said, 'Very likely.'

'The car is fascinating, a curiosity,' Rougvie stated, changing the subject, deliberately or not I wasn't sure. 'The car is an Argyll Turbo GT, extremely rare. Caused quite a stir when it was launched but the manufacturers weren't prepared to leave Lochgilphead, so it never took off. The car used bits and pieces from other cars – Volvo dashboard, Triumph suspension, Morris Marina door handles, the original hybrid.' Rougvie had done his homework.

'No doubts that is the car that I saw and we even have the owner's name. I am pretty certain that it's the person I saw that night.'

'Good, I'll ask my brother, Rich, who is a computer nerd to try and find out more about Murdoch W. Birse and, hopefully, where he lives. Shouldn't be difficult.'

'That would be great.'

'Okay, I've got to go but I'll be in touch soon. Take care and look after Jess.'

'Will do.'

The track eventually stopped at a farm where the two roads joined. I heard the mooing of cows and minutes later saw them being led from the fields to the milking parlour to be milked and watched as they were led past me. Jess's head was still down, focused on the screen.

'Let's head back,' I said, and she looked up briefly and turned around, still distracted.

37

The next day was the boys' last day at the Centre and I could see the sadness etched on their faces. To some this would have been the most wonderful experience of their lives; a glimpse of what life could be, before they returned to less than ideal circumstances. Duncan, Jim and the Centre staff had done an excellent job. Robbie was at the front of the house waiting for us, especially pleased to see Jess, who it was obvious he had a crush on. Teachers knew how to handle that but Jess less so, and she was embarrassed by his attention, which just encouraged Robbie.

We joined the group for breakfast and Darren came bustling in, talking quietly to Mark before coming over to our table, the blue eyes intense as usual as he searched our faces.

'Still intending to leave today?' he asked.

'Best to get started and we're feeling a lot better, thanks.'

'You need to collect your cars.' A statement not a question.

'Mark can take Jess to Loch Stroan to collect her car. Better that you are not seen.'

That made sense and Duncan chipped in, 'I'll take Finn along to collect his car,' and he seemed keen to take me, so I agreed.

Darren then pulled back a chair and sat down to talk to the

boys, asking them what they had enjoyed most about their trip, listening carefully to their feedback.

•   •   •

Mark and Jess left half an hour later to collect her car and Duncan brought his car to the front of the Centre. I got in quickly as the weather had turned wet, the wipers already working hard.

As we drove away from the house, I said, 'It's been a super trip for the boys.'

'Hasn't it,' he replied, as he reached the minor road that ran past the Centre grounds.

'There'll be a few tears today as they return home. However, the course has boosted their confidence and Jim and I have to step back – we've done all we can.'

'You made a massive effort. Also thanks for being in the right place at the right time.'

'We were glad that we could help.'

There was a question that I wanted to ask Duncan. 'The Centre gets funding from Sir Archibald's trust, doesn't it?'

'Has for several years.'

'I have caused him problems, haven't I?'

'Darren has high standards, strict moral values. He offered you sanctuary, an old biblical idea. In the Old Testament cities of refuge were established where innocent people could go and be safe, protected from their enemies. In the Middle Ages, if someone accused of a crime could escape his pursuers and reach the altar of a church they were safe. You needed help and he offered it. He wouldn't tell you himself that they received funding, not wanting to put any pressure on you or compromise his decision.

210

'The funding from Sir Archibald is now under review by the Centre. The Centre trustees are scrupulous in their sources. Unfortunately, when I was chatting to Mark I discovered that the funding from Sir Archibald was crucial last year, so if it's withdrawn then the Centre could find it difficult to continue. Darren will make the right decision whatever the consequences.'

'I am sorry for the problems I've caused.'

'They don't blame you but they are worried about you.'

We had now reached the busy A75 and Duncan twisted his head studying me for a moment, before spotting a gap in the traffic after a number of trucks trundled past, the spray from their tyres drenching the front of the car, before turning onto the main road.

'You face a lot of problems, many challenges and you don't have the same resources as Sir Archibald. They've already shown their ruthlessness. Are you sure that you want to go on?'

I was now used to this line of questioning, accepting that Duncan was only trying to be helpful, but also explaining why he wanted to take me in his car, so that he could talk in confidence.

'Seeing my father murdered has screwed up my life,' I admitted. 'Now I know that there has been a cover-up I have to go on, can't back down. I must expose the wrongdoing.'

He studied me again. 'These people are both dangerous and influential,' he said, repeating his warning.

'Yes, and they know my name, so they can come after me even now, so I have no choice. It's them or me,' and I know that sounded melodramatic, but it was the truth. They would not give up, they had too much to lose.

'Would you be better on your own? Jess is young.'

'Again, yes, but Jess is determined and she also lost her dad.'

'Listen Finn, it doesn't look good, a teacher on the run with a young woman who has just left school. It could be misrepresented, and Sir Archibald's men told me that you had abducted her, so the rumours have started. Your career could even be at stake.'

'I appreciate that, but there is nothing between us. She has a boyfriend, Danny,' and I found myself stroking my jaw, even though Duncan didn't appreciate the significance of that.

I saw Duncan grip the steering wheel tighter. 'Have you seen the way she looks at you? Jim commented on it, so it's not just me.' He wasn't for giving up and I appreciated his concern but... 'She is vulnerable, her choice of boyfriend suggests that and he sounds a controlling type. Jess is troubled, no doubt caused a lot of problems at her school. You must recognise that fact given your experience as a teacher. She needs support, counselling. You are not doing it deliberately but you are becoming a key figure in her life.'

'A father figure.'

Duncan turned his gaze towards me again. 'Maybe. Just be alert, don't give her false hope.'

'I appreciate what you're saying, but I don't agree. Let's just leave it.'

'You won't want me asking about Gillian then?' I felt my face flush. I guessed that this was where we were heading.

'I know that my life is a mess. I bitterly regret it and hoped that this summer I could find out the truth and move on, hoped that Gillian and I could get back together.'

Duncan meant for the best but I had made up my mind. To hell with the consequences. Now or never.

We had reached Castle Douglas, passing Carlingwark Loch with the rain sweeping in over it.

'My car is beside the Co-op on Cotton Street,' and I directed him. 'You can stop here,' an edge to my voice, signalling that I wanted the questions to end.

Duncan pulled over and parked, switching off the engine, as if he wanted to say more. The silence between us grew more intense. I grabbed the door handle and opened the door.

'This is not what I wanted,' I said, eventually, leaning back into the car, 'but it is what it is. I am aware of the dangers, pulling out wouldn't make a difference,' and I shut the door firmly. He wasn't pleased, but he quickly restarted the engine and pulled away from the kerb.

• • •

When I returned Duncan and Jim and the boys were up at the zip wire, which started at the top of the slope beside the house and stretched across the grounds between two tall trees some distance apart. That suited me, I was fed up with questions and I was anxious; it was taking Jess and Mark longer than I expected to get back. Was the car still beside the loch? Was someone waiting for them? I was relieved to finally see Mark's car appear at the corner near the start of the driveway, followed by Jess in the Fiat.

Jess parked in front of the house beside my car and I was waiting for her.

'So no one there?' I asked, anxious.

'Just a fisherman in his car hiding from the rain. My car has been searched but I don't think that anything was taken. Probably looking for identification.'

'Good. Let's not waste any time. Transfer what you need to my car and we'll be ready to go.'

'I'll leave my tent, just take clothes and a few other things.'

Why was I nervous? Maybe because it all seemed too simple, the car had been left alone, not what I expected from AGL. I was getting paranoid. I helped Jess transfer her possessions, rearranged some of mine and we were ready.

'Darren said to take your car around the back and put it in the garage,' I told her, and Jess drove her car away from the front. Mercifully, the rain had stopped though the sky was still overcast, so probably only a temporary halt to the downpour.

I suppose I felt bad that my last words with Duncan had been tense, not a good way to end. He and Jim were still with their group at the zip wire and Mark had now joined them. I headed across the lawn, climbing the slope towards them, watching as Davie screamed as he sped down the wire, twisting and turning in his harness. As I got closer Robbie gave me a wave and as I reached them Duncan smiled, which broke the ice. I thanked him and spent a few minutes bantering with the boys. Down below I could see the back of the house and Jess taking some small items from the car. I saw her step back and take out her phone. A few seconds later my phone rang.

'Finn, I found a phone in the glovebox under the car handbook. Is it yours?'

That was strange. 'No, the iPhone was smashed by AGL. I've only got the cheap mobile which I'm using now.'

'It's not Danny's. Don't know whose it is.' She sounded puzzled.

Something wasn't right. Why would a phone be left in a glovebox?

I stood there wondering whose phone it was when I felt a tug on my arm, looking down it was Robbie. I smiled at him but before I could speak he said, 'That's great, Mr McAdam.'

'What do you mean, Robbie?'

'We get to play the hiding game again,' and he pointed down to the driveway. Speeding up it was a white pickup. We had been discovered, tracked. They must have used the phone as a tracking device.

38

The white pickup was being driven fast up the driveway, braking hard in front of the house, stopping a few feet from my car, effectively blocking our escape route whether they realised it or not.

'That's the pickup we saw in the forest,' Jim declared, and Mark agreed. I took out my phone, dialling Jess. The phone rang repeatedly. I looked in despair at the others.

Instantly Mark used his radio alerting Darren. We watched as the doors of the pickup were flung open and two men jumped out, one in a tartan shirt worn loosely over shorts, the other, who had a long straggly beard, wearing dark clothing, rushing towards the front porch. I looked towards the back of the house and saw Jess entering the boot room unaware, having just left her car in the garage. 'Answer,' I screamed in frustration.

'We must get Jess,' I declared, 'before they catch her.'

Mark spoke into his radio. 'Delay them, Darren, until we get Jess.' He handed the radio over to me before he ran down the slope, muttering that it would keep me in touch with what was happening down at the house.

Then I finally saw Jess take her phone out of her pocket, putting it to her ear.

'Yes,' she said.

'Jess, Archibald's men are here. Don't go into the house. Join us now up at the zip wire.'

Before we could do anything else I saw Robbie, fixing his glasses firmly on his face, starting to run down the slope after Mark. Duncan shouted at him to come back but was ignored.

Then I heard Darren using the radio on his desk to let us know what was happening inside the house.

'Usually people ask to come into my office, don't just barge in. You've upset my staff. What are you wanting?' he demanded.

'Where are McAdam and his girl?'

'I don't know.'

'Don't try and be funny. We tracked them here. Sir Archibald wants them. You better not play games,' he stated loudly.

'Maybe he does want them, but could he not just pick up the phone and speak to me. Be civilised as befitting his position in society.'

'Don't waste our time and don't expect any more funding. Where are they?' The man was almost screaming.

Darren remained calm. 'I told you that I don't know. I am now going to contact the police and have you removed.'

'You're speaking on the radio, alerting others,' one of the men shouted, as they spotted the radio hidden behind files. There was a crashing sound and then silence.

While we listened I saw Jess emerging from the boot room, Mark leading her and Robbie not far behind, heading over to the games room and slipping around the back, hiding from view, huddled down. A minute later both of Archibald's men appeared in the boot room and flung open the door, the bearded one glancing at his phone and pointing in the direction of the garage.

Jess and Mark took the opportunity to slip away and start to

216

climb up the slope towards us, using the few bushes on the slope as cover.

We watched as they worked their way towards us. 'We need to get away in the car,' I stated, as the two of them finally reached us. Jess out of breath as she arrived, shaken, her face pale.

'They used the phone you found in the glovebox to track us,' I explained, and Jess muttered something under her breath at my revelation.

'Let's get down to the car.' Already I was working out that we would need to drive over the lawn to get away.

The two men were racing around, the one in the tartan shirt heading back into the house, the other checking the outbuildings. Suddenly I saw the one who was checking outside look up and spot our group. He started towards us, surprisingly fast, covering the ground between us rapidly with giant strides.

For a moment I was transfixed with the impending danger and then I snapped out of it. Time to go. I pulled at Jess and pointed towards the car and we started to run down the slope which led towards the lawn, keeping low, hoping that he wouldn't spot us. Duncan and Jim ushered the boys away, and Mark stood his ground ready to confront AGL's henchman.

The slope was slippery after the rain, and while we picked up speed it was difficult to control our footing, we half slid, almost falling several times, adrenaline keeping us going. Glancing behind I saw Mark blocking the man as they faced up to each other, Mark trying to counter his moves, a shadow dance, and trying to prevent him getting around him. I heard shouts and then turning I saw Mark being hit. Duncan ran towards them, diving at the man and knocking him over, wrestling him to the ground, giving us precious seconds.

We reached the gravel surface that ran around the house,

which helped to make our footing more secure, finally reaching the car. Jumping in I started the engine, throttling it in my haste, the engine revving high, and then I slipped it into reverse gear and the car moved back. Robbie suddenly appeared beside us from the direction of the pickup and shouted to Jess, who lowered the window as he threw something into the car.

'Good luck, Miss,' he shouted.

There was a roar and the henchman in the tartan shirt emerged from the entrance to the house racing towards us, pushing Robbie over in his haste. In my mirror I also saw the first man now running down the hill followed closely by Duncan and Mark.

Having created space by reversing, I spun the car around onto the lawn, the only means of escape, the wheels spinning, losing traction, before we shot forward, the tartan-clad man trying to jump on the bonnet, screaming at us to stop, but as he tried to keep a grip on the car he slipped and fell off. Quickly, however, he picked himself up and gave chase. I accelerated, the tyres spinning, gouging the soft ground, heading towards the driveway, the car slipping to the side as I fought to control it, narrowly missing a large tree.

Jess screamed, 'The other one is getting into the pickup. He'll be after us soon.'

With a bump we regained the driveway further down, nearer the entrance to the Centre. I turned the car sharply onto the driveway, our chaser giving up, signalling furiously towards the pickup.

I concentrated on my driving. 'Where are they now?' I asked, trying to sound calm but failing.

'The pickup won't start and the driver has just jumped out, looking very angry. '

I looked down at the car floor in front of Jess and relaxed.

'Maybe because Robbie threw us their keys. I hope that he's okay.'

Jess picked them up as we drove out of the Centre onto the minor road that ran alongside it and tossed the keys over a low stone wall into a field.

'That'll confuse the cows,' I said. 'At least we got away,' I added, 'thanks to Robbie and the others.'

'They won't give up, will they?' Jess stated and I saw tears trickle down her face. 'This is a nightmare, one big bloody nightmare.'

'We've got them rattled, we just need to discover what they're hiding and clear our fathers' names.'

I didn't mean it to sound simple, it wasn't. Sir Archibald was a determined foe, but he was a worried foe, even desperate. Desperate people often make mistakes, take risks. I had to hope so.

39

Quickly we reached the A75 and turned south. We'd agreed that we had to visit Urquhart and this was the direction. The car windows were steamed up, given the weather and our exertions, but the fan soon cooled us down and demisted the windows.

'It seems that we can never let down our guard.' Jess agreed, whilst stretching into the back seat, unzipping her bag and removing a towel, which she used to wipe her face.

'We're safe for the moment, they won't be moving in a hurry.'

'Thanks to Robbie. I hope he's okay, that brute knocked him over.'

'Robbie has probably had a lot worse, but we can phone Duncan when we next stop.'

I drove on past Gatehouse of Fleet and several caravan parks on the coast side of the road. As we saw Wigtown Bay I noticed a sign for a smokehouse and cafe and suggested that we stop. Jess nodded her agreement. We sat at a picnic bench in the courtyard beside the ruins of Carsluith Castle and I went into the shop and got coffee. It was good to draw breath, sip the hot liquid and try to calm down.

'I'll phone Duncan,' I suggested, and took out my phone.

Duncan answered almost immediately. 'Are you both okay?'

'Yes, thanks again, you're making a habit of keeping me safe.'

Duncan chortled. 'Chaos here. We have two very angry and frustrated punters sitting in their pickup, embarrassed that a small boy prevented them catching you. Their language is choice but nothing that the boys haven't heard before. Darren has phoned Sir Archibald, told him to remove his truck and men and threatened him with the police. He also informed him that he would be returning funding received in this financial year.'

'That will hurt them, surely.'

'Darren always believes that it is better to do what is right.'

'I respect his values but hope that he can get financial support from elsewhere.'

'They live by faith, he won't lose sleep.'

'How about Robbie?'

'Robbie has joined Davie in acquiring hero status for saving the day. His story is getting embellished already and I just hope that his mother doesn't believe him or she'll contact the head teacher to complain. Stories about this trip will, no doubt, last a lifetime. He's beside me now and sends his best wishes to Jess and to you. We are just packing up and none of the boys want to leave. Jim's in their rooms checking that they left them as they found them and then we must head off.'

'Mark?'

'A bit sore.'

'Do thank him.' That seemed inadequate. 'Tell him I appreciate what he did.'

'I will,' and then after a pause, 'What's next for the two of you?

'We've stopped for a break and then we're going to visit the policeman. We'll see what happens after that.'

'You'll both have to be very careful, you've unlocked a Pandora's Box. The odds don't look great.'

I acknowledged his comment.

'I was thinking about our conversation this morning,' continued Duncan. 'The concerns are still there but if you are going to go for it, there is no better time. They are unlikely to leave you alone. Seize the moment, someone once said.'

'Thanks, I couldn't have put it better,' and added, 'we have no choice as I don't think they'll stop searching for us now. We'll go for it and expose their secrets,' and if that sounded confident, it wasn't how I felt.

'Good luck,' and the conversation finished. I didn't know if our paths would cross again but if they did I owed him a drink. On second thoughts I would find another way to thank him – it would appear strange if I was drinking only soda water and lime.

I swirled the dregs of the coffee around the bottom of the cup before swallowing them. They tasted bitter.

I looked at Jess. 'Ready to go?' She stood up very slowly, giving the impression that every movement was a struggle and pursed her lips, anything more would have been too much of an effort. We headed to the car.

40

We were soon passing by the mudflats and salt marshes of
Wigtown Bay and taking the road that led down through the
Machars, bypassing Wigtown and taking the route to the Isle
of Whithorn that avoided the farms near Garlieston. I so didn't
want to be seen by Gillian's parents or even Gillian, who might
be spending some of her summer holidays with her parents.
Last year we had spent time at the farm together and it had gone
well, both relaxed and happy for one of the last times. Again, as
I did most days, I wondered where she was, how she was doing,
whether she would have me back.

Jess was sleeping beside me, her head slumped against the
window, which can't have been comfortable. Duncan's concerns
made me alert to any misunderstandings, but first Jess and I had
to work together, sharing a common goal or should that be foe.

Reaching the outskirts of the Isle of Whithorn, we drove
through the village, slowing down as we passed Urquhart's
house. It was impossible to tell at a glance if he was in. I
continued past the hotel, all the parking spaces on the harbour
front occupied, people drinking at the picnic benches outside
the hotel in warm sunshine, the clouds having moved on. I
remembered that there was an overflow car park in a field to

223

the rear of the harbour front buildings and found a space near a stone wall, beside a boat and trailer. Archibald's men would have noted the type of car I had and possibly the registration, so I was pleased that the car was out of sight.

I woke Jess gently and she jumped nervously, immediately sitting up, rubbing her neck, eyes open quickly staring around, a sign of anxiety, but after what we had been through, only to be expected. Leaving the car we wandered back to the harbour. Even on a summer's day wisps of smoke curled skywards from several chimneys, but checking Urquhart's house, I noticed no smoke, which was hardly conclusive, so we headed in the direction of the house. We strolled past the hotel, which was very busy, the restaurant full and the lounge and public bars packed. I stood outside looking in, scanning for Urquhart in the public bar but there was no sign of him, so we continued towards his house.

We walked beyond the church which protruded out into the sea. Opposite Urquhart's house was a low stone wall with a drop on the other side to a stony beach at low tide, but at high tide the water lapped at the base of the wall. As we passed his lounge window I told Jess to glance in. 'No one there,' she said, adding, 'and what a mess.' Somehow, I always thought that he would be at home. I expected him to be there and wondered what we should do next. Suddenly I felt tired, this was all such an effort.

Some distance beyond Urquhart's house was a lane which led down to what appeared to be a sewage plant and its concrete top provided a good vantage point to survey the rear of the row of terraced houses, all different heights and widths.

Jess was using her finger, quietly counting. 'According to the rows of chimneys, that must be his house,' and she pointed to it, a dirty-white colour. At the back there was an enclosed area with clothes poles peaking above the garden walls but no sign

224

of any washing drying. A high stone wall stretched up from the shoreline to just above the level of the gardens. The tide was out so we scrambled over seaweed coated rocks until we reached his house. Some of the houses had gates to access the shore and steps leading down, but Urquhart's didn't and the wall would be difficult to climb up. A nearby house, however, had several stones jutting out of the wall, which made climbing possible. Hopefully, we wouldn't need to access the house that way, but at least we had done the recce.

'This bit here was originally sea but was filled in many years ago,' I said, 'blocking the gap between the mainland and the island,' remembering what my father had once told me as he tried to explain how the landlocked village got its name, but I was really giving myself time to decide what to do next.

'I know,' I exclaimed, 'we'll ask at the hotel,' and decision made we worked our way back to the lane and around to the hotel. We entered through the doors leading to both bars, turning left into the public bar, which was packed and were making our way to the counter when Malcolm appeared, clutching empty pint glasses in his hand, which he had collected from the tables.

'Nice to see you again,' he said recognising me, glancing at Jess, no doubt assessing her age. He took our order, both soft drinks and as he poured them, I asked, 'Is Jimmy Urquhart about, Malcolm?'

'Popular guy, you're not the first person to ask for him this week, a woman was in yesterday. Anyway, he's away until tomorrow visiting his sister in Musselburgh.'

I had a sudden thought. 'Was the woman about this height?' and I held my arm up to my shoulder.'

'Yeah.'

'Dark shoulder-length hair?'

'Know her?'

'A friend from his police days, I think.'

Malcolm's eyebrows rose slightly as he handed over our drinks. 'Good for him, I thought his only love was the Famous Grouse.'

We found a space by the window. 'Sounds like Tania has been here from the description but we have the chance of being first to him. At least we don't have long to wait, but we'll need to stay somewhere tonight. What about here?'

'It's busy, no one will notice us,' Jess replied.

I worked my way back to the bar. 'Malcolm, do you have a couple of rooms for tonight?'

He shook his head, 'Only one left, but it's a good room with a harbour view.'

I turned to Jess, who nodded. I didn't know of any other hotels in the area and we were close to Urquhart's house, so we could keep an eye on it. It would be awkward sharing a room with Jess, but no one was likely to know.

'We'll take it.' Malcolm handed me the key and we walked upstairs, finding the room. It was a good-sized room with a double bed and en suite bathroom and, as Malcolm indicated, a great view over the harbour, although the church blocked our view of Urquhart's house.

'I'll sleep on the chair. I'm so tired I'll have no trouble sleeping anywhere.'

'Okay,' Jess's face gave no reaction.

'I'll get the bags in and then we can get something to eat.'

41

We sat in the conservatory to the rear of the hotel, lessening our chances of meeting someone we knew and ate our meal, conversation sporadic and the food, despite being good, of little interest, the events of the day catching up. I did wonder if we could keep going and realised that Jess's support was increasingly essential, each helping the other.

Coffee completed the meal and having paid up we walked out to the front of the hotel, the sun strong in our faces as it began to edge down towards the houses on the far side of the village, across the harbour. Jess excused herself and I walked towards the edge of the pier, lost in thought.

'Finn, what are you doing here?' The voice was familiar, interrupting my thoughts, jolting me.

'Hello, Stuart,' I replied turning around, my eyes taking a second to adjust.

Gillian's father was short, stocky in build, his thick hair now white, the nose angular, the cheeks ruddy, which always suggested that he'd had a dram.

I was lost for words, tiredness fogging my brain but panic mounting about this unfortunate encounter – the last person I wanted to see.

'You know this area is special,' I said, not knowing if Gillian had talked about our problems, or kept them to herself. I saw Sheila coming out of the hotel, approaching us, slimmer, shorter than Stuart, her face so like her daughter's. Gillian's parents were practical, hardworking farmers, no time for hair dye or frivolities. If Sheila was surprised to see me she hid it well.

'Hi Finn, good to see you,' her smile appeared genuine enough, but there was something in her expression which suggested that she knew more than Stuart. I was fond of them, always kind, generous, welcoming and I know that I had been a disappointment.

'Where's Gillian?' Stuart asked. Sheila frowned.

'You know, Stuart. Leave them to it.' Gillian had told them.

'She's broken-hearted,' Stuart stated, and he could be blunt, fiery when aroused. 'You have to put the past behind you or you will lose our daughter. You don't deserve her.'

Sheila placed a restraining hand on his shoulder but he ignored it, his face becoming more flushed.

'We did everything for you and what did you do?'

'Stuart, this doesn't help.'

'No, Sheila, some things must be said. Your place is beside Gillian, not hurting her.'

'I love Gillian, but for us to have a future I have to sort the past,' and that sounded like a line from a poor movie. Stuart shook his head but before he could speak again, Sheila pulled him away.

'Leave the young folks to sort out their issues. If my father had interfered you would have been angry, resentful.'

'I'm learning a lot about what happened that night,' I tried to explain. 'That's why I'm here, to speak with someone tomorrow. Please give me time.'

'She's away with friends, but she needs you,' and Sheila was

228

almost pleading with her eyes, trying to convey that she wanted it to work out, despite the pain I was causing her daughter.

'She'll be back soon. Call her, Finn.'

They were on the point of leaving when I noticed Jess standing behind them listening and realising who they were, edging away, hoping not to be seen, when Stuart turned. Wearing ripped jeans, a baggy tee shirt, Jess looked young, vulnerable and exhausted. What would Gillian's parents think of her?

'Who is this?' he demanded. Sheila's eyes quickly filled with tears.

'I'm Jess. I know Finn, but I'm only a friend, nothing else. I'm already engaged.' That comment only drew attention to a possible relationship.

Stuart interrupted. 'You look as if you're not long out of school,' whilst casting me a contemptuous look.

'My father was Dougie Hamilton,' Jess said, ignoring the jibe, and Stuart looked blank. 'He was murdered the same night as Finn's dad. I looked Finn up on Facebook and we're helping each other. I know that Finn loves Gillian as he talks about her all the time.' I'm sure I hadn't but Jess was trying to be helpful. 'I would love to meet her and Finn is going to arrange it. Once we've discovered the truth about the murders we'll go our own ways. I promise you that.'

Stuart appeared unconvinced. I think that Sheila was hoping that Jess was speaking the truth. The sun beat strongly on their faces, my face becoming hot with both the sun and the tension, the situation too much at the end of a long day. I looked pleadingly at Sheila, but there was little compassion left in her face.

'I'll phone Gillian next week and explain everything to her.' Now please go, was what I was really saying.

'Come on, Stuart, we may not approve but it is not our business, for the moment. Let him be,' and they walked away towards their car, which I could see was parked near the sailing club, where the road turned sharply left. Neither turned around but their body language was negative. Stuart appeared to be doing the talking, gesticulating, with Sheila more passive, absorbing his wrath. I did wish that I could change things, hoped that I could in the future, but at the moment, I could do nothing more.

'That was awkward. I hoped that I wouldn't run into them but they must have been here for a meal in the main restaurant.'

Jess had the sense to keep her distance from me, knowing that a backward glance from either of Gillian's parents would only cause more complications if they saw us walking close together. I felt sick, fed up and I wandered back towards the hotel, while Jess said that she wanted a walk up to the white cairn and headed in that direction after borrowing my car keys.

I returned to our room, thankful that Gillian's parents did not find out that we were sharing it. The sun was still strong, the room hot, dust motes danced in the air, so I opened the windows, the fresh sea breeze wafting in, bringing with it the noise of the rigging pinging against the masts as the boats in the harbour bobbed about. I slumped on the easy chair which was to become my bed. It was hard and uncomfortable.

Jess returned an hour later, bringing her sleeping bag and sat on the edge of the bed.

'You sleep on the bed. I'll use my sleeping bag on the floor and put some pillows under me. No arguments, that chair is too hard and the wrong shape.'

I relented and Jess seemed cheerier, starting to chat.

'A man walking his dog at the white tower talked to me and pointed out the hills of the Lake District in England and the Isle of Man, also showed me the memorial to a crew who lost their lives when their boat sank. I then watched a fishing boat heading out to sea with new respect. I didn't realise how dangerous it could be.' Jess was not usually so eloquent and I suspected that she was trying to cheer me up, changing the subject.

'When this is all over, you should bring Danny here. You'll both enjoy it – more comfortable than a tent,' and I attempted a smile.

Jess got up suddenly and clasped my head in her hands, forcing my head up as she looked directly into my eyes.

'Finn,' she said, 'don't give up. I need you to be strong.'

42

I did sleep well and woke early, slipping into the bathroom and having a shower. Jess was awake when I came out dressed.

'Thanks,' I said, pleased that she had given me the bed, 'I had a good sleep. Yourself?'

'Once the pub quietened, I slept well.' I hadn't heard any noise from the pub.

We went down together to breakfast, which was in the main restaurant overlooking the harbour. The tide was out, the boats stranded, with only a few pools of water remaining, patches of seaweed clinging to exposed rocks. The skies were grey, but it didn't look as if it would rain any time soon. Breakfast over we packed the car and walked back towards the village, wondering if Urquhart would be back. Jess was a few steps ahead turning the corner when she jumped back.

'It's Tania. We need to hide,' and she grabbed me and we raced back towards the field where the car was parked, crouching down behind the stone wall.

'She must be going to see Urquhart.'

'Did she see you?'

'I don't think so.'

'What was she driving?'

'A blue Range Rover.'

We waited a few minutes and I risked poking my head above the wall. There was no Range Rover. Emboldened, I motioned for Jess to stay and I ran to the corner, carefully peering around it. There was no sign of the vehicle. I ran forward nipping into an entrance to a block of flats and looked again along the road past the hotel. I couldn't see the Range Rover and my view of Urquhart's house was blocked by the church. I walked on to the hotel and back up to our room, which gave a better vantage point. Still no Range Rover. My phone rang, it was Jess.

'I can't see Tania's car,' I explained.

'Maybe she parked it down the lane we went to yesterday, with the sewage plant at the end? I'll walk out to the end of the pier and check.'

I watched Jess as she walked out onto the pier, keeping to the far side, her head turned away from the village. There was a lower section to the pier, complete with a navigation light and Jess wandered down the steps to reach it. She looked and quickly turned away retracing her route. I saw her take out her phone and a minute later my phone rang.

'She's parked down the lane. There's a light on in his lounge, so he must be back. Hold on, I see her at the front door and she has just gone inside. I'll meet you at the entrance to the hotel.'

Shortly after we met up.

'With the tide out we can work our way around the back of the church and keep low behind the stone wall, check what she's up to. Take photos, so we can prove she was here.'

We clambered over the rocky ground exposed by the low tide behind the church and keeping low worked our way until we were level with Urquhart's house. The sea wall loomed above us a few feet, so I linked my hands together and Jess using them as a step manoeuvred herself up, peering over the wall.

'They're standing in the lounge talking,' she said, as I lowered her down. 'He doesn't appear alarmed or concerned.'

'Something's not right,' I replied, remembering how aggressive Urquhart became when I spoke to him. 'We better wait until she leaves.'

'I'll take photos,' she said, and she walked along the stony beach until she was opposite the lane. The sea wall wasn't so high at this point and she managed to take some photos of the Range Rover, which would prove that Tania had been here. Hopefully, we could trace the car back to AGL.

We waited huddled against the wall for some time, before Jess moved back towards the church, lurking there where it was easier to observe what was happening at his house. We were conscious that we could be seen so wanted not to be appearing to act suspiciously. I picked up stones and put them down as if I was searching for something. Jess sat on a rock near the church.

Suddenly, I saw her sit up and she started taking photos and then crouching ran towards me and then past me. She held her phone up and started taking more photos, before sitting down, giving me the thumbs up after she checked her screen.

I joined her a minute later, as I heard Tania's vehicle turn onto the road and drive off. Jess quickly showed me the photos and I could see Tania leaving Urquhart's house and then walking towards her vehicle. We had evidence of her visit and that might prove useful.

'Send them to Rougvie,' and she worked on her phone for a few seconds before I heard a whizzing sound as the photos were sent.

'Shall we visit Urquhart?' and we clambered over the sea wall at a low point and walked towards his house. I glanced in as we passed his window. Urquhart was slumped on his sofa, head tipped to one side. Something was wrong. I tried the door but it was locked.

'Where is Rougvie when you need him?'

Jess was concerned. 'He looks unconscious.'

'We better get to him,' but we couldn't break down the door without alerting others. 'I'll try the back, climb the wall.'

'Be quick, I don't like this,' she replied.

I raced to the lane and ran down it, cutting across the marshy clumps of grass next to the water and reached the base of the high wall. At Urquhart's house there was no easy way to get up, so I went to a neighbour's house, where there was a series of steps and climbed up them, trying the wooden gate at the top, but it was locked. I heaved myself onto the top of the wall and straddling it I moved along until I reached the rear of Urquhart's house and flopped onto the ground inside his garden. The garden was a mess, mostly mud and weeds, with a grey plastic bin and a plastic box overflowing with empty glass bottles.

I grabbed the door handle and pushed in. On the kitchen table was a pile of newspapers which had been soaked in whisky, the smell permeating the room and on top was a lit candle. Tania had left a tealight burning, its flame flickering as I came in. The flame was intended to ignite the papers after she left, probably burning down the house and as I glanced into the lounge I saw Urquhart's slumped body, realising that he would be unable to save himself.

43

The tealight was burning down, the heat drawing out the whisky vapour from the newspaper, the volatile mix about to ignite. I dashed forward swiping the tealight hard sending it flying across the kitchen. It landed on the floor but the whisky soaked paper ignited anyway and I grabbed the lit newspapers, dumping them on the kitchen floor, stamping on them, whilst grabbing a mug from the dish rack, filling it with water and pouring it on the flames. There was a burning smell but the flames were quickly extinguished. A few minutes later I would have been too late.

I saw Jess staring anxiously in the lounge window, relieved to see me. I ran to the front door unlocking it and letting her in, explaining what I had found.

'Take pictures in the kitchen,' I said, as I went to try and rouse Urquhart. He smelt of whisky even this early in the day, his face very pale, his breathing shallow. Grabbing him by the shoulders I shook him. There was no response, his body sagging and he flopped back on the sofa.

'Jess, he's in a bad way. I suspect he's been drugged,' and I looked around, noticing an overturned whisky glass on the carpet and a wet stain beside it, so he had not drunk it all. When I lifted the glass there was a smell that I couldn't identify. Jess went into the kitchen to look at the remains of the fire.

As I followed her into the kitchen, I saw Jess examining a twist of paper on the kitchen surface which had been unfurled, traces of a white powder beside it. Why hide evidence when it will all be consumed by fire.

Jess touched the powder with her finger and smelt it. 'It's bitter,' she said, touching it with her tongue, 'probably a sedative,' and she immediately washed out her mouth at the sink. She seemed very confident in her assertion. I presume that it was Danny who had initiated her.

'We need evidence, Jess,' but she was ahead of me, taking photos of the powder and the mess on the kitchen floor.

'We got here just in time,' I said, as I went to the sink, cleaning a dirty glass and filling it with water, taking it through and propping Urquhart up, trying to make him drink. It didn't work. His shirt was soaked with whisky, his body unresponsive.

If we hadn't managed to stop the fire I could imagine what the headline in the newspaper would have been: 'Man burned to death in house fire, suspected of being drunk.' The bottles at the back in the refuse box would support that scenario, even before his reputation at the hotel confirmed the likelihood of it, so there would be minimal investigation and his former colleagues knew about his drinking habits so they wouldn't be surprised.

I flung the water in his face and slapped him. There was a low groan and I shook him by the shoulders. Jess watched my efforts while I cursed myself for not paying more attention during first-aid talks.

'Should we phone for an ambulance?' she ventured.

'Probably, but difficult to explain why we're in here.' I stated, as I continued with my efforts.

'Come on,' I said, 'wake up,' and continued to shake him.

'Jess, we might not get much sense from him in this state, even if he does wake up. I'm going to search the house while we

237

have the chance, you keep an eye on him.'

Jess moved over to him and I looked around the room. There were piles of newspapers, often, I noticed, opened at the day's racing tips, the names of some horses circled. On the coffee table there was a dirty mug and a plate with crumbs on it but also some letters – mostly circulars, an electricity bill and a charity appeal. On the wall next to the hall was a glass-fronted cabinet filled with rows of glasses, an empty vase and a few bottles of whisky. But there were two drawers underneath. I pulled out the first one, which had coasters, place mats, paper napkins. I shoved the top drawer back in and pulled out the one below. It was stuffed with papers and I started to examine them. More bills, some photos and some bank statements. I checked them, they were from the bank that Sis worked at, but a different branch, located in Dumfries.

I scanned the statements. There were cash withdrawals, several purchases from an off-licence, a standing order for his electricity and a regular payment from his police pension.

'He's waking up, Finn,' and I heard grunting, muttering and saw his eyelids flicker.

'Offer him water,' but Jess was ahead of me. There was spluttering and coughing and he stirred, eyes rolling, out of focus.

I examined the bank statement again. There was a payment into his account for several hundred pounds on the fifth of the month. A BACS transfer. I turned to the next statement and there it was again on roughly the same date.

'Jess, I think I've found something, come here.'

I pointed out the payments to Jess. 'Could be a private pension but it is a large sum.' Jess busied herself taking photos and I grabbed a few of the statements, stuffing them in my pocket.

There was movement on the sofa and Urquhart groaned, shaking himself. I quickly shut the drawer and stood up.

'What the hell are you doing here?' he exclaimed, looking around, trying to make sense of what he saw, easing himself up whilst holding on to an arm of the sofa for support.

'We were passing and saw that you were unconscious. We've been trying to help you.'

'Crap, you're rummaging through my possessions.'

'Do you not remember Tania visiting you,' stated Jess. His expression said no, though it made him look thoughtful, some vague memory surfacing and I was aware of a strong smell of urine; he had peed himself. Jess was aware as she sniffed the air. 'Probably a side effect of the sedative,' she mouthed quietly.

'And who the hell are you?'

'Dougie Hamilton's daughter. He was murdered beside John McAdam. You were at the scene. Remember?'

I didn't know whether Urquhart was playing for time or was still confused, but he dropped his shoulders, putting his head in his hands, groaning.

'Quite a mess,' I said quietly, 'and you would have been burnt alive if we had not come in. Tania was trying to kill you. She drugged you and left you to die. Look in the kitchen, if you don't believe us, and you will see how she was going to do it.'

Urquhart lifted his head, his face white and blotchy and ran his hand through his thinning hair.

'Go look in the kitchen, see what Tania was trying to do,' I said brusquely.

He slowly got up and made his way to the kitchen.

'How do I know that you didn't do this?'

'Because we would have just left you to die.' I think that even in his confused state he saw the logic of that.

'Why was Tania here?' I demanded.

He stared back at me and then turned quickly as he belched and then was sick in the sink, retching, whatever he had taken disagreeing with him. He washed his face and I gave him a towel to dry himself.

So I told him. 'Tania was here to ask if we had visited you, to see if you had been talking about us. We knew she was coming because we overheard Sir Archibald talking to her, ordering Tania to visit you and check that you were keeping quiet. Keeping your side of the bargain.'

At the mention of Sir Archibald's name, he lowered his head, avoiding eye contact.

'He's paying you, isn't he, to keep quiet? Helps pay your drink bill and whatever you owe the bookies.'

He sat down hard on one of the kitchen chairs, eyeing the pile of whisky soaked newspapers and the tealight on the floor. There was still a faint whiff of smoke in the kitchen.

'He was making sure that you couldn't talk. Tania was sent to kill you,' I repeated.

I let him absorb my statement, deliberately kept quiet, let him work out for himself the seriousness of his situation. He must once have been an able, intelligent man, not that I felt much pity for him.

'Better to talk and then get back to your sister in Musselburgh.'

'How did you know about her?'

'People talk.'

'Malcolm at the hotel,' and he seemed pleased to have worked that out for himself, as he wandered unsteadily back into the lounge.

'Who pays you the money each month, your slush fund?' but I could see that he was thinking, weighing up options as the effects of the drug wore off and his brain started to work again.

240

'You are both well in above your heads, no clue as to what you are facing. They'll squash you, destroy you to keep their own safe.'

'Who are "they"?' but he just laughed at me as he became bolder.

'I'm saying nothing more and you can't make me.'

'You're pathetic,' Jess said, 'weak and just a drunkard. Can you not see that what you are covering up is destroying you?'

'Oh very profound, Miss. Can you not see it already has. I don't need redemption, I just want to be left alone. I've made peace with my demons.'

'Until they try and kill you again,' I added.

I saw him glance covetously at the whisky in the cabinet. He was a lost cause.

'My advice is to let your fathers rest in peace,' he declared. 'You'll just cause trouble for yourself if you go raking up the past. They have the resources to find you and kill you.' He spat the final words out, his arrogance returning.

'They didn't manage with you,' Jess stated defiantly, 'and that should have been easy. Come on, Finn, let him drown in his own self-pity. The only people who will miss him are the whisky companies and the hit on their profits.'

'Who are they,' I enquired, curious, not willing to give up, 'who have the power to kill people?'

Urquhart just stood, his eyes darting from side to side as he tried to avoid answering.

'Sir Archibald and Julian Montgomery,' I said suddenly, and for a second the mask slipped, a momentary look of fear gripped him. Urquhart slumped on the sofa, his hands trembling, either a side effect of the drug wearing off or his body's desperate need for a drink. We glanced across at each other, Jess also having registered Urquhart's flicker of fear.

Without saying anything more we left by the front door. The sea air outside refreshing after the putrid smells inside the house. Urquhart was of no further use but maybe we had some evidence of the price of his silence and who had bought it.

44

Walking fast we reached the car and sat for a moment drawing breath.

'If we can prove the payments are from AGL, then they have a lot of explaining to do,' I suggested.

'Will anyone believe us,' Jess replied. 'Urquhart is correct, we are up against powerful people, horrible people,' and she shivered at the thought.

'Let's get away from here. I can't believe that Tania was willing to murder someone, just on someone's say-so. What type of person is she? How does AGL exert such a sinister influence over people? If we hadn't been around, Urquhart would be dead, burned alive.'

That was a terrifying thought. And if they caught us, what then? This was deadly serious stuff and it took me a moment to compose myself before setting off.

We drove along past the hotel and as we reached the community cafe, I turned right up the road towards Garlieston where Gillian's parents had a farm.

'I thought that you didn't want to go near the farm?'

'I don't but I bet Tania is waiting on the road to Whithorn, where the fire station is located, waiting for the fire engine to pass, checking that the house has caught fire.'

'Okay, I didn't think of that.'

'Nor would I a week ago.' Life was changing for both of us.

We passed close to Stuart and Sheila's farm but didn't see them and soon reached the distillery at Bladnoch, beside the bridge over the River Bladnoch, and turning right at the roundabout we drove up to Wigtown, Scotland's book town, commanding high ground overlooking Wigtown Bay.

Wigtown was a small town with most of the shops on Main Street, which was divided in two by a central park and bowling green, with the county buildings at the eastern end. I had been here with Dad, visiting book shops, another of his favourite pastimes. Memories of dusty tomes, percolating coffee to tempt you in and Classic FM playing in the background. As we reached the Main Street, I spotted a cafe and I pulled over and parked close to it. Jess wondered why I was stopping.

'I need a coffee, a chance to catch breath and plan our next steps,' I suggested. 'Even just one of those would be good,' and Jess smiled and added, 'Coffee would be my first choice.'

Soon we were sitting in a corner of the cafe, as far from other people as possible for some privacy, giving our order to a young waitress, who must have been about the same age as Jess. We waited until our order was delivered, the coffee excellent – which always helped my mood – before we began to talk.

'Did you notice the look of fear on Urquhart's face when I linked AGL's name with Julian Montgomery's?'

Jess nodded, adding, 'He is terrified of them and what Tania did will not have helped.'

'I agree. I wonder what Urquhart meant when he said, "You are both well in above your heads, no clue as to what you are facing. They'll squash you, destroy you to keep their own safe." Who are they hiding? Who are their own? They both

244

seem very well connected, with friends in high places who can protect them. They also have a habit of killing people – our fathers, now an attempt on Urquhart – to defend their interests. Pretty ruthless and they get away with apparent impunity.' Jess appeared puzzled by my last sentence. 'Escape the consequences of their actions,' I explained, and she agreed.

'However, the positive is that we might have evidence that Urquhart is receiving payments from them, which will leave him with some explaining to do, especially to his former colleagues in the police. I'll contact Sis, who works for the bank that Urquhart uses and see if we can trace the source of the payments. But she'll probably not help me. There will be some bank rule abut confidentiality. Still, worth a try.'

Jess checked her phone. 'Rougvie sent a text earlier,' and she looked hopeful as she scanned it quickly. I waited patiently.

'Rougvie's brother has found the birth certificate for Murdoch Walter Birse, he's now 73 and was born in Finzean, a village near Banchory, but no death certificate, so he must still be alive. However, his name does not appear on any electoral register or appear on the valuation roll as a tenant, proprietor or occupier. It is like he doesn't exist. He's tried different spellings of the name, he says, but with no success.

'He says that Birse is a common name in that area of Aberdeenshire, there being a Forest of Birse, a Birse castle, three churches with Birse in their name and a minister called Birse. He says that he could go on and on.'

'It's strange that he's disappeared, gone missing. Maybe he's moved abroad. I wonder what he is up to. Could our two foes be hiding him? But why? Rich seems thorough, which is good. Ask Rougvie if AGL or Julian Montgomery own any property in the area. If they do maybe he stays there.'

Jess typed in the question. 'He'll get back to us, he says. I think he is enjoying the mystery.'

'I'm glad that someone is. What about the car that Birse drives?'

Jess looked at the long text, scrolling down.

'He has some information. The car is extremely rare, the few that remain mostly in museums or in private collections. Rich can't find a list of owners or any Argyll owner's club. Manufacture of the car started in the early eighties but there was no more than a dozen manufactured. It won't be considered a classic car until it's forty years old, so it's not exempt from having to pay road tax or having an MOT but there's no MOT record for it. Rich believes that it must be off-road, lurking in some garage, not driveable or written off.'

'No great progress there, then.'

'What is our next step?' Jess enquired.

'Hopefully, Sis will be helpful, but don't count on it. She and Mum won't talk about the incident, blanking it out.'

'Is that not strange?' Jess suggested. 'I know that we've talked about it before but my mother wouldn't talk about my dad either. When I was a wee girl she even told me that he worked at a railway station. I believed her for years.' It was exasperating. We were covering familiar ground and not getting any further.

'What was the name of the station?' I asked, curious, but also to stop our conversation going round in loops with no apparent exits.

'Wylies.'

'That sounds more like a person's name, not a place name,' I said immediately. 'If he worked in a secret establishment, he maybe just spun a tale so that you couldn't boast to your friends about what your dad did. I am sure my father did that as well.'

'Maybe our next step should be to follow up Darren's suggestion of visiting the museum, the Devil's Porridge, about the history of the munitions works. Our fathers worked in that area and given that the Ministry of Defence owned a lot of the ground, they must have worked on part of the site. Maybe someone at the museum would have information that could help us or point us to someone who does. Is it far from here?' It was worth a try and we had few options.

Jess used her phone to find out. 'The museum is located in Eastriggs, which is east of Annan, seventy-five miles away and is open every day from 10 am. Should take us a couple of hours at most.'

I finished my coffee, pondering what we had discussed. Eventually I asked for the bill and while I waited, I composed a text to Sis asking for her help about the origin of the payments made into Urquhart's account and sent it off, not expecting much cooperation. It was disappointing that Rougvie's brother had not come up with more, but it was always a long shot and he was still searching.

45

No one describes the A75 as a good road. Passing lanes are few and not all villages have been bypassed, but once we reached the trunk road at Newton Stewart we kept going, overtaking where possible, Jess driving, me busy on my phone.

Over an hour later we reached the outskirts of Dumfries, passing the site of the new hospital. Lurking behind it was an industrial park, once the site of an ICI factory developed during the Second World War as a cordite factory, an important part of Dumfries and Galloway's contribution to the war effort.

Memories of my Higher Grade History project came back to me. Several satellite munitions factories were located around the south-west of Scotland to disperse the production of munitions from the main explosives factory at Ardeer, in Ayrshire, ensuring that production was less vulnerable to air attack. Importantly they were all connected to the then extensive rail network in the region. I restricted my studies to the Second World War, but researching on the Internet now made me aware that during the First World War a massive munitions factory, stretching over nine miles from Dornock in Scotland over the border to Longtown in England, had been built, at a time of national crisis due to a shortage of shells, which was crippling the war effort by 1915.

Farms were compulsorily purchased along the sparsely populated northern shore of the Solway Firth and a large factory built – the biggest in the world at the time, all to produce cordite, the propellant for shells. Factories, generators for power, railways to move materials around and thousands of construction workers and then production workers were required. Townships at Eastriggs and Gretna were built complete with churches, halls, picture houses and shops, all in a remarkably short time.

Dangerous chemicals were mixed together to produce the vital cordite in what was a dangerous process. It was Sir Arthur Conan Doyle who described the mixing by hand of nitroglycerine and guncotton as akin to the Devil's Porridge and the name stuck. As soon as the war was over, much of the site was mothballed or demolished and some parts used to store ammunition. Somewhere in this sprawling site my father worked along with Jess's father and others on a top-secret project.

I explained to Jess what I knew about the site from knowledge gleaned during my history project and from looking up the various websites. The Devil's Porridge Museum told the story of the First World War factory, known officially as HM Factory Gretna, along with the story of the worst railway accident in British history at nearby Quintinshill.

We turned off the A75, west of Annan, drove through the small town on the Solway Coast and soon reached Eastriggs. The museum had moved into modern premises not long ago. As we approached I was not sure how helpful the visit would be, but it was certainly a popular tourist attraction, the car park almost full. The museum had an attractive glass frontage, with sections of wood panelling and inside along with the exhibitions, a cafe.

Having paid the entrance fee we started to work our way around the exhibits. The first section was largely devoted to the Quintinshill railway disaster, which told a gruesome story, but was not our focus of interest.

We were a nation in peril, so it seemed, the shortage of shells meant that there was barely enough to repel the German army, let alone go on the offensive. The solution was bold and the resources committed substantial. Out of farmland, largely turned to mud during construction, a factory emerged quickly, with for the times, an unusually large female workforce. Social barriers were being broken down, wars often did that.

Jess studied the exhibits, looked at the historic maps, like me not sure what she was looking for. I was examining a large stoneware basin where the cordite paste was mixed, marvelling at the bravery of the workforce, never far from a cataclysmic explosion if a tiny error of judgement was made, when I heard Jess gasp. She was looking at a map of the factory, detailing all the different processes and I could see her excitement as she pointed out a name to me.

'Wylies Platform,' she said, 'that's what my mother talked about, where Dad worked. It exists.'

To the north of what, on the map, appeared to be canteens and general administration buildings, was Wylies Platform, part of an extensive railway network. There had to be something in the story that Jess had been told by her mother.

One of the museum assistants was nearby talking to another lady, who looked as if she worked in the cafe, wearing an apron.

'Excuse me,' I said, 'what can you tell me about Wylies Platform?'

I always felt it must be quite boring being a museum assistant standing around keeping an eye on visitors, so being asked a question breaks the monotony. She looked as if she was retired, grey-haired, probably a volunteer.

'The platform took its name from one of the local farms

250

which were compulsorily purchased. It was not generally staffed or had good facilities, hence it is best described as a halt, not a railway station, but it was very busy ferrying workers in from Eastriggs to other parts of the site. At one time there were about 30,000 workers on the site.' She knew her stuff.

'Wow, that is big,' I replied, adding, 'when did it stop being used?'

'At the end of the First World War, almost a hundred years ago.'

'Is anything left?'

'No, but you can see where it was located if you go along the Annan Road. Just outside the village, on the left, is a minor road which crosses the railway siding into the plant.'

'My father is dead,' said Jess, probably impatient with the overkill of detail, wanting to get to the point, and that got the attention of the two ladies who appeared suddenly sympathetic.

'He talked of working near Wylies Platform, about twelve years ago.'

The assistant was puzzled. 'The site was used as an ammunition dump until recently. Did he work in the storage bunkers?'

'No, he worked on some project on the site, along with Finn's father. They were chemists working on a special project.'

'I don't think that I can help you. I have not lived in the area that long,' and she looked at her colleague for help. Much the same age, the second woman had been listening carefully and appeared willing to help.

'My husband worked on the site as part of security for many years, after he retired from the police. He might know something.'

'Can you ask him, please?' pleaded Jess, 'I want to know as

much about my dad as possible. He died when I was only six. Finn and I are on journey,' and she stepped closer to me, 'to discover more about him and his dad, who also died.' Whether or not she was acting, she did look convincing. Was that tears in her eyes?

'Oh sorry, that must have been difficult. Was it an accident?'

'Something like that,' Jess stated.

'I will ask my husband, Sam, who is now retired from his security duties. He's at home, not far from here.'

'Oh that would be wonderful,' and Jess gave both women her biggest smile. Sunshine after the rain.

'I finish in an hour, can you wait?' and Jess nodded vigorously.

Both women seemed pleased. 'I'm Sally,' said the cafe assistant. 'I'll see you later.'

'We'll have some lunch and look around the other exhibits.' I smiled, adding my approval.

The story of HM Factory Gretna was one of incredible success on a scale difficult to appreciate. The terrible conditions for workers, the inevitable accidents, tales of woe and bravery quickly passed the time and when we reached the cafe Sally was busy cleaning a table but took our order and disappeared into the kitchen to soon return with soup and a sandwich.

Twenty minutes later she came back, her coat on.

'I usually walk home, but if you have a car maybe you could give me a lift.'

Sally was chatty as she guided me, Jess sitting in the back of the car. 'Here we are,' said Sally, 'Vancouver Road. All the roads were named after our colonies at the time,' and we stopped outside a brick terrace house with a small garden and a wide pavement with a grass verge.

'These houses were built for the workers,' she said, as she got out and we followed her to the door of the house.

Sam opened the door as we arrived, silver-haired with a trim goatee beard, he welcomed us, a cautious look on his face as he showed us into a small lounge with a large TV and a three-piece suite, with barely room for a small folding table. Sally had obviously phoned ahead to alert him.

Sam pointed to the sofa and we sat down.

'When I retired from the police I got a job as a security guard at the gate, so I saw most traffic and people in and out. From what Sally told me you must be Dr McAdam's son.'

'Finn,' I replied.

'And you, Miss, must be Dr Hamilton's daughter.'

'Correct. Jess is the name.'

That wasn't hard, few murders around here, especially involving folks who worked in top-security compounds.

'Where did our fathers work on the site?' I enquired.

Sam chuckled. 'I'm still bound by the Official Secrets Act, so I can't tell you, but there are many storage bunkers on site and one was converted for their use. Good idea, a remote site hidden underground would not attract attention. They sure brought in lots of equipment, fancy instruments and lots of pipes, ventilation pumps. Above my pay grade but the rumour was they were working on nerve gases or antidotes to them. We called it the Devil's Cauldron, because they were brewing up dangerous chemicals, for good or ill, we weren't sure. If the state requires it, who are we to argue?'

That made sense, probably a progression of my father's PhD work on organophosphates.

'I knew your father, Finn. He was a gentleman, always had time for everyone. I was very upset when I heard that he was dead. Your father, Jess, was also a nice man, larger than life. For one to die was terrible – for both was awful. We were all affected very badly.'

Sally came in with cups of coffee for everyone but left quickly.

'After their deaths the site was swamped with security officers and we were told to say nothing. Hints about what took place were dropped, never very convincingly in my opinion. They seemed totally out of character.'

'Like what?' I asked intrigued.

'About a squabble over a woman.'

'And as a result my father killed Jess's and then committed suicide.'

'You heard,' Sam said. 'I'm glad that I didn't have to tell you.'

'But you aren't convinced,' I added, studying his expression.

'No, I knew the woman, a lovely girl, very attractive, blonde, mid-twenties, who worked alongside them as a technician. I mean they were carefully chosen, background checked and she didn't seem to me to be the type to encourage flirting or sleep around.'

'What was her name?'

'Julia Finneston, she boarded with one of Sally's friends, who spoke very highly of her, enjoyed her company.'

'What happened to her?'

'I don't know. The project was quickly shut down, the equipment removed and within weeks the bunker was being used again as storage for ammunition. As if it had never been there.'

'How many worked on the project?' Jess enquired, clearing her throat as she spoke, an indication of how tense she was.

'Only four people,' and before I could ask, he added, 'the

fourth member was Dr Adrian Shaw.'

'What was he like?'

'I believe that he worked as a student for your father, Finn, which I suppose explained his presence, but he was different. Said little, always appeared distracted, gave you little eye contact, but a brilliant chemist, so I am told.'

'Where is he now?'

'I never saw him around the site again, don't know where he went. Disappeared, if you like but the security forces didn't appear to be interested in him, never asked questions about him, which they certainly did about your loved ones.'

'Do you believe my father murdered Jess's dad?'

'Not for one minute. I had been in the police, had contacts. There were lots of rumours. The consensus was that there was a massive cover-up, but they certainly put the frighteners on us. I have never spoken about it before today but, hey, I am retired now, they can only stop my pension. I felt that there was a great injustice done, it's a relief to talk about it.'

'Was Urquhart involved?'

Sam's expression changed, suddenly more guarded, cautious. 'How did you know about him?'

'I heard his name being mentioned.' I deliberately said nothing more, not wanting Sam to clam up.

'He was the senior investigating officer but the cover-up was above even his level and he thought that he was next to God.'

We now had names of all the members of the group who worked beside Dad. I glanced at Jess, who looked very thoughtful. 'You both were young at the time. I can understand your curiosity,' Sam stated, 'but can I caution you. It was a high level cover-up. Those involved will be very concerned if they discover what you are attempting to do.'

I decided to level with him. 'I was there on the night and I saw my father being murdered. I know that there has been a cover-up.'

Sam studied both of us. 'That's interesting, confirms what I thought about your father. He was not the type to have affairs.'

'What about my father?' asked Jess.

Sam hesitated for a moment and looked down at his feet and then looked up at Jess. 'I honestly don't know,' Sam eventually answered, 'but I doubt it, fishing was his big thing, although I don't believe that they found any fishing rods at the murder scene.'

Sally opened the door from the kitchen, joining us. I was sure that she had been listening to our conversation.

'I think that our visitors are just about to leave,' Sam stated.

'Thanks, you have been very useful. I appreciate your candour,' I added.

Sally showed us to the door, while Sam remained seated in the lounge. 'Sally, give them Mrs Shields' address. She was Julia's landlady. I suspect that you will want to talk to her,' he suggested. As I was leaving Sally handed me a piece of paper, tightening my hand around it, and smiling. 'Good luck,' she said, 'I hope that you find answers.'

46

After leaving their house I drove along the Annan Road and found the side road that crossed over the railway siding into the depot, stopping on the bridge and getting out. Security fencing lined both sides of the road and also both sides of the railway. From my recollection of the map Wylies Platform was at the far end, beyond a passing loop, but the site had changed with the removal of the factory at the end of the First World War. Somewhere though in the still vast site, now mostly vacant, my father worked underground creating chemical brews. I hoped that it was a search for antidotes to nerve gases that consumed him, but I would probably never know. Jess joined me staring into the site, her hands thrust deep into her pockets.

I pulled out from my pocket the note that Sally had given me. On it was a name, Mrs Shields, an address, a phone number and scribbled underneath was the message: 'Mrs Shields was Julia's landlady, but she now does bed and breakfast.' I showed the message to Jess, adding, 'I think that we have found our accommodation for tonight.'

Mrs Shields lived in a detached red sandstone villa on the road that led to the local distillery and made us welcome to her home on the outskirts of Annan. She was quite elderly, slightly stooped, her permed hair highlighted by a purple rinse. She stood at the door watching us unpack the car, and I had a feeling that she was very curious about the two of us. Our rooms were basic but clean and the beds looked comfortable. When we had unpacked she told us to come down to the lounge for a cup of tea.

When we arrived a tray was set for us with freshly baked scones and jam. As we sat down on the sofa, Mrs Shields joined us from the adjoining kitchen, bringing a pot of tea, and sat down on one of the other chairs.

'I was hoping that you would come after Sally phoned me,' and I suddenly became alert, hoping that she might be able to help us.

'I was very fond of Julia. She arrived just after my husband died and she was bright, cheery company, helped me a lot, and then she suddenly announced that she had to leave. The events surrounding your fathers' deaths quickly led to her work being stopped and then she was gone. I missed her.'

'Sam described her as a very friendly, attractive woman,' I said.

'Julia was a lovely girl, dedicated to her work,' a note of hesitation crept in and she paused. 'The events changed everything.'

'Two of her co-workers found dead must have been very distressing,' I suggested, gently probing.

'Two fathers, two families destroyed. That was terrible, Julia was most upset, very pale when she left, even unwell. I was worried about her. I never heard from her again,' and there was a tinge of sadness in her voice.

'Where did you think she went?' Jess asked.

'I don't know. I wrote to her home address but there was no reply.' For such a friendly relationship, and I had no reason to

258

doubt Mrs Shields' account, to cease so abruptly was strange. Possibly it meant a dead end for our searching.

'One of my friends, who works at a local farm, did say that her partner met Julia at a farmers' market in Ayrshire, a year later, and she was married with a child. He talked to her husband, knew where his farm was, and he seemed very nice.'

'So it turned out alright for her,' I said, adding, 'Do you have any idea where the farm is located?' Now we knew about Julia it would be good to talk to her.

'Near Ochiltree – High Skares, a dairy farm. I wrote to her, to say how happy I was for her, but again there was no reply.'

'That must have been upsetting,' Jess stated, 'but she must have wanted just to start again after losing both workmates and her job.'

'You must be right, dear,' but something was bothering her. I waited, hoping that she would continue, disclose more, not wanting to push her.

'You know that two weeks after Julia left I got visitors,' she eventually said. 'Two men arrived, asked to come in. I wasn't sure, they seemed respectable but not too friendly, quite officious. They flashed some identification but they weren't police. They were asking questions, wanting to know if Julia had told me anything about your fathers' deaths.' She was watching for our reaction.

'Did they take the opportunity to spread rumours about them?' and I raised an eyebrow quizzically.

'They said that...'

Jess, bless her, interrupted Mrs Shields. 'We have heard these stories. They are not true,' she added emphatically.

'I don't believe them myself, knew that they were false. Although I never met either of your fathers, Julia spoke highly of them both. Sam hinted that the rumours were untrue. I also wanted to tell you that the other man in the group, Dr Shaw, came around a few times, this was before the deaths. I didn't like him, but Julia treated him just as a work colleague and he seemed lonely. The night of the murders I was out but came home, quite late, to find Julia very distressed. She wouldn't tell me what went on but he had been here.'

Mrs Shields let us absorb the information as she sipped her tea, but she was not finished.

'A few years later I was travelling to a big shopping centre, near Glasgow, and made a detour to her farm, still sad that we had lost touch. I was going to call in unexpectedly and I found the farm, very easily, a road running past the farmyard. I saw a child playing outside the farmhouse, children's toys lying about and then I saw the farmer, who matched the description my friend gave, and a woman, who was pregnant, standing beside him. It wasn't Julia so I drove on.'

'Maybe Julia had separated from her husband and he had found someone else. The relationship simply didn't last.' Inside my mind was working overtime and a quick glance at Jess told me she was also trying to work out what this new information meant. Adrian Shaw was interested in Julia. Mrs Shields had doubts about him, or was I reading too much into what I had been told. Julia was upset on the night of the murders after his visit. Could it be that he had informed her of our fathers' deaths, which would explain her reaction? News like that would have been devastating. Or did something else happen between them? There could be many possible explanations, some very simple, even innocent, but Dr Shaw had disappeared off the face of the earth and Julia couldn't be traced. And she had a baby not long afterwards. Was that coincidence or was I becoming paranoid?

We needed time to think, so when Mrs Shields disappeared into the kitchen I suggested to Jess that we went out. Mrs Shields seemed disappointed but we had to talk alone, so we walked into town and found an Indian restaurant to eat in. Times like this I missed the comfort of alcohol and a good bar.

'I would like to meet Dr Shaw,' began Jess, after the waiter left, 'and find out what he was up to that night. Was he telling her about the murders or did something else take place?'

'I was thinking much the same. Sam thought him strange but Dad got him the job, so I suspect that he was a good chemist.'

'But maybe not a good person.'

'Julia was attractive, naive, maybe he was obsessed with her. We know that she had a baby not long after but was living with someone on a farm. But who was the father. Was it the farmer, and if so, why did she not stay long at the farm? Or could Shaw even be the father?'

Our meal was mainly eaten in silence as we wrestled with the new information.

'It strikes me as odd that rumours were put around about affairs but no one appeared interested in Shaw,' I stated. 'There were only four people working at the Devil's Cauldron, but her visitors wanted to know only if Julia had told them anything about the murders, dropping hints about affairs involving our fathers, but not asking about Shaw.'

'Maybe the cover-up also involves Shaw who then disappears,' Jess concluded, and I agreed.

'But why was he allowed just to walk away?'

'One person might know,' and Jess looked up, 'my Sis might have met him. Dad's students frequently visited the house. I was young and often in bed when they arrived and my mother didn't like offering them meals – too much work. Sis might remember him and it would be useful to have a photo of him. Tomorrow we go to visit my sister.'

'That makes sense,' replied Jess.

• • •

Next morning I was down first for breakfast and Mrs Shields busied herself cooking my order. As she placed the plate down in front of me, she informed me, 'Sam phoned last night and wanted your phone number in case he thought of anything else that might be of use to you.'

I liked Sam and he could be useful so I wrote my number down and handed it to her.

'Ask him if he has a photo of Dr Shaw. It's unlikely that I ever met him but I would be curious to know what he looked like.'

She hung around the table, asking if I wanted more tea or toast. I was getting a bit irritated by her, too intrusive, even though I realised that she was probably very lonely.

'You are such a nice couple...'

'Jess and I are just friends,' I replied in a clipped tone.

There was movement at the door and I saw that Jess had appeared, she quickly turned away, but I saw the look on her face and quietly cursed Mrs Shields.

• • •

The next step was to visit Sis who lived in Moffat with her husband, Paul. She had not responded to my request about the source of Urquhart's payments. To be fair, even if she agreed it could take time. Now we had additional questions for her about Adrian Shaw.

We waved to Mrs Shields, who was standing at her door, but before I could drive off my phone rang, so I stopped. I didn't recognise the number, which was from a landline. It was Sis, which was convenient, saved me phoning her.

'Don't answer me,' which was a decidedly strange way to

start. She spoke very fast, as if she wanted off the line as soon as possible. 'Do you remember the cafe in Dumfries that we used to visit when we were finished Christmas shopping?'

I had to think for a minute. 'Yes,' I replied, finally.

'How soon can you meet me?

'About an hour?'

'See you then,' and she hung up.

I looked at Jess puzzled.

'Sis wants to meet with us. Strange conversation and she sounds anxious. We have to meet her in an hour, so we better go.'

47

Situated in the heart of Dumfries, the restaurant was located down a side street off the pedestrian zone in the town centre. If Sis didn't want to be seen, she had chosen well. The restaurant was dimly lit with cubicles and a lot of dark-stained wood panelling. At Christmas it was always more brightly lit and there had been lots of festive decorations festooning the walls, the restaurant providing a treat at the end of a long day's shopping. She was waiting for us, a coffee cup half-empty, she was that type of person. Still only in her late thirties, there were grey streaks in her hair, which she made no attempt to hide. The serious expression was a younger image of her mother, maybe not with so many lines but that would no doubt come in time. I called her Sis because she was only half a sister, more an extension of mother and there was always a unity between them, mirrored, I suppose, by my closeness to Dad. A family cleaved in two, each half worked independently. My parents' relationship survived because Dad was probably so involved in his research that he didn't need much emotional support from Mum. What he lacked from Mother he got from me.

As I approached the table I saw her observe Jess and I knew instantly that she wasn't enamoured. So far what I expected.

'So you are Jess,' and she offered her a limp handshake, quickly turning her attention to me. I could sense that Jess was both bemused and a little annoyed.

'Switch off your phones, now,' Sis stated firmly, in her usual bossy manner, and waited expectantly until we obeyed. 'So what are you up to, Finn?' she added, ignoring Jess.

'This is Jess,' I said, 'Dougie Hamilton's daughter, who has been a great help in our joint quest to discover the truth about our fathers.'

Sis was forced to look at Jess. 'You are younger than I imagined,' and turned her attention quickly back to me.

'Age does not always improve people,' Jess observed icily and I saw a flicker of irritation on Sis's face. Well done, Jess.

'So why the meeting. What news do you have for us?' I said quickly, before Sis could formulate a reply to Jess.

She shifted in her seat, looking uncomfortable, not sure where to start.

'I have discovered that Paul has been asked to inform his Inspector if he finds out your whereabouts. Direct instruction texted to him while he is off on sick leave.'

'You read his texts?'

'Past experience has taught me that it keeps me fully informed of what he is up to,' and that uncomfortable look reappeared. That gave weight to the rumours that Paul had had an affair with a young constable.

'It seems that there is a general alert to keep an eye out for the two of you and to inform other people of what you are doing. I suspect that they will be tracing your whereabouts using your phones and they have details of your car.'

'Paul has been cooperative then.' He never liked me.

Sis ignored that comment. 'You are both in a lot of trouble.'

'I told you that there was a high level cover-up of what really happened when Dad was murdered, but you never believed me, dismissed me.'

'You were young and drugged.'

'I know what I saw,' but I wanted to change tack, this conversation was just starting to go over familiar ground, like a train being shunted to a dead end.

'Dad was not having an affair as you were led to believe but we think that a Dr Adrian Shaw might be involved. Did you ever meet him? I believe that he was one of Dad's best students or he wouldn't have involved him at Eastriggs.'

Sis thought for a minute. 'Father never brought home anyone from that project, it was all so secret. I knew that Dad went fishing with your father,' and motioned towards Jess, 'but that was all.'

'Think back, he sometimes brought home students and we believe that Shaw was one of his students.'

'I don't know, but I'll think about it later. More importantly, what are you going to do now? They will find you and then what – you could be arrested, Mother will be upset and your job put at risk. Think of the consequences, Finn.'

I ignored her litany of possible woes. She drained her coffee cup.

'I could buy another phone. Maybe you could let me use your car. We are not giving up,' and I met her disapproving stare with my most determined face.

'What about Gillian?' I think that was intended as her trump card.

'Gillian knows my feelings. If I don't find out the truth, I can't settle. I've tried, really tried. It hurts me to say that. I need your help and I do appreciate you meeting us.'

Sis saw that we weren't going to be put off.

266

She had one last go. 'This won't help Mother.'

'I'm sure that knowing the truth will help her and you,' and I faced her down. 'Before I forget, did you discover the source of payment to Urquhart?'

Surprisingly, Sis rummaged in her handbag and produced a piece of paper. 'I could get into a lot of trouble for this,' she said.

'The money comes from a bank account in London, but the source is an overseas account operated by the "United Umbrella Holdings", a trust fund set up in Barbados.'

'Wow,' and I saw Jess sit up, her mind no doubt thinking of that strange photo from AGL's hut. Could there be a connection? There had to be.

'The trust fund was set up in the early nineties. I can see that my information means something to you.'

'It could, might be important. Certainly a strange source of income for a policeman. Thanks, Debbie.'

Sis searched back in her handbag and produced her car keys. 'Take care, Finn,' she said, and for a second I felt a connection and responded with a smile.

She gave me directions to her car and as we got up she hugged me, nothing too powerful, but I appreciated it and responded, pecking her on the cheek. I handed her my spare key for the Focus.

I went to the nearby Argos store and purchased a new phone, adding the cost to my credit card. I found Sis's car parked nearby and drove it down close to the banks of the River Nith, where my car was, but parked the car up a side street. Jess and I collected our stuff from my car and we took a circuitous route back to Sis's Nissan Qashqai. It would give the CCTV operators more work to determine where we had gone. We still had our phones and I switched mine on for a final check and saw that I had missed two calls, both having left messages. I didn't recognise the first number and clicked play. It was a message from Mrs Shields. 'Just to let you know that shortly after you left I had two visitors, like the ones I told you about last night. They were looking for you – "very urgent", they said. I didn't like them and told them nothing. Good luck,' and the message ended.

I knew who the second message was from. 'Finnbar,' exclaimed Mother, almost shouting, being slightly deaf, she always bellowed. 'Stop this nonsense now. I have had people at my door asking about you. I am sure if you return they will treat you nicely.'

'Naive as always, self-centred,' I said to Jess.

I checked my phone again to get Rougvie's address, which he had given me before he left.

'Has Rougvie got all the photos?' I asked, and Jess muttered, 'Up to date and I've transferred the photos to the new phone.'

'They're closing in, whoever they are. No going back, eh Jess?' We drove west out of Dumfries, crossing the bridge over the River Nith and Jess threw our old phones into the river as we did.

48

'What's our next move?' Jess asked, as we drove west reaching the outskirts of Dumfries, deliberately avoiding the A75 and taking a road that led to Dalbeattie, the small town that I had visited the previous week. How things had changed since then, I mused.

'I was wondering about a visit to the farm that Mrs Shields mentioned and to Rougvie's house. His nerdy brother can do some more research for us. I hope he can help us find out more about the United Umbrella Company and also Adrian Shaw.'

'I thought a visit to my mother might also be useful. She has a box of old photos, they might include one of our elusive Dr Shaw. Both my parents were very sociable, lots of party photos,' she added wistfully.

'Agreed. The farm is nearest and I'll try and use back roads where possible, as I'm sure that the police use a network of roadside cameras to follow suspect vehicles.'

Jess grimaced. 'It's so unreal.'

We reached the outskirts of Dalbeattie in silence and once through the town I took a road which led to Haugh of Urr. Through that small village we would have to cross the A75 but hopefully our transit would not be recorded.

'Your sister is very unfriendly,' Jess suddenly stated, as we headed north towards Ayrshire.

'Nothing unusual in that, a bit of a cold fish. The age difference doesn't help, we never really connected but at least she was useful in finding the source of Urquhart's funding. Were you thinking of that strange picture with all the men? I didn't notice any women holding umbrellas pointing towards the photographer.'

'Must be some strange society, but it seems to have lots of money...'

'...and power,' I added. 'Enough power to buy senior policemen, to squash the truth. Jess,' I replied, turning towards her to reinforce my feeling, 'we are starting to unravel their secrets.'

With the use of the satnav in my sister's car we navigated, as far as possible, along minor roads, eventually reaching Ayrshire. High Skares farm was near Ochiltree and we found the farm on a low hill, just outside the village, a farmyard with a whitewashed stone cottage side- on to the road, the entrance facing into the yard with a rusting metal barn opposite and outhouses on the other sides, surrounded with fields populated by cows. On another hill in the distance I could see the village of Ochiltree. This was land once much scarred by coal mining but was now slowly being reclaimed.

I continued past the farm, noticing a plaque with the farm name bolted to the side of the house, rust stains spreading down the whitewashed stonework from the screws that held the sign in place and underneath the name of the farm on the same plaque was 'Finneston', which was Julia's second name. Both of us studied the layout, looking for signs of life. I noticed a porch with washing hanging from a pulley to dry and outside some kids' bikes abandoned. Importantly, the door to the porch was open, so someone was in.

'Something doesn't make sense,' I said. 'If Julia's surname is Finneston and she married here then the name would probably be her husband's name.'

'Julia's family must own the farm.'

'That doesn't help us to work out who the father of the child is.'

We both thought for a minute, puzzled.

'We won't get answers if we don't talk,' I stated. 'I'm not sure how to even begin to broach the subject with whoever is in there.'

'We're here now. No time like the present. We'll think of something.'

I turned the car into the farmyard and parked next to an outhouse. I heard a dog barking and as we got out I saw movement in the house and a woman, probably in her thirties, wearing jeans and a loose-fitting red top appeared at the door of the house and came out through the porch, accompanied by a white and tan Jack Russell terrier. She seemed friendly and welcoming, smiling as she approached us, wiping her hands on a towel. The dog was also friendly, its tail wagging as it sniffed us.

She held up her hands. 'I was kneading bread,' she explained, dough still clinging to her fingernails.

'Hi,' I said, trying to be bright and breezy, 'we're doing a bit of family research and we wondered if you could help us.'

She looked puzzled, but the smile didn't leave her face.

'If I can.'

'I'm Finn and this is Jess. Our fathers worked together along with a colleague called Adrian Shaw.'

The reaction was immediate, she breathed in sharply, audibly, and crossed her arms, the smile vanishing.

'My husband will not want to talk to you about him and I

271

don't know anything,' but she said that too quickly. She knew more than she was letting on.

'It is really important to us,' Jess said, 'our fathers were murdered and our findings suggest that Dr Shaw could help us understand what happened.'

'My husband won't talk about him.'

'But could you help us?' pleaded Jess.

'Any help would be appreciated,' I added.

She was very reluctant, too polite to say no, I felt.

'Could we talk inside?' The woman was not convinced. 'Sorry, I don't know your name,' and Jess appeared anguished, pleading for help.

'Vicki.'

'Vicki, we would appreciate your help, really appreciate it.' Jess was no longer the shy young girl, now she was nuanced, convincing, without the attitude I had encountered when I first met her.

I stepped forward in the direction of the house, the teacher trick of trying to encourage a recalcitrant pupil to follow, and then paused trying to encourage her as she stood still, my effort failing. Vicki still appeared uncertain and Jess added, 'We'll be away in a few minutes, before your husband returns.'

'John won't be happy and the kids are due back any minute from school. They'll be dropped off by taxi.'

'It's your husband's farm, isn't it?' Jess probed.

'Off course,' and Vicki appeared surprised by the question.

'Julia was John's sister?' I asked, and Vicki nodded and when she saw our reaction as we worked out the relationship, she relaxed.

'Come in,' she said, and we followed her inside, 'excuse the mess,' and she washed her hands, dried them and then lifted some clothes from the back of a wooden chair and invited us to sit down around a kitchen table, already set for a meal. I counted five place settings, so maybe three kids. The dough she had been kneading was in a large plastic bowl and she covered the bowl with a damp tea towel, leaving the dough to rise. To one side was a kitchen range, a pot boiling, steam rising from it – a traditional farm cottage with low, exposed roof beams.

'Where is Julia now?' I asked.

Vicki looked startled. 'Did you not know?'

It was my turn to appear puzzled. 'No.'

'She's dead, killed in a car accident, ten years ago.'

'That's terrible,' exclaimed Jess, looking genuinely shocked.

'A car was going too fast trying to overtake her on the road to Ayr and forced her off the road, and her car crashed into a tree. The driver didn't stop. Tim was okay, he was in the child seat, which saved him, but poor Julia was killed outright.'

'I understand why your husband finds it hard to talk about it.'

Vicki looked quickly at each of us, her expression hard to decipher. I still didn't think that we had the full story.

'Julia was staying here with her brother?' I enquired.

The worried expression had returned, uncertainty written again in her face.

'Was John helping out his sister in the circumstances?' I asked, trying to be diplomatic.

'Julia's parents would not accept her pregnancy, didn't approve. Too old-fashioned to accept a child outside of wedlock. John and Julia were very close and John had done well. Farming is his great love and he had managed to get a tenancy of High Skares, so he was able to care for Julia and she helped out around the farm,' a satisfied smile emerged on her face as she talked of John's accomplishments.

'John has done very well, especially in helping his sister but

273

I am so sorry about Julia's accident,' I said, but I was stumped, not sure how to raise the question of the father – was it Adrian Shaw?

'Julia left her work at Eastriggs very suddenly,' stated Jess, 'was that because of the pregnancy? We have heard all sorts of rumours, some quite distressing to us.'

'Only John knows what took place, but he won't talk about it. I'm not even sure of the details.'

Outside I heard another vehicle drive into the farmyard and seconds later, doors being slammed. Vicki looked up. 'That's the kids,' she said, her expression telling us it was time to go.

Two young boys entered the kitchen, one flinging his arms around his mum and hugging her and the other, older boy, hanging back shy in front of the strangers. By my calculation someone was missing as neither of the boys seemed old enough to have been involved in the car accident. Vicki seemed reluctant to introduce us and I edged towards the door as Vicki asked the boys, 'Where is Tim?'

'Outside, Mum, he knows that there are strangers here.'

'We'll go,' I said. 'Thanks for your help,' and Jess edged towards the door. We left the kitchen and went out through the porch looking for Tim, the taxi having driven away. I saw him lurking at the door of a barn. Ten or eleven I reckoned, the right age, fair curly hair. The Jack Russell ran past us wagging its tail vigorously, barking and headed towards the boy, jumping up on him, licking him. The boy knelt down and hugged the dog.

'Tim,' I said, and the boy looked up but quickly turned his head away, but I briefly saw his large staring eyes.

'Tim,' shouted Vicki, 'come in now, please.'

The boy ignored her, hugging the dog, letting the dog continue to lick his face.

While we stood another vehicle drove into the farmyard,

a battered pickup with a young calf tethered in the back and parked inside one of the barns beside some straw bales. A man emerged quickly from it, looking around, acknowledging us with a quizzical expression.

'You must be John,' I exclaimed, holding out my hand towards him. He was stocky, a crop of blonde hair, unshaven, wearing dirty blue overalls and mud-splattered Wellington boots.

'Who are you?' he asked warily, not shaking my hand.

I decided to be upfront, test what he knew. 'I'm Finn McAdam and this is Jess Hamilton.' In the background I saw Vicki ushering Tim quickly inside.

After a moment there was a dawning recognition.

'I don't want to talk with you, leave,' he demanded.

'We're very upset to learn about Julia but our fathers were murdered and we are just seeking the truth.'

'Your fathers did nothing to help Julia and I heard rumours...'

I cut him off. 'They're dead, so leave them out of this. Adrian Shaw got Julia in trouble, didn't he?'

His face darkened, eyes narrowed. 'Don't mention his name.'

'I'm right, your expression tells me that.'

He didn't speak for a moment, but the inner turmoil, the tension, was evident on his face, as he pondered how to react. One thing for certain, he was extremely uncomfortable.

'Get out. Get off my farm. You are not welcome here,' he stated angrily, waving his arms towards us, any indecision about a course of action resolved.

'Adrian Shaw is Tim's father,' Jess declared, and John's hands balled into fists. 'We are really sorry about what happened to Julia but it wasn't anything our dads did,' said Jess, 'but we're also suffering, our fathers' reputation destroyed to cover up what Shaw did. There needs to be justice.'

275

'Julia was a lovely person, maybe innocent, but vibrant and a joy to be around. We were very close. She was taken advantage of and should have stopped the baby, but that wasn't her nature. Her life was ruined.'

'I'm sorry,' I replied, 'all the more reason to seek justice.'

'It's too late for Julia to get justice. They couldn't even find the person who drove her off the road.'

'I'm sorry,' I said again. I saw Vicki looking anxiously from the door of the porch, wringing her hands. 'We have brought back painful memories, sorry.' Further words failed me, so I turned to Jess and we headed back to our car.

'If you ever find the bastard let me know,' shouted John, 'but you probably won't because I've searched and he's disappeared. The coward is hiding, though the men who visited me said he was dead, but they were lying.'

As we drove off I saw Vicki putting her arms around her husband, his head was lowered but he glanced up as we left, biting his lip, attempting to stifle his emotions.

The consequences of what took place in the Devil's Cauldron continued to exert a harsh price in relationships, lives destroyed, people murdered and yet those who caused the damage continued to escape justice. There had to be a reckoning, such carnage could not go unpunished. But then the reality sank in – how? We were discovering more, but everything just became more complicated.

49

'I doubt my mother can help,' Jess said, 'but let's try there next. I remember a box of photos on the top of a wardrobe in her bedroom. Mum never looked at them but she wouldn't throw them out. Maybe Mum can identify Shaw in one of the photos, he knew both our fathers as a student, and at least we would know what the bastard looked like.' She stopped speaking and looked at me, puzzled at my reaction. 'Why are you smiling?'

'Because unlike the woman I first met about a week ago you don't often swear these days, although probably with what we've been through you have more reason.'

Jess thought about what I said. 'I have changed, even in a week, what we're discovering is changing me. I care about something, I want to know answers, then I can get on with my life. I don't have to let the anger I feel eat away at me.'

'What we've done has helped me also, made me realise that it's not my fault what happened that night. The possibility of finding answers motivates me. I just think that we're missing something important but I don't know what.'

I used the satnav to guide me to Jess's mum's house. She lived in Paisley near Glasgow Airport, an area I didn't know. We drove into the centre of Paisley, past old mills and Paisley Abbey and out until we reached Arkleston Road and found her house in a side road. Jess's mum lived in a brick built bungalow with a red-tiled roof. We pulled into the driveway and stopped.

'I don't know how I will find Mum. She can't move on and sometimes drinks to ease her sadness.'

Jess fumbled in her bag and found a key.

'You call the shots. I wouldn't want to stay at my mother's for long,' something else we agreed on.

As we approached the front door, I could see through the frosted glass a figure in the hall.

'That doesn't look like your mother, more like a man's profile.'

Jess turned the handle. 'It's unlocked,' and she pushed in.

A man was standing in the hall and looked surprised as the door opened.

'Jess,' he said, 'good to see you. Your mum's okay but I was just about to phone the police.'

'Why Sean?'

'She's been burgled while she was out. Quite shaken.'

He was elderly, balding, wearing brown corduroy trousers and a checked shirt.

'This is Finn, a friend,' Jess stated. Sean acknowledged me. 'Sean is our neighbour. Did she call you?'

'Yes, very upset, didn't want to stay in the house. She found a window at the back had been forced open.'

'Where is she?' Sean motioned with his head towards the back of the house.

Jess shouted on her mum and proceeded into the kitchen. As the door was opened I saw Jess's mum sitting at the kitchen table, a glass in front of her, a sherry bottle beside her. She was startled by Jess's sudden appearance, quickly moving her body to hide the sherry bottle.

'Oh Jess, nice to see you,' she said.

'Mum, that won't help,' Jess said, pointing to the bottle. 'What's happened?'

'Someone broke in whilst I was out shopping.'

'Not too much damage,' said Sean, 'just a bit of a mess in the lounge and her bedroom.'

Immediately Jess and I exchanged looks, neither of us thinking that this was a coincidence. While Jess sat down with her mum, gently pushing the glass away from her, I went into the lounge. There was a sideboard with cupboards at each end and three drawers in the middle. All the drawers had been rifled, contents scattered over the floor. The end compartments seemed to contain only bottles of various drinks and glasses and had been left untouched. Not amateurs, who would have probably gone for the drink.

I then went across the hall and opened a door which led into her mum's bedroom. There was a chest of drawers with a mirror fitted on top, various perfume bottles and medicines on the surface. The drawers had been pulled out. Old cases had also been hauled from under the bed and prised open but they seemed to contain only clothes. On the far wall was a wardrobe, the doors left ajar, clothes on hangers roughly pushed aside, but I immediately looked at the top. Nothing was there, where I hoped to see a box of photos. I stood on a chair beside the wardrobe and checked the top. There was a layer of dust, but I could see the outline of where a box had been. Glancing around the room I didn't see any box. It had gone. This was no random burglary, the intruders knew what they were looking for.

Sean watched me, perplexed. 'Not much of this around here. I'll double-check my locks tonight.'

'If they want to get in, they will,' I replied, and then I saw concern on his face, quickly adding, 'I'm sure that they've gone, you'll be safe.'

Jess was talking to her mum, trying to cheer her up, as I re-entered the kitchen, shaking my head as she glanced up.

'Mum, I'll put the kettle on and make a cup of tea.'

She looked up at her daughter, a sad expression on her face. 'I still miss him, you know, especially at times like this.'

Jess busied herself filling the kettle. 'Mum, I wanted to show Finn photos of the family, me as a young girl, where are they?' I doubted that, hearing my name, Jess's mum would make a link to my family and there was no flicker of recognition and she only briefly looked in my direction.

'On top of the wardrobe, dear.'

I shook my head. 'Too late,' I muttered.

There was a cough behind me and I turned to see Sean standing awkwardly.

'Sorry,' he apologised for coughing, 'it's the mould in the air.' I noticed black mould was growing on the kitchen wall beside the window, and I was already aware that there was a dank smell in the house.

'Sean, thanks for all your help, we'll tidy things up.' I saw Sean to the door and Jess joined me, also thanking him.

'If we involve the police they'll know where we are,' Jess muttered as we shut the door.

'Not a good idea. I'll try and repair the window.'

The handle that opened the window was hanging loose and I did what I could to jam it. She could get a joiner in later, but it would hold.

I made myself coffee and went through to the lounge whilst mother and daughter talked. There were no photos in the room, apart from one of Jess at primary school.

I was watching a documentary on the television when Jess came through sometime later.

'She doesn't remember much. There could have been a Dr

280

Shaw at the house when they lived near Annan. However, I wouldn't trust any recollections.'

'They must know that we're onto Shaw and were ensuring that there is no evidence of him. I imagine if Rich does a search then nothing will show up about him. They are trying to frighten us, but how would they know that we were coming here? I don't think that we should stay.'

'I've told Mum that we have to go.'

'For the best, I think. Will she be okay?'

'She might start drinking after we go, but there is nothing we can do, we must move on.'

'You are a nice boy,' said Jess's mum, standing at the door to say goodbye, finally acknowledging me, 'hopefully, I'll see you again.' Jess pecked her on her cheek as she left.

I smiled. 'Nice to meet you,' and we headed to the car.

50

As I reversed the car out of the driveway, I looked up and down the road, not knowing what I would do if I saw people lurking in a car ready to tail us. Jess was doing the same. Paranoia was not far away. We reached the centre of Paisley without noticing anyone behind us and I headed south towards Kilwinning where Rougvie lived.

Jess was very quiet and I left her to reflect on her mum. Suddenly she sneezed, not once but three times.

'I always react like that when I visit Mum's house, the mould is getting worse,' she said by way of explanation and she opened the glovebox searching for a paper tissue. Glad to find a packet she extracted a tissue and blew her nose. 'Another reason not to visit,' she stated and I saw her go to shut the glovebox but she stopped and pulled out a small black plastic box with a green LED light shining.

'What's this,' she exclaimed, turning it over. 'It says Tracker GPS.'

'It's a tracker, so they can follow us,' and looking at it again, 'it seems fairly basic. Google the name.'

Jess got out our phone and entered the details. 'It is a tracker, pretty cheap, only a few pounds.'

I thought about it for a few seconds. 'Probably Paul checking on his wife's whereabouts. I'm sure security services would use something more sophisticated.' It seems that neither Paul nor Sis trusted the other. I knew that Paul had a wandering eye, but I wondered what Sis was getting up to.

'But Paul has been asked to keep an eye open for us and the gadget appears to be working, so he could be using it to trace where we are and he'll let his superiors know and they can pass it on. Get him some much-needed brownie points. Are you on the voter's roll at your mum's address?' I asked suddenly, changing tack.

'Yes, Mum insisted, not that I believe in voting.'

'But a quick check and they would guess where we were going when they saw the car heading towards Paisley.'

We were approaching a garage and I indicated and pulled over.

'We need fuel,' I explained and I drew up beside a pump. As I filled the tank a truck drew up to use the pump on the other side, belonging to a gardening firm, the back had high wire sides and was filled with cut-up branches and other garden refuse. I finished filling the tank and leant into the car, 'Give me the gadget,' I said, and Jess handed it over. I took it and as I went to pay I tossed the gadget in among the garden refuse.

As I returned to the car, I added, 'As long as he is not going in the same direction that should confuse them.'

• • •

Rougvie's house was on the outskirts of Kilwinning, a small town in North Ayrshire, south of Paisley, which we approached from the north, the tower of the local Abbey prominent and the island of Arran on the horizon with the sun edging down towards the ragged mountain tops on the island, the sea between the mainland and the island glowing orange. Probably the houses had once belonged to a local estate, quite separate from a more recent housing estate a few hundred yards away, and were located down a side road as you entered the town. There was a wood behind the houses and a field with cows to the front. I recognised Rougvie's Jeep parked at the far end of the short row of houses. The trees masked more of the sun, the house sitting in shade.

We had phoned ahead and got a lukewarm welcome from Rougvie, maybe not surprisingly, but I had assured him that we would be discreet. He was waiting at the entrance to the driveway wearing heavy-duty black work trousers and a sweatshirt. His beard had been trimmed, his hair not so tousled, neatly combed, quite unlike the person we had met only days ago.

'What took place at the campsite, remains there,' I reassured him, as I got out the car, 'we just need to talk with your brother, ask him to do some searches.' Rougvie appeared embarrassed, eyes down, not meeting our gaze.

'He means me,' a voice proclaimed from the side of the house where a figure was lurking in the shade behind a green plastic coal bunker. 'I'm Rich, Rougvie's son,' and he let the meaning of his words sink in as I saw him eye up Jess. 'I've heard a lot about you two. Dad told me,' and he smirked at his dad, who shuffled his feet uncomfortably. Rich was in his late teens, about Jess's age, his appearance striking, with his hair gelled into a spike and dyed purple, his arms tattooed with the names of heavy metal bands, his tee shirt brandishing the dates of some band's tour with chains dangling from his belt and ripped jeans.

'I thought you would have more trust in an older person. Just a small distortion,' Rougvie explained.

'Be sure your sins will find you out,' Rich stated, almost gloating. My first impressions were that Rich had some hold over his father, and my confidence in his ability to help us rapidly faded, like the setting sun. I suspect that Jess felt the same.

'Come in,' said Rougvie, still uncomfortable, hands fumbling with the gate latch. 'Cathy has prepared some food for you. You must be tired.' We followed him into the house and were greeted at the door by Cathy, a small woman, elflike, smiling as she greeted us, wearing a pinafore with a company name emblazoned on it. She appeared nervous, restless. Rich disappeared up the stairs leaving us, and we were shown to a table in the kitchen where cutlery had been already set.

'Rougvie and Rich have already eaten but I kept some back for yourselves,' and plates of stew were quickly placed in front of us. My stomach was rumbling and I was soon enjoying the food, and Cathy relaxed, noting our appreciation.

We finished and Rougvie took us through to a lounge which faced onto the field opposite, the head of a cow appearing as it stretched for some grass that had grown up through the hedge. The walls of the room were painted deep red, there was a three-piece suite, a low bookcase and a log burner, which was unlit, logs stacked up beside it. In two corners large speakers were perched on corner shelves, wires leading to an old-fashioned music centre, with a rack of LPs beside it.

As we sat down Cathy appeared at the door pulling on an anorak. 'Nice to have met you,' she said, 'I'm going out to work, you may be gone by the time I return, but Rougvie will show you where you can sleep,' and with that she left.

'Cathy works night shifts at a local care home,' Rougvie explained, but he seemed relieved that his wife had gone.

'Rougvie, thanks for your help,' I started, just as Rich entered the room and sat down on the floor just beside the music centre.

'It's okay,' Rougvie explained, 'Rich knows what happened at the campsite, 'and his son smirked, which I could see Jess didn't like, not making eye contact with him.

Quickly I updated Rougvie and Rich with Jess's help.

'Sounds like a real conspiracy,' Rich said, his eyes widening. 'Wild sex,' and he seemed to relish using both words, observing their impact, especially on Jess, 'and the United Umbrella Company.'

Rougvie cautioned him. 'This is real, people's lives have been destroyed by these events.'

He didn't add that ours were also still at risk but he could have, but Rich was not intimidated.

'You're getting chased around the country by government agents working for a secretive organisation known as the United Umbrella Company. Wow. This is good. Should be fun.'

'We need your help, Rich,' Jess said. 'Can you help us find out more about the United Umbrella Company, also find out what you can about Dr Adrian Shaw.'

'Okay, I'll start now. Come upstairs, Jess, and I'll show you my computers, you'll be impressed.'

Jess appeared reluctant, not surprisingly, but got up and followed Rich out of the room. Rougvie took out his phone and switched it off, placing it on the floor.

'Don't worry, Finn, it's mainly teenage angst but he does know his stuff. So how are you doing? You've been through a lot since I left.'

'Jess and I were talking about this earlier, we've raised our game, a chance to right wrongs, maybe get justice. Jess has been wonderful, although I think that we've helped each other. She is very different now from the girl I met at the campsite.'

'You seem closer, working like a team.'

'Yes, we are and I'm very fond of her. Probably uniquely, I

286

can understand her torment, but that's it though, once this is over we'll go our separate ways and I'll get back to Gillian. I love Gillian and want my marriage to work.'

We sat in the lounge as the light faded. Rougvie got up and brought in a candle on an old saucer and placed it on the top of the log burner and lit it. Its flickering flame was mesmerising and I realised how tired I was, my eyes drooping, yearning for sleep, but I tried to stay alert listening for Jess returning, concerned that she was alright. Rougvie appeared relaxed, not concerned at the length of time that they were upstairs, which helped me.

I woke with a start as I heard them return, looking outside it was pitch black and I was alone in the room. I heard Rougvie in the kitchen switching on the kettle.

'This is exciting,' Rich proclaimed, while Jess was less effusive and said nothing. Rich switched on a lamp and sat down on the floor, chairs didn't seem his thing, probably too conventional. The light from the lamp shone on him and he was enjoying the limelight. I looked at both of them expectantly.

'Wait until he comes back,' Rich said, his tone no less patronising than earlier about his father. Rougvie's head appeared at the door. 'Coffee?' and I gratefully accepted.

'We've found a number of scientific papers co-authored by Shaw and a Prof. Rankin, including a few with your father also listed,' and he nodded towards me. 'Chemistry isn't my subject but they all seem very specialised, lots of big words that I couldn't pronounce.'

'But none after the project at Eastriggs began,' Jess added, ignoring Rich.

I didn't imagine that the government would want their work at Eastriggs made public. Prof. Rankin must know Shaw, which was another line of enquiry, I realised, we could follow up.

'Any pictures or personal information?'

'No pictures and no personal information. No record that he existed in the last twelve years. People can now apply for information about themselves to be removed from the Internet.'

'I half expected that.'

'How about the United Umbrella Company?'

Rich's eyes gleamed in the light from the lamp and he leant forward, pausing for effect.

'I'll need to hack into the bank which keeps their funds and that will be very difficult, but they do own property in the UK.' I waited, letting Rich enjoy the moment.

'They part-own several hotels and conference centres, which appears to be their thing. Mainly south of England, but one in Scotland. Peter's Place, it is called, originally built in the 1930s, located near Banchory, in the Forest of Birse. It is close to Peter's Hill, hence the name,' his eyes blank as he recited the information.

'Any link to Murdoch W. Birse?'

'Just coincidence. There are lots of places called Birse around there. I told you that already.' So he had, but he might have uncovered some new information.

'Peter's Place is a grand house, three storeys high, rooms opening out onto a landing at each level, overlooking a central hall, converted by the partnership which includes the United Umbrella Company, about fifteen years ago. Specialises in weddings, several coming up in the next few days as it happens.'

'Well done,' and I smiled warmly at Rich.

I glanced at Jess. 'We need to speak with Prof. Rankin, he was a friend of my father's and obviously knows Shaw. I've got his address at home. He's a great guy, full of energy, never stops. We visited him on holiday once in Banchory. He has a chalet there by the banks of the River Dee, so he knows the Banchory area, which could be a bonus. Keep working, Rich, you're doing a good job.'

'You need to move fast,' he replied, 'with their resources they'll soon track you down. Keep in touch. I've shown Jess a few things,' and he gave what I thought was a creepy smile, 'that will enhance your phone,' he added, almost as an afterthought, enjoying the slight delay in completing the sentence.

'So,' Rougvie began, 'there is a link between Urquhart and the United Umbrella Company. He has been paid to keep quiet. You found out that Adrian Shaw probably made Julia pregnant. The final step is to work out why Shaw is being protected.' It was a neat summary and reflected more the Rougvie who had assisted us to take the photos and not the embarrassed guy who had greeted us earlier tonight.

'Seems like it and Prof. Rankin might be of help,' I confirmed.

The discussion had concluded, not by any conscious decision but because we were all tired.

'Cathy prepared a bed for you upstairs in our spare room,' Rougvie stated. 'Maybe you'll want a sleeping bag,' he added as an afterthought. 'I'll show you where it is. I've got work tomorrow,' and with that he stood up and pointed to the door.

'I'll get a sleeping bag and our gear from the car,' and I started towards the door, but Jess stopped me. 'I'll go,' she said, and took the key from my hand before I could object. No big issue, I suppose, so I let her. She returned a few minutes later with what we needed and we climbed the stairs. Rougvie pointed to a small room with a double bed and an old wardrobe. On the wall above the bed was a framed picture of a red squirrel holding an acorn in its claws.

'I'll use the sleeping bag,' Jess said, and unrolled it. Rich followed us upstairs before disappearing into another room, where I caught a glimpse of laptops, computer stacks and two large monitors.

'The bathroom is in there,' Rougvie stated, and he left us, going back downstairs.

'You go first, Jess,' and she left me alone in the bedroom. It was awkward getting ready for bed but eventually Jess crawled into her sleeping bag and I lay beside her under the sheets. I put the light out and there was silence. My eyes were closing, sleep overwhelming me, when I heard Jess sob. I turned over towards her.

'What's wrong,' I whispered.

'Nothing,' she replied.

'Rich didn't try anything on?' I asked.

'No, though he is creepy. He seemed to know what his father was up to, blackmailing him. I'm just tired, sometimes this is all too much. I'll be glad when it is over.'

I resisted putting a consoling arm on her though I sensed that she wouldn't have objected.

'So will I,' I answered. 'Tomorrow we go to my house, collect his address and then visit Prof. Rankin. He will know Shaw and your father.'

'Let's hope that he can help. I just want this over. Goodnight,' and there was silence again. Sleep rapidly overwhelmed me.

51

The distance from Rougvie's house to my own in Irvine was short – a few miles. I took the back roads which provided almost uninterrupted views across to Arran, where storm clouds were beginning to obscure the ragged mountain silhouette, blocked only by a few church spires and some high-rise flats in Irvine. I lived in a seventies housing estate, built to provide new homes for people from Glasgow among others, just north of Dreghorn, a former mining village and close to the school I taught in. My street was lined, on both sides, with terrace houses with access lanes to the rear. The house was modest, Stuart and Sheila had wanted us to buy something bigger but we felt that the house was appropriate for our needs and declined their offer of a larger place. Gillian and I wanted to make our own way, be independent.

The front door opened directly onto a fairly small living space, with the kitchen to the rear and with stairs leading up to a landing which overlooked the living space and contained a master bedroom, a smaller bedroom and a bathroom. We were happy, or had been.

After last night Jess had been quiet. I understood her tears of frustration and shared her wariness of Rich, who lacked maturity and was too full of himself. However, on him we depended whether we liked it or not.

I parked some distance from the house and Jess, wrapping herself in an anorak and keeping her head down, walked along my street. Following my directions she returned via the access lane at the rear and flopped down on the seat beside me.

'All very quiet, no suspicious people sitting in cars waiting for us, so I think that it is safe. The only person I saw was one of your immediate neighbours peering out of her window.'

'That's probably Margaret, typical, always wanting to know what's going on. Okay, here's the key, you go in and let me in the back door.' Minutes later the back door was opened and I slipped in. It was strange being back in the house which had an air of not being lived in. I nipped upstairs aware of a slight muskiness that reminded me of Gillian's perfume but it wasn't strong. She did sometimes return to collect things but I usually arranged to be out. I went into the small bedroom and went to the bookcase. Dad's PhD thesis was there and I pulled it from the shelf and opened it. Inside was the business card that Prof. Rankin had given me years ago. He lived near Callander, in the Trossachs, a popular area with tourists to the north of Glasgow. I slipped it in my back pocket and got ready to leave.

Ever cautious I pulled back the net curtain in the bedroom and looked out to check no one was around only to see Gillian's car. Of course Jess would never have recognised it. Gillian had to be visiting Margaret, who she was quite friendly with. I let the net curtain fall back in place and quickly headed downstairs.

'Gillian is next door,' I said to Jess, who was sitting on the couch. 'I don't want to meet her at the moment.' Jess was startled and immediately jumped up.

'I'll just visit a place and then we can go,' and she headed upstairs quickly. I waited now quite anxious, enough

292

complications in my life. Jess was only away a minute when I was aware of a fleeting shadow across the window and my heart sank as a key was inserted in the door and Gillian pushed the door open.

She had cut her brown hair shorter, pageboy style, and I briefly felt hurt that she had not consulted me, but then reality sank in. Her face was serious, her lovely smile vanished and I knew who was responsible. Guilt kicked in. A silver cross on a chain hung over her blue sweater, moving slightly as she stepped into the living area, her jeans as figure-hugging as I remembered. I closed my eyes, probably trying to avoid the inevitable confrontation.

'I'm so pleased to see you,' I said, and I meant it, just not now. Before she could reply I heard the toilet flushing and Gillian's gaze broke instantly, her eyes averted, as a second later a door shut and without looking up I knew that Jess was standing on the landing taking in the scene. I went forward and hugged her, but her body was stiff, unresponsive and I removed my arms quickly.

'So this is Jess,' she said in a low voice, not angry, but trying to conceal her emotion. 'Just as Mum and Dad described her. You are getting around.'

I couldn't reply, lost for words, any response would sound faltering, inadequate, hollow. I heard Jess coming down the stairs and not wanting to turn around, I waited for her to reach us, as Gillian pushed the still open door shut behind her.

'I didn't expect another girl, Finn. This doesn't seem to be fighting for justice, redeeming your father's name, this is...' and she paused, '...moving on.' I saw the tremble in her bottom lip, the eyes blinking and I was lost. This was not what I wanted.

It was Jess who spoke up, softly but her voice carried much-needed conviction. 'This is not what it seems,' and Gillian cocked her head slightly to one side, her eyes widening, 'Finn and I are not in a relationship, we are helping each other to resolve a burning issue in both our lives and we are making a lot of progress, just a little more time and we will breathe freely and Finn will return to you. I know he desperately wants to.'

Well said, Jess, but would she convince Gillian.

'I did meet your parents and they seemed nice people. I hoped that I hadn't hurt them. You are a lucky person, Gillian, to have Finn. Many a woman would want him, but he hasn't been anything but loyal to you and talks about you all the time.' Not strictly true for obvious reasons but I didn't want to upset Jess and add further complications. 'But,' she continued, 'he needs and wants you, believe me.'

'I wish I could, but the burning issue, as you describe it, has driven us apart and he's disappeared only to return with a new woman.'

'Gillian,' I pleaded, 'give me ten minutes to explain what we have been doing, what we have discovered, please,' and I pointed towards the sofa. Gillian didn't move but Jess intervened again. 'I'm going back to the car to leave you two alone. You need to talk and please, please believe him, Gillian,' and without waiting for a response she headed out the back door.

'Please sit,' I urged, when I heard the door shut and what followed was a fumbling attempt to explain what I had done, how I had met Jess and what we had discovered. Gillian listened, her expression difficult to decipher. I knew what I said sounded incredible.

'I can't promise you that we will succeed but you need to know why we have done it.'

'In case you end up in jail.'

'Possibly, but Dad was innocent. In modern parlance I have probably been suffering from post-traumatic stress disorder and I should have sought help before. I will when it is over, if you think that I need it. Promise.' Gillian had listened carefully, giving me more eye contact as I told my story. She took a pink hankie from her pocket and blew her nose, trying to hide the tears that were gathering. I blinked myself and stretched forward, but Gillian pulled back.

'Not now,' and she started to cry.

'I love you,' I said, 'can't wait for this to be over, and from the bottom of my heart I am sorry for what I have put you and your family through. I need your love and support more than ever.'

Gillian no longer attempted to hide her tears and we hugged each other, giving us a moment to appreciate what we were in danger of losing.

'I am so sorry,' I kept repeating, as we clung together on the sofa, stirring memories of past romantic moments. Minutes passed and then Gillian's body stiffened and she pulled back searching my face, her gaze intense.

'You better go,' she said, 'I trust you, but promise me you will come back.' We both stood up as one, synchronicity returning to our relationship, even if only briefly, we were a couple again, provisionally.

'Go before they find you, and take care of Jess. I can see that she is very fond of you, don't hurt her.'

'I have been aware of her behaviour changing towards me, but I have been totally loyal, in thought and deed, always will be,' and Gillian dipped her head, no longer able to meet my gaze.

'Go,' she repeated, as there was a knock at the door.

'It's Margaret,' said Gillian, as she recognised the outline of her neighbour, 'nosing about,' she added.

With a last lingering look, I turned away and quickly reached the back door. This was now even more personal, no longer did events just mess up my past and disrupt the present, but they could destroy my future. I had to succeed. I raced along the lane back to the car. Jess was waiting and as I got in, she said, 'So where does Prof. Rankin live?' Now with her it was business, no other issues clouded the situation. I was more determined than ever, switching on the wiper blades as the storm front reached Irvine.

52

By now we had to assume that they, whoever 'they' were, knew that we were driving Sis's car, so was there any point in taking back roads and avoiding motorways? Probably not, but we took a less direct route in the hope that it did and eventually we stopped for coffee in a small village called Buchlyvie. The coffee was drunk in silence as had been most of the journey, Jess almost mute, not unfriendly, just not wanting to talk. At least we knew where we stood with each other, and I was delighted that Gillian had supported me. Once this was over, whatever that meant, I would make every effort to rebuild our relationship.

We took a twisting road which wound past the Lake of Monteith, aware that ahead was the southern edge of the Trossachs and the Highlands, high hills which stretched for miles, dominating the horizon. Fortunately, our destination was closer and we would only skirt the edge of them. The journey continued through moorland, with several wooded areas and then we approached Callander, the hulking mass of Ben Ledi towering over the town, passing the local secondary school, before we crossed a narrow bridge over the River Teith. We turned south through the long main street, lined with tourist and outdoor shops selling gear for hill-walkers, before reaching the housing estate where Prof. Rankin lived, according to his business card. He had retired many years previously but like many academics had continued with research projects that interested him, funding never an issue for someone with his reputation.

His house was at the end of a short cul-de-sac, a roughcast detached villa showing signs of age, patches of moss staining the roof, the front garden separated from its neighbours by beech hedges, with several rose bushes in a circular plot in the centre of the small lawn. A short driveway led to a garage with a metal door, which flipped up for access. It was open, the garage filled with cardboard boxes. Beside the garage was a faded yellow Volkswagen Beetle, with floral decals. Stuck in the lawn was the explanation for the boxes – a sign for an estate agent with a sold sticker plastered over it.

Jess closed her eyes, rubbing her forehead, a gesture of despair. I felt similar, were we too late?

I got out and went up to the door, ringing the bell once, then again. Inside I heard movement and shuffling as someone reached the door. As the door opened, with much relief, I saw the diminutive figure of Prof. Rankin, just over five feet, small in stature, high in personality. His frizzy hair was now more white than red, also more sparse, the jowls heavier, but the smile just as bright as he recognised me.

'Come in, Finn, good to see you. You've grown a beard since I last saw you. Glad you came now, another week we would be away. To what do I owe this honour?' He looked beyond me as he gripped my arm. 'Ah, a friend,' he said, 'bring her in.'

As I waved to Jess she quickly got out the car, like me relieved and seconds later we were sitting in a lounge denuded of furniture, only a sofa remaining with bare floorboards. On the floor were several cardboard boxes, filled with books.

After introducing Jess, whose hand Prof. Rankin shook warmly, he said, 'I am so pleased to see you both, let me put the kettle on,' and he disappeared into the kitchen.

'Only mugs left,' he explained, as he returned several minutes later. He appraised us both carefully, as was his way, and then fetched a stool from the kitchen, his feet barely touching the floor when he sat on it.

'I can see so much of your father in you, Finn. He would be proud.' We spoke briefly about Mother and Sis and I updated him. He quickly sensed that I was not here to talk about them and he appeared thoughtful, his hand rubbing his chin, a gesture I had seen him give in lectures, whilst thinking of a response to a student's question, which in some cases would be angled so as not to deflate the student's confidence.

His gaze turned towards Jess and he smiled warmly. 'And who are you, young lady?'

'Dougie Hamilton's daughter,' was the succinct reply.

'Ah, interesting. Your father was another of my students, many years ago. A very good student, full of life and intellectual curiosity and a keen, no, passionate fisherman, if I recollect correctly. So this is not just a social call, welcome as that would be,' and his gaze flitted between the two of us seeking confirmation.

'I tell you what, you both appear tired and probably hungry. Jennifer has gone to visit our daughter, as we are moving closer to Zoe and her family. Age thing. Better now when you have got a choice. Anyway, I'll send out for pizza, have to be out of the cardboard box, mind you and afterwards you can tell me what is on your minds. I'll help if I can.'

'We would appreciate that very much,' and Jess added. 'Thanks, that is most kind.'

'It would be a pleasure,' and he left the room and I heard him

299

on the phone placing an order.

The pizza arrived half an hour later and was eaten quickly, followed by more coffee. Prof. Rankin cleared away the cardboard boxes and collected the mugs after offering us more, which we declined, but he sensed it was time to concentrate on the reason for our visit.

He returned and sat down on the stool again, leaning forward, his toes now just touching the floor.

'Call me Fred,' he stated.

'There's a bit of background,' I began.

'I have all the time in the world.'

I tried to explain, prompted a few times by Jess, his face looking more troubled as the tale progressed.

'My goodness, what a time you have had and what resilience you both have shown. Finn, I didn't know that you had witnessed your father being murdered, how traumatic. I did think when you were at university, the little I saw, that you were a troubled young man but didn't realise why and, Jess, you were younger, never really knowing your father but the sense of him being taken away from you and your mother's issues must have made life difficult. You have both done well.

'To more recent issues, however, and maybe there I can cast some clarity. I know, Finn, that your father met Sir Archibald, he told me, and the link was Adrian Shaw. Shaw was being sponsored by Sir Archibald, a favour for a friend, who wanted to ingratiate himself with your father and ensure that Shaw's career pathway was made easier. That's often how the upper classes work, making connections, looking out for each other.

'Shaw himself was a strange bloke, totally focused on work, obsessively so, I thought. Your father helped me put him through his PhD but Shaw had few social skills, a strange manner and was happiest working on his own. However, his credentials were

300

such that when your father was offered the Eastriggs project he certainly was the best equipped candidate with expertise in the area that was available. Sir Archibald backing him was not really necessary.

'John visited High Mossdale Lodge and he took along your father, Jess. John did not go back but Dougie was attracted by the fishing and made friends there and I suppose it suited Sir Archibald.

'When John and Dougie were killed I was heartbroken, couldn't believe it and the rumours that circulated seemed unbelievable. I too had a visit from two men planting what I believe we now call "fake news".

'Shaw disappeared after the murders, he certainly wasn't at either of your fathers' funerals. I was told that he had left the country and had been killed in a car accident.'

He saw the look on both of our faces. Another car accident.

'The story wasn't true. I saw him three years ago walking along the main street in Banchory with another man. I crossed the road to greet him but the other man ushered him away and neither would speak to me. Most strange. He looked older, his fair hair going grey, almost white. Still very curly, clamped to his head, but the eyes were the giveaway, protruding, staring, but often avoiding contact with you.'

My mind was racing – Shaw was still alive and living, possibly, near Banchory. The descriptions of Shaw and Tim were very similar, their look, their behaviour. My stomach was tightening, breathing faster. After a few seconds I managed to say, 'Your description of Shaw is also a good description of Tim, Julia's son.'

I believe that Fred had already reached that conclusion. 'You think that Shaw fathered Julia's child, born under a year after the loss of your parents. It's possible. I don't have any pictures of Shaw but the person we are describing, put it this way, is too uncannily similar.'

Fred lurched to his feet, uttering, 'Time for more coffee, helps me to think,' and he quickly went into the kitchen. 'Same as before?' he shouted, and we agreed.

'The photos, Jess, where are they?' I asked. Jess looked vague. 'Somewhere in my bag.'

'In the car? I can get them.'

'I'll get them soon, don't worry.'

Fred returned with the coffee, handing over mugs.

'I gave away photos from my university days, to the university archives. They pestered me for them, lots of group photos. Pity.

'Anyway, where was I. Oh yes, let's sum up what we know and what you need to do,' and he looked for confirmation to go ahead, modest as ever, as if his ideas were of little significance.

'Shaw is very clever, obsessive and strange. I am sure that psychiatrists would give a more detailed appraisal, pin a diagnosis on him, but we don't need their opinions. We have to deal with him regardless. Shaw would have had a bright career, lost in academia but Sir Archibald goes out of his way to get him promoted. Your father employs him for his ability and knowing John I am sure that is true. Shaw makes a co-worker pregnant and she bears him a son. But Shaw disappears after two people are murdered, not dead but,' and he paused, 'hiding is the word, I suppose, or maybe being kept out of sight. That suggests that in some way he is responsible or they would not have tried to cover it up.

'The events on the night of John and Dougie's death are not clear. Dougie contacts John and invites him to fish. Your father takes you along, Finn, leaves you in the car and you hear a gunshot. Other's arrive, most likely Sir Archibald's people and

302

eventually grab you, take you to his estate. He doesn't want you and you are taken to a lonely road and witness your father's execution.

'You know, Finn, they made one critical mistake,' and he paused again. 'They should have also killed you and there would have been no gaps in the cover-up,' and he looked at me for confirmation.

'Yes, but what could a twelve-year-old boy do to disrupt their plans?'

'Apparently, a lot. Sir Archibald wasn't ruthless enough, strange as it seems. The cover-up goes to the highest level. Police bribed, the resources of the state used to suppress the truth. Everyone warned off and fake rumours spread. Someone has contacts at the highest level and has used them ruthlessly. It has to be Julian Montgomery and I think that I can tell you why.'

We were now both sitting on the edge of the sofa, our faces, I am sure, a study.

'I saw the link immediately but wanted to be sure before I told you. The gravity of the situation merits its disclosure, although I am not in the habit of divulging confidences or spreading speculation. Forty years ago I was at a conference at Oxford University, I was a young lecturer at the time, nervously preparing to deliver a paper. I travelled down with Sophie Shaw, a postgraduate student in the Chemistry Department at the time. Very bright, very able, lovely person, attractive and charming, superlatives about her abounded. Anyway, on the first evening there was a drinks reception and she met an Economics student.'

'Julian Montgomery?'

Fred nodded, stabbing his finger in the air to underline that I had reached the correct conclusion. 'There was a massive attraction between the two of them, love and lust at first sight and they were together all night. The next morning over breakfast I saw her slipping back into our college. A few months later she abandoned her postgraduate studies. Later I heard that she had had a baby – a boy. Adrian Shaw is Julian Montgomery's son. I don't think he ever officially acknowledged him, he was already married at the time, but he did want to support him.'

We sat stunned as Fred added, 'Even twelve years ago Julian Montgomery was in government, working at the Ministry of Defence as a junior minister. He had the clout to suppress events…'

'…and the money?' Jess enquired.

'The United Umbrella Company, I would think, supplied the means and you have proof that they are paying Urquhart. No wonder they are concerned and determined to silence you. You could end Montgomery's career, even threaten the Government, who are not currently popular and have only a small majority. I would say that you need to be very careful, many people have a vested interest in ensuring that you never reveal the truth.'

'What would you do, Fred?'

'Simple. Find out if Shaw is still living near Banchory, Peter's Place might be a good place to start, and get a confession,' and he laughed, acknowledging that what he suggested was anything but easy.

'I think I know how to do that,' Jess said, interrupting us and as we both switched our attention to her, she added, 'but first I have a confession to make.'

53

Jess had the attention of both of us. Fred leant forward towards her, encouraging her to continue. I waited, curious, not sure where this was going.

'When we were at Rougvie's, Rich invited me upstairs to see his computers,' she began. 'Show off more likely. He pressed a few keys and we were listening to your conversation with Rougvie. It was wrong. I heard your declaration of love for Gillian. Understood what you said. It cleared my head.'

That helped to explain Jess's reaction last night. Maybe it was not a bad thing that she heard. However, I concentrated on what she was going to say next while Fred looked perplexed but held his silence, also assuming that there was more to come. But one thing puzzled me. 'I saw Rougvie switch off his phone.'

'Doesn't matter, switched on or off, the way the phone is set up, it still acts as a listening device and he can listen in.'

'Sneaky,' said Fred, 'but useful,' as he considered the potential of the device.

'That's why I've kept the phone away from us, because he installed the app on our phone, thought it would be useful, keep him up to date and able to alert police if we were in trouble. If I send him a text he'll record any conversations we want him to but I don't trust him, he's sleazy, and I am sure he would listen in when we don't want or need him to.'

'Like at bedtime,' and Jess agreed. 'I put the phone out in the car to stop Rich listening to us.'

'I understand,' I said, 'but the app would be, could be, very useful,' realising the potential for recording a confession. 'Fetch the phone and we will assume that there is another person present.'

'Forewarned is forearmed, Jess, thanks for your honesty,' added Fred.

Jess was gone for a few minutes before she returned clutching the phone, switching it on and bringing up the photos we took at AGL's hut. Fred got up and shut the curtains, as if it was getting dark. I felt that it was more a subconscious gesture towards privacy, but it would do nothing to prevent the technological intrusion provided by the phone.

We all moved to the sofa, Jess in the middle.

'I presume you have studied the photos before,' Fred said, as on the screen came the first photo. He took the phone, removed his glasses and scrutinised it carefully.

'Never saw the point in fishing,' he exclaimed, after some time. 'Don't know these people,' and he flicked to the next photo. He took longer but eventually shook his head and moved on to the photo of the fishing rods.

'These fishing rods are your father's, the ones you mentioned earlier?'

Jess nodded. 'I have seen similar ones, there's no doubting it.'

'Not conclusive evidence, difficult to prove anything, but possibly more than coincidence,' and he brought up the next photo.

'Your father is in the front row, Jess. I don't recognise the woman. Which one is Sir Archibald?' as if Fred didn't want to dwell on Jess's father's apparent liaison. I leant over to point him out, as Fred gasped, 'There is Adrian Shaw,' and his fingers enlarged the photo. 'Definitely.' We both peered closely. Shaw was in the back row, staring at Hamilton's woman – very curly fair hair, protruding eyes, not dissimilar to Tim, Julia's son.

'The elusive Shaw, caught at AGL's mansion, ogling someone else's woman,' I blurted out and cursed my insensitivity as I said it, but Jess ignored my crassness.

'It's true, Finn, but at least we know what he looks like, now we only have to find him.'

'Next photo,' and Fred brought it up.

'Shareholder's meeting for the United Umbrella Trust, no doubt,' as he saw the cluster of people with their protruding umbrellas. 'They seem like a bunch of rich people, bonding together, pledging loyalty to help themselves and each other. I have known groups like that forged at university, networking for their own selfish ends, and there is Julian Montgomery next to Sir Archibald.

'Now you have a motive. Sir Archibald was trying to promote Montgomery's son, helped get him a plum post and then had to cover up for him as his obsession with one of his co-workers cost two people their lives. Curse them,' and the anger was palpable as he spat out the words, 'Two excellent scientists killed to hide the truth that Montgomery's son was a troubled man. This has to be exposed,' and his finger jabbed at the screen, and then he sighed and sat back heavily in the sofa, both feet momentarily leaving the ground, an expression of anger on his face. I had never seen Fred so worked up, his calm demeanour gone, raging at the unnecessary loss of two people he valued highly and worked beside, not just colleagues but in the case of my father also a dear friend.

'I think you said that there were six photos,' he remembered, as he tried to regain his composure, and he swiped the screen to expose the last photo.

'Ah,' he said loudly, 'that's the man I saw in Banchory with Shaw,' and he enlarged the photo with his fingers. 'No doubt,' he exclaimed, as he studied the photo again. 'I wonder if they were sent to that area to hide. Murdoch W. Birse,' he repeated several times, considering the name. 'Birse is a name local to that area,' but then he added, 'I wonder what the relationship is between Shaw and Birse. My impression was that Birse was taking care of him, when I think about what I saw in the street. Shaw now needs a minder, the price of his lusts, and a family friend offers or is asked to help out. You say that the United Umbrella Trust own or part-own Peter's Place. They could easily install them at the property, it would be good cover.'

Fred had nailed it. 'So they are likely resident at Peter's Place and that must be our next destination,' I stated, turning to Jess, whose hand was at her mouth as she tried to absorb all the new information.

The phone buzzed, distracting us, a text message from Rich. Glad that progress is being made.

We all stared at each other, confirmation of Jess's fears that Rich could listen in at any time, alerted by any activity on our phone. However, we needed him to record any confessions, be on our side.

I typed a message in response: Rich, thanks for your help. You know our plans. Record any confessions and be ready to broadcast them on the web so that everyone learns the truth, newspapers, police, radio, TV, maximum circulation. Go for it, the truth must be spread.

A few seconds later several thumbs up appeared on the screen and then a further message.

Finn, do you have a smartwatch? If I'm trying to record a

message and can't hear you clearly I can buzz the smartwatch, make it vibrate to alert you. Two buzzes and I can hear you. One buzz if the recording is too faint.

I shook my head. 'I've got a smartwatch,' Fred stated, and he immediately undid the strap, took it off and handed it to me.

Okay, we have one – anything else? I texted Rich.

Now Bluetooth your smartwatch to your new phone.

Minutes later I texted Rich back. He sent a message and I felt the watch vibrate twice. We were almost ready, I hoped.

54

As we prepared to leave the next morning, Fred insisted that we take his wife's car and it did make sense. 'Take Jennifer's car,' he said, 'and I'll make it up to her. No one will expect you to be travelling in the Beetle, they will be searching for Debbie's car. Drive straight up to Peter's Place,' and he handed us a well-thumbed map book, his finger tracing the route. 'Go via Perth, Dundee and over the Cairn o'Mount down to Finzean and travel west.'

We had breakfasted on toast and coffee, Fred still agitated by the fate of his former colleagues. His questioning of events sharp and incisive as usual.

'If your Internet friend doesn't succeed, please be assured that I will spotlight these nefarious events. I still have some credibility. But take care, Finn, these people are ruthless and your poor mother has suffered enough. You too, Jess, your mother would struggle to cope,' already does, was the unspoken end to the sentence.

He followed us out to the car. 'Jennifer is very proud of Flora,' which presumably was her name for the ancient Beetle, 'otherwise with its lack of green credentials she would have got rid of it, but,' and Fred smiled, 'one mustn't encourage her to get rid of ancient things, I might end up in the dustbin myself.'

I was losing count of the number of times we had transferred our belongings to a different vehicle but set about the task with the unexpressed hope that this would be the last time. Certainly, we would soon need to wash our clothes or buy new ones, as we were left with only old jeans and tee shirts, but we were beyond caring.

Fred had disappeared into the house and came out with a wide-brimmed straw hat and a pair of secateurs, much to Jess's bemusement. 'This should help disguise you, Jess,' and he handed the hat over with the instruction to wear it in the car, and then he bent down and snipped a rose from one of the rose bushes in the garden and told Jess to place it in the flower holder on the dashboard.

As Jess took the rose, she hugged Fred and thanked him, and I noticed how touched Fred was by the gesture.

'Both of you take care and I'll see you soon,' he said, as I started the engine, hearing the engine turn over, roaring rather noisily into life, creating clouds of exhaust. Fred stood and watched as we drove away and gave a final wave as we turned the corner.

We reached Perth within the hour and navigated the maze of roundabouts and slip roads, heading out along the flat ground beside the River Tay, passing the polytunnels filled with ripening berries, towards Dundee. The traffic slowed us down as we edged around the busy city and took the A90 north in the direction of Aberdeen. After another hour we turned off towards the village of Fettercairn and started to climb the foothills of the Grampians, and the high pass which led towards Deeside. The road was narrow and twisting and it was about lunchtime, so we decided to stop and noticed a sign for the Clatterin Brig restaurant and soon reached it, nestled beside the road, a car park to the rear, the restaurant on higher ground above it.

Jess reached down for her handbag as I drove into the car park and stopped beyond a few cars, the car park being mostly deserted. I got out, stretched my legs and we headed up to the restaurant. Neither of us had much appetite, anxious about what lay ahead, and ordered soup and bread and some coffee, taking our time over the soup, conversation perfunctory.

We had come a long way, much further than I seriously had expected, a path opening up for us which had brought us unexpectedly to Deeside. As we lingered over the coffee, we said little but I knew that Jess, like me, was girding herself for what lay ahead. I settled the bill as Jess visited the Ladies Room and wandered through to a small exhibition room with photographs of the restaurant and the area, instead of going down to the car. I knew the signs, it was like before an interview and I was stretching out the last moments, psyching myself up.

Jess appeared at the door and then visibly stiffened, closing the distance between us with great speed, which startled me, and flinging her arms around me and squeezing me, as she muttered, 'Shush, it's them. I don't think they saw me,' and from the entrance I heard Tania's voice say, 'I'll be with you in a minute, Sir Archibald.' I was glad that lunch had been light.

I heard the toilet door slowly shut and Jess released me and edged back to the door.

'Quick,' she said, 'he's not looking our way,' and we both edged out and ran towards the entrance, running down the steps towards the car park. There, next to the Volkswagen Beetle, was the Aston Martin with the lime-green strip down the middle. I didn't need to check the registration.

Jess jumped into the Beetle and I was about to when I had an idea. I ran to the Aston Martin, removed the dust cap on the front tyre nearest to me and used the Beetle's key to release air from the tyre. The air whistled out as I anxiously scanned the restaurant for any sign of them. Jess urged me on as gradually the tyre softened, then the sides bulged and compressed down. I didn't know whether they had a spare or a foot pump but I knew we had gained time, vital time.

I jumped back into the car, reversed and spun around heading out of the car park, resuming the steady climb towards the summit. Both of us released a sigh.

Jess spoke first. 'At least we have delayed them and we know they are in the area. If they had arrived unexpectedly that would have blown our plans.'

'I bet he makes Tania inflate the tyre,' and Jess laughed. 'They must be heading for Peter's Place, surely,' I added, 'which confirms, I hope, what we thought, but it won't make our task any easier.'

By now, as the road twisted, there was open moorland, heather-clad hillsides all around, snow poles lined the road and the views I noticed in the rear-view mirror extended all the way to the North Sea. We reached a car park at the summit, where some people were looking at a map and taking in the panoramic views. There were wind turbines in the distance, well-suited to utilise the savage winds which could scour the high hills, their blades slowly rotating on what was a calm day.

Hills dominated the scene as we continued, with the distinctive granite torr of Clachnaben astride a high ridge to the west, the road undulating, eventually reaching forests as we lost height and returned to the gentler green valley. We crossed a bridge over a fast-flowing river and turned left through a small village. All along the road there was a smattering of houses, fields and woodland, with steep hills to either side of the valley.

Jess was busy studying the map and suddenly cursed. 'We

should have gone left there, but hang on, we can get back on track if we turn left just further on. Just look out for school signs.'

A couple of miles on, I spotted signs for the school and turned down the road.

Ahead, the valley was broader, with the granite torr of Clachnaben to the left and a ridge of hills stretching west. Clouds caressed the top of the highest peak. 'That's Peter's Hill, the summit cloudy, we're getting closer.'

Jess was proving a good navigator, but I saw a farm shop ahead and pulled over, parking in front of it. The locals usually know a lot and I had spotted a group of men walking towards the farm shop from the car park, who looked local, wearing working clothes, probably gathering for a meeting or a coffee.

I quickly got out the car and approached them. 'Could you help me?' I asked, and a farmer, clad in orange overalls, with a cloth cap, stopped.

'Could you direct me to Peter's Place?'

'Oh aye,' he replied, removing his cap and rubbing his bald head, a man possibly in his sixties. 'Down the road, take the road to the right at the church and you'll meet the road to the venue. A couple of miles on and turn off the road at the mill, cross the bridge and you can't miss it. It's a posh place,' he added. 'Late for the wedding?' and he raised his eyebrows, probably thinking that I wasn't properly dressed.

'Helping out,' and on a whim, I asked, 'do you know Murdoch W. Birse?'

'Aye, Disney. I do.'

I was puzzled and the group, who by now had stopped just outside the door of the farm shop, waiting for their friend, laughed. 'Murdoch Walter Birse,' he paused, as I still didn't follow. 'Walter, Walt Disney,' and I smiled, finally appreciating the joke, as the farmer added, 'He disnae work. He does nothing but fish,' and he looked at the group, a few of whom were smiling at his comments, before continuing, 'don't see so much of him these days or that other fellow.'

'Fair curly hair?' I probed.

'That's a younger version than the one I know. Strange fellow.' My heart missed a beat.

'Do they both stay at Peter's Place itself?

'I think so, somewhere in the big house.'

'Thanks for the directions,' and I turned back to the car to tell Jess, who had quickly put away the mobile phone as I got back in the car.

'Interesting,' she said, 'but it's what happens next that bothers me.'

'Likewise, a step at a time,' I replied.

I veered right at the church and followed a narrow road down to where it joined another road. A car sped by and its occupants looked dressed for a wedding. I followed the car along and gradually the fields next to the road turned to a mixed woodland before we reached a small community of a few houses beside a river. The car ahead turned left and crossed a bridge and we followed it, spotting the water wheel of a mill as we did.

A few hundred yards on, a man, wearing plus fours, dressed in tweed, was standing directing cars. We joined a short queue and waited. The cars were directed into a field and we eventually drew up beside him.

'Staff use the next entrance,' he said, and waved us on dismissively.

'We know our place,' I muttered, and we continued on the road. After a bend, I saw Peter's Place, a three-storey building with gothic trappings, standing in extensive grounds fringed by woodland. Peter's Place was ostentatious, built on a whim by

315

a rich railway magnate from America, who never lived to see it completed, now a wedding venue and also used by shooting parties who scoured the nearby hills for grouse in season.

A young man appeared from behind a hedge and pointed to a gravel road which wound around to the back of the house, our tyres making a crunching sound as we drove along slowly. Behind the house was a courtyard surrounded by a high brick wall, with cars and a minibus parked up against the far wall. A white van belonging to a catering group was in the middle of the courtyard, with boxes being carried from it to the basement of the house. At the far end of the courtyard were double doors opened flat against the walls revealing a garage under the house. I spotted a parking space and stopped.

'Here goes,' I said, trying to give a reassuring smile to Jess whose face was pale, her mouth narrow, the strain showing. As I opened the door, a woman came across. 'From the catering company?'

'Yes,' I said, what else could I say?

'You're late,' she snarled, obviously under pressure, and added, 'Did they not tell you how to dress? I doubt I can use you for serving. I'll be raising this with your boss, but in the meantime, we are very short-staffed. Sign in,' and she pointed towards an open wooden door, 'and collect aprons, they're on the table by the door.' She continued to scrutinise us and frowned, shaking her head. 'I hope that you are better than you seem. Hurry along,' and we walked slowly towards the door. At least we had gained access to the house.

316

55

The basement was busy and noisy, staff scuttling around. To the right of the door was a large kitchen area and I heard a chef berating someone, swearing loudly. Steam was rising from large pots of water on a kitchen range and one of the kitchen staff was carrying a large metal tray towards an oven, with what appeared to be small chickens for roasting.

'Sign in and collect an apron,' shouted a rotund figure, who interrupted giving someone instructions to let us know what to do, pointing to a table by the door. There was a sheet sellotaped to the table. I scribbled a false name and Jess did the same. The man observed us as we put on the striped aprons, the moustache on his top lip flexing as he spoke. 'Next time, black trousers and white shirts, please. Surprised Jemina let you in. Join Ted over there,' pointing to someone about Jess's age, fair-haired, who smiled in a friendly fashion towards us as the other man gave instructions. 'Help with getting the wine bottles out and uncorked,' and he turned away to accost someone else.

'I'm Ted,' he said, with a broad smile, as we approached, 'you get used to abuse here. They are too mean to hire the right number of staff,' he added, lowering his voice, not wanting to be overheard. 'Help me upstairs with the boxes of wine and put them out on the table by the door. Then it is one bottle of red for every four people, we'll uncork them later. Then we fill up the wine buckets with ice and plop a bottle of white wine in each bucket. Ice machine is in the garage.'

It made sense to play along and I picked up a case of wine and followed Ted upstairs to the main banqueting area. Half the area in the banqueting hall was set for the guests to eat, long tables covered with white tablecloths, arrangements of flowers set at intervals. At the far end was a platform, and instruments and speakers were being set up for a ceilidh. A woman, wearing tartan trousers, was practising on an accordion, accompanied by a man playing drums. Between the stage and the tables was a tiered wedding cake on a circular table draped in a white cloth.

All of this I could have expected, but my real interest was in looking for a flat or rooms that could hide Shaw and Birse. Three tiers of balconies surrounded the compact banqueting and dance area. On each level were black metal railings, with alternative motifs of a thistle and an eagle incorporated in them, topped by a polished mahogany handrail, a sort of trans-Atlantic kitsch; they surrounded the banqueting hall, allowing guests to lean on and watch the activities below. I could see rooms to the outside and guests already arriving, suitcases outside doors, and in each corner swing doors which must lead to stairs. On the top floor the pattern changed. On one side, directly above the platform for the musicians, there was a wall immediately behind the railings. It extended about three-quarters of the length of the side and was probably a flat. I pointed it out to Jess, but before I could say anything, Ted shouted.

'You've had a look and it is impressive but we must get busy. As you can see, the guests are arriving.' He slit the tape at the top of a box of wine and started pulling out the bottles. 'Remember one bottle for every four places,' and he started distributing the

318

wine. Jess and I followed his example, busying ourselves. For some time we fetched boxes of wine from downstairs and carried them up to the hall, absorbing all that was going on.

Jemina appeared, casting her usual critical eye on proceedings and ordered us over to her.

'Go to the garage and collect the bottles of champagne, put them in the ice buckets by the door,' before she turned away, frowning. 'That should already have been done.'

Following her order we went downstairs and outside, heading to the garage that I had spotted on our arrival. Inside the garage, strip lights lit up the scene, and I immediately spotted two cases containing the champagne. Jess grabbed my arm. 'There's a car over there in the corner, under a protective cover,' and I immediately knew what she was hoping for. I walked smartly across and lifted the cover. There at the front was a narrow grill and on the bonnet above was a thistle on a blue background, with the name Argyll underneath it.

'Quickly, take a photo,' I said, and Jess produced the mobile, the flash going off as she took it. I heard footsteps and dropped the cover, sprinting back to the boxes, hefting one up, just as Jemina appeared. 'What's keeping you,' she said, eyeing us suspiciously, but I was holding one of the boxes and Jess was lifting hers off the ground. 'Hurry,' she ordered, 'they should have been chilled already; otherwise, they will be all frothy when opened.'

We followed her back into the house and up to the banqueting hall, unpacking the cases and plunging them into buckets of ice. Jemina seemed satisfied with our efforts.

'Two more workers from the catering company have turned up,' the man with the moustache exclaimed, appearing perplexed.

Jemina looked at us, a puzzled expression on her face, before

319

saying. 'Never rains but it pours. We can use them.' She quickly turned away and disappeared downstairs.

'Time we headed upstairs,' I muttered, and we edged towards the nearest stairwell, gathering speed and pushing through the doors, a flight of stairs in front of us. We ran and as we reached the top floor, we discarded our aprons, emerging onto the balcony. Crouching and hugging the walls of the rooms, so that we couldn't be seen from below, we ran along towards the flat.

The doors at the end nearest the flat swung open. Instinctively I tried the handle of the nearest guest room and we dived in, pulling the door shut behind us, tense, wondering if we had been seen. Footsteps echoed along the balcony but continued past the door. Then we were aware of someone in the en suite bathroom and a voice calling, 'Is that you, Hilary?' We quickly left the room as a figure emerged from the bathroom, a towel around his waist, shouting, 'Who are you?'

We bolted along through the swing doors at the end of the balcony and found the door to the flat. I tried the handle but it was locked. There was no bell, so I banged on the door. Inside I heard someone coming to the door and a minute later it was opened.

'Hello Disney, I am the ghost of Christmas past,' I said, and we pushed in, Jess shutting the door quickly behind us.

56

Disney was startled, struggling to take in what we were doing, as we pushed into the hallway of the flat, Jess quickly shutting the door behind us. The hallway was fairly dark, light only at the far end where the lounge was located. Birse appeared much older than the photo of him beside the Argyll. The intervening years had not treated him kindly, only tufts of hair around his ears remained, his complexion blotchier, his lips thin with a purple tinge. Initially the shock of strangers pushing in overwhelmed him but you could see the eyes darting, assessing how to react. He was dangerous, quick-witted. It was important we kept the pressure on him.

'I'm Finn McAdam,' and I let my name sink in, 'we have met before, the night my father was murdered. You were there with your friend, Sir Archibald.'

Recognition dawned, he drew a deep breath. 'Sir Archibald is on his way, he'll...'

'He's had an accident, don't count on him arriving soon.'

'What do you mean?'

'He's been delayed, which conveniently gives us time to talk,' and I pushed him along the hallway towards the lounge, keeping him, literally, on the back foot. Jess was busy opening the doors of the corridor, the first was a bedroom, no one in it, the next was a bathroom and the final one another bedroom.

'Leave him,' Birse growled, but Jess ignored him and switched on the light as the room was in darkness, blinds drawn. I saw a figure stirring in the bed, turning towards the light, confusion on his face.

'He is resting,' Birse shouted, 'leave him,' his voice more strident.

'No,' I countered, 'we have lots of questions to ask Shaw. Get him up,' I ordered Jess, who moved to the bed, rousing Shaw, pulling back the bed clothes, exposing him lying there with purple pyjamas on, shielding his eyes from the light. Shaw was another one who had aged, the curly hair now white, the face pinched, the eyes, however, still giving a distant look, avoiding direct contact. Meekly he moved his legs over the edge of the bed. He must be drugged, this shadow of a man, so far removed from the person capable of raping Julia and murdering people, but I felt no sympathy. I noticed boxes of medication lying on the bedside cabinet, blister packs of pills, some opened.

'Come on,' Jess demanded, grabbing a dressing gown from a hook behind the door and throwing it at him, 'get up, we need to talk.'

'Leave him,' Birse shouted, 'you can see he is not well.'

'And we know why. Move it,' I demanded. Shaw looked up at me, no recognition in his face, but took the dressing gown and pulled it on as he stood up, his face vacant, conveying no emotion.

'Sir Archibald will be furious.'

'We are assuming that,' I replied curtly to Birse, 'and we know that he is capable, you do too,' and I glared at him, 'of having people murdered when he is in a rage.' We had reached the lounge door and I pushed Birse inside. 'Sit on the sofa,' I ordered, and Jess led Shaw into the lounge, directing him to the sofa beside Birse.

The lounge was situated at the far corner of the flat, windows on two sides with views to Peter's Hill, with a small kitchen, the width of the hall, recessed off the room. Simply furnished with a flat screen television in the corner. Jess grabbed a large knife from the drainer beside the sink, brandishing it.

Shaw was still disorientated, staring at the far wall. Jess had alerted Rich to be ready to record our conversation whilst we had waited outside. The smartwatch vibrated twice.

'Adrian,' I softened my tone, 'we know that you raped Julia Finneston. Why?'

'Don't answer, Adrian, they're trying to trick you.'

'Shut up,' I snapped angrily at Birse, before turning my attention back to Shaw. 'Tell us.'

'I loved her. Thought... she wanted me.'

'Can you not see he is unwell, leave him, his mind is disturbed.'

'Is that why you murdered my father, so you could have Julia to yourself?' Jess spoke quietly, but her message was clear, delivered with conviction, recognition on Birse's face as he realised who Jess was, but it appeared lost on Shaw.

Birse tried to get up but I pushed him down hard and stood over him, clenching my fists.

'Go on, Adrian,' I said, trying to sound sympathetic, 'tell us everything.'

'I loved her but she didn't want me, wanted...' and he paused.

I added: 'Dr Hamilton?' He nodded.

'Say it, Adrian.'

Birse interrupted again. 'Don't put words in his mouth,' and he tried to get up again but this time I hit him hard on the face and he recoiled moaning, a trickle of blood from his nose.

'I won't warn you again,' I said to him, rage coursing through my veins.

'Did you feel that you had to get rid of Dr Hamilton?' Jess asked, trying to coax him into speaking. Nervously Shaw wiped his mouth, whether he was fully compos mentis I didn't know, but I wanted a confession, hear it from his own lips. Shaw nodded again.

'No, Adrian, say it. Did you murder Dr Hamilton?'

His hand movements became more pronounced, agitated, erratic.

'He couldn't have her. I wanted her.'

'So you killed him by the lochside?'

'Yes, I am sorry,' he finally admitted, his head slumping on his chest, the effort of speaking draining him.

'A confession under duress is inadmissible,' Birse snarled, pinching his nose, but he pulled Shaw towards him, extending a comforting, protective arm around him.

'He had a breakdown,' Birse tried to explain.

'Some breakdown. Jess's father murdered and you watched as my father was shot on Sir Archibald's instructions. Did Sir Archibald have a breakdown?'

'I saved your life,' Birse began, and that got my attention.

'How?'

'Sir Archibald also wanted you killed so that there were no witnesses. I demanded that you be drugged, you were too young to die, innocent of what your father had done.'

'My father? He is the murderer,' I shouted, and pointed to Shaw's slumped figure.

'I was the doctor for Sir Archibald and his family, and also a close family friend,' he added, so I became familiar with Adrian, and his problems. Overwork, excessive demands made by your father and the nature of the work, creating a new generation of toxic nerve gases, drove him over the edge. That doesn't excuse what he did but helps explain it. I look after him here. We have an arrangement.'

'You're shielding a murderer,' but my mind was racing with this new information. Could I believe him?

'I saved your life,' Birse repeated. 'I don't expect you to be grateful but I did stop a worse tragedy. I had no choice. When your father saw me while I was fishing further along the loch, he was desperate, trying to lead Shaw away from you. I contacted Sir Archibald and...'

'The rest is history.' Gotcha, I screamed inside me, hoping that Rich was recording. He must have been listening. The watch vibrated twice.

Marshalling my defence of Dad, I stated, 'It helps if you have an important father pushing for you, getting you the job at Eastriggs,' and Birse closed his eyes in resignation at the extent of our knowledge. 'Someday it was all going to come out. Sir Archibald helped to exert pressure on my father, to get him to employ Shaw. Thought that he was doing his friend Montgomery a favour. Ironically, Dad would have chosen him anyway, but if your father is a minister at the Ministry of Defence, it was going to happen,' I added.

I turned to Jess, anxious, knowing that Sir Archibald would be here soon. 'Time to leave?' but Jess ignored me and grabbed at Shaw's shoulder forcing him to raise his head and stare into her eyes.

'You ruined my life and my mother's,' she stated, but Shaw's expression was unfocused.

'You better go,' Birse said. I looked around the lounge, spotting a phone by the television. I went across and pulled it out from its holder, going across to the kitchen and throwing it on the ground and crushing it underfoot. I grabbed Birse and checked his pockets, no mobile.

'Watch them,' I said to Jess, and I ran along the corridor to the first bedroom, which I presumed was Birse's, and searched the room. There was a mobile on the bedside cabinet and I grabbed it, threw it on the floor and jumped on it, grinding it into the floor with the heel of my shoe until I heard the plastic crack.

'Right, Jess, let's go,' and as she came out of the lounge I heard someone arrive at the door. Too late. The handle was turned and the door pushed open. Immediately Tania reached inside her jacket and produced a gun. Sir Archibald was beside her.

'Well,' Sir Archibald said, 'this is convenient.' Tania motioned us back along the hall.

57

Sir Archibald stood absorbing the scene, listening as Birse shouted, 'They forced their way in,' whilst holding his nose, which gave his voice a strange nasal tone, blood seeping through onto his fingers. Jess had let the knife drop on the floor when Tania pointed the gun at her. Tania's eyes darted from Jess to me and then to Birse, they expressed little sympathy for any of us, just a cold fury, reflected by her boss.

'Lounge,' Sir Archibald spat out the word and Tania motioned with her handgun. Faintly I could hear the sound of laughter rising from the banqueting hall, incongruous with our plight, as presumably the best man or bridegroom was giving their speech.

In the lounge Shaw was still sitting on the sofa and Sir Archibald went across and gently pulled him up. Birse began to check him out. Simple actions which seemed further at odds with our situation.

'Take Adrian away,' Sir Archibald said to Birse, adding, 'you maybe don't want to stay.'

'Oh,' I said, 'not going to stay to watch history repeating itself with the next generation of McAdams, or have you learnt your lesson.'

Birse stepped forward suddenly and hit me hard on my face, narrowly missing my nose, but the pain was still real, my jaw jarring. Fortunately, it was the other side that Danny hit. He turned away abruptly and led Shaw from the lounge, leaving Jess and I alone with the two of them.

'Sit on the sofa,' and Tania pointed the gun at us again, reinforcing his command, as more laughter erupted from the hall, a surreal backdrop. He stepped forward and frisked us, removing my phone. 'Switch it off,' he demanded, which I did, making a show of it and he threw it on the floor, the phone skidding across the carpet, bouncing back off one of the legs of the television stand, stopping a few feet from me.

'You let down the tyre, didn't you?'

'Anything to help you,' I replied, and he moved closer, clenching his fists, fighting his emotions, trying to retain control.

'So here we are, we meet again,' he started, after a pause, 'and I warned you of the consequences.' The watch vibrated only once. Rich couldn't pick up his voice.

'Indeed,' I screamed, startling him, 'glad to meet you. The man who ordered the murder of my father. The man who is too cowardly to pull the trigger himself but has to ask others to do it.' I was goading him, hoping that he would get angry and raise his voice, be recorded.

He just laughed and turned to Tania. There was no flicker of response from her.

'At least tell me why you had my father murdered.'

Sir Archibald stood rubbing his chin for a moment, pondering what to do next, my fate to be decided by his next utterances.

'Loyalty comes at a price,' he stated.

'So you can kill anyone as long as you remain loyal to your friends, or is it because you would lose out financially. I know all

328

about the United Umbrella Company, that you and Montgomery are both members,' and his thin lips curled as he discovered that I had worked out the connection between him and Montgomery. 'I have proof of the cover-up. We watched as Tania visited Urquhart and tried to kill him by setting his house ablaze. We snuffed out the candle. Not very good, Tania, are you? You left evidence of bank payments to Urquhart, which we've passed on. Your game is up.'

I saw the first sign of annoyance register on Sir Archibald's face. He scowled at Tania.

'Incompetence, I would say,' and he shouted at me to shut up.

'I assumed the candle went out and I went back, but he had gone.'

'To the pub, probably.'

'Who's got the information?'

'Everyone by now, I expect. Word gets around.'

'Who?'

'You tell me first what happened to our fathers. Fair deal.' The blow to my stomach was as severe as it was unexpected, Archibald snapping. I doubled up and fell on the floor, my arm hitting something sharp, adding to my discomfort. It was the phone. As I staggered up I dragged the phone closer with my foot, noticing for the first time a sheen of sweat on Sir Archibald's forehead. He was worried.

'You don't think that I came here without making preparations, in case I don't return. It's not looking too good for your friend Julian. Loyalty is everything, I suppose, but he won't appreciate it when he has to resign. Career over,' and I stiffened waiting for another blow.

'Tell us, please,' Jess pleaded.

'Okay,' and I saw Tania glance quickly at him.

'Do you think…'

329

'Shut up, Tania, I'll deal with this,' he snapped.

'Adrian had a breakdown, pressure of work. Did you know that your fathers were creating a new nerve gas, so deadly that the work had to be carried out away from Porton Down, the usual research centre, so that few knew about it? Your fathers were going to be mass murderers. Think so highly of them now?' he sneered, and it was a jolt, confirming what Birse had claimed.

'They pressurised Adrian, as they had to get results, and he couldn't cope, became obsessed that your father was having an affair with Julia,' and he had turned his attention to Jess. 'He had form you know,' the eyes barely conveying his fury as he spat out the words.

'Adrian was staying with me, took one of my guns and went to the loch where Hamilton was fishing and shot him.' The watch vibrated once then twice. I could show no emotion, no reaction.

'The great Dr McAdam, father of the new nerve gas, turned up unexpectedly and found him. He saw Adrian with the gun lurking in among the trees and ran away, in the opposite direction to you. How brave to save one life but be capable of destroying thousands, maybe millions. Fortunately, he ran into Murdoch, who was fishing another stretch, and he let me know.'

'And Shaw ran away and assaulted Julia.'

'Pretty much.'

'Ruined her life. You know that she had Shaw's child?'

'Oh yes.'

'Did you have her killed?'

'No, I did hear about that but it must have been an accident.'

'My father had to die to cover up what Shaw had done.'

'Yes, loyalty trumps all.'

The watch vibrated twice.

'Now, I presume you told your sister about Urquhart? She

will never tell. Debbie and your mother were disgusted when I told them what your father was doing, with a few extra details about experiments on animals to convince them. Deadly stuff, the great Dr McAdam developed.'

From the hall below I could hear instruments being tuned up, a sound check on the microphones.

'Later, in an hour or two, the fireworks will start. You can watch the display from here. It will be the last thing you do, either of you,' and he gave that thin smile, a sneer of arrogance.

58

The band was tuning up for what seemed like an eternity and then the music began, a Scottish reel, with encouragement from the master of ceremonies. I could hear the sound of the guests joining in, sensing the vibration of many feet jumping about. Sir Archibald sat in the chair opposite, while Tania stood, her gaze never wavering, the gun in her hand. I was still trying to absorb what he had told me about my father. It hurt, didn't fit my image of him, but it was what it was. Jess's head was down, turned away from me, so I couldn't read the expression on her face.

Rich had recorded the conversation, so hopefully he would be broadcasting it to the world, something which gave me quiet satisfaction. Whether either of us would live to discover the consequences was another matter. Surely Rich would realise our predicament and ensure that the police were on their way?

After half an hour Sir Archibald got up and made himself a mug of coffee, not offering any to Tania and wandered out of the room. I heard him speaking to Birse and Shaw but couldn't make out what he said, a muffled conversation. He returned after a few minutes and sat down again, minus the mug. In my heightened state of anxiety I noticed all these small details. Time dragged, tension mounting, the sky outside darkening and from the front of the house I heard a few voices and a sudden whoosh as a firework soared above the window and I saw a series of flashes, followed by the sound of small explosions. Was this a signal for the fireworks to begin or a trial run? Sir Archibald got up and looked out the window, having given Tania a knowing look. Time was running out.

The master of ceremonies was speaking again, his voice muffled. I thought that he was announcing the start of the firework display but to my relief another reel began. Sir Archibald pulled the blinds down and sat back in the chair. I felt like screaming and could no longer bare to look at Jess. I regretted involving her, sorry that my determination was largely responsible for her being here. I was distracted from my thoughts as Sir Archibald was drumming his fingers on the top of the television, keeping rhythm with the reel, his frustration at the delay showing. Tania stayed impassive, more like a cyborg than a human, something chilling about her. I closed my eyes, breathing deeply, the silence in the room unnerving.

An explosion shattered the silence and the entrance door burst open, slamming against the wall, the lock smashed. From the end of the hall, I heard footsteps and before I could react, saw someone flop to the ground at the door of the lounge and then a flash. Tania's hand blew apart, the handgun dropping to the ground, cloaked in her blood. It was Danny, dressed in dark clothes, his shaved head glistening in the light, scrambling to change his position and fire his rifle again but Sir Archibald stooped, picking up the handgun. Jess screamed, flinging herself at Sir Archibald as the handgun was fired at point-blank range and Danny's body jumped, his arm twitching. Sir Archibald leapt over him and raced down the hall, still clutching the handgun, slamming the door behind him, but it bounced open such was the force he used.

Chaos reigned. Tania grabbed a towel from the kitchen to staunch the flow of blood from what remained of her hand, her face pale, and she slumped against the wall, groaning. Jess was down at Danny's side, crying, pressing her hands against his arm, blood oozing out.

From Shaw's bedroom I heard a noise and saw him emerge. Birse tried to stop him but failed, and he ran out the door of the flat, dazed, looking around and seeing all the people below, some, presumably now attracted by the sound of gunshots, looking up. He climbed on the banister, fighting to keep his balance, and I heard the first screams from below as people saw him, alarmed at what he was going to do next. He manoeuvred his body until he was sitting on the banister, legs hanging over it, perched above the banqueting hall. He then tried to stand on the banister but slipped. For a moment his body seemed stationary, then slowly it fell forwards, his arms flailing, gravity taking over, and then he was gone. The music became discordant, screams intensified. By the time I reached the banister his body lay motionless on the floor below, a circle of people edging back as if a stone had hit the surface of water, a ripple spreading out. The shape of his body was awkward, unnatural, blood oozing from his head.

Birse was now standing beside me. 'Why couldn't you have let things rest? None of this would have happened. I wish I had let Sir Archibald have you killed,' and he turned away before I could reply.

59

The armed response unit appeared shortly after, edging out from the stairwell, peaked caps covering tense faces, with what appeared to be sub-machine guns in their hands, skeletal triangular butts, magazines angling to the front. They edged into the flat, kicking open the first bedroom door and then the bathroom door, checking for occupants. I stood, holding up my hands.

'Two wounded, everyone else okay. One rifle on the floor,' I shouted, but was rewarded with an officer training his weapon on me, crouching, a red dot on my chest. He motioned me to sit down and shouted, 'Hands on head.' I obliged and seconds later I was being frisked and told to remain seated, handcuffs slipped on.

Minutes later search over, radios crackling, paramedics streamed in, going to Tania and Danny, tending to them. A police inspector came into the flat and was quickly updated.

'Finn McAdam,' he started, 'we are taking you to the police station for questioning.' I told him that he should be searching for Sir Archibald Graham-Linton, who had a handgun and was potentially very dangerous, there was little reaction. He read me my rights and I was frisked again and led away, an officer holding each arm. Was the cover-up underway? Jess was getting similar treatment. Dr Birse, as I suppose I should call him, stood up, his hands and clothes covered in blood from a brief examination of the two wounded, walked with an officer out of the flat behind me, shaking his head in fury when he saw me glance back.

The smartwatch was silent. I was on my own awaiting developments.

• • •

After a drive of about an hour I was placed in a cell, the door locked and I was left on my own. The world could have been ending outside and I wouldn't have known. Time is the policeman's friend, softens you up, really makes you think hard about what has brought you to this confined space. My mind went into overtime, imagining the worst.

Shaw had been troubled, unstable, had Dad exacerbated his mental condition, intentionally or otherwise? Did that justify Shaw's actions? Birse would not be a positive witness for me. Would he have influence? And what about the work Dad had been doing. It left me uneasy. At least I had found out what took place on that fateful night. Hopefully, we had the evidence to allow the police to bring charges. Where was Sir Archibald now? And what the hell was Rich doing? Time played slow, hours stretched, confidence dwindled.

60

The mobile rang several times before I picked it up, my hand fumbling to find it and answer the call. I said nothing, wary. Who was calling me so early in the morning? It was a relief to hear Jess's voice. We were not supposed to talk, part of the deal. Gillian was asleep in the bed beside me and so I slipped out of the room and crept downstairs to find a quiet spot, suspecting that I knew the reason.

'That's better,' I said, 'I can speak now. How are you?' but she ignored the question.

'Have you heard?'

'What?'

'They have found Sir Archibald's body at the bottom of the Big Water of Fleet viaduct. Suicide they say,' but her tone was sceptical.

'I knew but I haven't had the chance to slip away from Gillian to phone you. Sam phoned me last night. He had heard from his friends still working in the police. Archibald had been hiding in the area. Rumours are that it was not suicide; he was pushed. A cover-up to protect others, I believe. I'm glad that he's dead. Pity though that we couldn't force him to tell his story in court.'

I paused, but Jess said nothing, absorbing the information.

'How's Danny?' I added.

'Recovering. They have charged him with going AWOL and stealing a rifle.'

'That all?'

'Yes.'

'Is that not surprising, or is it also part of the cover-up?'

'He'll get a dishonourable discharge.'

'That's good news. It could have been far worse. How are the two of you doing?'

'Okay, I've outgrown him, going to go to college and then try to get into a university course. But I can't leave him yet, not fair.'

'Thanks for all you did. Danny saved the day, pity you didn't tell me that the cavalry were on the way.'

'Not sure that he would make it on time. He had gone AWOL from his barracks and was trying to reach us. He was an insurance policy. I kept him updated. I contacted him whilst you were talking to the farmers outside that shop, to give him final directions.' There was a pause. 'How are you getting on?'

'Gillian and I are doing very well.' I still suspected that Jess would have wanted a different reply. 'Sis and Mother are still a bit distant,' I added to cover any awkwardness.

'Do you think that the truth will ever come out?' This was the main purpose in her call, I felt.

'We did a deal, no charges, keep quiet. No choice really and I can still teach. They found out about Rich early on. We didn't realise that it wasn't him who was signalling me, but some security geek.'

'But they must have kept the recordings,' Jess pointed out.

'I am sure that they did, as they would be useful for blackmail purposes.'

'I wonder who "they" are,' she mused, but upstairs I heard

338

Gillian stirring, getting out of bed.

'I only know that someone has kept them,' I replied. 'What they do with them is no longer our business. We have justice for the murder of our parents. Shaw and AGL are both dead, even if very few will ever find out what really happened.'

We ended the call and as I went to switch off the phone, I was alerted by a newsflash:

BREAKING NEWS: *After the surprise resignation of Prime Minister Susan Brooks, Julian Montgomery is the first to declare his candidacy. 'I have the values and experience to lead this country,' he claims.*

Cover photographs credits:

Front cover – Hitler's Grave carving – Alasdair Wham
Back cover – Big Water of Fleet viaduct – Alasdair Wham

Acknowledgements

My special thanks to my wife, Christine, sons Martin and Scott, for their support and encouragement and in particular to Gillian Wham for the cover and book design. Thanks also to Mike Clayton for the initial editing and Sue Roy's final edit.

The story of the Devil's Porridge is fascinating. I first became aware of it whilst researching 'Exploring Dumfries and Galloway's Lost Railway Heritage'. During the First World War, there was a severe shortage of cordite for artillery shells. Britain's response was to build HM Factory Gretna, a vast factory dispersed along the Solway Firth's northern shore. The site employed 30,000 people at its peak of production and also involved building several new townships. Sir Arthur Conan Doyle gave the Devil's Porridge its name as he witnessed workers mixing the cordite paste.

The Devil's Porridge Museum is dedicated to telling the story of HM Factory Gretna and the harrowing tale of Britain's worst railway disaster at nearby Quintinshill and is well worth visiting.

The Devil's Porridge Museum is situated on Annan Road, Eastriggs, DG126TF. Further details are available at www.devilsporridge.org.uk

Alasdair Wham
May 2021

Who can you trust?

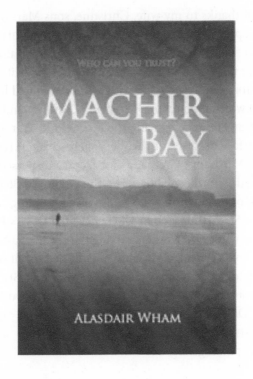

'.... a fast moving plot full of suspense it becomes a real page turner.' *Jean Cook, Women Together magazine*

'Machir Bay is quite excellent and worthy of your attention' *Ileach*

Sequel to Machir Bay

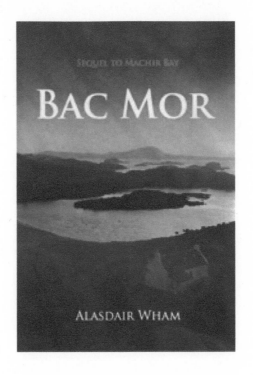